ADVANCE AND RETREAT

HARRY TURTLEDOVE

ADVANCE & RETREAT

A Baen Books Original

Baen Publishing Enterprises
P.O. Box 1403
Riverdale, NY 10471
www.baen.com

ISBN: 0-7434-8820-2

Cover art by Tom Kidd

First paperback printing, April 2004

Distributed by Simon & Schuster
1230 Avenue of the Americas
New York, NY 10020

Production by Windhaven Press, Auburn, NH (www.windhaven.com)
Printed in the United States of America

WIZARDS OF MASS DESTRUCTION

Waving to the north, the military wizard Alva said, "The northern mages are up to something, sir."

"What is it this time?" Doubting George was amazed at how scornful he sounded. Before finding Alva, he would have been worried. Northern magecraft had plagued the southron cause all through the war. Now? Now in this weedy young wizard, he had its measure.

Or so he thought, till Alva's head came up sharply, like that of a deer all at once taking a scent. "It's . . . something big," the sorcerer said slowly. "Something very big."

"Can you keep it from hitting us?" George asked.

"It's not aimed at us," Alva answered. "It's aimed . . . somewhere far away." Then he said, more to himself than to Doubting George, "I didn't think they could manage anything like that." He sounded both astonished and admiring.

Shouts from the pickets and encampments said somebody was alarmed about something. Soldiers in gray tunics and pantaloons pointed up into the sky. "A dragon!" they shouted. "A gods-damned dragon!"

Doubting George threw back his head and laughed. "Is that all the traitors could cook up? An illusion?"

Quietly, Major Alva said, "Sir, that is not the illusion of a dragon. That is . . . a dragon, conjured here from wherever it lives."

"A real dragon?" George, who'd served in the east, had seen them before, flying among the peaks of the Stony Mountains. "What can your magic do against a real dragon, now that the beast is here?"

"I don't know, sir." Alva answered. "Not much. Magic isn't what drove dragons out to the mountains. Hunting is."

Stooping like an outsized hawk, the dragon dove towards a knot of tents. Flame burst from its great jaws. Then the tents—and several soldiers—burst into flame. some of the screams that rang out were anguish. More were terror, as the men realized the beast was real—real, angry, and hungry. . . .

BAEN BOOKS by HARRY TURTLEDOVE

ADVANCE AND RETREAT

I

Off to the north and west, an army loyal to King Avram marched through crumbling northern defenses in Peachtree Province toward the Western Ocean. Due west, in Parthenia Province, another southron army loyal to Avram laid siege to Pierreville. If the great fortress fell, Nonesuch, the capital of the rebel Grand Duke Geoffrey—he called himself King Geoffrey, a title no one but his fellow traitors acknowledged—would also fall, and in short order.

General Hesmucet led the soldiers marching through Peachtree. Marshal Bart led the soldiers besieging Pierreville.

Doubting George? Doubting George sat in Ramblerton, twiddling his thumbs.

The war between brothers in the Kingdom of Detina was deep into its fourth year now. When King Avram ascended to the throne, he'd let the world know he intended to make citizens of the blond serfs who labored on the nobles' great estates in the northern provinces. And Geoffrey, his cousin, had promptly led the nobles—and the rest of the north—into rebellion, declaring Avram had no right to do any such thing.

A few southron men, reckoning provincial prerogative more important than the true succession—or sometimes just wed to northern women—had thrown in with the uprising against Avram. And a few northerners, reckoning a single Kingdom of Detina more important than holding the serfs in bondage, had remained loyal to the proper king, the rightful king. Lieutenant General George was one of those men. Geoffrey had promptly confiscated his estates in Parthenia.

That was how the game was played these days. Duke Edward of Arlington, who commanded Geoffrey's most important force, the Army of Southern Parthenia, had had his estates close by King Avram's Black Palace in Georgetown. Avram had confiscated them as soon as his soldiers overran them in the early days of the war.

I got the same punishment for being loyal as Duke Edward did for being a traitor, George thought. *Is that fair? Is that just?*

"I doubt it," George said aloud. He used the phrase a lot, often enough to have given him his nickname. He was a burly man in his early forties, with a typical dark Detinan beard, full and curly, that gray was just beginning to streak.

He muttered to himself: not words, but a discontented rumble down deep in his throat. The Lion God might have made a noise like that when he contemplated chewing on the souls of sinners.

"No good deed goes unpunished," Doubting George said when the mutters turned into words again. He'd done as much hard fighting as any southron officer in the war. If it hadn't been for his stand, there on Merkle's

Hill by the River of Death, the whole southron cause in the east might have unraveled under the hammer blows of Count Thraxton the Braggart's sorcery.

And what was his reward? How had a grateful kingdom shown him its appreciation for all he'd done, for all he'd sacrificed?

More words emerged: "Here I am in Ramblerton, twiddling my gods-damned thumbs."

Ramblerton was the capital of Franklin. It lay by the bank of the Cumbersome River, in the southeastern part of the province. Doubting George might have been farther out of the fight down in New Eborac City, but not by much. He'd done the work, and others had got the glory. The war looked well on the way toward being won. He was glad of that. He would have been even gladder to have a bigger part in it.

A sentry stuck his head into Lieutenant General George's office. "Beg your pardon, sir," he said, "but Major Alva would like to see you, if you've got the time."

"Oh, yes, I've got the time," George replied. "By the Thunderer's beard, to the seven hells with me if I can think of anything I've got more of."

The sentry withdrew. A moment later, Major Alva came in. He looked preposterously young to be a major. But, for one thing, a lot of officers in this war *were* preposterously young. And, for another, he was a wizard, and so an officer at least as much by courtesy as because he was expected to command soldiers in the field.

Major Alva, in fact, was short on just about everything that made soldiers what they were. His gray wizard's robe hung from his scrawny frame. His beard hadn't been combed any time lately. He plainly needed to remind himself to salute Lieutenant General George. But he was also far and away the best wizard in

Doubting George's army—maybe the best wizard in *any* southron army. Before the war, southron mages had done most of their work in manufactories, which didn't suit them for battle magic. Wizards in the north had worked hard to keep the serfs in line and over-awed, which did. In the early years of the war, northern prowess at wizardry had helped hold back southron numbers. Now . . .

Now Doubting George hoped it wouldn't any more. Nodding to Alva, he said, "What can I do for you, Major?"

"Something's going on," Alva said. Lieutenant General George folded his arms across his broad chest and waited. Alva was swarthy, but not swarthy enough to keep his flush from showing. "Uh, something's going on, *sir*."

Back in the days when Alva was a mere lieutenant, he wouldn't have had the faintest idea what George was waiting for. Now he knew, though he still plainly thought the idea of military courtesy absurd. George didn't care what Alva thought. He cared what Alva did. "Do you have any idea *what's* going on, Major, or where it's going on?" he inquired.

"Something to do with the traitors . . . sir," the wizard answered.

"I had suspected that, yes." Doubting George's voice was dry enough to make Alva flush again. "I doubted you'd have come to me with news of a barge wreck on the Highlow River—although you never can tell."

"Er, yes," Major Alva said, visibly off-balance. Like a lot of mages, he conceived of generals as a stiff, stodgy lot. Evidence to the contrary, which Doubting George gave now and again, flustered him.

"And how do you know what you think you know?" George asked.

With a lot of wizards, that would have spawned an

endless epistemological discussion. There was one vice, at least, of which Alva was free. He said, "I feel it in my bones, sir."

George would have thrown most wizards out of his office after an answer like that. With some, he wouldn't have bothered opening the door first. He paid Alva a high compliment: he took him seriously. "What else can you tell me?" he asked.

"Not much, sir, not yet," Major Alva said. "But the northerners are stirring, or thinking about stirring. And when they come, they'll come hard."

"Best way," Doubting George agreed, which flustered the young wizard all over again. George went on, "Do you think you could find out more if you did some serious sorcerous poking around?"

"I don't know for certain, sir," Alva replied. "I could try to find out, though."

"Why don't you do that, then?" George said. "Report back to me if you find anything interesting or important." Alva was one of those people you needed to remind of such things. Otherwise, he was liable to forget.

He nodded now. "All right. I'll do that. Snooping is fun. It's not like General Bell has any wizards who can stop me." He certainly owned all the arrogance a good mage should have.

"Good enough," George said. "You're dismissed, Major."

"See you later," Alva said cheerfully, and touched the brim of his gray hat as he might have back in civilian life. Doubting George coughed. Major Alva turned red again. Little by little, George kept on persuading him he was a soldier. In even smaller increments, the lessons took. Mumbling, "Sorry," Alva gave him another salute. He coughed again. Alva's stare held nothing but indignation. "Now what?"

"'Sorry, sir,'" George said, as if to a four-year-old.

"'Sorry, sir,'" Alva repeated, obviously not sorry in the least. "What the hells difference does it make?"

"Magic has rituals, eh?" George said.

"I should hope so," the young wizard answered. "What's that got to do with anything, though?"

"Think of this as a ritual of the army," George said. "You don't need to salute me because you like me or because you think I'm wonderful. You need to salute me because you're a major and I'm a lieutenant general."

Alva sniffed. "Pretty feeble excuse for a ritual—that's all I've got to say."

"Maybe. Maybe not, too," Doubting George said. "But I'll tell you this—every army in the world has rituals like that. Every single one of 'em. If there ever were armies without those rituals, the ones that do have 'em squashed the others flat. What does that tell you?"

It told Alva more than George had expected it to. The mage's foxy features shut down in a mask of concentration so intense, he might have forgotten George was there. At last, after a couple of minutes of that ferocious thought, he said, "Well, sir, when you put it that way, you just may be right. It almost puts you in mind of the Inward Hypothesis of Divine Choice, doesn't it?"

Doubting George gaped at him. "Not that gods-damned daft heretical notion!" he exclaimed. On the far side of the Western Ocean, back in the mother kingdom, the land from which the Detinan colonizers left for their newer world, a mage who called himself Inward had proposed that the gods let beasts compete over time, those better suited to whatever they did surviving and the others failing to leave offspring behind. Every priest in the civilized world immediately started screaming at the top of his lungs, the most common shriek being, *With an idea like that, who needs gods at all?*

"It makes a lot of sense, if you ask me," Alva said. George had long known his wizard lacked conventional piety. He hadn't known Alva followed the Inward Hypothesis. As far as he was concerned, the wizard who'd proposed it had known what he was doing when he chose a false name. Now Alva went on, "You said it yourself, sir. Armies that develop these rituals survive. Those that don't—don't."

He hadn't even been insubordinate this time. He'd left Doubting George nothing to do but repeat, "Dismissed."

Major Alva saluted. "A pro-survival ritual," he said thoughtfully. "I won't forget." And out he went.

Doubting George drummed his fingers on his desk. He'd scorned the Inward Hypothesis from the moment he first heard about it. But now, though he hadn't even known he was doing it, he'd argued in favor of what he'd thought he scorned. What did that say? Nothing good, he was sure.

If I hadn't tweaked Alva about saluting, he wouldn't have tossed a firepot at my thoughts. George sighed. Alva hadn't even meant to be inflammatory. As far as George was concerned, that made the wizard more dangerous, not less. "What *am* I going to do with him?" he wondered aloud. Asking was easy. Finding an answer wasn't.

And what am I going to do if the northerners really are up to something? he wondered. That was about as puzzling as what he would do with Major Alva. The problem was, he didn't have all the men he needed. General Hesmucet had gone traipsing across Peachtree toward the Western Ocean with all the best loyal soldiers in the eastern part of the Kingdom of Detina. He hadn't expected the northerners to be able to mount much of a challenge here in Franklin. If he was wrong . . .

"If he was wrong, gods damn it, I've got my work cut out for me," Doubting George muttered.

He scowled. That would do for an understatement till a bigger one came along. Among the men Hesmucet had taken with him were a good many from the wing George had commanded on the campaign that ended up seizing Marthasville. The soldiers Hesmucet hadn't taken made up the nucleus—the small nucleus—of the force George had here in Franklin.

Along with those men, he had garrison troops scattered through countless fortresses in Cloviston and Franklin. They guarded not only towns but also the glideway line that kept men and supplies moving. That meant they were scattered over the two provinces— one of which had stayed in the Kingdom of Detina but still furnished soldiers to Grand Duke Geoffrey's army, while the other had tried to leave but was, after a fashion, reconquered—and not in the best position to fight if they had to.

I'd better concentrate them, Doubting George thought gloomily. Then his scowl blackened as he shook his head. *If I do, Ned of the Forest's unicorn-riders will play merry hells with the glideways*. Ned of the Forest was no ordinary commander of unicorn-riders, no ordinary raider. When he hit a glideway line, he didn't just damage it. He wrecked it. His troopers and mages knew their business altogether too well.

Doubting George shrugged. Keeping the glideway lines intact mattered less than it had earlier in the year. Hesmucet's men weren't tied to them for food and firepots and crossbow bolts any more. They were living off the country now, living off the country and by all accounts doing well. Raids against the glideways would still be a nuisance. They wouldn't be a disaster.

That decided Lieutenant General George. He hurried over to the scryers, who had their headquarters next door to his own. When the gray-robed mages looked up from their crystal balls, he said, "Send word to all garrisons of company size and above: they're to move at once, to concentrate here at Ramblerton."

"Yes, sir," the wizards chorused. Unlike Major Alva, they knew how to obey orders. Also unlike him, they were utterly ordinary when it came to sorcery. Doubting George usually thought Alva's talents outweighed his shortcomings. Sometimes, though, he wondered.

Lieutenant General Bell looked down at himself. The northern officer was a big, strong man, with a bushy beard and a face that for years had put men in mind of the Lion God. These days, he looked like a suffering god. His left arm hung limp and lifeless at his side. He'd been with Duke Edward of Arlington and the Army of Southern Parthenia down at Essoville when he'd taken the crippling wound. And later that same summer, here in the east at the River of Death, a stone flung from a catapult had smashed his right leg, which now ended a few inches below the hip.

He was not a man much given to whimsy, Lieutenant General Bell. Nevertheless, surveying the ruins of what had been a redoubtable body, he nodded to Ned of the Forest with something approaching geniality and said, "Do you know what I am?"

"What's that, sir?" the commander of unicorn-riders asked.

"I am the abridged edition," Bell declared.

That brought a smile—a cold, fierce smile—to Lieutenant General Ned's face. "I reckon we ought to see what we can do about abridging us some o' those stinking southrons," he said, a northeastern twang in his voice. Unlike most high-ranking northern officers, he held not a drop of noble blood in his veins. He'd been a serfcatcher before the war, and enlisted as a common soldier when fighting between the two halves of Detina broke out. He'd risen to his present rank for one reason and one reason only: he was overwhelmingly good at what he did.

Bell knew perfectly well how much he needed such a man. He said, "With your help and the help of the gods, Lieutenant General, I look forward to doing just that."

"Good," Ned said. "A pleasure to have a man I can work with in charge of the Army of Franklin."

"Yes." Bell nodded. "I was wounded, I think, when you had your . . . disagreement with Thraxton the Braggart."

"Disagreement, hells. I was going to kill the son of a bitch," Ned said matter-of-factly. "He had it coming, too. But did you ever run across a miserable cur dog not worth wasting a crossbow bolt on? By the Thunderer's beard, that's Thraxton. So I let him live, and I daresay the kingdom's been regretting it ever since."

"Er—yes," Bell said. Count Thraxton's patronage, along with that of King Geoffrey, had got him the command of this army when Geoffrey sacked Joseph the Gamecock outside of Marthasville. Joseph hadn't fought the oncoming southrons; he'd stalled for time instead, hoping to make King Avram and his folk weary of the war. Bell *had* fought—and Marthasville *had* fallen. Bell remained convinced that wasn't his fault. Coughing a couple of times, he added, "You are . . . very frank."

"What's the point of talking if you don't say what you mean?" Ned returned. He leaned forward. "Now, then—what do you mean to do about the southrons down in Franklin?"

"General Hesmucet has marched west—he's off the

map," Bell said, and Ned of the Forest nodded to show he followed. Bell went on, "Not only has he marched west, he's taken all his best soldiers with him. That leaves nothing but odds and sods to hold Franklin and Cloviston. All we've got to do is win once, maybe twice, and we can get all the way to the Highlow River. What could stop us?"

Ned's eyes gleamed ferally as he thought about that. "You're right. And wouldn't Avram look pretty with egg all over his ugly mug? Thinks we're licked, does he? Thinks we're flat? Well, he'd better think again."

"That's right. That's exactly right. I think we're going to get along just fine together, Ned," Bell said.

"You tell me what to do. If I can, I will. If I can't, you'll hear all about the reasons why, I promise you," Ned said.

Bell was his superior. Bell was also, or had also been, a ferocious fighting man in his own right. He'd never been one to encourage insubordination. Even so, he didn't demand immediate, unquestioning obedience of Ned of the Forest, as he would have from anyone else. He just nodded and said, "Yes, we'll get on fine."

"Good." Ned gave him a sloppy salute he found himself gladder to have than many neat ones from lesser officers. The commander of unicorn-riders ducked his way out of General Bell's pavilion. Bell wasn't sorry to see him go. The commander of the Army of Franklin looked like a suffering god because he suffered—on account of both the ruined arm he still had and the ruined leg he no longer owned. The leg might be gone, but its ghost of sensation lingered, and that ghost was in constant, unending torment.

Working awkwardly with his one good hand, Bell opened the leather pouch he wore on the belt that held up his dark blue pantaloons (one leg, of course, pinned up short). He pulled out a little bottle of laudanum and yanked the cork with his teeth. Then, tilting his head back, he took a long pull from the bottle.

Odd-tasting fire ran down his throat. Laudanum was a mixture of brandy and poppy juice. If it wouldn't kill pain, nothing would. Only two things were wrong with that. One was, sometimes even laudanum wouldn't kill the pain Bell knew. The other was, he'd been taking the stuff ever since his arm was ruined at Essoville. After close to a year and a half, he needed much bigger doses to quell his agony than he had at first. By now, the amount of laudanum he took every day would have been plenty to kill two or three men who hadn't become habituated to the drug, or to leave six or eight such men woozy.

After he put the laudanum bottle away, Bell waited. He remembered the strange, almost floating sensation he'd got from laudanum when he first started taking it: as if he were drifting away from the body that still suffered. No more. Now laudanum was as much a part of his life as ale was part of a farmer's.

Little by little, the anguish receded in the dead arm and the missing leg, the leg that didn't seem to know it was missing. Bell sighed with relief. Laudanum didn't fuzz his wits any more, or make him sleepy. He was sure of that. He was just as sure he would have had trouble thinking without it. The few times the healers had run short of the drug—the north didn't have enough of anything it needed, except men who despised King Avram—he'd suffered not only from his dreadful wounds but from the even more dreadful effects of giving up laudanum.

He shuddered. He didn't like to think about that. As long as he had the drug, he was still . . . at least the shadow of a fighting man. So what if he couldn't bear a shield? So what if his stump was too short to let him sit a unicorn unless he was tied to the saddle? He was still a general, and a general who'd kept the surviving chunks of the Army of Franklin intact despite everything Hesmucet's superior force had done to destroy them. He still had bold soldiers, and he could still strike a savage blow. He could—and he intended to.

That sentry stuck his head into the pavilion. "I beg your pardon, sir, but Brigadier Patrick would like a moment of your time, if you have it to spare."

"Of course," Bell said expansively. As the laudanum made him feel better about the world, how could he refuse?

In strode Patrick the Cleaver. "Top o' the day to you, General," he said, saluting. The young brigadier's voice held the lilt of the Sapphire Isle, where he'd been born. After a career as a soldier of fortune, he'd crossed the Western Ocean to fight for King Geoffrey. He'd risen swiftly. Bell reckoned him among the finest wing commanders in northern service.

"What can I do for you now, Brigadier?" Bell asked, returning the salute. Yes, Patrick the Cleaver was one of the finest wing commanders in northern service. Bell doubted he would ever rise above the rank of brigadier, though. Even by Detinan standards, Patrick was devastatingly frank. Earlier in the year, he'd suggested that Geoffrey arm blond serfs and use them against King Avram's armies. Geoffrey had not been amused. No one else had had the nerve to make that suggestion since.

"What can your honor do for me?" Patrick repeated. "Why, sir, you can be after telling me when we set ourselves in motion against the gods-damned southrons."

"Soon," Bell said soothingly. "Very soon."

"And when exactly might 'soon' be?" Brigadier

Patrick inquired. "Sure and we shouldn't be letting 'em set themselves to meet us, now should we?"

"I don't intend to do anything of the sort," Lieutenant General Bell said. He also didn't intend to order the Army of Franklin into motion right this minute. Laudanum filled him with a pleasant lassitude, almost as if he'd just bedded a woman. Since the drug made it harder for him actually *to* bed a woman, that was just as well.

"Well, if you won't let those southron spalpeens set themselves, when are we to move?" Patrick the Cleaver demanded. "For would it not be a fine thing to be having the Army of Franklin in the province of Franklin once more? Better that nor hanging about down here in Dothan, I'm thinking."

"Yes, and yes, and yes," Bell said. "Yes, but how can we move till we gather supplies? Harvest time is long past. We can't live off the country. Whatever we eat, we'll have to take with us. The mages won't be able to conjure it up—that's certain. And we need more than food, too. Too many men in this army have no shoes on their feet. They're wearing pantaloons and tunics they've taken off of dead southrons—either that or they're wearing rags. We have to be ready before we march. Winter isn't far off, and it can get cold down in Franklin."

Brigadier Patrick mournfully clicked his tongue between his teeth. "Mighty fine does this sound, your Generalship, sir, but are you sure there's sense to it? For won't the southrons, may they find themselves in the hells or ever the gods know they're dead, the scuts, won't they be mustering and resupplying faster nor we could ever hope to? If I was in charge of this army, now, I'd—"

That was too much for Lieutenant General Bell's always fragile patience. "You are not in command of this army, Brigadier," he said in a voice like winter. "Nor are you ever likely to be. And you know why, too."

"I do that." Patrick matched him glare for glare. "I'm not in good odor in stinking Nonesuch, is why, the reason being I was man enough to tell King Geoffrey the plain truth, the which he cared to hear not a bit."

"Put pikes and crossbows in the hands of our blond serfs?" Bell shook his head. "We can't win the war with such so-called soldiers."

"The gods-damned southrons use 'em, and too many of our own brave lads dead in the dirt they've stretched," Patrick said. "You tell me we can't win the war with such soldiers? Well, I tell you this, Lieutenant General Bell, the which is the gods' own truth: we can't win the war without 'em. And that said, your Excellency, gods give you a good day." He bowed stiffly and stomped out.

"Miserable bog-trotting hothead," Lieutenant General Bell muttered. No, it was no wonder at all that Patrick the Cleaver would never enjoy a higher command.

Bell reached for his crutches. He got one under his good shoulder and used it to help lever himself upright. Then he put the other one under his bad arm. That shoulder still hurt despite the laudanum. Making it bear some small part of his weight only made it hurt worse, too. If he hadn't been a man who could stand pain, he would long since have cut his own throat or fallen on a sword.

Moving like an inchworm, one hitching step at a time, he made his way out of his pavilion. His sentries, surprised to see him outside, stiffened to attention. He ignored them. He wanted to look at the encampment. It didn't look much different from others he'd seen: a place full of tents and soldiers and lines of tethered unicorns. The woods of southern Dothan blazed with autumn colors around the campground. The day was bright and clear and crisp, without a cloud in the sky.

But he could see the differences when he looked for them. As he'd told Patrick the Cleaver, too many of his men wore gray pantaloons and sometimes even tunics captured from the southrons. That didn't just mean they couldn't get enough uniforms of the proper color, though they couldn't. It also meant that, in battle, the rest of his soldiers might start shooting at the wrong men.

That was why he'd issued an order that captured pantaloons and especially tunics had to be dyed King Geoffrey's indigo blue. A couple of kettles boiled and bubbled in the camps, with men taking out their newly dyed garments with sticks. Bell nodded in somber, leonine approval.

Here came some of Ned of the Forest's unicorn-riders. Bell eyed them.

Unicorn-riders in the Army of Southern Parthenia were aristocrats one and all, their mounts the finest they could provide. They took pride in grooming the beasts, not just to keep them clean and healthy but to make them look as smart as possible before going into battle.

By contrast, Ned's men looked like so many teamsters. Their uniforms were even shabbier than those of Bell's crossbowmen and pikemen. Slouch hats held the sun and rain out of their eyes. Their unicorns were in good enough condition, but nothing special. They didn't look like men who'd been able to keep all of eastern Franklin and Cloviston in an uproar behind southron lines, or like men who'd routed a southron army three times the size of their own in Great River Province. But they had. No matter what they looked like, they could fight. Bell had to respect that.

Overhead, a hawk flew south. Bell took it for a good

omen, hoping it meant the Army of Franklin would succeed when it did move south. He would have been more nearly certain had the beast been a dragon. The dragon was Detina's emblematic animal, the kingdom flying on its banners a gold dragon on red. To difference his men from those of Avram, Geoffrey had chosen a red dragon on gold.

But dragons had been rare in western Detina even when the colonists from across the Western Ocean used iron and unicorns and sorcery to seize the land from the blonds then inhabiting it. A few of the great beasts were still said to survive west of the Great River, but Bell had never seen one. In the lands far to the east, in the Stony Mountains beyond the steppes, dragons not only survived but flourished. That did Bell no good with the omens, though.

He shrugged a one-shouldered shrug. Even that hurt. But then, what didn't? Omens or no, he—and the Army of Franklin—would march south.

Corporal Rollant liked garrison duty. He'd spent a lot of time putting himself in positions where strangers could kill him: at the battle by the River of Death, storming up Proselytizers' Rise, and all through the campaign from the southern border of Peachtree Province up to Marthasville. No, he didn't mind being back here in Ramblerton, well away from the fighting, at all.

Most of all, he enjoyed strolling—or rather, swaggering—along the streets of Ramblerton in his gray uniform with the two stripes on his sleeve showing off his rank. Northerners, men and women who would gladly have left the Kingdom of Detina when Grand Duke Geoffrey proclaimed himself king in the north, had to get out of his way in a hurry, for along with the uniform he wore a shortsword on his hip and sometimes a crossbow slung on his back.

They got out of his way as they would have for any ordinary Detinan soldier. If they hadn't, he and his comrades would have made them sorry for it. He was one of King Avram's soldiers, yes, but not an ordinary Detinan. Ordinary Detinans were swarthy, with dark eyes, dark hair, and, on the men, dark beards. Rollant was a blond, an escaped serf from Palmetto Province who'd fled south to New Eborac and made a good living as a carpenter till taking service with others from his city, from his province, to help liberate all the serfs in the north from their bonds to the land and to their feudal overlords.

That would have been bad enough for the Detinans of Ramblerton. Serfs in arms had been their nightmare ever since their ancestors overthrew the blond kingdoms of the north. Because they'd easily won those wars, they professed to believe blonds couldn't fight. The gray uniform on Rollant's back argued against that.

But the stripes on his sleeve were what really made the locals shudder. One of those locals called, "You there!"—not to Rollant, but to his friend Smitty, a common soldier walking at his side.

"You talking to me?" Smitty asked. *He* was as ordinary a Detinan as any ever born, but for a silly streak.

"Well, who else would I be talking to?" the Ramblertonian demanded.

"Oh, I don't know." Smitty donned an expression of exaggerated idiocy. "You might be talking to my corporal there. He's got more rank than I do. He's the company standard-bearer, and I'm not."

The man from Ramblerton shuddered. "He's a blond!"

Smitty looked at Rollant as if he'd never seen him before. "Why, by the gods! So he is!"

"By the gods is right! It's against nature, that's what

it is," the local said. "What do you do when he gives you an order?"

After grave consideration, Smitty answered, "Well, most of the time I say, 'Yes, Corporal,' and I go off and do it. Isn't that right, your Corporalship?"

"Not often enough," Rollant said gravely. "But most of the time, yes, that's what you do. That's what you'd better do." He tapped the stripes on his sleeve.

"I know it." Smitty looked fearful. In confidential tones, he told the Ramblertonian, "He beats me when I disobey. He's terrible fierce, he is. You wouldn't want to mess with him, believe you me you wouldn't."

Animal. Rollant read the word on the local's lips. But the fellow didn't have the nerve to say it out loud. What he did say was, "It's a disgrace to the Detinan race, that's what it is." He walked off with his nose in the air.

"How about that?" Smitty said. "How do you like being a disgrace to the Detinan race?"

"Me? I like it fine," Rollant answered. "But I thought he was talking about you."

"Was he? Why, that son of a whore! Of all the nerve," Smitty said. He and Rollant both laughed. Rollant looked back over his shoulder. The Ramblertonian's back had got stiffer than ever. The blond laughed again.

But the laughter didn't last. By proclaiming he intended to release the Kingdom of Detina's blond serfs from their feudal obligations and ties to the land, King Avram had also, in effect, proclaimed they were, or could at least become, Detinans like any others. The whole of the north set about forming its own kingdom and went to war sooner than admitting that possibility. Even in the south, blonds had a hard time of it although legally on the same footing as real Detinans. Rollant had seen that for himself as a carpenter. He'd had to be twice as good as his competitors to get half as far.

It was worse in the army. Detinans prided themselves on being a warrior race. They also assumed blonds couldn't fight. Smitty had told the local he obeyed Rollant's orders. And so he did—most of the time. A lot of his comrades had been less willing after Rollant won the promotion he would have had long since if his hair were properly black, his skin properly swarthy.

Of course, if his hair were properly black, his skin properly swarthy, he never would have had to flee from Baron Ormerod's estate because he wouldn't have been bound to the land in the first place. Detinans didn't think about such things. Why should they? They didn't have to. *They* weren't bound, as his people were.

"How do you suppose that bastard would like working somebody else's land his whole life long?" Rollant asked Smitty. "How do you suppose he'd like his baron flipping up his wife's skirt, and nothing he could do about it if he wanted to keep his head on his neck?"

"Oh, he wouldn't have to worry about that," Smitty said.

"Ha!" Rollant said. "Just shows you've never been a serf."

Smitty shook his head and repeated, "He wouldn't have to worry about that." Only when Rollant started to get angry did he condescend to explain himself: "Any woman *he* could get would be too ugly for a nobleman to want."

"Oh." Rollant felt foolish. "All right. You got me there." He laughed, a little sheepishly.

The true Detinan flag, King Avram's flag, gold dragon on red, flew above the keep at the heart of Ramblerton and on important buildings throughout the town. Displaying false King Geoffrey's reversed banner was illegal as could be. Several Ramblertonians languished in jail for letting their patriotism outrun their good sense. As far as Rollant was concerned, they could stay there till they rotted.

When he'd been back on Baron Ormerod's estate, he would have reckoned Ramblerton the grandest town in the world. No more. After New Eborac City, it seemed small and only half finished. Not a single street was cobbled. All of them were dirt: dusty in the summertime, muddy now that winter was on the way. People flung their slops wherever they pleased, which meant the place stank even worse than it would have otherwise. And, toward the north, Ramblerton just petered out, clapboard houses gradually giving way to woods as one low ridge after another marked the land's rise from the banks of the Cumbersome River.

"No, not so much of a much," Rollant muttered.

"What's not so much of a much?" Smitty asked him.

"This place," he answered.

Smitty wasn't a city man. He came from a farm outside New Eborac City, and hadn't liked going into town even when he'd had the chance. He shrugged now. "Just one more place we've got to hold on to," he said.

"I should hope so!" Rollant said. "I'd like to see the gods-damned traitors try to take it away from us. They'd be sorry to the end of their days, by the Lion God's fangs."

He swore by the Lion God, the Thunderer, and the other gods of the Detinan pantheon. He believed in them. He worshiped them. His own blond ancestors had had gods of their own before the Detinans crossed the Western Ocean and took this land away from them. He still knew the names of some of them. He even believed in them, after a fashion. Worship them? He shook his head. They'd let his ancestors down when those ancestors needed them most. If he was going to worship gods, he wanted to worship gods who delivered.

"We ought to head back to camp," Smitty said.

"That's true." Rollant kept on walking.

Smitty laughed. "I know why you don't want to leave. You want to keep showing off in front of the traitors."

Rollant thought that over. Solemnly, he nodded. "You're right. I do."

But, when Smitty turned back, he followed. Doubting George's army held more people than Ramblerton, and sprawled over a wider area, too. If it weren't for riverboats on the Cumbersome and all the glideway lines that came into the area, the army would have starved in short order. As things were, a swarm of blond laborers—runaway serfs—unloaded boats and glideway carpets and heaved crates and barrels into ass-drawn wagons that would take them exactly where they needed to go.

The laborers were working harder than they would have if they'd stayed on their liege lords' estates. Plainly, they didn't care. They were doing this work because they wanted to, not because they had to. Rollant understood that down to the ground.

He eyed the asses with a certain mournful sympathy. His ancestors had tried to use bronze axes and ass-drawn chariots against the thunderous unicorn cavalry of the Detinan conquerors. They'd tried, they'd fought bravely—and they'd gone down to the subjection a whole great segment of Detina had taken enough for granted to be willing to fight rather than see it abridged in any way.

As they neared the encampment, Rollant pointed ahead. "Something's going on."

"Sure is," Smitty agreed. "Whole camp's stirring like a beehive just before it swarms."

"Where the hells have you two been?" Sergeant Joram growled when Rollant and Smitty reached their company. "We're marching inside of an hour."

"Marching?" Smitty said. "How come? Where are we going?"

Rollant was content to let Smitty ask the questions. Joram could have made his life as a corporal difficult, if not impossible. He hadn't done that. But he wasn't any great lover of blonds, either. Rollant stayed out of his way as much as he could—which was also, on general principles, a good thing to do with sergeants.

"We're going up toward the Dothan border," Joram answered now. "Doubting George has given John the Lister a whole wing's worth of men, and we're part of it. Seems like General Bell may be getting frisky up there, so they need us to make sure he doesn't kick up too much trouble."

"What's he going to do?" Smitty said scornfully. "Invade Franklin? After all the lickings he took over in Peachtree Province, he hasn't got the men for that, I wouldn't think."

"Nobody much cares what you think, Smitty," Sergeant Joram pointed out.

"By the gods, somebody ought to," Smitty said hotly. "I'm a free Detinan, and my ideas are just as good as anybody else's—better than some folks' I could name. How's Bell going to invade Franklin if he couldn't stop General Hesmucet, Thunderer love him, from marching across Peachtree Province? He didn't even try."

Had Rollant been so insubordinate, he was sure Sergeant Joram would have raked him over the coals on account of it. He was only a blond, after all. But he'd also seen that Detinans were passionate about freedom (about their own freedom, anyhow; that blonds weren't free seemed to bother most of them very little). They insisted on doing and saying what they wanted when they wanted to, and didn't care what might spring from that. It made them difficult soldiers.

With such patience as he could muster, Joram said, "I don't know how Bell's supposed to invade Franklin with what he's got, either. That's our job—to go down toward the border and find out. And if he's dumb enough to try it, we're supposed to give him a good boot in the ballocks to slow him down. What do you think of that?"

Smitty mimed giving *somebody* a good kick. Maybe it was Bell and the traitors he led. By the way his foot was aimed, maybe it was Sergeant Joram, too.

"Come on," Rollant said. "Let's get ready to move."

They didn't have a whole lot of getting ready to do. They were veterans; throwing what was essential into their rucksacks took only minutes. Everything that wasn't essential had long since been lost or left behind. Rollant had tea, crossbow bolts and strings, hard bread and smoked meat, a skillet made from half a tin canteen nailed to a stick, and a couple of pairs of socks his wife, Norina, had knitted and sent from New Eborac City. He carried more bolts on his belt, and a water bottle in place of the canteen that had long since split. Smitty's gear was similarly minimal. They both slung their crossbows on their backs and were ready to march.

Rollant had one more piece of equipment to carry. He went to take the company banner from its shrine. Offering a murmured prayer—if he'd had wine or spirits in the bottle, he'd have poured a libation—he plucked up the staff and proudly brought it to the front of the company. Standard-bearers were always targets; he'd taken the job by seizing the banner and keeping it from falling when his predecessor was hit. He made a special target, being not just a standard-bearer but also a blond. He didn't care. As far as he was concerned, the honor outweighed the risk—and the way he'd taken up the banner and gone on afterwards had won him promotion to corporal, no easy thing for a blond to win.

"Good day, Corporal," said Lieutenant Griff, the company commander. Griff was young and skinny and weedy, with a voice that sometimes cracked. But he was brave enough, and he treated Rollant fairly. The company could have had a worse man in charge.

"Good day, sir." Rollant saluted. "Ready when you are."

Griff returned the salute. He was punctilious about military courtesy. "We'll be moving soon, I'm sure. Not everyone is as swift as we are."

"Too bad for the others," Rollant declared.

"I like your spirit, Corporal," Griff said. "You make . . . you make a good soldier." He sounded faintly surprised at saying such a thing.

Ordinary Detinans often sounded faintly—or more than faintly—surprised when they said anything good about a blond. More often than not, they left such things unsaid. That Lieutenant Griff had spoken up pleased Rollant very much. He saluted again. "Thank you, sir!"

"You're welcome," Griff replied. Horns blared just then. All through the ranks, men stirred. They recognized the call to move out. Griff smiled at Rollant. "Raise that banner high, Corporal. We've got some marching to do."

"Yes, *sir*!" Rollant said, and he did.

Ned of the Forest turned to one of his regimental commanders as he led the long column of unicorn-riders south. "Feels good to be on the move, doesn't it, Biff?"

"Yes, sir," Colonel Biffle answered. Gray streaked his

beard. Ned's beard remained dark, though his hair had some gray in it. "I just hope we can hit the southrons a gods-damned good lick, that's all."

"So do I," Ned said. He was a big man, and a quiet one till he got in a temper or found himself in battle. Then nothing and no one around him was safe. He wore his saber on the right side, where a lefthanded man could draw it in a hurry. He also carried a short crossbow and a sheaf of bolts.

He'd had the crossbow for years. The hilt of the saber was wrapped in leather, not with the gold or silver wire some officers a good deal less wealthy than Ned affected. Unlike a lot of northern nobles, he didn't fight because he loved war and glory. He fought because he'd chosen Geoffrey over Avram, because he wanted to do everything he could to aid his choice, and because he'd turned out to be monstrous good at war. But, to him, the tools of the trade were only tools, nothing more.

"We *can* lick the southrons, can't we, sir?" Colonel Biffle asked. "We've whipped 'em plenty of times, after all."

"Of course we can," Ned said stoutly. "Of course we have. And of course we will." He didn't like the doubt in Biffle's voice. He didn't like the doubt in his own heart, either. The raids he'd led had kept the southrons off-balance in Cloviston and Franklin and in Great River Province, too. He'd sacked fortresses—once, his men had turned on and slaughtered a couple of hundred blonds at Fort Cushion when they didn't yield fast enough—and wrecked glideways. He'd ridden into southron-held Luxor, on the banks of the Great River, and come within inches of capturing the enemy commander there. He'd heard that General Hesmucet, as grim a soldier as the south had produced, had said there would be no peace in the east till he was dead.

By the gods, I'm not dead yet, he thought.

But he felt no great assurance when he looked back over his shoulder at the force General Bell had scraped together. Even with his own unicorn-riders added in, this was a sad and sorry remnant of the army that had smashed the southrons at the River of Death—had smashed them and then failed to gather up their men who were trapped at Rising Rock in northwestern Franklin. Ned muttered under his breath, calling curses down on the sour, empty head of Count Thraxton the Braggart. Comparing what he could have accomplished with what he'd actually done . . .

Ned muttered under his breath again. He didn't want to think about that. The more he did think about it, the angrier he got. *I should have killed him.* He'd had his chance, but he hadn't done it.

Biffle said something. "Tell me again, Biff," Ned said. "I was woolgathering, and I missed it."

Colonel Biffle grinned. "I hope you were dreaming up something especially nasty for the stinking southrons."

"Well . . . not exactly," Ned said. Biffle had been along when he had his run-in with Count Thraxton. Even so, he didn't tell the regimental commander he'd been contemplating the untimely demise of somebody on his own side. "Let me know what's on your mind. I'm listening now, and that's a fact."

"I said, I don't like the look of those clouds there." Biffle pointed to the southwest.

His attention drawn to them, Ned of the Forest decided he didn't like the look of those clouds, either. They were thick and black, and spreading over the sky with startling speed. No sooner had that thought crossed his mind than the first harbinger of the wind that carried them reached him. It felt wet and cold, a warning winter was on the way.

"We ought to step up the pace," he said. "Best to get along as far as we can before the rain starts coming down—because it will."

"Yes, sir," Colonel Biffle said, but his voice was troubled. A moment later, he explained why: "We'll get a long ways in front of the pikemen and crossbowmen if we do, won't we, sir?"

Except in the heat of battle, Ned was a man who seldom cursed. He felt like cursing now. Relentless motion was what he depended on to win his battles. However much he depended on it, though, he couldn't use it now. A sour laugh helped him make the best of things. "When you're right, Biff, you're right. We've got to stay with 'em, sure as sure."

He hated that. He felt tethered. He wanted to range freely with his unicorn-riders, to hit the southrons where they least expected it. At the head of the riders, he could do that when they were on their own. When they were also the eyes and ears for the rest of the army, he couldn't, or not so easily.

The wind got stronger and colder and wetter. Before long, the rain he'd foreseen started falling. It was a hard, chilly rain, a rain that would have been snow or sleet in another few weeks. Even as rain, it was more than bad enough. For a little while, it laid the dust the unicorns—and the asses drawing the supply wagons, and the wagons' wheels—kicked up from the roadway. But then, when it kept falling, it started turning the road to mud.

Ned of the Forest still didn't curse. He felt like it more than ever, though. His unicorn began to struggle, having to lift each hoof out of the thickening ooze with a separate, special effort. What his unicorn was doing, he knew every other unicorn was doing as well. They wouldn't be able to go fast now, no matter how much they wanted to.

As Ned yanked his hat down lower to help shield his eyes from the rain, Colonel Biffle said, "Other trouble with this is, it plays merry hells with the crossbowmen's bowstrings. If we do bump into the southrons now, it'll be swords and pikes, mostly."

"Yes," Ned said discontentedly. That wasn't the sort of fight General Bell's men were likely to win. In almost every battle, the southrons could put more men into the field than could King Geoffrey. If both sides could only chop and thrust, who had the edge? The one with the most soldiers, surely.

Down came the rain. *Come on, Thunderer*, Ned thought in annoyance. *You're supposed to be on our side, aren't you? We need good weather to get where we need to be before the southrons know what we're up to.*

The Thunderer, of course, did what he wanted to do, not what Ned of the Forest wanted him to do. Lightning flashed. A few heartbeats later, thunder rumbled in the distance. Another lightning bolt crashed down. This time, the thunder came quicker and sounded louder and closer.

"They say you don't ever want to hear thunder the same time as you see lightning," Biffle remarked.

Ned nodded; he'd heard that, too. But . . . "Who are *they*?" he asked. "The ones who lived?"

"I suppose so," Colonel Biffle said. "I never really thought about that till now." His chuckle was a little uneasy.

"You've always got to think about these things," Ned said gravely. "The more you believe just because *they* say it's so, the worse things will go wrong if *they* turn out to be a pack of fools—and, a lot of the time, *they* do. The only things you ought to take on faith are the gods."

Biffle nodded. But then, with another chuckle, he asked, "Why even take *them* on faith?"

Ned scratched his head. He'd believed himself a freethinker, but doubting the power of the gods? That had never occurred to him. At last, laughing uncomfortably himself, he answered, "Don't take 'em on faith if you don't want to. The way they show themselves in the world, you don't need to."

"No, I suppose not," Biffle agreed. Lightning flashed again. Through the boom that followed, the regimental commander added, "Pretty hard not to believe in the Thunderer when you hear that, isn't it?"

"I should say so," Ned replied.

It started raining harder. The drops drummed and hissed off the ground, off growing puddles, off the unicorns and men. Ned had to lower his head to keep the rain from soaking his face. He did some more muttering. His riders and the footsoldiers who made up the rest of General Bell's army could keep going forward in such weather, but the supply wagons wouldn't have an easy time. Neither would the catapults and the repeating crossbows that made charges across open country so expensive.

"Captain Watson!" Ned called, pitching his voice to carry through the rain. When he had to, he could make his voice carry through almost anything. "Come up here, Captain, if you please. I need to speak with you."

"Coming, sir!" Watson called back. A moment later, his unicorn rode beside Ned of the Forest's. Colonel Biffle drew off a little way, so as not to eavesdrop; he was polite as a cat. Saluting, Watson asked, "What can I do for you, sir?"

Ned eyed him with more than a little affection, which only showed how things could change. When Viscount Watson first joined his unicorn-riders, Ned had thought himself the victim of somebody's bad joke. The alleged commander of engines had been a beardless nobleman of twenty, surely too young and too well-bred to know what he was doing or to be much use in the field. A couple of years of hard fighting had proved otherwise. Watson still couldn't raise much more than fuzz on his cheeks and chin, but Ned no longer cared. He could handle catapults and repeating crossbows and the men who served them. Past that, nothing else mattered.

Now Ned could ask, "Will your toys be able to keep up with us?" and know he would be able to rely on the answer he got.

Captain Watson nodded. "Yes, sir. I'll *make* 'em keep up, by the gods. If I have to, I'll unharness the asses hauling them and put unicorns in the traces instead. If that doesn't do it, soldiers hauling on ropes will keep the carriages moving."

"Good man," Ned said. "That was what I wanted you to tell me."

Grinning, Watson said, "You don't ever want to hear no from anybody."

"Not from anybody in my command," Ned agreed. "Not from anybody I'm relying on."

Watson nodded again. He already knew that. Nobody who served under Ned of the Forest could help knowing it. Ned would have been an impossible commander if he hadn't driven himself harder than he drove any of his men. They knew how hard he worked at war, and did their best to match him.

Something up ahead, half seen through the curtain of rain . . . Ned leaned forward, peering hard. It had been a white something, which meant . . . "Was that a southron scout on unicornback there, sneaking off into the woods before we could get a good look at him?"

"I didn't see him, sir," Captain Watson answered. Colonel Biffle shrugged to show he hadn't noticed anything out of the ordinary, either.

Wheep! Ned's sword came free from its scabbard.

"I'm going to have a look," he said. "If that *is* a southron, I don't aim to let him get back and tell his pals he's seen us." He spurred his unicorn forward.

Most commanders would have sent out scouts to hunt down an enemy. Ned didn't think like that, and never had. He was as good a fighting man as any he led. He'd been wounded several times, and had close to a dozen unicorns killed under him. As he rode toward the woods now, he leaned forward and a little to one side, using this mount's body as a shield in case that southron had a crossbow aimed at him.

Ned laughed softly. If the fellow did see him and tried shooting at him, he might not have much luck. In weather like this, bowstrings soon turned soggy and useless.

When Ned reached the woods, he slid down off the unicorn and tethered it to the branch of an oak. He could move more quietly and less conspicuously on foot. That southron—if there had been a southron, if Ned hadn't been imagining things—had gone in a couple of hundred yards from where Ned was now. Ned hurried forward, flitting from tree trunk to tree trunk like one of the ghosts the blonds believed to haunt the wilderness. Ned didn't believe in those ghosts, though he did want to send that southron's spirit down to the hells.

A flash of white—was that the enemy soldier's unicorn? Ned of the Forest drifted closer. Yes, that was the unicorn, and there sat the southron, still mounted. *Fool*, Ned thought. *You'll pay for that.* The gray-clad soldier had sword in hand, and no doubt felt very safe, very secure. What he felt and what was real were two different things, as he'd soon find out.

With a wordless bellow making do for a battle cry, Ned rushed him. The southron cried out, too, in horror. He had to twist his body awkwardly to meet Ned's attack, for the northern commander of unicorn-riders approached on his left side, and he, like most men, used his right hand.

Swords clashed. The southron managed to turn Ned's first stroke. The second laid open his thigh. The third tore into his belly. He shrieked. His blood poured down the unicorn's white, white flank. Ned of the Forest pulled him out of the saddle and finished him with a thrust through the throat.

That done, Ned sprang onto the unicorn's back. It snorted fearfully and tried to rear. He used his weight and the reins and the pressure of his knees to force it down again. Then he rode it back toward his own men, pausing to reclaim the animal he'd tethered before going hunting for the scout.

The troopers cheered when he emerged from the rain riding one unicorn and leading another. They knew what that had to mean. "Scratch one southron," somebody called, and the rest of the riders took up the cry. Ned waved, pleased with them and pleased with himself.

"Looks like you were right, sir," Colonel Biffle said.

Ned shrugged. "He got careless. The gods won't help you if you don't give 'em a chance."

"I expect you're right," Biffle agreed.

"You bet I am." But then Ned started thinking about some of the things King Geoffrey had done, most notably leaving Count Thraxton in command much too long, till far too much of the east was lost. *The gods won't help you if you don't give 'em a chance*. He wished he hadn't put it quite like that.

Captain Gremio squelched through mud that threatened to pull off his shoes with every step he took. The road would have been bad any which way. It was even worse because Ned of the Forest's unicorns had chewed it into a quagmire before any of General Bell's foot-soldiers marched down it.

"Come on! Keep it up! We can do it!" Gremio called to the soldiers of the company he commanded. The men from Palmetto Province slogged along in no particular order. But they did keep moving. Gremio didn't suppose he could ask for more than that.

One of the soldiers grinned a wet, muddy grin at him. "You going to send us to jail if we don't?" he asked.

Back in Karlsburg, Gremio had been a barrister. That made him unusual among northern officers, most of whom came from the ranks of the nobility. Baron Ormerod, whom he'd replaced, had owned an estate outside Karlsburg. But Ormerod was a year dead now, killed in the disastrous battle of Proselytizers' Rise. Gremio had led the company since he fell.

He knew he couldn't be too sensitive when soldiers teased him. If he were, they'd never give him any peace. He managed a grin of his own as he answered, "Not likely, Landels. My job back there was keeping people out of jail, not putting them in. Of course" — he stroked his bearded chin— "for you I might make an exception."

Landels laughed. He had to, for the men around him were laughing, too. Show you had a thin skin and you would pay and pay and pay.

Colonel Florizel, the regimental commander, rode up on a unicorn. No one held that against him; he had a wounded foot that had never healed the way it should have. "How are things, Captain?" he called.

"As well as can be expected, sir," Gremio answered.

Florizel nodded, apparently satisfied, and rode on. He hadn't asked the question that most needed asking, at least to Gremio: *how well can things be expected to be?* Like most soldiers in General Bell's army,

Florizel seemed to think everything was fine. After all, the Army of Franklin was moving forward again, wasn't it? Soon it would reenter the province for which it was named, wouldn't it? How could anything be wrong when that was so?

Some people—a lot of people, evidently—had no sense of proportion. That was how things looked to Gremio. A lot of people had trouble seeing what lay in front of their faces. The realm Grand Duke—now King—Geoffrey had fought so hard to form was in trouble. King Avram's men held the whole length of the Great River, cutting Geoffrey's kingdom in half. General Hesmucet, against whom the Army of Franklin had fought so long and so hard, was cutting a swath of destruction through Peachtree Province as he marched toward the Western Ocean, with no one able to stop him or even to slow him down very much. The Army of Southern Parthenia was trapped in Pierreville, with no chance for Duke Edward of Arlington to break free.

Gremio sighed. General Bell loudly proclaimed that his move south would set all the new kingdom's troubles right. Gremio hoped he knew what he was talking about. The barrister-turned-soldier didn't believe that. He was trained to examine evidence and see where it led. He didn't believe, but he did hope.

"Come along! Straighten it up!" Sergeant Thisbe called. "Look like men, gods damn it, not a shambling herd of goats!" Thisbe's light, true tenor pierced the noise of the rain like a rapier piercing flesh. Unlike those of most Detinan men, Thisbe's cheeks were bare of beard. The soldiers, as soldiers often will, paid more attention to their sergeant than they did to a captain.

Trouble seeing what lay in front of their faces . . . Gremio laughed, though it wasn't really funny. How long had he had trouble seeing what lay in front of *his* face? Only the whole war, up until a couple of months before. If Thisbe hadn't been wounded, Gremio knew he would still be a blind man. He also knew Thisbe wished he still were a blind man.

"How are you feeling?" he asked the sergeant.

"Just fine now, thanks," Thisbe answered. "You see? I didn't need to go to the healers after all."

"You were smart not to, Sergeant," Landels said. "Those bastards will help somebody every now and again, but they bury more than they cure."

"I was smart not to, sure enough," Thisbe said. The sergeant's eyes were on Gremio. He knew just what those words meant, or thought he did. Landels and the other ordinary soldiers marching down the muddy road didn't.

All I have to do is open my mouth, and Thisbe is gone from this company, Gremio thought. He and the sergeant both knew that. He could see some excellent good reasons for speaking up, too. On the other hand, the company would lose far and away its best underofficer if he did. And Thisbe would hate him forever, too.

He didn't know which of those worried him more. That he didn't know worried him all by itself. That he didn't know was, in fact, one of his better arguments for talking things over with Colonel Florizel.

He'd thought so for weeks. No matter what he'd thought, though, he'd kept quiet up till now. That he'd kept quiet worried him, too. He stole a glance at Thisbe. Thisbe, as it happened, was looking at him. The sergeant kept trying to pretend the wound and everything that followed from it had never happened. Gremio had gone along with that up till now. He knew it couldn't last forever, though.

How would it break down? What would happen when it did? He had no idea. Sooner or later, he would find out. Meanwhile . . .

Meanwhile, he kept marching through the mud. As long as he concentrated on putting one foot in front of the other, he didn't have to think about anything else. Sometimes, even for a barrister, not thinking came as a relief.

Darkness fell earlier every day. Getting a fire started with wet wood wasn't easy. "Where's a mage when we really need one?" somebody grumbled.

It was, Gremio thought, a good question. The north had held on as long as it had in this war because its mages were generally better than the ones the southrons used. Being better for battle magic, however, didn't necessarily mean being better for small, mundane tasks like starting fires.

Gremio looked around. He didn't see any blue-robed mages around, anyhow. He had no idea what they were doing. His mouth twitched in what wasn't quite a smile. A lot of the time, they had no idea what they were doing, either.

Some of his men still carried half-tents that they toggled together to give them shelter from the rain. More, though, had long since abandoned such fripperies or had never had them to begin with. Gremio's mouth twisted again. Tents weren't the most important thing on his mind right now. A lot of his men had no shoes. That was a far more urgent worry.

Eventually, by dousing wood with oil that wouldn't be used on wagons now, the soldiers got some smoky fires going. They huddled around them, trying to get warm. Some poked bare toes toward the flames. Gremio pretended not to see. The only way those men would get shoes again would be by taking them off dead southrons.

Along with his men, he toasted hard biscuits over the fire. Toasting made the weevils flee, or so people said. Gremio hadn't noticed that much difference himself. Every so often, something would crunch nastily under his teeth when he bit down. He'd learned to pay little attention. Weevils didn't taste like much of anything.

Smoked and salted beef accompanied the biscuits. No bugs got into the beef. Gremio suspected that was because they couldn't stand it. Every time he choked down a bite, he wondered who was smarter, himself for eating the stuff or the bugs for having nothing to do with it. He feared he knew: one more thing better left unthought about. But marching made a man hungry as a wolf. If you didn't eat all you could, how were you supposed to keep moving dawn to dusk? You'd fall over dead instead. Gremio had seen men do it.

Thisbe said, "Another day or two and we'll be back *in* Franklin."

"Seems only right, since we're the gods-damned Army *of* Franklin," a soldier replied.

"That's what it says on the box, anyways," another soldier said. "But this'll be the first time in almost a year we've really been there—since the stinking southrons ran us out after Proselytizers' Rise."

Low-voiced curses, and some not so low-voiced, made their way around the campfire. All the men who'd been with the regiment then still felt the Army of Franklin had had no business losing that battle. The southrons had swarmed straight up a steep cliff, right at everything King Geoffrey's men could throw at them. They'd swarmed up—and the northerners had run away, leaving the field to them.

"A regiment of men could have held that line," Thisbe said, exaggerating only a little, "but a whole army didn't."

"Thraxton the Braggart's spell went wrong." Gremio spread his hands, as if to say, *What can you do?* And what could they do—now? Nothing, and he knew it only too well. "The spell was supposed to fall on General Bart's men, but it landed on us instead. We didn't run because we were cowards. We ran because we couldn't help it."

"Well, to the hells with Thraxton, too," Landels said. "Scrawny old sourpuss never did lead us to anything that looked like a victory."

Heads bobbed up and down. Gremio and Thisbe nodded along with the ordinary soldiers. Blaming Thraxton the Braggart meant they didn't have to blame themselves. But they knew they'd fought as well as men could. Thisbe said, "The one time we had as many men as the southrons—when we fought 'em at the River of Death—we whipped 'em. And then Thraxton threw that away, too."

More nods, some angry, others wistful. If they'd laid proper siege to Rising Rock, if they'd starved General Guildenstern's army into submission . . . If they'd done that, the whole war in eastern Detina would look different now. Could they have done it? One man in four at the fight by the River of Death had been killed or wounded. Thraxton hadn't thought they'd had it in them. Maybe he'd been right. But if they couldn't follow up a victory, what were they doing fighting this war? No one seemed to have an answer for that.

A runner with his hat pulled low to keep rain out of his eyes came splashing up to the smoky, stinking fire. "I'm looking for Captain Gremio," he announced.

Gremio got up off the oilcloth sheet he'd been sitting on. He wondered why he bothered with it, since he was already good and wet. "You've found me."

"Colonel Florizel's compliments, sir, and he's meeting with all his company commanders in his pavilion," the messenger replied.

"Now?"

"Yes, sir—as fast as all of you get there."

"I'm on my way." As Gremio walked toward Florizel's tent, he reflected that that was one way to tell Geoffrey's men from Avram's when they spoke, for most of the differences between their dialects weren't great. But, while men in the northern provinces said *all of you*, those in the south had a separate form for the plural of the second-person pronoun, with a separate set of verb endings to go with it.

Sentries in front of Florizel's tent saluted as Gremio came up. The regimental commander was a stickler for the forms of military politeness. Returning the salutes, Gremio ducked inside.

He was glad to find only a couple of the regiment's other nine company commanders there ahead of him. "Good evening, your Excellencies," he said—both of them were barons, not that either was liege lord to much of an estate.

"Good evening," they answered together, an odd mix of caution and condescension in their voices. They were nobles, and Gremio wasn't, which accounted for the condescension. But he was not only a barrister but had more money than either one of them even if he didn't own land. That accounted for the caution.

One by one, the rest of the company commanders came in. They were noblemen, too. Gremio and they exchanged the same sort of greetings he'd given their fellows. When the last captain squeezed into the pavilion, Colonel Florizel said, "Gentlemen" —he nodded to Gremio, as if to make sure Gremio knew he was included among that elect group— "I want you to convey to your men the certainty that we can yet win this war."

"Hells, don't they already know that?" demanded Captain Tybalt, one of the two who'd been there ahead of Gremio. He had courage to spare and a temper hot as dragonfire, but no one had accused him of owning a superfluity of brains. He went on, "Of course we'll lick the gods-damned southrons."

It hadn't seemed like *of course* to Gremio for a very long time. While he tried to find some way to say that without actually coming out and calling Tybalt an idiot, Colonel Florizel said, "We're getting entirely too many desertions. Spirits are down. Some of the soldiers seem to think we're bound to lose. We have to fight that. We have to fight it with everything that's in us. Do you understand?"

Some of the soldiers have the sense of ordinary human beings, Gremio thought. But Captain Tybalt didn't seem the only company commander astonished at the idea that his men might need encouragement.

"Do you understand?" Florizel repeated.

"Yes, sir!" the captains chorused. Gremio made sure his voice was loud among theirs. He knew he would have to carry out the order. He also knew a lot of the men he led would laugh at him when he did. They hadn't given up hoping they would win, but more than a few had given up expecting it. He'd given up expecting it himself.

"Very well, gentlemen. Dismissed," Florizel said. "And remember, I want no more desertions from this regiment."

"Yes, sir," the company commanders said again. Again, Gremio made sure his voice rang out. He also wanted no more desertions. He knew better than to expect or even hope for that, though.

II

John the Lister looked over his shoulder from unicornback. He knew more than a little pride in the gray-clad army he led north from Ramblerton, the army that, from this hilltop, resembled nothing so much as a long, muscular snake. Turning to his adjutant, he said, "By the gods, I hope Lieutenant General Bell *is* coming south. I'll be very happy to meet him. We'll have a lot to talk about, don't you think?"

"Yes, sir," Major Strabo said. "And a sharp conversation it will be." Strabo was a walleyed man with a taste for bad puns, but a good officer despite that.

"Er—yes." John's eyes pointed as they were supposed to. He had, however, gone bald as a young man, and wore a hat at any excuse or none. He had a good excuse now: the rain that dripped from a sky the color of a dirty sheep's belly.

"Can we flagellate them all by ourselves, do you

think?" Strabo asked. He never used a simple word if he could find a long, obscure one that meant the same thing, either.

After a brief pause to figure out what the other officer was talking about, the southron commander nodded. "I expect we can manage that," he said. "Unless he's managed to scrape together more men than I think he has, we'll be all right. And even if he has, well, we can still hurt him."

"Here's hoping we get the chance," Major Strabo said.

"Well, my choice'd be to have the traitors throw in the sponge and surrender, but they're as much a bunch of stubborn Detinans as we are, so I don't expect that'll happen tomorrow, or even the day after," John the Lister replied. "We're just going to have to lick 'em. If we do have to lick 'em, I'd sooner do it up in northern Franklin than down around Ramblerton."

"There'd be a great gnashing of teeth if they got so far," his adjutant agreed.

The rain kept right on falling. It soaked the roads. It soaked the soldiers. It soaked the woods that covered so much of Franklin. Woods that had been gorgeous with the gold and crimson and maroon leaves of autumn only days before went brown and bare. The leaves lay underfoot, losing their color and smelling musty and turning dreadfully slimy and slippery in the rain.

When evening came—as it did earlier every day— the army made camp. Tents sprouted like toadstools in the rain. Considering the number of toadstools also sprouting, John found himself in an excellent position to make the comparison. More of his men carried tent halves than held true among the traitors. More supply wagons accompanied his army, too. He might not be able to move quite so fast as Lieutenant General

Bell's lean, hungry troopers, but he thought his men could hit harder when they got where they were going.

And there's not a thing wrong with taking whatever comforts you can into the field, he told himself. The traitors boasted of how scrawny they were, and did their best to turn their quartermasters' weakness and sometimes incompetence into a virtue. John preferred having his men go into a fight well fed and as well rested as they could be. Thanks to the manufactories and glideways of the south, he got his wish.

Hat still jammed down low on his head, he prowled through the camp, making sure everything ran to his satisfaction. Not everyone recognized him as the commanding general; like Marshal Bart, who led all of King Avram's armies, he wore a common soldier's blouse with stars of rank on the shoulders. But here and there, a man would call out, "How's it going, Ducky?"

Whenever that happened, John would wave back. He'd had the nickname a long time. When he was a younger man, he'd combed his hair so that it stuck up at the nape of his neck, putting people in mind of the southern end of a northbound duck. A lot of young men had worn their hair in that style twenty years before. He wasn't the only one who'd ended up getting called Ducky or the Duck on account of it, either.

He took out a mess tin and stood in line with ordinary soldiers to see what their cooks were dishing out. Once, a cook had been so surprised, he'd dumped a ladleful of stew on his own shoes. John had got the helping after that, and it had been pretty good. What he got this time was hard bread and cheese and sausage—nothing very exciting, but decent enough of its kind. He ate with real enjoyment.

"Halt! Who goes there?" sentries called as he approached his own pavilion. They were alert, but not alert enough to have noticed he wasn't in there to begin with.

"I'm John the Lister," he said dryly.

The sentries muttered among themselves. At last, one of them said, "Advance and be recognized, sir."

Advance John did. Recognize him the sentries did. They came to attention so stiff, they might almost have come to rigor mortis. "Am I who I say I am?" the general asked.

"Yes, sir!" the sentries chorused. One of them held the tent flap wide for him.

"You don't need to bother with such foolishness," John said as he stooped and went into the pavilion. "Just make sure you keep any traitors from sneaking in after me, all right?"

"Yes, sir!" the sentries chorused once more. They would do what he told them—unless they did something else, in which case the force he commanded would have a new leader shortly thereafter. John suspected it would do about as well under a fair number of other officers. He contrived to keep this suspicion well hidden. As far as his superiors knew, he was convinced he was indispensable.

His superiors . . . John the Lister let his broad-shouldered bulk sag into a folding chair, which creaked under his weight. Depending on how you looked at things, he had either a mere handful of superiors or a whole great list of them. In King Avram's volunteers, he was a brigadier. As long as the war against false King Geoffrey lasted, he could command a wing or even a small independent army, as he was doing now.

That was true as long as the war lasted. The minute it ended, he was a brigadier no more. In King Avram's regular army, the army that persisted in peacetime, John was only a captain, with a captain's pay and a captain's prospects. The best he could hope for as a captain would be to end up at a fortress on the eastern steppes, commanding a company against the blond nomads who preyed on the great herds of aurochs there—and on Detinan settlers.

Doubting George was a lieutenant general of volunteers. But Doubting George was also a brigadier among the regulars. If the war ended tomorrow, he would still be a person to reckon with. John knew only one thing could get him the permanent rank he so craved: a smashing victory over the southrons. Knowing what he needed was all very well. Knowing how to get it was something else again.

John gave Doubting George reluctant credit. George could have commanded this move up from Ramblerton himself. He could have, but he hadn't. He already owned as much permanent rank as he needed. John didn't. He had the chance to earn more here, if he could.

And if Lieutenant General Bell was really coming. John the Lister still found that hard to believe. If he'd commanded the force Bell had, he wouldn't have tried doing anything too risky with it. He would have held back, waited to see what the southrons opposing him had in mind, and hoped they'd make a mistake.

Waiting and seeing, of course, had never been one of Bell's strong points. If the situation called for him to charge, he would. If the situation called for him to wait and see, odds were he would charge anyway.

Besides, who could say if he was really so foolish? The way things looked, the north needed something not far from a miracle to beat King Avram's armies. Hanging back and waiting wouldn't yield one. Striking for the enemy's throat might.

John had a flask on his belt. He liberated it, yanked out the stopper, and took a swig. Sweet fire ran down his throat: brandy made from the most famous product of Peachtree Province. After that one swig, John corked the flask and put it back on his belt. One nip was fine. More? More and he would have been like General Guildenstern, who, reports said, had been the worse for wear during the battle by the River of Death. Maybe Guildenstern would have lost sober, too. No one would ever know now.

After pulling off his boots, John the Lister lay down on his iron-framed cot. He had a brigadier's privileges; a captain would have slept wrapped in a blanket or on bare ground, like a common soldier. The cot wasn't very comfortable, either, but it was better than bare ground.

As usual, John woke before dawn. He got out of bed and put his boots back on. That done, he scratched. Back in Ramblerton, he'd been able to bathe as often as he wanted to—even a couple of times a week if he was so inclined. He usually wasn't that fussy, though some of the more fastidious officers were. Out in the field, though, and especially when the weather wasn't warm . . . He shook his head. Some things were more trouble than they were worth.

When he came out of the pavilion, a couple of blond servants carried its light furnishings to a wagon, then took down the big tent itself and packed it on top of the cot and chair and folding table. "Thanks, boys," John said. They both nodded. John had to remind himself they weren't serfs. They worked for wages, just as a proper Detinan might find himself doing.

They probably think they are proper Detinans. John the Lister muttered under his breath. He didn't necessarily share that opinion. But he was sure Grand Duke Geoffrey had no business tearing the kingdom to pieces. That put him on King Avram's side, no matter what he thought about blonds and whether or not they were as good as Detinans whose ancestors had crossed the Western Ocean.

John watched the encampment come to life around him. Here and there, blonds cooked for soldiers and helped them knock down their tents. Most of those men and women were runaway serfs. They got wages these days, too. That they had fled their liege lords said they wanted to be free, even if they didn't always quite know how.

As John went over to get in line for breakfast, he plucked thoughtfully at his long, square-cut beard. Wanting to be free was what marked Detinans. Maybe some of those blonds had what it took after all.

"Here's Ducky!" Again, the nickname ran ahead of the general commanding. John pretended he didn't hear. He took his place in a line, got a bowl of mush with bits of salt beef chopped into it, and had a blond cook's assistant pour boiling water into the tin mug he held out. Like a lot of soldiers, he doubted he was a human being till he'd had his first mug of tea, or sometimes his second.

When he came back from breakfast, Major Strabo saluted, saying, "Greetings and salutations, sir."

"Hello." John politely returned the salute. Unlike his adjutant—perhaps in reaction to his adjutant—he kept his own speech simple.

Walleyed Strabo looked past him to the left and right. "Now we fare forth to find and flummox the fearsome foe."

"You should have been born a bard, Major," John said. "There are times when you sound like the singers who told the tale of our ancestors and how they conquered the blonds' kingdoms they found in this new land."

"You do me honor by the comparison, sir." Again, Strabo looked around John rather than at him.

Mounts gleaming whitely, unicorn-riders went north ahead of John's main force. General Guildenstern's disaster had taught southron officers one lesson, any-how: to make sure they didn't get taken by surprise the way he had. John the Lister didn't expect trouble from Lieutenant General Bell. He didn't expect it, but he wanted to be ready for it if it happened. Better to take precautions without need than to need them without taking them.

These days, General Guildenstern fought blond sav-ages out on the steppe. His ignominious departure from the scene of the important action was no doubt intended as a warning to others who made mistakes in battle against the traitors. John the Lister's shiver had nothing to do with the chilly weather. He knew any man could make mistakes—even the gods made mistakes.

On the other hand, things might have gone worse for Guildenstern. John considered the fate of Brinton the Bold, who'd led King Avram's army in the west for most of the first two years of the war. Brinton was handsome and brave, and had won a couple of small victories not long after the fighting started. But he moved with the speed of a tortoise, and his nickname soon seemed an ironic joke. Avram had asked, not altogether in jest, if he could borrow the army him-self, since Brinton didn't seem to be using it. These days, Brinton was a soldier no more. He went around the south making speeches that fell just short of treasonous, declaring that he would do a better job with a crown on his head than Avram could. If Detina hadn't had a long tradition of letting any freeman say what-ever he pleased as long as he didn't harm anybody, Brinton's body probably would have hung from a cross near the Black Palace as a warning to others.

As things were, the former general was merely an embarrassment to the army he'd left and to most of the people who listened to him. He had a hard core of supporters, but John doubted they'd ever come to much.

In any case, a soldier who remained a soldier had no business worrying about politics. John listened to the tramp of thousands of booted feet. That sound filled up the background of his days in the saddle. It got mixed in with the sound of his own blood flowing through his veins, so that it almost seemed a part of him. When the men fell out for a rest break, as they did every so often, he missed it.

At sunset, he chose a low swell of ground to make camp. "What's the name of this place?" he asked Major Strabo.

"This, sir, is Summer Mountain," his adjutant said after checking a map.

John the Lister snorted. "Mountain?" he said. "This isn't even a pimple next to the Stonies, out past the steppes to the east. Even here, it's hardly a hill."

"It's anything but insurmountable," Strabo agreed. "But Summer Mountain the map calls it, and Summer Mountain it shall be forevermore."

"Miserable excuse for a mountain," John grumbled. "It's not summer any more, either."

The unicorn-rider came galloping back toward Ned of the Forest. "Lord Ned!" he shouted. "Lord Ned!"

Ned was no lord, but he didn't mind being called one. No, he didn't mind at all. "What did you see, Ben?" he asked. "You must've seen something, to be yelling like that."

"Sure did, Lord Ned," the rider named Ben said. "The stinking southrons are camped on Summer Mountain, only a couple of hours' ride from where we're at."

"Are they?" A sudden feral glow kindled in Ned's eyes. "How many of 'em? Doubting George's whole army?"

"No, sir," Ben answered. "I don't even reckon they've got as many men as we do."

"Is that a fact?" Ned murmured. The unicorn-rider nodded. "Well, well," Ned said. "In that case, something ought to happen to 'em. You're sure about what you saw, now?"

"Sure as I'm on my unicorn's back," Ben said. "I'd take oath by the Lion God's mane."

"They aren't trying to set up an ambush, or anything like that?"

"No, sir. Nothing like that at all," Ben said. "They were just making camp, like they'd gone as far as they figured on going today and they were setting up for the night."

"Something really *ought* to happen to them, then," Ned said. "You come along with me, Ben. We're going to have us a little talk with Lieutenant General Bell."

"You reckon he'll pay attention to the likes of me?" the unicorn-rider asked.

"He'll pay attention, by the gods," Ned said softly. "If he doesn't pay attention to you, he'll have to pay attention to me." He smiled a thoroughly grim smile. He'd met few men who cared to stand up under the full storm of his anger.

He and Ben rode back toward Bell, who traveled with the pikemen and crossbowmen of the Army of Franklin. When he saw Bell on a unicorn, he sighed. The commanding general hadn't had an easy time of it. Ned had often wondered about Bell's common sense. No one could doubt the leonine officer's courage. Bell's adjutant had had to tie him into the saddle. The stump of his left leg was too short to give him a proper grip on the unicorn's barrel.

Ned looked down at himself. He'd been wounded several times, and still had the tip of a crossbow quarrel lodged somewhere near his spine. It had broken off; the surgeon had dug out most of the bolt, but not all. Men often died from a wound like his. He'd confounded the healers—he'd got well instead. He still had the use of all his parts, even if some of them had been punctured. Nothing on earth would have made him trade places with Lieutenant General Bell.

What was it like, to be a wreck of your former self? What was it like, to *know* you were the wreck of your former self? Bell knew those answers. Ned was glad he didn't.

Respecting Bell's bravery, he saluted the other officer. The commanding general cautiously returned the salute. With only one good hand, he had to be cautious about taking it off the reins. "What can I do for you, Lieutenant General?" Bell asked. As it often did, laudanum dulled his voice. His sagging, pain-racked features told the story of his suffering.

At Ned's prompting, Ben repeated his news for Lieutenant General Bell. Ned added, "Sounds to me like if we move smart, we can hit the southrons a devils of a lick."

"I don't want to go straight at them," Bell said. "We just use up our army that way, and we haven't got enough men to be able to afford it. But if we can flank the southrons out of their position, if we can get around behind them and make them retreat past us . . . If we can do that, we'll really make them pay."

"Yes, sir. I like that." Ned of the Forest liked hitting the enemy—he was one of the hardest hitters the north had. Hitting the enemy head-on was a different story. He saw that plainly, and wondered why more of King Geoffrey's generals didn't. Nodding with pleasure, he asked, "What do you want me to do?"

"Hold the gods-damned southrons in place with your men," Bell answered. "Don't let them come any farther north, and don't let them get wind of how many men we have or what we're doing with them."

"I'll try my best, General," Ned said. "Can't promise to hold off a whole army with just my unicorn-riders, though."

"Yes, I understand that," Bell said. "You can slow it down, though, and screen away the enemy's riders, eh?"

"I expect I can manage that much, yes, sir," Ned allowed. "Wouldn't be much point to having unicorn-riders if we couldn't do that sort of thing, would there?"

"I wouldn't think so," the commanding general said. "Well, go on down and take care of it, then. The men on foot will follow and outflank the southrons while you keep them in play. And when they realize we've got behind them and they have to retreat, they're ours. I wish I could ride with you."

"So do I, sir," Ned said, more or less truthfully. Bell was no unicorn-rider by trade, but everyone said he'd been a fierce fighter before he started leaving pieces of himself on the battlefield.

Bell paused now to swig from the bottle of laud-anum he always carried with him. "Ahh!" he said, and quivered with an ecstasy that almost matched a priest's when he had a vision of his chosen god. For a moment, Bell's eyes lost their focus. Whatever he was looking at, it wasn't the muddy road and the trees shedding the last of their leaves. But then, quite visibly, he came back to himself. "You there, trooper!" He nodded at Ben.

"Yes, sir?" the unicorn-rider asked.

"You're a corporal now," Bell said. "You took chances to get your news, and you deserve to be rewarded. Lieutenant General Ned, see that the promotion goes into your records, so his pay at the new rank starts from today."

"I'll do that, sir," Ned promised. "I was going to promote him myself, matter of fact, but better he gets it from the general commanding the whole army."

Ben—now Corporal Ben—looked from Ned to Bell in delight. "Thank you kindly, both of you!" he exclaimed.

"Don't you worry about that. You'll earn those stripes on your shirt, never fear," Ned said. "Now come on. We've got work to do."

He urged his unicorn forward with knees and reins and voice. Ben followed. Ned felt Lieutenant General Bell's eyes boring into his back. Bell could ride well enough to stay in the saddle, but he'd never storm forward in a unicorn charge.

Of course, Ned didn't plan on storming forward in a unicorn charge, either. More often than not, he used his riders as mounted crossbowmen, not as cavaliers slashing away with swords. Unicorns let them get where they needed to go far faster than they could have afoot. Getting there first with the most men was essential. And if you got there first with a few, most of the time you wouldn't need any more.

Back in the west, Duke Edward's commander of unicorn-riders, Jeb the Steward, had played at war as if it were a game. His men had fought as much for sport and glory as to do the southrons harm. They'd done quite a lot; not even Ned could deny it. But Jeb the Steward had died the summer before. He'd died a hard, nasty death, with a southron crossbow bolt in his belly. The war in the west had got grimmer since he fell.

Here in the east, the war had been grim from the start. With the southrons holding down Franklin and Cloviston but a lot of men in the two provinces still loyal to the north, brother sometimes faced brother sword in hand. No fight could be more savage than one of that sort. Some of Ned's own unicorn-riders had kin on the other side.

Ben pointed ahead. "There's our riders, sir."

"I see 'em," Ned answered. He raised his voice to a great bellow: "Blow *advance!*" The trumpeters obeyed. The men cheered the martial music. Ned went right on roaring, too. "We've got the gods-damned southrons ahead of us," he told the unicorn-riders. "We've got 'em ahead of us, and we need to hold their vanguard where it's at. Reckon we can do that, boys?"

"Hells, yes!" the troopers shouted. If Ned of the Forest wanted them to do something, they *would* do it, or die trying.

But even reaching the southrons proved harder than Ned had expected. He booted his unicorn up to a trot so he could lead the riders from the front, as he always did. One reason they followed him so well was that they knew he wouldn't order them to go anywhere he wasn't going himself.

He knew where Summer Mountain lay and how to get there. He knew the whole province of Franklin. *I'd better*, he thought. *By now, I've fought over just about every gods-damned inch of it.* He guided the troopers forward with confidence.

Despite that confidence, though, after about an hour Colonel Biffle rode up to him and asked, "Excuse me, Lord Ned, but should we be heading west?"

"West?" Ned stared at him. "What the hells are you talking about, Biff? I'm riding north, and that's as plain as the horn on a unicorn's face." But even as he spoke, he looked around. As he did, he started to swear. He wasn't usually a blasphemous man; only the prospect of battle brought foul language out in him—battle, and being tricked before battle. For, when he did look around, he saw that he *had* been riding west, and hadn't known it. Face hot with fury, he demanded, "Where in the damnation is Major Marmaduke?"

"I'm here, sir." His chief mage came up on donkey-back; few wizards could be trusted to ride unicorns without killing themselves. Marmaduke was a fussy little man who kept his blue sorcerer's robe spotlessly clean no matter what. "What do you need?"

"I need a wizard who's really here, not one who just thinks he is," Ned snarled. "Why the demon didn't you notice we've been riding west, not north?"

Major Marmaduke looked astonished. "But we're not riding—" he began, and then broke off. After a moment, he looked even more astonished, to say nothing of horrified. "By the gods, we've been diddled," he said.

"We sure have. I thought we were supposed to be the ones with the good wizards, and the southrons were stuck with the odds and sods." Ned scornfully tossed his head. "Seems like it's the other way round."

"Lord Ned, I am—mortified," Marmaduke stammered. "To think that I should be taken in—that I should let us all be taken in—by a spell of misdirection . . . I will say, though, that it was very cunningly laid. I did not think the accursed southrons had such subtlety in them."

"Well, they gods-damned well do," Ned growled. "And now we're going to have to backtrack and hope by the Thunderer's prong that they haven't gone and stolen a march on us. If they have, you'll pay for it, and you'd best believe that."

Marmaduke licked his lips. "Y-y-yes, sir."

With icy sarcasm, Ned went on, "You reckon you can see if they try any *more* magic on us while we're heading back? You up to that much, anyways?"

"I—I hope so, sir," the mage replied miserably.

"So do I. And you'd better be." Scowling, Ned

shouted to his men, "They've tricked us. When we catch 'em, we'll make 'em pay. Meanwhile, though, we've got to ride like hells to get back to where we were at so we *can* catch 'em. Come on! We'll do it right this time!"

They rode hard. Anybody who wanted to fight under Ned of the Forest had to ride hard. As his unicorn trotted back toward the place where they'd gone wrong—Ned hoped it was back toward the place where they'd gone wrong—he kept muttering morosely about Major Marmaduke. The wizard still seemed bewildered at what had happened. Ned wasn't bewildered. He was furious. As far as he was concerned, the southrons had no business outdoing northern men when it came to sorcery.

Riding up ahead of his troopers, he was one of the first to reach the crossroads from which his force had gone astray. He couldn't imagine how it had happened. He knew which fork he should have taken. He thought he *had* taken it. But the southrons' magic had led him astray, and had kept him from noticing anything was wrong. He muttered again. It had certainly kept Major Marmaduke from noticing. If Colonel Biffle hadn't finally spotted the trouble . . . Ned didn't care to think about what might have happened then.

And, riding up ahead of his troopers, he was one of the first to spy the southrons riding toward the crossroads. He threw back his head and laughed. "All right, you sons of bitches!" he shouted. "You reckoned you could lead us astray and get here first. Now I'm going to show you you aren't as smart as you figured." He looked around. As usual, a trumpeter rode within easy range of his voice. He waved to draw the man's attention, then called, "Blow *charge!*"

As the martial notes rang out, his sword leaped free from the scabbard. The blade gleamed in the watery autumn sunshine. He spurred his unicorn forward. The well-trained beast lowered its head, aimed its ironclad horn at the enemy, and sprang toward the southrons. "King Geoffrey!" Ned shouted. Sometimes dragoon work wouldn't do. Sometimes you had to get right in there and fight unicorn to unicorn.

Some of his men yelled Geoffrey's name, too. More, though, shouted, "Lord Ned!" They fought for him personally at least as much as for the north. Their swords also flashed free. Some of them fit arrows to the strings of the light crossbows they carried. That would do for one volley, anyhow; reloading on unicornback wasn't for the faint of heart.

"Let's get 'em!" Ned roared. "This is *our* road, by the gods, and they've got no business trying to take it away from us."

As soon as the southrons spied his men and him, they deployed from line to column. Their own gray-clad officers briefly harangued them. Then they too were charging. "King Avram!" they cried. "King Avram and freedom!"

"To the hells with King Avram, the serf-stealing bastard!" Ned yelled. His unicorn tore a bleeding line in the flank of the first enemy beast it met. He'd trained it always to gore to the right, to protect him on that side. A rider came up to him on the left. The other fellow would have had most men at a disadvantage. Not lefthanded Ned. He chopped the southron out of the saddle. How many men had he killed in the war? A couple of dozen, surely. Well, he'd killed before the war, too. A serfcatcher didn't have an easy life.

He had more men with him than the southron commander, who'd led a mere reconnaissance in force. Ned's men were fiercer, too, at least that day. They sent the southrons, those who lived, fleeing back in the direction from which they'd come as fast as they could gallop. Ned pushed them hard. He always did.

"They know we're here now," Colonel Biffle said as the pursuit at last wound down.

Ned nodded and spoke one word: "Good."

Rollant had served in King Avram's army for a couple of years now. He'd seen things go well, and he'd seen things go wrong. He knew the signs for both.

Unicorn-riders galloping back toward the crossbowmen and pikemen were not a good sign. He knew that only too well. Turning to Lieutenant Griff, he said, "Something's gone to the hells up ahead."

"It does look that way, doesn't it?" Griff's voice broke as he answered. He kicked at the muddy ground under his shoes. He was very young, and hated showing how young he was.

Plenty of crossbowmen in the company drew the same conclusion as its standard-bearer and commander. "Who ever saw a dead unicorn-rider?" they jeered as the men on the beautiful beasts pounded past.

Some of the riders pretended not to hear. Some cursed the footsoldiers who mocked them. And one fellow yelled, "Wait till *you* run up against Ned of the Forest's troopers! We'll see plenty of you bastards dead, and you'd better believe it."

After that, Corporal Rollant gripped the staff of the company banner so tight, his knuckles whitened. He tramped on in silence, grim determination on his face. Lieutenant Griff needed a while to notice; he wasn't the most perceptive man ever born. But at last he asked, "Is something wrong, Corporal?"

"Ned of the Forest," Rollant said tightly. "Sir."

"Yes, his riders really fight, no doubt about it," Griff said. "I wish we had more men as good, I truly do, but—"

"Fort Cushion," Rollant broke in. "Sir."

"Oh," Griff said. For a wonder, he had the sense not to say anything more. Fort Cushion, along the Great River down in Cloviston, had been garrisoned by blonds loyal to King Avram till Ned's men overran it. Stories of what happened next varied. Ned's men claimed the blonds had started fighting again after surrendering. They'd killed almost the whole garrison as a result.

"Yes, sir." Rollant's voice was bleak. "Whatever happens, I don't intend to let those bastards get their hands on me while I'm breathing."

"I . . . see," Griff said. "Well, Corporal, taking everything together, I can't say that I blame you."

As the southron army tramped north, Rollant waited for the order to deploy from marching column into line of battle. Where Ned's riders were, the bigger army of traitors couldn't be far behind, not if rumor came anywhere close to telling the truth. Rollant *wanted* to fight. Part of that sprang from knowing that a blond had to do better than an ordinary Detinan to be reckoned half as good. And part of it sprang from his own desire to pay back Ned's men for what they'd done down in the southeast.

But the horn call he waited for never came. Instead, after a little while, the trumpeters blared out *retreat*.

"What the hells are we retreating for?" Rollant burst out.

"I don't know." Lieutenant Griff sounded almost as perplexed as Rollant, if not quite so furious. "But we have to obey the order. We can't go on and attack the traitors all by ourselves."

Rollant, just then, was ready to do exactly that. Regretfully, he realized Griff was right. Even more regretfully, he turned back toward Summer Mountain.

"It *is* a good defensive position." Was Griff trying

to convince Rollant or himself? Rollant couldn't tell. Maybe the company commander couldn't tell, either. He went on, "If they have more men than we do . . ."

"How could our unicorn riders tell one way or the other, if they only ran into—ran from—Ned's riders?" Rollant asked.

"That's a good question, Corporal," Griff said. "I haven't got a good answer for you. I wish I did."

"We've been fighting this war for a long time now," Rollant grumbled. "Why don't we have generals who know what the hells they're doing yet?"

"I think John the Lister has a pretty good idea of what he's doing," Griff said. "If that *is* the traitors' whole army north of us, we've got to slow it down as much as we can. We haven't got the men to crush it all by ourselves."

"By the Lion God's claws, I'd like to try," Rollant declared.

Lieutenant Griff started to answer, then stopped and gave him a curious look. It wasn't quite the ordinary curious look he would have given had he been arguing strategy with another ordinary Detinan. It also held a certain amount—perhaps more than a certain amount—of surprise. Rollant had no trouble reading Griff's thoughts. *Here's a blond who's more interested in fighting the traitors than the commanding general is. Aren't his kind supposed to be cowards and weaklings?*

Wearily, Rollant hefted the company standard. Even more wearily, he said, "Sir, you didn't let me keep this because I was afraid to fight the northerners. You didn't promote me to corporal because I was afraid, either. The more of those bastards we kill, the sooner this gods-damned war'll be over."

"My," Griff said after a long, long silence. "You *have* got fire in your belly, haven't you?"

"Who better to have fire in his belly than somebody who grew up bound to a liege lord's lands and ran away?" Rollant replied. "I really know what we're trying to knock down. Sir."

That produced another silence, even longer than the first. Rollant wondered if he'd said too much, if Griff would take him for no more than an uppity blond from now on. At last, the company commander said, "If all blonds had your spirit, Corporal, we Detinans would have had a much harder time casting down the blond kingdoms in the north after we crossed the Western Ocean."

He means well. He's trying to pay me a compliment, Rollant reminded himself. He chose his words with care: "When we fight the traitors, sir, we've got crossbows and iron-headed pikes and unicorns and siege engines and all the rest, and so do they. What we fight with is even on both sides. If the blonds back in those days had had all that stuff instead of bronze maces and asses hauling chariots, and if they'd known more wizardry, the Detinans *would* have had a lot tougher time."

"So you think it was the quality of the equipment and magic, not the quality of the men?" Griff said.

"Of course, sir. Don't you?"

Again, Rollant wondered if he'd said too much. Griff startled him by laughing. "That isn't the lesson Detinans learn in school, you know," he remarked.

"Yes, I know it isn't. But don't you think it's true anyhow?"

Lieutenant Griff didn't answer right away. Rollant gave him credit for that; a lot of Detinans would have. At last, his voice troubled, Griff said, "There may be *some* truth in what you say, Corporal. But wouldn't you agree that the first Detinan conquerors were also heroes for overcoming so many with so few?"

Now it was Rollant's turn to think before he spoke.

He'd never tried to put himself in the place of those first Detinans to cross the Western Ocean. His sympathies lay with the blonds. Only reluctantly did he take the conquerors' side in his mind. No more than a couple of hundred of them had come on that first expedition to what was now Palmetto Province. They'd pushed inland till they found the blond kingdom closest to the Western Ocean—and they'd shattered it. They might have been villains. They hadn't been weaklings.

His voice as troubled as Griff's, Rollant answered, "There may be *some* truth in what you say, Lieutenant."

"Thank you," Griff said, which surprised him. The company commander explained, "I've heard blonds—educated men, men who'd lived all their lives in the south and were never serfs—say the first heroes were nothing but bandits and robbers, and should have been crucified for what they did. That goes too far, I think."

"Maybe," Rollant said. "But then, I've heard Detinans—educated men who'd lived all their lives in the south and were never liege lords—say blonds were nothing but cowards and dogs, and should have got even worse than what the first conquerors gave them. That also goes too far, I think."

"That's different," Griff said.

"How?" Rollant asked. "Uh, how, sir?"

"Why . . ." Griff stopped. Undoubtedly, he'd been about to answer, *Why, because that has to do with blonds*, or some such thing. Unlike a lot of ordinary Detinans, he saw that wouldn't do here. He gave Rollant a lopsided grin. "Have anyone ever told you you can be difficult, Corporal?"

"Me, sir?" Rollant shook his head. "I don't know what you're talking about. All I want to do is get to the bottom of things."

"And if that doesn't prove my point, I don't know what would." The lieutenant waved to the low swell of ground ahead. "There's Summer Mountain." Not even to Rollant's eye, trained by the low country of Palmetto Province, did it look anything like a mountain. Griff went on, "As I said before, it's a good defensive position."

"Yes, sir," Rollant agreed dolefully. "I thought the idea was to get out there and fight the enemy, though. I wonder why we're not."

"Difficult," Griff repeated, but he had a smile in his voice.

When they did return to Summer Mountain, Colonel Nahath promptly set the whole regiment to digging trenches and heaping the earth up in front of them for breastworks. Rollant didn't mind digging. On the contrary—the long campaign up in Peachtree Province the previous spring and summer had taught him, along with the rest of General Hesmucet's army, the value of trenches.

"Isn't this fun?" Smitty said, flinging up dirt.

"It's a lot more fun than getting shot," Rollant answered. "To the hells with me if I want to stand out there in the open for the traitors to shoot at."

"Well, there is that," Smitty admitted. "But it's a lot of work, too."

"I don't mind work," Rollant said. "This is the kind of work I chose for myself when I volunteered to be a soldier."

Smitty gave him a quizzical look. "You sure you're one of those shiftless, no-account, lazy blonds everybody's always talking about?"

Only a few men in the regiment could ask him a question like that without making him angry. Smitty, fortunately, was one of those few. Rollant paused in his own digging, thought for a moment, and then said, "You've got a farm outside of New Eborac City, so you work for yourself, right?"

"For myself, and ahead of that for my old man, yes," Smitty answered.

"You work hard, then, right?"

"I'd better." Smitty wiped his sweaty face on his sleeve. "Who'll do the job if I don't?"

"Now imagine your boss doesn't care about you—he just wants to get work out of you," Rollant said.

"I didn't know you'd met my father," Smitty said.

That threw Rollant off his glideway path of thought. He needed some effort to return to it: "Suppose he doesn't care about you, like I said. Suppose he can do anything he wants to you. Suppose you have to do what he says, no matter what it is. And suppose, no matter what you do, you don't get to keep a copper's worth of money from the crop you bring in."

"Doesn't sound very good," Smitty said. "Got any more supposes?"

"No, that's the lot of them," Rollant said. "Suppose they're all true. How hard would you work then?"

"I'd do the least I could get away with, I expect." Smitty paused, taking the point. "So you're saying blonds aren't lazy on account of the gods made 'em lazy. You're saying they're lazy on account of the liege lords give 'em the shitty end of the stick."

"Either that or they give 'em the whole stick right across the back." Rollant turned away so Smitty wouldn't see his enormous grin. He'd actually made an ordinary Detinan understand some small fraction of what serfdom was like.

"Here, I've got a question for you," Smitty said.

"Go ahead," Rollant answered.

"You know that book that lady wrote—*Aunt Clarissa's Serf Hut*? How true to life is that?"

Ten years before the War Between the Provinces broke out, *Aunt Clarissa's Serf Hut* had scandalized the south and north, though in different ways. It had outraged the south while infuriating northern nobles. They called it a pack of lies, wrote denunciations and rebuttals by the score—and banned it in their provinces to keep serfs from getting their hands on it.

"Well, I've read it," Rollant said. "Read it a while after it came out, because I needed to learn my letters first after I ran away from Baron Ormerod. I thought it was pretty good. The liege lord in the book was a lot nastier than Ormerod, but there are some like him. I never knew a blond who was made out of sugar and honey paste, the way some of the ones in the story are, but it tells about what a hard, nasty life serfs have, and that's all pretty much true. What did *you* think of it?"

"Made me want to grab the first northern nobleman I saw and give him a good kick in the teeth," Smitty said.

"Suppose you just get back to work instead," Sergeant Joram rumbled from behind him.

"Yes, Sergeant," Smitty said meekly, and dug in with the shovel. But working didn't keep him from talking: "Some of the people we've got set over us, they might as well be liege lords themselves."

He had a point. In a lot of ways, underofficers had more power over common soldiers than nobles did over serfs. Rollant hadn't thought of it like that before, but it was so. *Does that make me like Baron Ormerod?* he wondered. In spite of the warm work, he shivered. That was a chilling thought if ever there was one.

From unicornback, Colonel Florizel called, "Come on, men! Keep moving. If we get around behind the stinking southrons, we can bag the whole rotten lot of them."

"The colonel's right," Captain Gremio agreed. "If we move fast now, it pays off later. We can give King Avram's men just what they deserve."

Sergeant Thisbe was blunter about the whole business, as sergeants have a way of being: "Keep moving, you worthless slobs! We've got somewhere to get to, and we're going to get there, gods damn it!"

And the men paid more attention to Thisbe than they did to Gremio and Florizel put together. That didn't particularly surprise Gremio. He could order them into fights where they might get killed, but Thisbe had the power to make their everyday life hells on earth.

On they tramped, making the best time they could down muddy roads. They never saw a southron unicorn-rider. Captain Gremio assumed that was Ned of the Forest's doing. Ned was no gentleman, as far as he was concerned. Gentleman or not, Ned knew what he was doing with unicorn-riders.

At last, with evening twilight fading from the sky, they had to stop for the night. Thisbe sent the spriest men out to gather wood and fill water jugs. Other soldiers simply flopped down, exhausted. As fires began to burn, the weary men gathered around them to toast hard bread and meat and simply to get warm. All through the first part of the night, more and more stragglers joined them: men who'd marched as hard as they could, but hadn't been able to stand the pace.

Gremio held a chunk of hard bread over the flames on a forked stick. He didn't watch while he did it; he was one of those who preferred not to think about the weevils that were abandoning his supper. Sometimes, of course, he had to eat bread without toasting it first. He preferred not to think about everything that crunched between his teeth then, too.

Sergeant Thisbe sat at the same fire, looking as worn as Gremio felt. One by one, soldiers lay down where they were and started to snore. Thisbe yawned, but stayed awake. So did Gremio. After a while, with more and more snores rising around them, Gremio quietly asked, "Can we talk?"

"I don't really think we've got a whole lot to say to each other, sir," Thisbe answered. "Not about that, anyway."

"I know what I know," Gremio said. "I have the evidence." Yes, he was a barrister through and through.

"You'll do what you want to do, sir." Thisbe's voice was toneless.

"But—" Gremio couldn't shout. He couldn't even swear, not without . . . He shook his head. "I don't want to tell anybody about—"

"I'm glad," the sergeant said.

"I just want to—"

Sergeant Thisbe interrupted again: "To what, sir?" Normally, a sergeant who kept interrupting an officer would find himself in trouble in short order. Things weren't normal here, as Gremio knew too well. Thisbe went on, "There's nothing you can do, sir. There's nothing anybody can do till the war's over."

"But then—" Gremio said.

"But then, who knows?" Thisbe broke in once more. And, once more, Gremio let the sergeant do it without a hint, without so much as a thought, of reprimand. "I think you're the best company commander the regiment's ever had. To the hells with me if I know whether that means anything else." A shrug. "We'll find out then. Not now."

"You know what I think of you—some of it, anyhow," Gremio said. "You know I wanted to get you promoted to lieutenant."

"I didn't want that. You know I didn't want that." The harsh, flickering shadows from the fading fire exaggerated Thisbe's rueful expression. "Now I suppose you think you know why I didn't want it, too, gods damn it."

"Maybe I do," Gremio said, quite sure he did. He took a deep breath, then continued, "Well, here's something you may not know, Thisbe d— Sergeant. Once upon a time—"

"Before I got wounded?" Thisbe asked.

"Oh, yes, a long time before you got wounded," Gremio answered. "Once upon a time, a long time before you got wounded, I told myself that if I ever met a girl who could do the things you can, I'd marry her on the spot."

"Did you?" Sergeant Thisbe's voice held no expression whatever. When Gremio tried to read the under-officer's face, he found he couldn't. The brim of Thisbe's hat cast black shadow all across it, for the sergeant stared down at the muddy ground.

Gremio nodded. "That was what I said to myself, and I meant it, too. You can take it for whatever you think it's worth, Sergeant."

"It would be worth a lot, I figure, to a girl like that," Thisbe said. "But I'm not so much of a much. I expect you could find half a dozen girls who knew more than a dumb soldier like me ever dreamed of, just by snapping your fingers." The sergeant's light, true tenor was uncommonly earnest.

"You don't give yourself enough credit." Gremio had to fight to keep anger out of his voice. "For as long as I've known you, you've never given yourself enough credit, and I can't figure out why."

Thisbe still didn't look up. The sergeant's laugh seemed anything but mirthful. "You know me. You know where I am. Can't you figure it out for yourself?"

"Well . . . maybe I can," Gremio said.

"All right, then. And if you don't mind my saying so, sir, that's about enough of that for right now. That's too much of that for right now, if you want to know what I really think." Thisbe's yawn was theatrical, but probably no less real on account of that. "I'm going to wrap myself in my blanket and go to sleep. You ought to do the same thing."

"Yes, so I should." Seeing Thisbe yawning made Gremio want to yawn, too—not that he wasn't already weary after a long day's march. "Good night, Sergeant."

"Good night, sir." Thisbe's blanket was worn, almost threadbare. Gremio had a thicker, finer one. Were things different, he would gladly have given his to the underofficer, or at least invited Thisbe to crawl under it with him. He remembered doing exactly that, back in the days before Thisbe was wounded. He could no more imagine doing it now than he could imagine chasing all the southrons back to their own part of Detina singlehanded.

His hat made a tolerable pillow. He'd long since stopped worrying about having anything fancier. He fell asleep almost at once, as he always did when the Army of Franklin was on the move. Tramping along all day would knock a man out even if he wanted to stay awake, and Gremio didn't.

Horn calls pulled him out from under his blanket in the morning. He creaked to his feet, feeling elderly. Thisbe was already awake and sipping tea from a tin cup. The northerners called it tea, anyhow. Gremio didn't want to know from what all leaves and stems it was really made. The southrons' blockade kept much of the real stuff from getting into King Geoffrey's harried realm.

Gremio fixed himself a cup of his own. Even with honey added, the brew was bitter and nasty. But it was warm, and some of those leaves helped pry his eyelids apart, the way real tea did. He said, "That's better," and drained the cup.

"Couldn't hardly get by without something hot in the morning," Thisbe agreed.

Colonel Florizel limped up. "We'll be getting on the road soon," the regimental commander said. "So far, it doesn't look like the gods-damned southrons are stirring away from Summer Mountain. If we can get around behind 'em, we'll bugger 'em right and proper." He laughed loudly.

"Er, yes, sir," Gremio said. Florizel stumped off, looking miffed that the barrister hadn't laughed with him.

Gremio probably would have, if Thisbe hadn't been standing there beside him. The sergeant sent him a reproachful look. "*I* thought it was pretty funny, sir. I hope we *do* bugger the southrons."

Had the sergeant not been there, Gremio would have laughed. He knew that. He also knew he had to say something, and did: "I didn't think it was all that much of a joke. Besides, he shouldn't have said it—"

"When I was around?" Thisbe asked. When Gremio nodded, the sergeant looked even more reproachful than before. "What's that got to do with anything? I'm just one of the boys, and everybody knows it."

"Right," Gremio said tightly. "Shall we get the men ready to move, Sergeant?"

"Yes, sir." If anything bothered Thisbe, no sign of it appeared in the sergeant's face or bearing.

And the men *did* move. They might have moved faster if more of them had had shoes, but northern men were too stubborn to give in on account of something that trivial. As usual, no one begrudged Colonel Florizel his place on a unicorn. His wound wouldn't have let him keep up on foot.

Ned of the Forest's men were on unicorns, too, and seemed to be doing their job. Again, Gremio spotted not a single gray-clad southron rider. His guess was that the enemy really didn't know where the Army of Franklin was. He knew a certain amount of hope on account of that. The last time the southrons had been so fooled was before the battle by the River of Death, more than a year ago now. If they could be tricked again . . . Well, who could say what might happen?

We'd better not mess things up, the way we did then, Gremio thought. The Army of Franklin could have surrounded Guildenstern at Rising Rock and forced him to surrender. They could have, but they hadn't. And, in due course, they'd paid for the omission. General Bell was trying to make amends for that now. Maybe he would. Even a hardened cynic of a barrister like Gremio couldn't help hoping.

"Form column of fours!" he yelled. The men obeyed. Before joining King Geoffrey's army, Gremio hadn't dreamt how important marching drill was. Soldiers moved in column, fought in line. If they couldn't shift from one to the other in a hurry, they were in trouble. Getting caught in column was every commander's blackest nightmare.

Up at the head of the brigade, horns ordered the advance. A moment later, Colonel Florizel's trumpeters echoed the command for the regiment. The company had a trumpeter, too. The only trouble was, he wasn't much of a trumpeter. His notes assailed Gremio's ears.

"Let's go!" Sergeant Thisbe shouted. Away the Army of Franklin went, heading south. General Bell dreamt of reaching the Highlow River. If he could do it, he would give King Avram an enormous black eye. He might remind the provinces of Franklin and Cloviston of their allegiance to King Geoffrey—and, more to the point, bring their men and supplies into the war on Geoffrey's side, not Avram's. That would make the fight in the east a whole different struggle.

Captain Gremio's dreams were smaller. He would have been satisfied—no, by the gods, he would have been delighted—if the northerners could get around behind Summer Mountain and cut off the retreat of the southrons there. *One bite at a time*, he told himself. *If we can do one thing right, more will follow from that.*

Birds filled the sky overhead. They were flying north for the winter, flying north to escape the coming cold and snow and ice. Pointing to them, Thisbe said, "They're smarter than we are—they're going the right way for this time of year."

"I was just thinking the same thing," Gremio said, and beamed at the sergeant. Thisbe didn't beam back.

Every so often, a soldier would take a shot at the stream of birds. Every once in a while, a crossbow bolt would strike home and a bird tumble out of the sky. The lucky soldier would run over and grab it and put it on his belt to cook when the army stopped that night—if some other man didn't get it first. After Gremio broke up a couple of quarrels that were on the edge of turning into brawls, he ordered the men of his company to stop shooting at the birds.

"That's not fair, Captain," a soldier said. "We're hungry, gods damn it. Anything we can get is all to the good."

"It's not all to the good if you start stealing from one another and brawling," Gremio replied. "We'll do better hungry than we will if we can't trust each other."

"The captain's right," Thisbe declared. "Most of these birds aren't any more than a couple of mouthfuls anyway. They're not worth the trouble they're stirring up."

No one could say Gremio or Thisbe ate better than the common soldiers in the company. They didn't. The soldiers might have grumbled, but they followed orders. The only trouble was, not all commanders gave those orders, so quarrels over birds elsewhere slowed the company—and a crossbow quarrel shot at a bird came

down, point first, at Gremio's feet. Had it come down
on his head . . . One more thing he preferred not to contemplate. He stooped, yanked it out of the ground, and
held it high. "Here's another reason not to shoot things
up in the air," he said.

A voice rose from the ranks: "That's right, by the
gods. If we're gong to shoot our officers, we should
aim straight at 'em." The marching men bayed laughter.
Gremio managed a smile he hoped wasn't too sickly.

Along came a mage in a blue robe riding on the
back of an ass. He was muttering to himself, his fingers writhing in quick passes as he incanted. "An ass
on an ass!" another uniformed wit called. The wizard
affected not to notice—or maybe, preoccupied with the
spell he was casting, he really didn't. Whatever sort of
magic it was, Gremio hoped it worked.

It must have, for the company, the regiment—the
whole army—halted earlier than he'd expected. Colonel
Florizel rode up with a great big grin on his face.
"We've got 'em!" he said. "We've got 'em good, by the
gods! This is the only way they can retreat, and they
have to come right by us when they do. We'll land on
their flank, and then—!" He slashed a finger across his
throat. The soldiers raised a cheer, Gremio's voice loud
among theirs.

"General John! General John, sir!" The mage shouting John the Lister's name sounded on, or maybe just
over, the ragged edge of hysteria.

"What is it?" John asked. When people started
shouting in that tone of voice, it wasn't going to be
anything good.

And it wasn't. The mage burst into John's pavilion.
Horror was etched on his face. "They've used a masking
spell on us, sir!" he cried.

No need to ask who *they* were. "And what is this

masking spell supposed to do?" John inquired. "Whatever it's supposed to do, has it done it?"

"Yes, sir!" The mage sounded like a tragedian playing
in an amphitheater in front of images of the gods at
a high festival. "I'm afraid they've got round behind
the army, sir. We didn't notice till too late!"

What John the Lister felt like doing was kicking the
mage in the teeth. Botched wizardry had cost King
Avram's armies dear again and again. Now it looked
as if it was going to cost John. Instead of doing what
he felt like, he asked, "Didn't notice what?"

"Didn't notice General Bell's army on the move, sir,"
the mage answered miserably. "The wizards masked it
from us till just now."

"So did Ned of the Forest's unicorn-riders." John
the Lister's voice was unhappy and enlightened at the
same time. He'd wondered why Ned's men had been
so active, pushing back his own pickets and generally
doing their best to impersonate Bell's whole army. He
hadn't worried much about it, not till now. Ned was
always busy and active; he wouldn't have made such
a pest of himself if he weren't.

"What will we do, sir?" the gray-robed mage howled.
"What *can* we do?"

"Well, it seems to me that getting out of this mess
would be a pretty good idea," John replied. "Don't you
agree?"

"Y-yes, sir. But . . . how?"

"I don't know yet," John the Lister said. "I expect
I'll figure something out, though. Once I know where
the enemy is, that'll tell me a lot about what I can do."

"Sir, he's—he's behind us. Between us and Poor
Richard. Between us and Ramblerton." White showed
all around the irises of the wizard's eyes, as if he were
a spooked unicorn.

"That's not so good," John said, which would do for

an understatement till a bigger one came along. He tried for a bigger one in his very next sentence: "If there's one thing you don't want, it's the traitors sitting on your supply line, especially when the harvest is done and the foraging's bad."

"How can we hope to escape?" Despite John's calm, the wizard was the next thing to frantic. "If we stay here, we'll starve. If we try to retreat past the enemy, he'll hit us in the flank. He'll probably block the road, too, so we'll have no hope of getting by."

"This isn't the best position to try to defend," John said. "Too open, too exposed. Bell's men could make a clean sweep of us, and they wouldn't have to work very hard to do it, either. If we're on the move, though—"

"If we're on the move, they'll strike us in the flanks," the mage repeated.

"Maybe they will," John the Lister agreed politely. "But maybe they won't, too. Funny things can happen when you're on the move—look at how they just diddled us, for instance. They fooled us, so maybe we can fool them, too. How's *your* masking spell these days, Lieutenant?"

"Not good enough, sir, or they wouldn't have been able to do this to us." The wizard still seemed ready to cry.

John the Lister slapped him on the back, hard enough to send him staggering halfway across the pavilion. "Well, you and your friends should work on it, because I think we're going to need it soon. You're dismissed."

Muttering under his breath, the mage left. Once he was gone, John the Lister spent a minute or two cursing his luck and the incompetence of the wizards with whom he'd been saddled. A lot of southron generals had sent those curses up toward Mount

Panamgam, the gods' home beyond the sky. The gods, unfortunately, showed no sign of heeding them.

If nothing else, cursing made John feel better. General Guildenstern would have got drunk, which would have made him feel better but wouldn't have done his army any good. Doubting George would have loosed a volley of sardonic remarks that made him feel better and left his targets in despair. John tried to relieve his own feelings without carving chunks from anyone else. He didn't always succeed, but he did try.

Once he'd got the bile out of his system, he ordered a runner to find his adjutant and bring him back to the pavilion. Major Strabo came in a few minutes later. "What's the trouble, sir?" he asked. The commanding general explained. His walleyed subordinate seemed to stare every which way at once. "Well, that's a cute kettle of cod," Strabo said when John finished. "And what in the name of the cods' sort of coddity let the traitors hook us like that?"

"They outmagicked us," John replied. "They've done it before. They'll probably do it again. Now we have to figure out how to keep this from ending up a net loss."

For one brief, horrified moment, both of Strabo's eyes pointed straight at him. "You should be ashamed of yourself," the major said. "Sir."

"Probably," John the Lister agreed. "But I have more important things to worry about right now. So does this whole army."

"Your statement holds some veracity, yes." Major Strabo's eyes went their separate ways again. "What do you propose to do, sir?"

That was about as straightforward a question as was likely to come from John's adjutant. The commanding general answered, "I propose to get this army out in one piece if I can. If Bell forces a fight, then we give him a fight, that's all."

"Will you let him come to you, or do you aim to go to him?"

Two straightforward questions in a row—John the Lister wondered if Strabo was feeling well. He replied, "We're going back toward Poor Richard. If we can get there, it's a good defensive position. And if we stay here, Bell can starve us out without fighting. To the hells with me if I aim to let him do that. Draft orders for our withdrawal down the road to Poor Richard, warning it may be a fighting retreat."

"Yes, sir," Strabo said, and then, after some hesitation, "Uh, sir, you *do* know it may be a great deal worse than that?"

"Oh, yes, I know it." John nodded heavily. "I know it, and you know it. But if the men don't know it, they're likely to fight better if they have to. Or do you think I'm wrong, Major?"

"No, sir," Major Strabo answered. "I am of the opinion that your accuracy is unchallengeable. Not only that, but I think you're right."

"I'm so glad," John murmured. "Well, prepare those orders for my signature. I'll want to get moving this afternoon, so don't waste any time."

"I wouldn't dream of it," said Strabo, who was as diligent as he was difficult. "Will you want all your unicorn-riders in the van?"

Reluctantly, John the Lister shook his head. "No, we'd better leave half of them in the rear to keep Ned of the Forest off us. Hard-Riding Jimmy looks like he's still wet behind the ears, but he knows what he's doing for us, and those quick-shooting crossbows his riders have make a small force go a long way. Half the men at the van will do. And we *need* the rest back at the rear. We couldn't move very gods-damned fast if Ned's men kept chewing at the hind end of our column. Write 'em that way. With Ned back there, Bell won't have many unicorn-riders at the front of his army, either."

"That makes sense," Major Strabo said. "It may not be right, mind you, but it does make sense."

"I'm glad I have you to relieve my mind," John told him. Strabo smiled and inclined his head, as if he thought that a genuine compliment. Maybe he did; he was more than a little hard to fathom. John went on, "Draft those orders, now. The sooner you do, the sooner we see if we can't set this mess to rights."

"Yes, sir. You may rely on me. As soon as I pluck a quill from a goose's wing . . ." Strabo made as if to grab a goose from the sky. John made as if to strangle his adjutant. They both laughed, each a little nervously.

However difficult Strabo might have been, the marching orders he prepared were a small masterpiece of concision. Along with a detachment of unicorn-riders, he also posted most of the southron wizards in the van. John nodded approval of that. He wasn't sure how much good the wizards would do, but he wanted them in position to do as much as they could.

The army hadn't even left Summer Mountain before John realized *how* much trouble it was in. Sure enough, Bell's army *was* posted close to the road down which his own force had to withdraw. All the northerners had to do was reach out their hands, and his army was theirs. That was how it looked at first glance, anyhow. He hoped it wouldn't seem so bad as he got closer to the foe.

It didn't. Instead, it seemed worse. The northern army was drawn up in battle array perhaps half a mile west of the road leading south to Poor Richard. John felt like deploying into battle line facing them and sidling down the road crab-fashion. He couldn't—he knew he couldn't—but he felt like it.

Skirmishers rushed forward and started shooting bolts at his men. His repeating crossbows hosed them with death. Here and there, men on both sides fell. But it was only skirmishing, no worse, and didn't force him to halt his march and try to drive back the traitors.

A few northern catapults came forward, too, and flung stones and firepots at his long column. Most of the missiles missed. Every once in a while, though, one of them would take a bite out of the long file of men in gray tunics and pantaloons. The dead lay where they fell—no time to gather them up, let alone to build pyres and burn them. Soldiers with crushed limbs or with burns from a bursting firepot would go into the wagons, for healers and surgeons to do what they could.

Major Strabo said, "If their main force attacks, we are dead meat."

"Think so, do you?" John the Lister said.

"Gods-damned right I do," his adjutant answered. "Don't *you*?"

"Well, now that you mention it, yes," John said. "We've already got farther than I thought we would."

"What's wrong with them?" Strabo seemed almost indignant at not being annihilated. "Is our masking spell working *that* well?" He sounded as if he didn't believe it.

John the Lister didn't believe it, either. He had good, solid reasons not to believe it, too. "Can't be, Major," he said. "If it were, their skirmishers wouldn't know we're here."

Major Strabo's eyes slewed wildly as he watched the brisk little fight—and it was only a little fight—over on the army's right flank. "What's wrong with General Bell? Is he cracked? He's at liberty to attack us whenever he pleases, and what's he doing?"

"Nothing much." John answered the rhetorical

question. Then he asked one of his own: "Are you sorry?"

"No, sir. Or I don't think so, sir. The only trouble is, if Bell isn't attacking us here, I'd like to know *why* he isn't. What's he got waiting for us down the road?"

That was a good question, and anything but rhetorical. "I don't know," John admitted. He waved to the men in blue, most of whom still watched his army tramp past their positions. "What I do know is, he can't have too much, because that over there has to be most of the Army of Franklin. Or will you tell me I'm wrong?"

"No, sir. Can't do it, sir," Strabo replied. "Hells, I didn't think Bell had even that many men. But where's the plug on the road? That has to be it. As soon as they force us to stop, then they'll all swarm forward." Again, he almost sounded as if he looked forward to it.

"I don't know where it is. We haven't bumped into it yet." But even as John the Lister spoke, a unicorn-rider came galloping back toward the army. Ice raced up John's spine. For a moment there, he'd almost known hope. Now the bad news would come, all the crueler for being late. "Well?" he barked as the rider drew near.

"The road's clear, sir, all the way south," the unicorn-rider said. "The traitors aren't trying to block it, not anywhere we can find."

"You're joking." John said it automatically, for no better reason than that he couldn't believe his ears.

"No, sir." The rider shook his head. "By the Thunderer's lightning bolt, the way south is as empty of men as Thraxton the Braggart's head is of sense."

"Than which, indeed, nothing could be more empty—or should I say less full?" Major Strabo shook his head, too, and answered his own question: "No, I think not, for Thraxton the Braggart unquestionably is full of—"

"He certainly is," John the Lister said hastily. "But that doesn't really matter, especially since Thraxton's not in charge of the traitors any more. What matters is, they had us all boxed in" —he waved toward the men in blue still drawn up in plain sight, the men in blue who still weren't advancing against his own force— "they had us, and they didn't finish the job. I don't know how they didn't, I don't know why they didn't, but they didn't." Most of the time, John was a serious man. Now he felt giddy, almost drunk, with relief.

"Now General Bell's let us get away, and very soon, I think, he'll rue the day," Strabo declaimed.

"Has anyone ever called you a poet, Major?" John asked.

"Why, no, sir." Major Strabo looked as modest as a walleyed man could.

"Well, I understand why," John said. His adjutant sent him an injured look. The commanding general didn't care. Something had gone wrong for the traitors. John didn't know what, but he knew the only thing that mattered: he would gladly take advantage of it.

III

Lieutenant General Bell had taken what the healers politely called a heroic dose of laudanum, even by his own standards. He'd taken plenty to leave a unicorn flat on its back waving its hooves in the air, a silly smile on its face. For once, Bell felt no physical pain.

But Bell was sure all the laudanum in the world wouldn't have sufficed to take the edge off his towering inferno of wrath. Had he had two working arms and two legs, he would have done murder against his wing and brigade commanders. As things were, he could only scorch them with his leonine eyes, wishing each and every one of them into the most agonizing firepit of the hottest hell.

"You idiots!" he roared. "You bunglers! You fools! You knaves! How could you let the gods-damned southrons escape you? How? *How?*" The word came out as an agonized howl. "Are you cowards or are you traitors? Those are the only two choices I see."

His officers stirred. He didn't think any of them would have the effrontery to answer him, but Patrick the Cleaver did: "In that case, sir, you'd better get new fletching for your sight so it'll carry farther."

"Oh, unicorn shit!" Bell bellowed. "I watched you botching boobies there on the field. I watched you, and what did I see? Nothing! Nothing, gods damn it! You would not close with them. None of you would, you spineless squid! The best move in my career as a soldier I was thus destined to behold come to naught. To naught! You disgrace the uniforms you infest. A half-witted dog could have led an attack that would have swept the southrons away. Would I'd had one in an officer's uniform!"

The subordinate commanders stirred again, more angrily. A brigadier whose parents had given him the uncompromising name of Provincial Prerogative hissed, "You have no business to use us so . . . sir."

"You had no business to use *me* so!" Bell yelled, still in a perfect transport of fury. "Did I order you to attack the retreating southrons? I did. And did you attack them? You did not. They escaped. And whose fault is that? Mine? No, by the gods. Yours!"

A very red-faced young brigadier called Hiram the Cranberry said, "You have no business calling us cowards and dogs."

"You have no business acting like cowards and dogs," Bell raged. "You were supposed to act like soldiers. Did you? *Did you?*" He was screaming again. He half hoped he would have an apoplexy and die so he could escape this mortification.

"Sir, we did the best we could," said another brigadier, a short, squat fellow known as Otho the Troll.

"Then gods help King Geoffrey and his kingdom!" Bell said.

"You go too far, sir; you truly do," Patrick the Cleaver said. "Indeed and it's a sore trial to our honor."

"Have you any? It's news to me." Lieutenant General Bell wished he could simply turn his back on the wing and brigade commanders. Being a cripple brought with it all sorts of humiliations, some less obvious than others.

"For gods' sake, sir!" another brigadier burst out. That was his favorite expression; because of it, he was widely called For Gods' Sake John. Twirling one end of his fiercely outswept mustache, he went on, "You damage your own honor, sir, when you impugn ours."

"That's right. That is well said," agreed a brigadier known as Count John of Barsoom after the Peachtree Province estate where he'd grown goobers before the war. He thought very well of himself.

"I don't damage my honor. You—the lot of you— damaged my honor," Bell insisted. "If you'd only done what I told you to do, we would be celebrating an enormous victory right now. Instead, we have—this." He gestured in disgust. "You are dismissed, every single one of you. I wish I never had to see any of you ever again. The gods don't grant all wishes—I know *that*."

"Were you after calling us together for no better purpose than to be railing at us like your Excellency was a crazy man?" Patrick the Cleaver asked. "A bad business that is, a very bad business indeed."

Bell could at the moment think of no better purpose than the one Patrick had named. If the officer from the Sapphire Isle didn't agree with him—well, too bad for Patrick the Cleaver. "You are dismissed," Bell said again. "Get out of my sight, before I murder you all."

He couldn't make good on the threat. He knew that. His subordinate commanders had to know it, too. But if his look could have stretched them all dead on their pyres, it would have. They had to know that, too. By the way they hurried off, they feared his glare *might* strike them dead.

He took yet another swig of laudanum after they were gone. He hoped it would make him fall over. Again, no such luck. It didn't even quell his fury. All it did was make him a little woozy, a little sleepy. He heaved himself to his feet: no easy job, not with a missing leg and a useless arm. Laudanum or no laudanum, sticking a crutch in his left armpit brought a stab of pain. He welcomed it like an old friend; being without pain, these days, felt unnatural.

He pushed his way out through the tent flap. The sentries guarding the pavilion stiffened to attention. They saluted. General Bell nodded in reply; returning a salute while he was on his feet—on his foot, rather— wasn't easy.

The Army of Franklin was encamped not far from the road down which John the Lister's southrons had escaped. Healers still worked on some of the men who'd been wounded in the skirmishes of the day before. Bell growled something under his breath and ground his teeth. His army shouldn't have skirmished with the southrons. It should have crushed them.

One of the sentries pointed north. The motion swung Bell's eyes in that direction, too. The soldier said, "Looks like Ned of the Forest's unicorn-riders are coming in, sir."

"Yes, it does," Bell said. "I wish they'd been here yesterday. Say what you will about Ned, but he knows how to fight, which is more than most of the useless, worthless officers in this miserable, gods-forsaken army can do."

Prudently, the sentry didn't answer.

Before long, Ned's men were pitching their tents and

building campfires next to those of the footsoldiers in the Army of Franklin. Ned of the Forest himself rode toward Lieutenant General Bell's pavilion. He swung down from his unicorn with an easy grace Bell remembered painfully—and that was indeed the way he remembered it—well. "By the gods, Bell," Ned cried, striding up to him, "what went wrong?"

"*I* don't know," Bell answered, his bitterness overflowing. "What I know is, I'm surrounded by idiots. I know that right down to the ground."

"We had 'em," Ned declared. "We *had* 'em. All we had to do was bite down on 'em and chew 'em up. Why didn't we?"

"I wish I could tell you," Bell said. "I gave the necessary commands. I gave them repeatedly. I gave them, and I saw them ignored. The attack I ordered did not take place. I wish it had."

"We won't get another chance like that," Ned warned.

Lieutenant General Bell nodded. "That, Lieutenant General, I do know. I wish I could cashier every brigade commander in my army, but I can't, gods damn it."

"There was a squabble like this here one after the battle by the River of Death," Ned of the Forest said.

"So I've heard," Bell said. "If I hadn't been wounded in that fight, I daresay I would have been a part of it."

"Reckon you're right," Ned said. "Thraxton the Braggart wanted to get rid of all of *his* officers, too, and we all wanted to kill him." By the way Ned's hands folded into fists, he meant that literally. Bell remembered stories he'd heard while recovering from his amputation, and what Ned had said not long ago. After a moment, the scowl fading from his face, Ned went on, "Thraxton got his way, on account of he's pals with

King Geoffrey—you'll know about that, I expect. Thraxton got his way, all right—but the army was never the same again. Meaning no disrespect, sir, but it may be just as well you can't get rid of 'em all."

"I find that hard to believe—very hard, as a matter of fact," Bell said.

"I'm telling you what I think," Ned of the Forest answered. "If you don't care for what I think . . ." He didn't go on, but something nasty sparked in his eyes. *If you don't care for what I think, to the hells with you*, had to be what he meant.

Even full of anger as Bell was, he hesitated before provoking Ned. He shrugged a one-shouldered shrug instead. "Maybe," he said grudgingly.

"What are you going to do now?" Ned asked, adding, "Sir?" as an afterthought.

"We have to keep moving south," General Bell answered. "John the Lister got away this time. When I catch him, though, I'll make him pay."

"My bet is, he's heading toward Poor Richard," Ned said. "I know that part of Franklin—I know it right well." He spoke with great assurance. He'd fought all across Franklin and Cloviston and Dothan and Great River Province ever since the war began. Without a doubt, he knew them more intimately than most officers could hope to. He went on, "Some places around there, if the southrons dig in, they'll be mighty hard to dig out."

"Will John know those places?" Bell asked.

"If he doesn't, somebody in his force will," Ned said. "Plenty of traitors wearing southron gray." To a soldier who followed King Geoffrey, a northerner who stayed loyal to Avram was a traitor. A fair number of men from Franklin and even more from Cloviston had chosen Avram over Geoffrey. They fought their own small, bitter war with Geoffrey's backers in addition to and alongside of the larger struggle waged between the main armies of the two rival kings.

"Plenty of traitors to good King Geoffrey still in blue," Bell muttered. "If my commanders had done what they were supposed to—"

Ned of the Forest held up a hand. "Plenty of people—plenty of people with fancy uniforms on— are natural-born fools. I don't reckon anybody could quarrel with that. But you have to remember, there's a sight of difference between a natural-born fool and a traitor."

"Maybe," Bell said, even more grudgingly than before. "By the Lion God's claws, though, I wish you'd been at my van and not harassing the southrons' rear. You'd have blocked the road down to the Trumpeteth River and Poor Richard the way it should have been blocked."

"I hope I would," Ned said. "But it takes more than magic to let a man be two places at once. If I hadn't been harrying the southrons, they could've moved quicker, and they might've got out of your trap before you could spring it."

He was right. Bell knew as much. That didn't make his words any more palatable, though. "Bah!" Bell said: a reply that didn't require him to admit Ned was right. Realizing he needed something more, he continued, "I trust, Lieutenant General, you *will* lead the pursuit of the southrons now."

"Oh, yes, sir," Ned answered. "I'll send the boys after 'em. I'll do it right this minute, if you want me to."

"No, let it wait till the morning," Bell said. "Your unicorns are worn, and so are my pikemen and cross-bowmen. No point to a strong pursuit unless we're fit to fight."

"My boys are always fit to fight," Ned of the Forest declared. "If yours aren't, too bad for them." Having had the last word, he got back onto his unicorn and rode away, the beast's hooves kicking up dirt at each stride.

Bell started to growl at him, to order him to come back and explain himself and apologize. He left the order unspoken. He was as brave a soldier as any who served King Geoffrey. No one without great courage would, or could, have stayed in the field after the wounds he'd taken. But even he didn't care to antagonize Ned of the Forest.

"We'll get them," Bell muttered. "If we don't catch up to them on the road, we'll get them in Poor Richard. John the Lister might have slid by me once, but he won't do it again."

Where railing at his subordinate commanders hadn't done a thing, that did help ease his wrath. *All I need is another try*, he thought. *All the north needs is another try. We can still lick those southron sons of bitches. We can, and we have to. And so, of course, we will.*

He went back into his pavilion. A folding chair waited for him. With a weary sigh, he sank into it and leaned his crutches against the iron-framed cot nearby. With his one good hand free, he fumbled for the laudanum bottle. He pulled it out, yanked the stopper free with his teeth, and took one more long swig.

Little by little, the latest dose of the drug washed through him. He sighed. At last, he had enough laudanum coursing through his veins to stop worrying quite so much about what might have been. He felt much more alive with the mixture of opium and brandy than he ever had without it. There were times when he felt his mutilations were almost worthwhile. Without them, he never would have made the acquaintance of the wonders of laudanum, and he couldn't imagine living apart from it, not any more he couldn't.

But not even laudanum's soothing influence altogether stifled his rage against the men who had let him down. *How many times do I have to give the command to advance?* he wondered. *What can I do when they refuse to listen? I can't charge the gods-damned southrons myself, not on one leg.* He had charged them, many times. The catapult stone that had smashed his thigh by the River of Death was the reason he went on one leg these days.

"Next time," he muttered. "We *will* get them next time." Then the huge doses of the drug he'd taken overwhelmed even his laudanum-accustomed frame. A wriggle and a scramble shifted him from the chair to the cot. He twisted into a position that put the least weight on his bad shoulder and his stump, closed his eyes, and slept, dreaming of blood and victory.

"Here you are, sir," the gray-robed scryer said, standing up from the stool in front of his crystal ball so Lieutenant General George could take his place.

"That's true. Here I am." Doubting George sat down. John the Lister's image, tiny and perfect, stared out of the crystal ball at him. George said, "So you're on your way to Poor Richard now, are you?"

"Yes, sir," John answered. "By the Thunderer's beard, I'm glad to be past the traitors, too. I thought they'd cooked our goose at Summer Mountain."

"Never give up," Doubting George said. "Till they kill you, you're still in the fight. And after that, make 'em worry about your ghost."

"Haven't seen any ghosts on the battlefield, sir," John the Lister said. "It's the live sons of bitches who worry me. If Bell pursues hard, I could still wind up in trouble."

"What can I do to help you?" Doubting George asked.

"Another ten thousand men would be nice," John

replied. George chuckled. He'd made many such wry remarks himself.

But this one, unfortunately, he couldn't answer with more than a chuckle. He said, "I'd send them to you if I had them, but I don't. Do you know how much trouble I'm having pulling garrisons out of towns and off of glideway lines here and down in Cloviston?"

"I have some small idea." John sounded even drier than before. "You wouldn't have sent me up here to take a beating—I mean, to slow down Lieutenant General Bell, of course—if you thought it would be easy. Still, if you had them to spare, I could really use them right now."

"I haven't got them to spare. I haven't got them at all, as a matter of fact," George said. "You're commanding more men than I am right now. General Hesmucet did me no favors when he put me in charge of these provinces after he went and stripped most of the good soldiers out of them."

"Superiors don't usually do favors for subordinates they give hard, nasty jobs to," John the Lister said.

"Uh, yes." Doubting George felt skewered by the sort of dart he usually aimed at other officers. He'd given John a hard, nasty job, and was uncomfortably aware of it. "I am doing the best I can," he assured the man to whom he'd given it.

"I'm sure of that, sir." John didn't come right out and call him a liar, but he didn't miss by much. "If you can't give me reinforcements, can you send that hotshot mage of yours up to me?"

"Major Alva, you mean?"

"I forget his name. The one who actually knows what he's doing, even if he looks like an unmade bed and has no idea how an officer is supposed to behave."

"That's Major Alva, all right," George said. "I hate to lose him. He's far and away the best wizard around—gods only know why Hesmucet didn't take him along for the march across Peachtree."

John took a deep breath that was both visible and audible. "I wouldn't ask for him if he weren't good, sir. I'm trying to keep from getting slaughtered, you know. Anything you can do to help would be nice."

"You're right, of course," Doubting George said contritely. "I'll send him straight to you. Shall he wait for you in Poor Richard, or do you need him on the north bank of the Trumpeteth?"

"If you can get him all the way up here, I'll be glad to have him," John said. "The river's running high right now, what with all the rain we've had lately, and bridging it won't be easy. A good wizard would be a handy thing to have."

"Call Major Alva a thing to his face, and he'll make you sorry for it," George warned. "It's not just that he forgets he's supposed to be an officer. He'd be touchy even if he weren't one."

"Too smart for his own good, eh?" John the Lister asked.

"You might say so," George answered. "Yes, by the gods, you just might say so. Why I haven't wrung his scrawny neck . . . But I know why, as a matter of fact. I haven't wrung his neck because he *is* good."

"Well, fine. I can use somebody who's good," John said. "The mages I've got up here with me can't grab their backsides with both hands. They can't spell *cat* if you spot them the *c* and the *a*. They can't—"

"I get the idea," Doubting George said. "I'll send Alva to you as fast as I can, and I hope he does you some good."

"Thanks very much, sir," John said. "I am grateful for it. If we can get over the Trumpeteth and into Poor Richard, I think we'll give a good account of ourselves when Lieutenant General Bell comes to call."

"That's good. That's what I want to hear." *Especially if it's true*, George thought. He asked, "Anything else?" John the Lister shook his head. George gestured to the scryer in charge of the crystal ball. The man in the gray robe broke the mystical connection between this ball and the one John was using. John's image disappeared. The crystal ball went back to being nothing but a round lump of glass that twisted light oddly when you looked through it.

"Do you need to speak with anyone else, sir?" the scryer asked. "With Marshal Bart, maybe, or King Avram?"

"No, thanks," George said. "The only time they want to talk to me is when they think I've done something wrong. As long as they're happy leaving me alone, I'm happy being left. The less I do to remind them I'm around, the better off I am. This way, I get to run my own war."

Belatedly, he realized he might get in trouble if the scryer passed his sentiments on to Marshal Bart over in Pierreville, or to King Avram's henchmen in the Black Palace at Georgetown. Then he shrugged. Even if the marshal or the king did get wind of his sentiments, he'd probably escape without anything worse than teasing. What Detinan didn't think he could do almost anything? What Detinan didn't resent having superiors looking over his shoulder? George had the job here. He intended to take care of it.

He left the building where the scryers kept their crystals. As soon as he walked out onto the streets of Ramblerton, he flipped up his collar and stuck his hands in his pockets to protect them and his neck from the chilly wind blowing up from the south. He came from Parthenia himself, and had no use for the nasty weather that made winter so unpleasant through much of King Avram's realm.

Sentries came to attention and saluted when he returned to his headquarters. "Fetch me Major Alva, if you'd be so kind," he told one of them, adding, "and don't let him dawdle on the way any more than you can help."

"Yes, sir." The sentry saluted again and hurried off, crossbow slung on his shoulder, quiver full of bolts hanging at his hip next to his shortsword.

Alva arrived soon enough to keep Doubting George from getting too annoyed at him. He even remembered to salute, which warmed the cockles of the commanding general's heart. And when he said, "What can I do for you?" he tacked on, "Sir?" with a hesitation even George, who was looking for it, had trouble noticing.

"You can go to Poor Richard," George told him. "At once. Go pack. Be on the next northbound glideway caravan."

Major Alva gaped. "I beg your pardon?"

"Why? Did you fart?" Doubting George asked. Major Alva's jaw dropped. George ignored the histrionics. He went on, "I gave you an order. Please obey it, without fuss and without wasting time."

"Uh, yes, sir," Alva said dazedly. "But why?" The expression on his face said, *What did I do to deserve this?*

"You're not in trouble. It's even a compliment, if you like," George said. "John the Lister asked for you by name." That wasn't quite true, since John hadn't remembered Alva's name, but it came close enough. "He's having some difficulties with Lieutenant General Bell and his wizards, and he wanted a good mage on his side to make sure things don't go any wronger than they have already."

"Oh," Alva said, still a trifle stunned. "All right. I'll go."

"How generous of you," Doubting George said.

Alva needed a moment to notice the lurking sarcasm. When he did, his flush was unmistakable despite his swarthy skin. "I said I'd go," he muttered, voice petulant.

"You don't need to make it sound as if you deserve a decoration for doing what I tell you to do," George said. "I hope you do well enough to deserve a decoration." He paused, then shook his head. "No, I take that back."

"You hope I *don't* do well enough to deserve a decoration?" Alva asked. "Why?"

"I hope you don't need to do well enough to deserve a decoration," George answered. "I hope everything is simple and easy, and the traitors don't do a single thing to cause you any trouble. Wouldn't that be nice?"

"That would be lovely," the mage said in hollow tones. "That would be splendid. But I doubt it's going to happen. Don't you?"

"Me? Doubt? What a ridiculous notion," Doubting George said. "Why, I'm as full of positive thoughts as the inside of a daffodil is full of crossbow quarrels."

"Er, yes . . . sir." Major Alva looked like a man who wanted to leave. Rapidly. After a moment of very obvious thought, he found an excuse: "If I want to be on the next glideway carpet, I'd better get ready. May I be excused, sir?"

"Oh, yes. You're dismissed," the commanding general said. Alva had to remember to salute. He hurried out of the headquarters. Doubting George threw back his head and laughed. He'd put the fear of the gods into Alva, or at least done a good job of confusing him, which would serve every bit as well.

Now if I could only assemble an army that easily, he thought. Getting men to come to Ramblerton so they could actually do some fighting got harder by the day. News that General Bell had invaded Franklin should have made men rush together to defend their kingdom. Instead, it had made each little garrison want to stay exactly where it was, so it could defend its own little town or fortress.

If Bell wasn't altogether a fool—not the most obvious proposition George had ever thought of—he wouldn't want to fight at every little town and fortress. He'd bypass whatever he could so he could move south into Cloviston and head for the Highlow River, where he could do King Geoffrey some good and embarrass and perhaps even hurt King Avram. That seemed obvious to George. To his subordinates? No.

But Bell couldn't ignore a big army on his flank— or at least he would be a fool if he did. Maybe he would try to ignore it—Bell was the sort who would try to ignore whatever he could if ignoring it meant he could go after something else. George hoped Bell would ignore southron soldiers on his flank. That would make life easy for him personally, and for King Avram and the south in general.

Meanwhile, he still had an army to build up . . . if he could, if his own officers, men who were supposed to obey his commands, would let him. They were convinced they knew what was best for them, best for their own little forces. They didn't think about or didn't care what was best for the kingdom. If somebody tried to point out what was best for Detina as a whole, they didn't want to listen.

Colonel Andy came in and saluted. "What did you do to poor little Alva?" George's adjutant asked.

"Poor little Alva? I doubt that," Doubting George said. "After the war ends, he can get about as rich as he cares to. What did I do? I sent him up to Poor Richard, to give John the Lister a hand."

"Oh. *That* explains the kicked-puppy look I saw on

his face," Andy said. "He has to pack his carpetbag and go somewhere else, and nobody will take care of him while he's traveling."

"He's not all *that* helpless," George said. "Gods know I've seen mages who were a hells of a lot worse."

"I know," Andy said. "But he *thinks* he's helpless when he has to deal with the ordinary world, and so he acts that way, which also gives him the chance to annoy everybody around him."

"My, you're sour today," George remarked. "Feel like insulting anyone else while you're here, or can I have a turn?"

"Go right ahead, sir. You're the commanding general, after all," Andy replied. "Rank hath its privileges."

Doubting George snorted and held his nose. "Rank is mostly just . . . rank. Look at what *dear* General Hesmucet left me, if you don't believe that. Some people had to make bricks without straw. I get to make bricks without clay. There's good reason most of these odds and sods in Franklin and Cloviston were garrison soldiers. The more I see it, the plainer it is, too: they aren't worth a counterfeit copper in a real fight."

"And you blame Hesmucet for that?" Andy asked.

"Of course I do. You don't expect me to blame myself, do you? Not fornicating likely. Besides, Hesmucet's marching through Peachtree, and he's up against nothing but the same kind of odds and sods, except in blue uniforms. He'll whale the living stuffing out of them, and he'll be a big hero. Meanwhile, I'm still fighting against a real army. Do you think I'll let him get away without a few insults flying around his ears? That's likely the worst opposition he'll see."

"You don't like him very well, do you?"

"He's a brave soldier. He's a good general. I wish I were doing what he really is. I'd get to be a famous hero, too. The way things are, I've got a hard, ugly job to do, and nobody gets famous taking care of those." Doubting George sighed. "That doesn't mean they don't need doing, though."

Corporal Rollant looked toward the Trumpeteth River, which lay between John the Lister's army and safety in Poor Richard. He'd crossed the river coming north, on his way to Summer Mountain. At the ford, it hadn't come up past his waist. He'd taken off his pantaloons, got the bottom of his shirt wet, and gone on about his business. Things wouldn't be so easy heading south.

What with all the rain that had fallen, the Trumpeteth came up a lot higher than Rollant's waist now. It would have been up over his head, even at the ford. It wasn't quite out of its banks, but it wasn't far from flooding, either. Any army falling back toward Poor Richard would have to bridge the stream before it could cross.

Normally, that would have been straightforward work for John the Lister's artificers and mages. Things weren't normal now. Rollant wondered if things ever were really normal in wartime. When he said that out loud, Smitty snickered. "Of course they're normal," he said. "They're always buggered up."

"Well, yes," Rollant said. "But there's the usual kind of mess, and then there's *this* kind of mess." He scratched his head. "If there's a usual kind of mess, I suppose things *can* be normal during the war. But they're not normal now."

"Sure as hells aren't," Smitty agreed. "Not with the gods-damned traitors trying to sabotage everything we do."

"They always *try* to do that," Rollant said dolefully. "Trouble is, they're having too much luck at it right now."

Smitty shook his head. "That isn't luck. They're still better wizards than we are, even after all this time."

"I know," Rollant said, even more dolefully than before. "They wouldn't have dropped our latest try at a bridge into the Trumpeteth if they weren't."

"And the one before that, and the one before *that*, don't forget," Smitty said. "Something tells me they don't *want* us crossing over the Trumpeteth. They're sure trying like anything to keep us from doing it, anyhow."

"Lieutenant General Bell's probably still mad at us for sliding past him at Summer Mountain," Rollant said.

"I would be, if I wore his shoes—his shoe, I mean," Smitty said.

"I bet the traitors make that joke every day," Rollant said.

"I bet you've got a big mouth . . . Corporal," Smitty said. For a moment, he'd forgotten Rollant outranked him. Ordinary Detinans often had a hells of a time remembering blonds *could* outrank them. Hastily, Smitty went on, "And I bet General Bell's probably about ready to spit nails like a repeating crossbow on account of we did get by his bastards. Only goes to show the traitors can screw up a perfectly good position, too. Sort of reassuring, if you know what I mean."

"We already knew they could be as stupid as we are," Rollant said. "Remember Proselytizers' Rise."

"There is that," Smitty admitted. "Yes, there is that, by the Lion God's fangs. They should have slaughtered us."

Rollant laughed. "You sound like you're sorry they didn't."

"No, they're the ones who're sorry they didn't," Smitty said. "Only thing I'm sorry for right now is that I've got to stand in this miserable, muddy trench."

"They've got soldiers along with their wizards,"

Rollant said. "If they overrun us, we don't get another chance to build the bridge. Besides" —he touched his crossbow, which leaned against his leg, ready to grab and pull and shoot— "anybody who tries overrunning me'll have to kill me first."

That wasn't just bravado. He meant every word of it. Detinans had forced blonds in the north into serfdom because the blonds hadn't been able to fight enough, all those centuries ago, to keep their kingdoms from being overwhelmed. Ever since then, northern Detinans had figured blonds couldn't fight— and had taken elaborate precautions to make sure they never got the chance. The Detinans didn't notice the paradox. Blonds did—but who cared what blonds noticed?

If Lieutenant General Bell's men captured Smitty, he'd go into a prisoners' camp till he was exchanged for some northerner. If Bell's men captured Rollant, he'd go, in chains, back to the estate from whose lands he'd presumed to abscond with himself. He knew his old liege lord was dead. He'd shot Baron Ormerod himself, up at the top of Proselytizers' Rise. But whoever owned Ormerod's land these days still had a claim to the serfs tied to it. Whoever that was had a claim under the laws of Palmetto Province, anyhow. Rollant was rude enough to think himself entitled to the fruits of his own labor, and ready to fight to hold on to that freedom to work for himself.

Out beyond the trenches were holes in the ground sheltering the pickets who would slow down any northern attack. Out beyond the pickets were the scouts and sentries who would spot the attack before it rolled over the southrons. That was how things were supposed to work. Most of the time, they did. Every once in a while . . . Rollant didn't want to think about all the things that could go so gruesomely wrong.

For now, Bell's soldiers didn't care to close with John the Lister's men. Soldiers who followed both Avram and Geoffrey had, in this fourth year of the war, become very cautious about rushing earthworks. That wasn't to say they wouldn't, but it was to say they looked for the likelihood of reward before pressing an assault to the limit. Rollant had seen up in Peachtree Province how important entrenchments were. Bell's men had fought there, too. They were traitors, but they weren't morons.

An ass-drawn wagon driven by teamsters in King Avram's gray rattled past the sentries, past the pickets, and through a gap in the entrenchments not far from the position of Rollant's company. Another followed, and another, and another. They carried logs with one end sharpened to a point: pilings for the southrons' next effort at a bridge.

Smitty watched them go by with world-weary cynicism. "Wonder if they'll do any better than they did the last time," he said, and then, before Rollant could answer, "Don't suppose they could do much worse."

"We have to get over the Trumpeteth," Rollant said. "We *have* to. Once we're back in Poor Richard, Bell won't dare give us any trouble."

"Who knows what Bell will dare?" Smitty said.

"Well, he'd be an idiot if he did," Rollant said. "If he wants to be an idiot, that's fine with me."

"Me, too." Even the argumentative Smitty didn't seem inclined to disagree with that. "Now, if I were Bell, I'd dress some of my boys up in gray and let 'em sneak through our lines. They could have us trussed and tied before we even know what's going on."

"That's a dreadful idea!" Rollant exclaimed in horror.

Smitty bowed, as if at praise. "I like it, too."

For a heartbeat, Rollant thought the farmer's son

had misheard him. Then he realized Smitty was just being his perverse self. Acknowledging him only made him worse. Rollant said, "One of these days, Smitty . . ."

"I know," Smitty said. "But I'll have fun till then."

At dawn the next morning, heavy stones and firepots started landing in and around the entrenchments. "The traitors must have brought their engines up during the night," Rollant said.

Smitty bowed again. "Thank you so much for that brilliant deduction, Marshal Rollant, your Grace, sir."

"Oh, to the hells with you," Rollant snapped. "Can't anybody say anything without getting it twisted around and shot back at him?"

At that moment, a stone slammed into the parapet in front of them, showering them both with dirt. Rollant rubbed at his face. Smitty spat—spat brown, in fact. "Wouldn't you sooner have me shooting words at you than the traitors shooting big rocks?" he said, and spat again. "My mouth's full of grit."

"So is mine," Rollant said, "but I got some in my eye, too."

About fifty yards down the trench line, another stone thudded home. Two men shrieked. Rollant and Smitty exchanged dismayed glances. Rollant wondered whether the stone had hit any other soldiers and killed them outright before maiming the two who cried out. It could have. He knew that altogether too well.

Lieutenant Griff said, "We are going forward, men, to capture those engines or destroy them or make the northerners pull them back."

No one grumbled, even though coming out of the trenches was risky. This way, they could hit back. Nothing was harder to bear than staying in place and taking a pounding without being able to repay the damage in kind. Even Rollant, who would carry the company standard and wouldn't do any actual fighting out in the open till he got close enough to the enemy to chop with his shortsword, only nodded.

Out of the trenches swarmed the men in gray. "Avram!" they shouted. "Avram and freedom! King Avram!"

Crossbow bolts hissed through the air at them. Bell had brought men forward to defend his engines, too. Rollant sighed. He'd known Bell would. "Geoffrey!" the northerners shouted, and, "Provincial prerogative forever!"

Provincial prerogative, as far as Rollant was concerned, meant nothing except the privilege of treating blonds like beasts of burden. He waved his standard, gold dragon on red, high above his head. False King Geoffrey's partisans flew the same flag with the colors reversed.

Pok! A crossbow bolt tore through the silk. The standard had already taken a number of such wounds. Another bolt hissed past Rollant's ear, this one not from in front of him but from behind. One of his own comrades was shooting carelessly at the traitors. Rollant hoped the fellow was shooting at them, anyhow.

Bell's men hadn't had time to entrench as well as Rollant was sure they would have liked. Some of them crouched behind stumps and rail fences. Others stood or knelt on one knee or lay on their bellies in the open. Seeing the men in blue—some of them in southron gray ineptly dyed blue—roused Rollant to fury, as it always did. These were the men who wanted to tie him to a little plot of land for the rest of his days. He whooped with glee when one of them crumpled to the ground, clutching at himself and kicking.

"Come on!" he shouted to his own comrades, waving the standard again. "Let's get rid of all these bastards!"

They didn't get the chance. Perhaps Bell hadn't

expected John the Lister's men to sally so aggressively against his men. In this part of the field, southrons outnumbered northerners, though Lieutenant General Bell's army was a lot bigger than John's. The traitors hitched their catapults to asses and unicorns and hauled them away. The crossbowmen and pikemen protecting them fought a rear-guard action till the valuable engines had escaped. Then they too fell back.

Rollant was all for charging after them. His superiors weren't. The trumpeters blew *withdraw*. Reluctantly, he returned to the southrons' trench line. Litter bearers hauled back the wounded and the dead. Healers and surgeons would do what they could for the wounded. Soldiers and runaway serfs now laboring in Avram's army would have to chop wood for the pyres of the dead. Rollant likely would have drawn that duty before he got promoted. Not now, not as a corporal.

Both forces had lost a few men, seen a few men hurt. The little fight wouldn't change how the war turned out, not in the least. He wondered why either side had bothered making it. You could, if you had the right sort of mind, then wonder if even a big battle meant much in the grand scheme of things. Rollant didn't have that sort of mind. He knew what those battles meant—serfs escaping from bondage who would still labor for their liege lords if southron armies hadn't won and given them hope and protected them when they fled.

Axes were still thudding into lumber when a messenger came up to the trenches from the direction of the Trumpeteth. Lieutenant Griff called, "Men, we're to pull back from this line toward the river. The bridges are said to be ready to cross." By the way he spoke, he had trouble believing it. He was very young, and he'd been callow when he joined the company. He'd seen a lot since then, as had the men he commanded.

Rollant certainly had trouble believing it, too. Turning to Smitty, he said, "What do you want to bet the traitors' wizards will have sunk these so-called bridges by the time we get there?"

"You're a corporal. You already make more money than I do," Smitty said. "If you think I want to give you any of mine, you're mad."

"If you think I want to give you any of mine, you're mad, *Corporal*," Sergeant Joram growled. That Rollant was an underofficer counted for more with him than that he was a blond. Not all Detinans, even in the south, felt the same way.

When they got to the river, Smitty started to laugh. "I should have taken you up on that one, your Corporalship," he said.

"Yes." Rollant tried to hide his astonishment. The bridges—which, by their faint glow, seemed compounded more of magecraft than of mere material things—did indeed stand. Men were already tramping over them toward the south bank of the Trumpeteth.

A scrawny young mage in a gray robe stood on the north bank of the river. He looked weary unto death. Even as Rollant watched, the mage swayed—he supposed under yet another sorcerous assault from the northern wizards. But, though the mage swayed, the bridges held. They didn't suddenly vanish and pitch the burdened soldiers on them into the Trumpeteth, where those men would without a doubt have drowned.

Seeing others safely cross the river, Rollant didn't hesitate when his turn came. He held the company standard high as he set foot on the bridge. It felt solid under his shoes, even if it was mostly magical. How it felt was all that mattered. If he let out a sigh of relief when he got to the far bank of the river—well, if he did, maybe nobody noticed. And if anybody did, he wasn't the only one.

❖   ❖   ❖

Ned of the Forest rode his unicorn up to the south-ern bank of the Trumpeteth River. He actually rode the great white beast *into* the river; muddy water swirled around its forelegs. Turning to Colonel Biffle, he said, "Well, Biff, they slid through our fingers. They might have been greased, the way they slipped by us."

"'Fraid you're right, sir," Biffle agreed mournfully.

"And look at what's left of this here bridge." Ned pointed. Only a few wooden pilings emerged from the Trumpeteth. "Look at it, I tell you."

"Not much *to* look at," his regimental commander said.

"Sure isn't," Ned said. "Sure as hells isn't. And it doesn't look like the stinking southrons burned their bridges once they'd used 'em, either. They couldn't have, by the Thunderer's lightning bolt—we'd've seen the flames. No way on earth they could've hidden those from us."

"You're right again, sir," Colonel Biffle said.

"And what does that mean? There's hardly a thing left here, but the southrons didn't burn what there was." Ned made a harsh, chopping gesture with his left hand. He couldn't have been more disgusted if he'd heard Thraxton the Braggart was returning to command in the Army of Franklin. He shook his head. No, on second thought, he could.

Biffle said, "It means they used magic to get over the river. It can't mean anything else."

"You're right. You're just exactly right. That's what it means." Ned of the Forest repeated that chopping gesture. "And how did *they* get away with using magic to build their miserable bridge when *we're* supposed to have the best wizards in Detina? How, Biff? Riddle me that."

"Either they've got themselves some good ones from

somewhere, or else ours aren't as good as they've been telling folks they are," Biffle said. "Maybe both."

Both hadn't occurred to Ned. When Colonel Biffle suggested it, though, it made entirely too much sense to him. "Wouldn't be a bit surprised," he said. "But it's purely a shame and a disgrace, that's what it is. The southrons have got more men than we do. They've got more of just about everything than we do, except grit and wizards. If they start licking us when it comes to magecraft . . . Well, Lion God's tail tuft, Biff, why keep on fighting in that case? We're whipped, grit or no grit."

"Yes, sir," Biffle said. "But what can we do about it? Us unicorn-riders, I mean."

"Not much," Ned said morosely. "Still and all, I'm going to hash it out with Lieutenant General Bell. Maybe he knows something I don't. Or maybe he'll give *me* some laudanum. Then I won't care any more, either."

"Lieutenant General Bell's doing the best he can," Biffle said. "If he didn't have *something* to hold back the pain, he'd be hard up."

"Oh, I know that, Biff," Ned answered. "I really do. He's not like Thraxton the Braggart, that cowardly, conniving, shriveled-up little unicorn turd of a man. Bell *does* try hard, and he's a good fighter himself— or he was, before he got ruined. I don't reckon it was his fault this army didn't lay into the southrons at Summer Mountain. By the way he carried on, he gave the right orders, but the fellows under him didn't do what he told 'em to."

"By the way *they* carried on, his orders weren't as good as he said they were," Colonel Biffle replied.

That was also true, and worried Ned of the Forest. It reminded him much too much of how things had been during the unhappy command of Thraxton the Braggart. Ned tugged on the reins, jerking his unicorn's head around. He gave Biffle a few orders, then got the beast moving with the pressure of his knees and rode off toward the north, toward the main encampment of the Army of Franklin.

Lieutenant General Bell's pavilion was at least twice the size of any other officer's tent there, and dwarfed the miserable little shelters under which some of Bell's soldiers slept. The rest of Bell's men had no shelter at all. True, Bell was the commander of the army. True, his wound might have made him need more space— or be happy with more space—than a whole officer required. Even so . . .

Trying to hold in his unease, Ned announced himself to the sentries in front of the commanding general's pavilion. One of them ducked inside. He returned a moment later, saying, "Lieutenant General Bell will see you, sir."

"He'd better," Ned rumbled; the idea that Bell might not see him filled him with fury. He ducked through the tent flap and into the pavilion.

His eyes needed a moment to adjust to the gloom inside. Bell sat in a folding chair. As Ned came in, the general commanding put a small bottle back into a leather pouch at his belt. "Good day, Lieutenant General," Bell said, licking his lips. "And what can I do for you?"

Ned peered at him before answering. Once upon a time, people had spoken of Bell as the reincarnation of the Lion God on earth. These days, those leonine features might have been carved in cold butter that was then set in front of a fire. His face sagged. He had great dark bags under his eyes. His cheeks drooped. Even through Bell's thick beard, Ned could see how jowly he'd become. The commander of unicorn-riders shivered. Pain and forced inactivity did dreadful things to a man.

Bell had asked him a question. He needed a moment to remember that, and then to answer: "I want to know where we're going, sir, and what we're going to do about the southrons now that they've holed up in Poor Richard."

No matter how bad Bell looked, he hadn't lost the urge to fight. "We're going to hit them, that's what," he said. "We're going to hit them, and we're going to rout them, and then we're going on to take Ramblerton. It must be done, and so it will be done."

"Yes, sir," Ned said. Bell was right—taking Ramblerton was something the northern cause desperately needed. Ned went on, "I've ordered Colonel Biffle, one of my regimental commanders, to lead the unicorn-riders across the Trumpeteth so we'll be ready to hit the southrons that good hard lick you want just as soon as we can."

"Have you?" Bell raised an eyebrow in surprise, like a lion thinking it might have scented prey. "Without waiting for orders or permission from me?"

"Yes, sir," Ned of the Forest said again. His voice warned that he was another lion, not a lumbering buffalo. "They're my men. I reckon I can tell 'em what to do without a by-your-leave from anybody, especially when it comes to putting them closer to the enemy."

He waited to see how Lieutenant General Bell would take that. Bell started to cloud up, then checked himself and nodded. "All right. I will not complain of any man who *wants* to close with the southrons. That compares well with the miserable cowards commanding my crossbowmen and pikemen. They had a golden chance, a chance sent by the gods, to strike John the Lister a deadly blow, and did they take it? *Did* they? No! They sat inert, the spineless wretches, and let this magnificent opportunity dribble through their palsied fingers."

Carefully, Ned said, "Sir, there's a difference between things going wrong because somebody's a coward and things going wrong just on account of they go wrong, if you know what I mean."

"I know what you mean, which doesn't mean I think you're right," Bell replied. "Wouldn't *you* have attacked the gods-damned southrons if they were marching across your front? Of course you would have—you make a proper man. Those fools, poltroons, brigadiers . . . But I repeat myself."

"When we get to Poor Richard, sir, it won't be that bad," Ned predicted.

"By the Thunderer's holy foreskin, it had better not be." Bell sounded very much like an angry lion.

"You'll see." Ned of the Forest spoke with all the confidence he could muster. He would, in due course, be proved right, if not in precisely the way he meant when speaking to Lieutenant General Bell.

Bell waved the words aside with a motion of his good hand. "Anything further to report, Lieutenant General? The southrons continue to flee before us, having even less spirit than my own brigade and wing commanders, and your men are crossing the Trumpeteth, which is actually not bad news." By his scowl, he never expected to hear anything but bad news ever again. "Nothing more? Very well, then. You may rejoin your riders, and my congratulations for the spirit they—and you—have shown."

"Thank you, sir." Ned saluted and left the pavilion. His strides were lithe, pantherlike. He didn't care to think about the crutches leaning close by Bell's chair. Bell would never advance at anything but a caterpillar's hitching crawl. No, Ned didn't want to think about that. He'd already suffered several wounds. One instant of bad luck and he'd be no better off than the commanding general.

If everybody thought about those things, who'd go and mix it up? he wondered. *How would you, how could you, fight a war?*

He saw no answer, not at first. But as he swung up onto his unicorn—one more thing Bell would never do unless someone tied him to the saddle—he realized the answer was that most men *didn't* think about such things. He didn't want to think about them himself, as he'd just proved, and he was as far from a coward as any man breathing. He shrugged and scowled and went on riding.

When he got down to the Trumpeteth, he found only a rear guard of his unicorn-riders still on the northern bank. The rest had crossed over with their animals on a motley little fleet of rowboats and rafts. Ned piled into a boat with the ordinary riders he commanded. They chivvied his unicorn aboard a raft, although the great white shining beast didn't like the journey at all. Once on the southern bank of the Trumpeteth, Ned had to gentle the unicorn down again before it would deign to bear his weight.

"You know how to handle 'em, Lord Ned," a trooper said admiringly.

"I ought to." Ned of the Forest was not sentimental about unicorns, or about anything else that had to do with battle. "I've had enough of them killed out from under me."

"That's on account of you always head for where the fighting's hottest," the soldier said.

"I'm going to tell you a secret about how to be a general," Ned said. "Do you want to hear it?"

"Yes, *sir!*" The trooper leaned forward. If he could have pricked his ears ahead like a unicorn, he would have done that, too.

"All right, then. Here it is: if you want to be a general, you have to want to go where things are the hottest, and you have to make your men want to follow you. If you can manage that, you'll do all right."

"Lord Ned, sir, you make a *hells* of a general," the soldier said.

"Thank you kindly." Ned's smile was a little less carnivorous than usual. He liked praise, and being called Lord Ned. Unlike most of the officers who fought for King Geoffrey, he was no noble. He'd made a good living before the war as a serfcatcher. A lot of blond serfs ran away from the land and liege lord to whom they were bound, and Ned had more than a little genius for poking through the jungles and woods and swamps where they liked to hide and bringing them back. That was how he'd come to be known as Ned of the Forest.

But serfcatching, while it might bring money, didn't bring respect. Thraxton the Braggart wasn't the only officer who looked down his nose at Ned for his work and his low birth. Most of the scornful ones, though, had learned to keep their mouths shut. For one thing, Ned had proved an even better commander of unicorn-riders than he was a serfcatcher. And, for another, he'd made it plain he had no qualms about killing men supposedly on his own side who were rash enough to insult him.

He booted his unicorn into motion. It was a big, sturdy beast. It needed to be, to carry a man with his big, sturdy frame. He brought it up to a fast trot.

Unicorn-riders waved as he went past. He waved back, or sometimes lifted the broad-brimmed felt hat from his head for a moment to greet the troopers. That made them wave even more, and cheer, too.

Before too long, he caught up with Colonel Biffle at the head of the column. "What's the word, sir?" Biffle asked.

"Well, Biff, I'll tell you," Ned answered. "When the

whole army gets down to Poor Richard, the stinking southrons had better look out for themselves."

"All right." But Biffle frowned. "That won't be an easy position to crack, not if John the Lister digs in like he can."

"Bell thinks we can lick 'em. Even more to the point, Bell thinks we should've licked 'em at Summer Mountain," Ned said. "Somebody's going to pay on account of we didn't."

"Somebody's going to pay, all right," Colonel Biffle agreed gloomily. "I tell you, Lord Ned, if we go at 'em at Poor Richard, it's liable to be us."

"We've got to do some fighting. Bell's dead right about that," Ned said. "John the Lister won't disappear if we don't. Neither will Doubting George, down in Ramblerton. We went into this war talking about what a bunch of cowards the stinking southrons were. Well, by now we know that isn't so. If we want to shift 'em, we'll have to *shift* 'em. You know what I mean?"

"I sure do," Biffle replied. "And don't I wish I didn't?"

"Can't be helped," Ned of the Forest said. "Everything'd be a lot easier if we only had to fight when we were sure of winning. But sometimes we have to stand up there and prove we *are* men. Don't you reckon that's right?"

Colonel Biffle gave him a reluctant, half shamefaced nod. They rode on together toward Poor Richard. It wasn't far.

John the Lister looked back toward the Trumpeteth from the position he'd chosen for his army, just outside the little town of Poor Richard. His men dug like moles at the high end of a long, bare stretch of ground that ran north for a couple of miles. Turning to his adjutant, he said, "If the traitors care to attack me here, I will give them a warmer greeting than they care for."

One of Major Strabo's wandering eyes looked towards one stretch of the lines the southrons were preparing, the other toward another. "The devils in the seven hells might give them a warmer greeting than we can. No one else, I think."

"They cannot flank us out here, as they did before," John said.

"No, indeed," Strabo said, looking around his superior. "They would be idiots to try, which may not stop them."

"We've got a glideway line straight back to Ramblerton," John the Lister said. "Doubting George can send us all the food and bolts and firepots and fodder we need, and the line's well fortified."

"Yes, sir." Major Strabo pointed toward the line of entrenchment; his finger, unlike his eyes, went straight. "As you say, they'll likely be through if they try to go through us."

"They'd be idiots to try to do that, too," John said. "In fact, if you ask me they were idiots to mount this whole invasion. Why isn't Bell fighting General Hesmucet? As far as I can see, none of the traitors is off fighting Hesmucet. How can they call themselves a kingdom if he marches across Peachtree Province to Veldt and the Western Ocean?"

"Simple, sir," Strabo answered. "They can lie."

"That's about what it comes down to, sure enough," John the Lister said. "As a matter of fact, that's just what it comes down to. Hesmucet was right: once you crack the shell, there's nothing but wind and air behind it."

"Some of that wind and air is coming this way," his adjutant pointed out.

"Let 'em come," John replied. "If they want to

charge up that slope, in the face of everything we can throw at 'em, they're welcome to try. Have we got the engines lined up where they're supposed to be?"

"Yes, sir. Catapults and repeating crossbows both," Major Strabo said. "And we've got plenty of stones and firepots and bolts for them. If all the traitors in the world want to charge up that slope against us, I think we can murder the lot of them."

John eyed Strabo with more than a little surprise. His adjutant was no blithe optimist. Strabo, in fact, was inclined to see difficulties whether they were there or not. If he thought the southrons would have no trouble holding this position, he was likely to be right. John certainly hoped he was right.

At the same time, John wondered what Lieutenant General Bell would do when he saw what sort of position the southrons had at Poor Richard. He wouldn't have an easy time assailing it, even if his army was close to twice as big as John's. He couldn't ignore it and keep marching south, either.

What did that leave? Nothing John saw just then. *Maybe Bell will give up and go away. Maybe he'll throw his hand in the air and march back to Dothan.* John the Lister laughed.

"What's funny, sir?" Major Strabo asked. John explained. Strabo laughed, too. "The likelihood of that is most unlikely," he said, a sentence obscure even by his standards.

"Uh, yes," John said.

"Bell's options are impenetrable in their opacity," Strabo added.

"Not only that, nobody has a real good notion of what the son of a bitch will do," John said.

"Indeed," Strabo said. "And in fact."

"That, too," John agreed gravely. "Now, in fact, I'm going to round up the famous Major Alva, see what more help he thinks he can give us here, and have another look at our works, make sure everything is sited just the way I want it."

"Yes, sir," Strabo said. "The one thing we haven't sighted is the traitors."

John thought about groaning at that, but decided not to bother. Strabo's plays on words were frequent enough—and bad enough—that acknowledging them only encouraged him to do worse. John sometimes thought he couldn't do worse, but his adjutant kept proving him wrong.

He waved for a runner. "Yes, sir?" the young man in gray asked.

"Tell Major Alva to meet me at the top of the slope there." John pointed. "Tell him I want to see him as soon as he can get there." Doubting George had warned him Alva was a free spirit. From everything John had seen so far, Doubting George had understated things.

But the wizard got to the field fortifications in good time, only a couple of minutes after John the Lister himself. And Alva did remember to salute. He looked as if he was reminding himself of something before he did it, but he did salute. Then he said, "Tell me, sir, what do you think of the Inward Hypothesis?"

Of all the questions John had expected to get on what might become a battlefield, that one might have been the very last. He blinked, wondering if he'd heard rightly. Deciding he had, he answered, "I don't really know, Major. It's not something a soldier needs to worry about, is it?"

He'd done his best to dodge the question. He learned trying to evade Alva wasn't a good idea. The wizard's eyebrows shot up, as if he couldn't believe his ears. He said, "Don't you think it's important for every Detinan—for everyone in the whole world—to wonder about how the gods fit into the scheme of things? If they say, 'Be,' and something *is* the very next heartbeat, then we look at them one way. But if they say, 'Be after you go about shaping yourselves and changing for thousands or maybe millions of years,' then we look at them another way altogether. Or I do, anyhow. What about you, sir?"

"When I need to worry about the gods, I'll worry about them," John the Lister said. "Till then, I'm going to worry about Lieutenant General Bell more, because I expect he'll be here sooner."

He waited to find out how the contentious wizard would take that. To his surprise, Alva beamed. "Well said, sir. I couldn't have put it better myself. Worrying about things of this world ahead of the gods is always a good idea—as far as I'm concerned, anyway."

"You must have some interesting talks with priests," John remarked.

"Oh, I do, sir," Alva said earnestly. "They can believe what they want, as far as I'm concerned. They're free Detinans, after all. But they don't seem to understand that I'm a free Detinan, too. They want me to stop thinking what I think. It doesn't seem fair."

"I can see how it wouldn't," John said. "But then, how often do they run into someone who doesn't believe in the gods?"

"I believe in the gods, sir." Alva sounded shocked that John should doubt him. "I just don't believe they're very important."

"Do you? Or do I mean, don't you?" John the Lister shook his head. "I can see how priests might have trouble drawing the distinction."

"Can you? Could you explain it to me, sir? I've never been able to figure out how anyone wouldn't want to draw the finest distinctions he could."

He's not joking, John realized. *He does want me to*

explain it. Can I? Picking his words with care, he said, "To somebody who's a priest, to somebody who thinks about the gods all the time, not believing in the gods at all and not believing they're very important probably don't seem much different."

"Hmm." Alva thought it over. John had the odd feeling he was taking a test. When Alva suddenly smiled, he decided he'd passed it. "Oh. Perspective!" the mage said. "I should have figured that out for myself." He thumped his forehead with the heel of his hand to show how stupid he thought he was.

"It's nothing to worry about." John the Lister almost added, *by the gods*, but at the last instant checked himself. Given what the conversation was about, the phrase didn't fit.

"But I was wrong. I don't like being wrong." By the way Major Alva said it, he didn't like it at all. He gave a partial explanation: "A mage can't afford to be wrong very often."

"From everything I've heard and from everything I've seen, you're not wrong very often," John said.

"I don't dare," Alva replied. "Sir, I started with nothing. The only reason I've got anything at all is because I'm good at wizardry. I'll ride it as far as I can here in the army. When I get out, I'll go even further. This is what I can do. This is what I'm good at. I'm going to be as good at it as I can."

"All right, Major." John the Lister nodded. "You sound like a proper Detinan to me: out to paint your name on the wall with the biggest letters you can. This is a kingdom where men do things like that."

"This is the best kingdom in the world, sir—in the whole gods-damned *world*." Major Alva spoke with great conviction. "Anybody can be anything here, if he's good enough and works hard enough. That's why the northerners are such fools to want to leave. Do they think they'll be able to climb to the top with all their pigheaded nobles clogging the road up? Not likely!"

"I don't know whether they worry about getting to the top so much as keeping blonds on the bottom," John said.

"But that's stupid, too." Alva, plainly, had no patience with stupidity, his own or anyone else's. He pointed to a blond in the trenches, a blond with a corporal's emblem on the sleeve of his gray tunic. "Take a look at him. He's getting ahead because he's good at soldiering. If he were an ordinary Detinan, he'd probably be a lieutenant by now, but even blonds *can* get ahead here."

John the Lister had no enormous use for blonds. He wasn't thrilled at the idea of unbinding them from the land and making them citizens like proper Detinans. If it weren't for splitting the kingdom, he would have been happy to let the north take most of them out of Detina. "Next thing you know," he said, "you'll be talking about women the same way."

"Oh, don't be silly, sir," Alva said. "Some people do, but they're a bunch of crackpots."

"Well, we see eye-to-eye about something, anyhow," John said with a certain amount of relief. The wizard, plainly, was a radical freethinker, but even he had his limits. The general commanding went on, "Now, is there anything you notice in these works that could be stronger from a wizardly point of view?"

"Let's see." Alva didn't want to commit himself without looking things over, which made John think better of him. He paced along behind the rearmost of three lines of entrenchments, looking out over them toward and along the north-facing slope. At last, he said, "Would Lieutenant General Bell really be dumb enough to try to drive us out of this position?"

"*I* don't know," John said. "Only Bell knows how

stupid he really is. But *we'd* be stupid not to give him the warmest reception we could, wouldn't we? How can we make sure of doing that?"

"Sir, I think you've done it," the mage replied. "I saw a few engines you might bring up closer so they'd throw farther. Other than that . . ." He shook his head. "I can *feel* the defenses you've set up against the traitor's battle magic. They should work."

"You're the one to say that. You put most of them up."

"I told you—I'm good." Alva had no false modesty—and probably little of any other sort.

"How soon do you think they'll attack?" John asked.

Now the wizard looked at him in some surprise. "*I* don't know, sir. I deal with enchantments. You're the fellow who's supposed to be a soldier."

I've just been given the glove, John the Lister thought. His voice dry, he said, "I do try to impersonate one every now and again, yes."

Alva looked at him in surprise of a different sort. "Have you been listening to Doubting George, sir?" he asked reproachfully.

"Not for a while now," John answered. "Why?"

"Because I don't run into a lot of men who are supposed to be soldiers" —Alva seemed to like that phrase, while John didn't, not at all— "who know what it is to be ridiculous."

"That only shows you haven't spent enough time paying attention to soldiers," John the Lister told him. "The only officers who don't know what it is to be ridiculous are the ones who've never led men into battle. Those sons of bitches on the other side will do their best to make a monkey out of you, and sometimes they'll bring it off."

"What have they got to say about you?" Major Alva asked.

"If I'm doing my job, they say I'm trying to make a monkey out of them, too," John replied. "Whichever one of us does best, the other fellow ends up swinging through the trees." He mimed scratching himself.

"Sounds like the Inward Hypothesis in action to me," Alva said. John glared at the wizard. Alva mimed scratching himself, too, carefully adding, "Sir," afterwards.

IV

Captain Gremio's shoes thudded on the bridge the northerners had thrown across the Trumpeteth River. His company wasn't so loud crossing over the bridge to the south bank as he would have liked. Not enough of them had shoes with which to thud. Bare feet and feet wrapped in rags made hardly any sound at all.

Unicorn hooves drummed quite nicely. From atop his mount, Colonel Florizel called, "Step it up, men! They're waiting for us in Poor Richard."

So they are, Gremio thought unhappily. *And they've had a little while to wait now, too—plenty of time to dig trenches to fight from.* Trenches saved lives. Without them, Joseph the Gamecock wouldn't have been able to delay Hesmucet up in Peachtree Province for nearly so long as he had. *And then Bell brought us out of our trenches and hit the southrons as hard as he could. And we lost Marthasville, and we're losing the rest of Peachtree, too.*

"Keep moving," Sergeant Thisbe said. "We have to whip the southrons."

"The sergeant's right," Gremio said. "We've got more men than John the Lister, and we'll swamp his whole army."

I hope we will. We'd better. Gods help us if we don't. Maybe they won't have dug too many trenches. Maybe.

His shoes stopped thudding and started thumping on dirt. "Over the river," Thisbe said. "Not far to Poor Richard now."

On they marched. One of the soldiers in the company exclaimed in disgust. "What's the matter, Ludovic?" Gremio asked.

"I just stepped in some unicorn shit," Ludovic answered.

"Well, wipe it off your shoe and keep going," Gremio said.

"Captain, I haven't had any shoes for weeks now," Ludovic said.

"Oh. Well, wipe it off your foot and keep going, then," Gremio said. "I don't know what else to tell you. You can't stop on account of that."

"Make the southrons pay when you get to them," Thisbe said.

"Wasn't the gods-damned southrons. Was our own gods-damned unicorn-riders. I'd like to make those sons of bitches pay, them and their shitty unicorns." Ludovic scattered curses with fine impartiality.

"If you find the fellow whose unicorn did it, you have my permission to pick a fight with him," Gremio said gravely.

Ludovic pondered that. Like the weather on a changeable day, he brightened and then clouded up again. "How the hells am I supposed to do that,

Captain? Gods-damned unicorn didn't leave any gods-
damned calling card, you know. Not except the one I
stepped in."

Snickers ran up and down the long files of marching men. Gremio said, "No, I suppose not. In that case,
you'd better just slog along with everybody else, don't
you think?"

"You aren't making fun of me by any chance, are
you, sir?"

"Gods forbid, Ludovic." Gremio had to deny it, even
though it was true. A free Detinan who thought
himself mocked would kill without counting the cost.
An apology would have made Gremio lose face. A simple
denial didn't.

Ludovic nodded, satisfied. "That's all right, then,"
he said, and marched on without complaining any more
about his filthy foot.

When the Army of Franklin camped that night, the
southrons' fires brightened the horizon to the south.
"They're waiting for us," Gremio said as he seared a
chunk of beef from one of the cows from the herd that
shambled along with the army. It wasn't very good
beef—it was, in fact, vile, odious beef—but it was ever
so much better than no beef at all.

"We knew they would be." Sergeant Thisbe, sear-
ing another gobbet of that odious beef, didn't sound
worried. The only time Thisbe had ever sounded
worried was about going to the healers after taking that
wound in southern Peachtree Province. Other than that,
nothing in army life that Gremio had seen fazed the
underofficer. "We'll lick 'em."

"Of course we will." Gremio couldn't very well deny
it, not in front of his men. Colonel Florizel had wanted
his company commanders to make the men believe the
war was still winnable. Gremio didn't know whether
it was or not. No matter how much he doubted it—

and that was almost enough to make him his own side's Doubting George—he couldn't show his doubts. He understood why not: if the men thought they couldn't win, why would they want to risk their lives for King Geoffrey?

"Poor southrons'll be sorry they ever heard of Poor Richard," a trooper declared.

A few men from the Army of Franklin *had* deserted. The ones who remained still kept plenty of fight. Maybe returning to the province for which the army was named helped. Maybe they were just too stubborn to know they were beaten. Whatever it was, Gremio didn't want to disturb it. He wished he had more of it himself.

Thisbe pulled the ragged, sorry beefsteak from the flames. The sergeant sniffed at it and made an unhappy face before taking out a belt knife and starting to haggle off bite-sized chunks. "Better than nothing. Better than your belly rubbing up against your backbone," Thisbe said.

"Yes, that's true." Gremio cut a bite from his own beefsteak. He stuck it in his mouth and chewed . . . and chewed, and chewed. Eventually, with a convulsive gulp, he swallowed. "Not a whole lot better than nothing," he said.

"I think it is." Thisbe, as usual, was determined to look on the bright side of things. "When you're empty, you can't hardly do anything. You feel all puny and sickly. It's not a wonderful supper, gods know, but it's a supper, and any supper is better than no supper at all."

"Well, I can't say you're wrong. I was thinking the same thing a little earlier, in fact." Gremio didn't want to argue with Sergeant Thisbe. He wrestled another bite of meat down his throat. "Now I know why so many men in the company have no shoes. The drovers have been butchering them and called the shoeleather beef."

Thisbe did smile at that, but then grew serious again. "I wonder what they're doing with the hides of the cattle they're killing. If they're just leaving them for scavengers, that's a shame and a disgrace. The Army of Franklin must have plenty of men who know how to tan leather. Maybe they could make shoes, or at least patch the ones that are coming to pieces."

"That's a good idea. That's a hells of a good idea, as a matter of fact." Gremio made fewer bites of the rest of his beefsteak than he should have. A couple of times, he felt like a small snake trying to choke down a large dog. When at last he swallowed the final bite, he jumped to his feet. "I'm going to find out whether we're doing anything like that—and if we aren't, why not."

He hurried to Colonel Florizel's pavilion. The regimental commander was gamely—which did seem the proper word—hacking away at a slab of meat no finer than the one Gremio had eaten. When Gremio explained Thisbe's notion, Florizel paused, swallowed with no small effort, and then said, "That *is* clever. I have no idea what we're doing with the hides. We should be doing something, shouldn't we?"

"If we have any sort of chance to, we should, yes," Gremio said. "If you don't know, sir, who would?"

"Patrick the Cleaver, I suspect," Florizel answered. "He sticks his nose into all sorts of things."

The other side of that coin was, *I can't be bothered sticking* my *nose into all sorts of things*. Calling Florizel on it would have been worse than useless. Gremio saluted and said, "Thank you, sir. I'll speak with him."

"I hope something comes of it." Colonel Florizel did mean well, as long as he didn't have to put himself out too much. He *was* a brave leader in battle. Gremio

wished he were a better administrator, but Gremio, a
barrister himself, highly valued organization in others.

He'd never spoken to Patrick the Cleaver before,
and wondered how much trouble he would have getting to see the wing commander. He had no more than
he'd had seeing Colonel Florizel. As he had with
Florizel, he explained himself. "This is your notion,
now?" Patrick asked him.

"No, sir," Gremio answered. "My company's first
sergeant thought of it. H—uh, his—name is Thisbe."

"It's a good notion, indeed and it is," Patrick said.
"My hat's off to you, Captain, for not being after claim-
ing it for your own."

"I couldn't do that," Gremio said.

"No, eh?" The brigadier eyed him. "Plenty could,
the which is nobbut the truth."

"I don't steal," Gremio said stiffly. From anyone but
Thisbe, he might have. From the sergeant? Never.

"Well, good on you," Patrick the Cleaver said. "If
you're after giving this sergeant the credit, you might
also be thinking of giving him lieutenant's rank to go
with it."

"Sir, I tried to promote the sergeant during the
fighting south of Marthasville, for bravery then,"
Gremio said. "Thisbe refused to accept officer's rank.
I doubt anything has changed . . . his mind since."

Patrick chuckled. "Sure and there are sergeants like
that. Most of 'em, I think, are fools. The army could
use officers o' their stripe—better nor a good many
of the omadhauns giving orders the now."

Thisbe had reasons for declining that Patrick the
Cleaver probably hadn't contemplated. Gremio saw no
point in discussing those reasons with the wing commander. He asked, "Is there any chance of doing what
the sergeant suggested, sir?"

"By the gods, Captain, there is that," Patrick

answered. "Once we're after driving the gods-damned southrons from Poor Richard, I'll see to it. You may rely on me."

"Thank you, sir." Gremio believed him. Patrick was one of the youngest brigadiers in King Geoffrey's armies, but he'd already acquired a reputation for reliability to go with his name for hard fighting. Gremio said, "May I ask you one thing more?"

"Ask what you will," Patrick said. "I do not promise to answer."

"That's only fair," Gremio said. "What sort of ground will we be fighting on at this Poor Richard place?"

"It's open," Patrick the Cleaver replied. "It's very open." His face, which had been very open a moment before, all at once closed. "If I were Lieutenant General Bell . . ." He didn't go on.

"If you were Bell . . ." Gremio prompted.

"Never you mind," Patrick said. "I've told the general commanding my opinions, and I need not repeat 'em to another soul."

Had he stood in the witness box, Gremio could have peppered him with questions as with crossbow quarrels. That wasn't how things worked here. A man who tried to grill a superior not inclined to be forthcoming wouldn't find out what he wanted to know, and would wind up in trouble.

Patrick said, "Give my compliments to your clever sergeant, if you'd be so kind, and the top o' the evening to you."

That was dismissal. Captain Gremio saluted and left the wing commander's pavilion. He made his way back to his own regiment's encampment. "Well, sir?" Sergeant Thisbe asked when he sat down by the fire once more.

"Well, Sergeant, Brigadier Patrick says you ought to be promoted to lieutenant for your cleverness," Gremio replied.

Thisbe stared into the flames. The sergeant said nothing while a soldier dumped more wood on the fire. Then, in a low voice, Thisbe said, "I don't want to be promoted. I told you that, sir, the last time you were generous enough to offer that to me. I'm . . . content where I am."

Gremio looked around. The soldier with the wood was building up another campfire ten or twelve feet away. A couple of men lay close to this blaze, but they were already snoring thunderously. Gremio spoke in a low voice: "Do you have the same reasons now as you did then?"

"Yes, sir," the sergeant answered.

"Are they the same reasons that kept you from wanting to see a healer when you were wounded?" Gremio persisted.

Thisbe looked into the flames again. "My reasons are my reasons. I think they're good ones." The sergeant would not meet Gremio's eyes.

"Are they the reasons I think they are?" Gremio asked.

That made Thisbe look at him. It didn't get him a straight answer, though. With what might have been a smile, the underofficer said, "How can any man know what another man is thinking?"

Gremio took a deep breath. He'd never asked Thisbe a direct question about the matter that interested him most. Even as he started to ask one now, he stopped with it unspoken. Thisbe might give him a truthful answer. But even if the sergeant did give him that kind of answer, it might preclude further questions. One of these days—very likely not till the war ended, if it ever did—Gremio hoped to have the chance to ask those questions.

All he said now was, "Sergeant, do you know how difficult you make things?"

"I'm sorry, sir." And Thisbe really did sound sorry.
"I never wanted to be difficult. All I ever wanted was
to do my job, and to do it as well as I could."

"You've done it very well—well enough to deserve
promotion," Gremio said.

"I don't want to be a lieutenant," the sergeant said.

"I know. You deserve to be one anyhow," Gremio
said. They eyed each other, back at their old impasse.
Thisbe shrugged. Gremio smiled a rueful smile. And
then, in spite of everything, they both started to laugh.

Doubting George wished he could go north to Poor
Richard. All hells were going to break loose up there,
and he sat here in Ramblerton gathering soldiers a
dribble at a time. Actually, he knew he *could* go up to
Poor Richard. John the Lister was hardly in a position
to shoo him away if he hopped on a glideway carpet and
sped up there. But John was only a captain in King
Avram's regulars. If he could hold Bell off or beat him,
he would surely gain permanent rank to match his ability. George already had it: less than he craved, less than
he thought he deserved, but a sufficiency.

And so he stayed behind the line, and did the things
a good regional commander was supposed to do, and
didn't do anything else. If he sometimes drummed his
fingers on his desk and looked longingly toward the
north . . . well, he was the only man who knew that.

Colonel Andy came in, a troubled look on his round
face. "Sir," he said, "word from the scryers is that
Lieutenant General Bell is getting ready to attack John
the Lister."

"John's got himself ready at Poor Richard, hasn't he?"
George asked.

"As ready as he can be, yes, sir." His adjutant
nodded.

"Better Bell should attack him there than when he

was on the march and vulnerable by Summer Mountain, eh?" George said.

"Well . . . yes, sir, put that way." Andy nodded again, but reluctantly. "Even so, he's badly outnumbered."

"There is that," Doubting George allowed. "How imminent is this attack? Can we down here do anything about it?"

"I don't think so, sir." Colonel Andy looked very much like a worried chipmunk. "From what the scryers say John says, Bell will be on him this afternoon at the latest."

"We could send men by glideway that fast, if everything went perfectly," George said. "We couldn't send so many as I'd like, and we couldn't send much in the way of equipment with them, not on such short notice, but they would be better than nothing."

"That was the other thing I wanted to tell you," Major Andy said unhappily. "The northerners have desorcerized a stretch of the glideway line between here and Poor Richard. I don't know whether Bell got wizards past John and Alva, or whether these are local traitors sneaking out and making trouble now that we've recalled so many garrisons to Ramblerton. Either way, though, till our mages repair the break, we can't use that line to move soldiers."

"Well, gods damn the northerners, then," George said. "I was just thinking John had the chance to make a name for himself. I doubt he would have wanted quite such a good chance, though."

"Yes, sir. I doubt that, too," Andy said. "I wish we could do something more."

"So do I." Doubting George drummed his fingers on the broad desktop, right out there where Andy could see him do it. He'd sent John the Lister north to delay Bell, not to serve as a snack for him. After a moment, he brightened. "Bell's not what you'd call a very clever fellow, and he's bound to be spitting mad because John got away from him once. He'll go in as quick and as hard as he can, no matter what's waiting for him."

"If he has enough men, how much will it matter?" Colonel Andy asked bleakly.

"Always an interesting question," George admitted. "Of course, there's another interesting question—what do you mean by 'enough'? The north has never had enough men for all the ground false King Geoffrey needed to cover at the start of the war. That's why they're losing."

"In general terms, that's true, sir. But whether Bell has enough to smash John is a rather more specific question, wouldn't you say?"

"Unfortunately, I would. Anything I can do to help our wizards fix the desorcerized stretch of glideway? Would sending more sorcerers help?"

"Probably not, sir," Andy answered. "They're doing all they can, and half the time more wizards only mean more quarrels."

"More than half the time," Doubting George said. "All right, then. We'll do everything we can. If we can't do enough, John the Lister will fight his own battle." He brightened slightly. "I *did* send him Major Alva before the traitors got at the glideway line. That's something, anyhow."

"Yes, sir," Colonel Andy said. "And he has Hard-Riding Jimmy's unicorn-riders with him."

"Hard-Riding Jimmy hasn't got very many men, not if he wants to stand against Ned of the Forest." Doubting George sounded even more dubious than usual.

His adjutant spoke soothingly: "They carry those newfangled quick-shooting crossbows, though. There may not be many of them, but they can put a lot of bolts in the air."

Hesmucet had offered Doubting George the same

sort of consolation when he'd given him Hard-Riding Jimmy's brigade. "Newfangled crossbows are all very well," George said now, "but one of the reasons you take newfangled weapons into the field is to find out what goes wrong with them. Tangling with Ned of the Forest's unicorn-riders is liable to be an expensive way to find out."

"That's if they don't work as advertised," Andy said.

Doubting George raised one dark eyebrow. "When have you ever known a newfangled weapon that did, Colonel?"

Andy frowned. After a moment, he shrugged. "Well, you've got me there, sir. But these *have* seen some use—and besides, there's bound to be a first time."

"Yes, so there is," George agreed. "But has the Lion God come down from Mount Panamgam and whispered in your ear that this is it?"

"Uh . . . no, sir." Colonel Andy looked as if he wasn't sure whether George was serious.

Since the commanding general wasn't sure whether he was serious, either, that suited him fine. He gave Andy his blandest smile. "Have you got any other delightful news for me, Colonel?"

"Uh . . . no, sir," his adjutant repeated.

"All right. You're dismissed," George said. "I'm going to review our works here. Unless John the Lister takes Lieutenant General Bell's army clean off the board, Bell's heading this way. Or do you think I'm wrong?"

"No, sir." Andy sounded sure about that. "And it's not very likely that John can smash Bell, is it, not when he's so badly outnumbered?"

"I thought I just said that. Maybe I'm wrong." Doubting George dug into his map case. Andy departed, shaking his head.

The maps showed what George already knew: Ramblerton was a town fortified to a faretheewell. The southrons had taken it away from King Geoffrey's men when the war was barely a year old, and they'd held it ever since, even when Thraxton the Braggart mounted an invasion of Cloviston. To hold it with the fewest possible men, they'd surrounded it with a ring of trenches and forts as strong as any in Detina save perhaps those of Georgetown itself.

Doubting George shook his big head. The works at Pierreville, north of Nonesuch—the works Marshal Bart was now besieging—were probably this strong, too. He hadn't thought of them for a moment because they belonged to the traitors. But that was wrong. Detina was still *one* kingdom. If not, why fight for Avram?

He hadn't dwelt on such things for a while. And he'd already given his own answer, to himself and to Detina. As far as he was concerned, his homeland was and could be only one kingdom. If that meant it would be one kingdom without serfs, then it did, and he would worry about what, if anything, that meant later on. He'd felt the same when he declined to follow Duke Edward of Arlington after Parthenia Province declared for Geoffrey and against Avram: that even though he'd been a liege lord himself, over a small fief in Parthenia.

False King Geoffrey had solved his problem there long before King Avram could have worried about it. George chuckled. Now, at a distance of more than three years, he could find it funny. He didn't need to worry about serfs if he didn't own that estate any more. And he didn't, not according to Geoffrey, who'd taken it away from him.

If the south won the War Between the Provinces— no, *when* the south won the War Between the Provinces—he could go back again. He could take his place among his neighbors as a minor nobleman. He could, yes, but how much good would it do him? He would be a minor nobleman without blonds to work the land.

Under those circumstances, what point to going back at all?

That was one obvious question. Another question, equally obvious, was, what would his erstwhile neighbors, who were also minor nobles in Parthenia Province, do after the south won the war? How would they bring in their crops without plenty of blond serfs to do the hard work for them? Would they labor in the fields themselves, with their wives and children?

"I doubt it," George said, and went back to the maps.

But maps could show him only so much. They chiefly showed him the places he needed to see with his own eyes. He put on a wool hat and a gray overcoat and left his warm headquarters to give his own eyes the looks they needed.

Ramblertonians glowered at him as he made his way north up a muddy street (and, when it rained, Ramblerton had no other kind of street). King Avram's soldier's had held Franklin's metropolis—such as it was—for two and a half years now. The locals still resented them. Doubting George laughed. The locals did more than resent. They hated southrons, with a hatred that had curdled and grown more sullen over time because it was so impotent.

"Bell'll bundle you bastards back where you belong!" somebody shouted after George walked past.

He stopped and looked back. That was exactly what the Ramblertonian had wanted him to do, of course . . . whichever Ramblertonian it was. Six or eight Detinans in civilian clothes sent mocking stares his way. He judged they would all mock him if he said, *I doubt it*. What he said instead was, "Well, he's welcome to try." Then, tipping his hat to them, he went on his way.

They muttered behind him. He doubted they would have the nerve to rush him, and he proved right. They could jeer, but that was all they could do. *And Geoffrey's so-called kingdom is no better off than they are*, George thought, and smiled again.

The maps had got behind the fortifications they were supposed to represent. Doubting George had hoped that was so, but hadn't dared to expect it: if he assumed the worst, he was unlikely to be disappointed. Here, though, areas that had seemed weak on parchment looked rugged in reality.

Blonds did most of the ongoing work, under the orders of Detinan engineers. Runaway serfs dug trenches, carried dirt in barrows and hods, and raised ramparts where none had stood before. Some of them wore gray tunics and pantaloons of a cut not much different from that of southron uniforms. Others had on the rags of the clothes they'd worn while fleeing their liege lords' estates. All of them were probably working harder than they ever had back on those estates.

What struck Doubting George was how happy the blonds looked. Detinans, especially Detinans from the north, thought of blonds as a happy-go-lucky lot, always smiling regardless of whether things called for a smile. That, George now suspected, was a mask serfs wore to keep Detinans from knowing what was really in their minds. These blonds, by contrast, looked and sounded and acted really happy, no matter how hard they were working.

One of them recognized Doubting George. Waving, the fellow called, "General, we want you to use these works to kill loads and loads of those stinking northern nobles."

"We'll do our best," the general commanding answered. He wondered if the blond knew *he* was a stinking northern noble. He had his . . .

"Kill 'em all," the blond said. "Bury 'em all. Stick

'em in the ground. Don't give 'em to the fire. Don't let their spirits rise up with the flames and the smoke."

The rest of the runaways now laboring for King Avram nodded. Back in the old days, before the conquerors came, most blonds had buried their dead. Now they followed ordinary Detinan usage, and looked on burial with as much horror as ordinary Detinans did. Odds were these fellows hadn't the faintest idea what their ancestors had done.

Are they savages, or just savage? Doubting George wondered. *And if people had done to me what we've done to the blonds for generations, wouldn't I have good reason to be savage?*

He walked up and down the line, from one end to the other. It was anchored at both east and west by the Cumbersome River. A solid fleet of catapult-carrying war galleys rowed up and down the Cumbersome. All of them flew King Avram's gold dragon on red. The northerners had no galleys on the Cumbersome, and none on the Great River, either, not any more. Several river fights and the losses of Old Capet and, after a long siege, Camphorville had made sure of that.

In the center, the line bulged out toward the north, swallowing up the whole town of Ramblerton and taking advantage of the high ground out beyond the edge of settled territory. The more George walked, the fewer the doubts he had. He didn't see how Lieutenant General Bell and the Army of Franklin could batter their way through these works and into Ramblerton.

Of course, what he saw and what Bell saw were liable to be two different beasts. "I hope they're two different beasts," Doubting George muttered. The mere idea that he and Bell might think alike offended him. And if it also offended Bell . . . George did some more muttering: "That's his worry."

❖   ❖   ❖

It was already past noon when Lieutenant General Bell and the Army of Franklin neared John the Lister's defensive position by Poor Richard. Bell looked across the wide, empty fields toward the three slightly concave lines of entrenchments awaiting him. King Avram's banners fluttered on the earthworks.

He glanced over toward his wing and brigade commanders. With a brusque nod, he said, "We attack."

"As simple as that, your honor?" Patrick the Cleaver asked.

"As simple as that," Bell said. "Unless you haven't the stomach for it, as you hadn't the stomach for it at Summer Mountain."

Like most men from the Sapphire Isle, Brigadier Patrick was swarthy even by Detinan standards. That didn't keep him from showing an angry flush now. "I'll show you what sort of man I am," he growled. "Sure and you've shown me now what sort of man *you* are."

That did nothing to improve Bell's temper. Neither did the pain he could never escape. "We can discuss this further at your leisure, Brigadier," he said.

Patrick bowed. "I am at your service in that as in all things."

"And I," Brigadier Provincial Prerogative said. "When you insult Brigadier Patrick, you insult all your officers."

"That's true," Otho the Troll said in a rumbling bass.

Brigadier John of Barsoom bowed to Bell. "As a proper northern gentleman, I would be remiss if I said this did not also hold for me."

"And me, for gods' sake," For Gods' Sake John added.

Hiram the Cranberry turned even redder than usual and nodded without speaking.

Bell wondered if he would have to duel with every officer in the Army of Franklin, down to the rank of lieutenant. He had a hells of a time cocking a cross-bow, but he could shoot quick and straight with one hand. If they wanted to quarrel with him, he would give each of them a quarrel, right in the ribs.

Ned of the Forest said, "I thought we were supposed to be fighting the southrons, not each other."

"Theory is wonderful," Provincial Prerogative said, still glaring at Bell. He'd been one of the leaders in the attack on Sumptuous Castle in Karlsburg harbor, the attack that had started the War Between the Provinces. Bell glared back. He didn't care what Provincial Prerogative had done in what now seemed the dim, distant, dead past.

"We'd better fight the southrons," Ned said. "Anybody who doesn't care to fight them can fight *me* instead."

That produced a sudden, thoughtful silence. No one was eager to fight Ned. Lieutenant General Bell said, "I require no proxies."

"I'm not doing this for you, sir," Ned of the Forest answered. "I'm doing it for the kingdom. Seems to me a lot of folks here have forgotten about the kingdom."

Some of Bell's brigadiers still looked angry. But several of them nodded. "For gods' sake, he's right!" For Gods' Sake John burst out. No one disagreed, not out loud.

Ned said, "Sir, by your leave, I'd like to take my riders over to the left and back into the southrons' rear. When you lick 'em, we'll be there in perfect position to fall on 'em as they're running away."

Bell didn't need to think long. Anything but victory was unimaginable. This time, he'd follow up victory once he got it. He nodded to Ned. "Good idea. Go do it."

Ned of the Forest started to leave the assembled officers, then stopped and turned back. "Matter of fact, sir, I reckon we can flank 'em right out of their works. If you'll hold up a little, you won't even need to charge 'em. That there's liable to be a hard line to take by assault."

Several brigadiers brightened. One man after another nodded. The longer Bell watched them, the angrier he got. He shook his leonine head. "No. We *will* attack."

The commander of unicorn-riders scowled. "Why the hells do you want to pick a fight when you don't have to . . . sir?" he asked. "Give me a brigade of footsoldiers to go with my riders and I will agree to flank the southrons from their works within two hours' time. I can go down the Folly-free Gap, the one the Ramblerton road goes through, and sneak behind 'em before they even know I'm around."

"What a fine notion you're after having there!" Patrick the Cleaver exclaimed. "We're asking for naught but trouble, crossing such a broad stretch of open space towards earthworks the Thunderer's hard prong couldn't pierce."

Brigadier Benjamin, called the Heated Ham because he'd made a bad schoolboy actor, also nodded. The wing commander said, "Sir, I think Ned and Patrick are right. I don't like the looks of this fight here. The southrons have a good position, and they're well fortified."

"No," Bell said again. "My mind's made up. Ned, you may use your flanking move, but with unicorn-riders only. You, at least, have shown you are not afraid to manfully fight out in the open."

Ned of the Forest looked even angrier than he had before. The wing and brigade commanders started screaming at Lieutenant General Bell all over again, louder than ever. "How dare you call us cowards, for gods' sake?" For Gods' Sake John demanded.

"How dare you act like cowards?" Bell retorted,

which might have been a new firepot bursting among his subordinates. Ned of the Forest stamped away, throwing up his hands in disgust.

John of Barsoom cried, "At least have the decency to tell us why you're sending us off to be slaughtered."

"I will tell you exactly why," Bell said in tones of ice. "I have made the discovery that this army, after a forward march of more than one hundred fifty miles, is still seemingly unwilling to accept battle unless under the protection of breastworks, and this has caused me to experience grave concern. In my inmost heart I question whether or not I will ever succeed in eradicating this evil. It seems to me I have exhausted every means in the power of one man to remove this stumbling block from the Army of Franklin."

"Meaning no disrespect, sir, but it seems to me you don't know what the hells you're talking about," Benjamin the Heated Ham said.

Bell wondered how he would have spoken had he meant disrespect. The commanding general gave one of his one-shouldered shrugs. "I do not care how it seems to you," he said, his voice even colder than it had been a moment before. "It seems to me that some of my subordinates have a great deal to learn about obeying orders."

"It seems to *me* somebody has a deal to learn about *giving* orders," Otho the Troll muttered.

"What's that? What's that?" Bell said. "By the Lion God's claws, King Geoffrey trusts me to give orders for the Army of Franklin. That's the truth, and anybody who doesn't like it can go to the devils!"

"King Geoffrey trusted Thraxton the Braggart to give orders for this army, too," Otho the Troll snapped. "Fat lot of good *that* did us."

"If I report that to his Majesty, you'll be sorry for it," Bell said.

"I'm already sorry for all sorts of things. What's one more?" Brigadier Otho waved toward the southrons' lines. "Besides, if we go up against that, how many of us are coming back, anyhow?"

"We're not planning on coming back. We're planning on going through the gods-damned southrons and on to Ramblerton," Bell said.

None of the assembled brigade and wing commanders said a word. The silence seemed to take on a life of its own. Bell's stump hurt. His right leg hurt, too, though he had no right leg. His ruined left arm was also full of anguish. He longed for laudanum. Taking it here and now, though, taking it in front of his brigadiers, would be an obscure admission of weakness and defeat.

Instead of using the drug he craved, he tried to hearten himself and his officers with hope: "By the gods, we *can* do this. We outnumber them. We'll roll over them like an avalanche."

More silence, colder than the late autumn afternoon. Lieutenant General Bell's wounds throbbed and burned worse than ever. Of itself, his good hand again started toward the little bottle he always carried with him. He made it hold still: far from the easiest thing he'd ever done.

"Well," he said at last. Again, silence all around him. He stood as straight as he could. "Well," he said again. It seemed a complete sentence. In case it wasn't, he spoke once more: "I have given you your orders, gentlemen. I expect you to show me what manner of men you are in the way you obey them."

Mechanical as if they were so many machines stamped out by the manufactories of the south, the wing and brigade commanders saluted. Still, though, not one of them spoke to Bell.

He didn't care. He was past caring. He was as sure

of what wanted doing as if the Lion God had growled the plan into his ear. "We will go forward," he said. "Brigadier Patrick!"

Directly addressed, Patrick had no choice but to answer. Saluting once more, he said, "Yes, sir?"

"Do you see the path there, the one going through the field toward the center of the enemy line?"

"Yes, sir. I see it, sir." Patrick the Cleaver was offensively polite.

Bell matched him in fussy precision: "Good. Form your men to the right of the path, letting your left overlap the same. Give orders to your soldiers not to shoot a crossbow bolt until you run the southron skirmish line out of the first line of works, then press them and shoot them in the back as they run to their main line. Then charge the enemy's works. Poor Richard is the key to Ramblerton, and Ramblerton is the key to independence."

Patrick the Cleaver smiled grimly. "Sure and you have given me the hottest part of the fire to quell, your honor. Well, that is as it is, and no help for it. I will take the southrons' works for you, sir, or I will die trying." His salute was, of its kind, a thing of beauty. He turned and walked over to his unicorn, which was tethered to a nearby oak: no doubt a splendid tree in summer, but bare-branched and skeletal now. Mounting with a grace that roused nothing but envy in Lieutenant General Bell, Patrick rode off to the soldiers he commanded.

Did I put his men in the most dangerous position on purpose, because he has caused me so much trouble? Bell wondered. After a few seconds, he shrugged another of his painful, one-shouldered shrugs. *What if I did? Someone has to be there, and Patrick the Cleaver has never been a man to shrink from striking a mighty blow. We need a mighty blow right now.*

He nodded to himself. If he'd ever had any serious doubts, that stifled them.

One by one, the other wing and brigade commanders straggled off toward their soldiers, some riding, others walking. Those who stayed on foot all went with bowed heads and stooped shoulders, as if trying to bear the weight of the world on their backs. They did not look like officers heading into a battle for which they were eager. Bell had seen many such officers in the early days of the war. Up till the battle by the River of Death and his second maiming, he'd *been* such an officer. He didn't think many of that sort were left in King Geoffrey's army.

A victory will make more, he told himself. *We have to have a victory. Because we have to have one, we'll get one. It's as simple as that.*

Last of the subordinate commanders to stay by Bell was Benjamin the Heated Ham. He looked as gloomy as any of the other brigadiers. "Are you sure you want to do this, sir?" he asked. "Are you sure we've got men and engines enough to do the job?"

The soldiers were starting to shake themselves out into a battle line. "I am sending everything I have," Bell answered. "What more can I do? What more can Geoffrey's kingdom do? If everyone gives all he has, our victory will be assured."

Benjamin still looked as mournful as a man planning his own cremation. He said, "Yes, sir," in a way that couldn't possibly mean anything but, *No, sir.* Then, shaking his head, he too went off to command his wing.

Bell stroked his beard, deep in thought. Where to get more men? All his soldiers were here, all except those riding off for that trip around the southrons' flank with Ned of the Forest. "By the Thunderer!" Bell exclaimed, and shouted for a messenger.

"Yes, sir?" the young man said.

"Ride after Lieutenant General Ned," Bell told him. "Kill your unicorn if you have to, but catch up with him. Tell him I am recalling two of his regiments. They are to report back here to me at once, for direct use against Poor Richard. Have you got that?"

"Yes, sir," the messenger said again, and repeated it to him.

"Good—you do have it straight. Now go, and ride like the wind," Bell said. Nodding, the messenger dashed to his unicorn, sprang aboard, roweled it with his spurs, and went off like a crossbow quarrel. Bell nodded. That would take care of that. Ned might grumble, but Bell was prepared to ignore grumbling. *He* commanded here, and the fight came first.

More long files of northern soldiers moved out over the field, forming themselves into a battle line. Their brave standards, red dragon proud on gold, fluttered in the chilly breeze. For all the carping and whining and grumbling Bell had heard from his brigadiers, the men complained not at all. They knew they had a job to do, and they were ready to give it everything they had in them.

With a nod, Bell turned to the trumpeter beside him. "Blow *advance*," he said.

Ned of the Forest listened to Lieutenant General Bell's messenger with a mix of fury and disbelief. "You can't mean that," Ned said when the youngster finished. "You can't possibly mean that. Gods damn it, Bell can't mean that."

"I do, sir. He does, sir," the messenger replied. "He requires the men at once, to help in the attack on Poor Richard."

"That's half my force!" Ned exclaimed. The messenger merely rode his unicorn alongside the commander of unicorn-riders without a word. Ned tried again.

Maybe the young soldier would see reason: "It'll help his attack a hells of a lot more if I can strike at the southrons' flank with all the power I've got."

"I'm sorry, sir," the fellow said uncomfortably. "I don't give the orders. I only send them on from the general commanding."

"This is a fool's order." Ned of the Forest thought hard about disobeying it, about pretending he'd never got it, even about making something unfortunate happen to this messenger so he could be convincing when he pretended that. Reluctantly, he decided he couldn't justify something unfortunate. He didn't *know* how things were back by Poor Richard. Maybe Bell *did* desperately need two regiments of unicorn-riders to turn John the Lister's right flank or for some other reason. Maybe. Ned of the Forest still had a hard time believing it. But, hard time or not, he turned to the trumpeter trotting along close by and said, "Blow *halt*." The words tasted putrid in his mouth, like salt beef that had gone off.

A quarter of an hour later, two regiments of unicorn-riders trotted back with the messenger. The rest of Ned's force pressed on. Colonel Biffle, whose troopers Ned had kept with him, muttered into his beard. He didn't need long to stop muttering and come right out and say, "This is a bad business, sir—a very bad business."

"Don't I know it?" Ned said bitterly. Then he laughed, and that was more bitter still. "Bell only half wanted to let me go in the first place, and so he's ending up letting me go with only half my men. I reckon that leaves me just about half a chance of doing anything worthwhile. How do you cipher it, Biff?"

"About the same, sir. Don't suppose anybody *could* cipher it any different. What the hells do we do now?"

"The best we can," Ned of the Forest answered.

"Don't know what else there is *to* do." He raised his voice to call to a couple of men riding farther away from him than Colonel Biffle: "Captain Watson! Major Marmaduke!"

By strict protocol, he should have named Marmaduke first. But he couldn't bring himself to put a mere wizard ahead of the man who led soldiers and engines. Both the sorcerer and the commander of catapults answered, "Yes, sir?" and guided their mounts—one unicorn, one ass—closer to his.

"Are you ready to do everything—and I mean *everything*—to make up for the loss of the soldiers Bell just stole from us?" Ned asked them.

"Yes, sir!" they chorused again. Ned knew he could rely on Watson. No matter how young he was, he'd fought like a veteran from the day he'd taken service with the unicorn-riders. Major Marmaduke, on the other hand . . . Ned of the Forest sighed and shrugged. Counting on a wizard was always a roll of the dice. That was one problem the southrons had, too. It might have been the only problem they had worse than King Geoffrey's men, as a matter of fact.

A scout rode back, calling, "Folly-free Gap just ahead, sir. There's southrons at the far end of it, too."

Ned swore. He'd hoped he could get through the gap and into the southrons' rear before meeting up with their unicorn-riders. Then he would have had the edge, or more of it, even if Bell had robbed him of half his force. He shrugged again. What you hoped for in war and what you got were all too likely to be different animals.

He turned to Watson and Marmaduke. "You heard that?" he asked. They both nodded. He went on, "All right, then. We're going to have to shift the gods-damned sons of bitches. Do everything you know how to do."

"Yes, sir," they said once more. Watson added, "I'll bring the engines up as close to the enemy as I can."

"I know you will," Ned said. Major Marmaduke made no such promises. Odds were, he didn't know how he would be useful till the moment came. Ned hoped he would figure it out then.

Colonel Biffle had heard the scout's report, too. As the leading unicorn-riders entered Folly-free Gap, the regimental commander asked, "You aim to move as near as we can mounted and then attack on foot, sir?"

"Best way to do it, far as I can see," Ned answered. "I wish we had more cover coming down on 'em, gods damn it." In summertime, the low, gentle slopes of the gap would have offered plenty of concealment, and he might have sneaked around the southrons before they knew he was there. No chance of that now, not with all the branches bare. If he wanted to unplug the gap, he'd have to knock the enemy riders out of it.

Colonel Biffle pointed ahead. "Nice little stand of woods there where we can tether our unicorns. We'll only need to leave a handful of men behind to watch 'em."

"I don't want to leave *any*, not after Bell went and robbed me." Ned of the Forest drummed the fingers of his left hand against his thigh. "You're right, though, Biff. We've got to leave a handful, I reckon. By the Thunderer's beard, we won't leave many."

Tiny in the distance, southrons on unicorns rode back toward their main body of men. Ned could easily see the unicorns because they were so very white. He laughed. One of these days, if he ever got the chance, he would have to slap brown paint on his men's beasts so they wouldn't stand out so much from the terrain over which they rode. That might let him give King Avram's unicorn-riders a nasty surprise.

No surprises here. This would be straight-up,

toe-to-toe slugging. Ned hated this kind of fight, but the ground dictated it. So did Bell's insistence on slamming straight ahead at Poor Richard. Ned muttered into his chin whiskers. If only Bell had had some sense to go with his undoubted courage . . .

The unicorn-riders reached the copse Colonel Biffle had seen. They scrambled off their mounts, tethered them, and trotted toward the southrons. They didn't move in neat lines, as footsoldiers did. All they wanted to do was close with the enemy or find some way to outflank him. Once they managed that, they were convinced the rest would be easy. It usually had been up till now.

A few of Ned's men stayed behind to guard the tethered unicorns. A few of the unicorns went forward: those ridden by officers, Ned among them, and those pulling Captain Watson's catapults and repeating crossbows. Major Marmaduke went forward still mounted, too. Again, though, Ned had trouble taking a man who rode an ass seriously. A fellow who rode an ass was all too likely to be one, too. . . .

As usual, Ned sent his unicorn trotting out ahead of his men. He wanted to make the southrons start shooting at him, so he could discover where they were. He also wanted them to see him, to know who he was. He won as much by intimidating the enemy as by outfighting them.

A firepot arced through the air and burst about twenty feet in front of him. The unicorn sidestepped nervously. He fought it back under control. Waving his sword, he pointed to the stand of trees from which the firepot had flown. "Captain Watson, there's some of what the bastards have waiting for us!" he shouted.

"Right, sir," the young officer said gaily. He waved the siege engines he led forward. Because he came forward with them—ahead of them, in fact—the men who served the catapults and repeating crossbows didn't hesitate in advancing. They set up in the open and got to work shooting at the southrons' engines.

Dismounted soldiers in gray came up in the same irregular way as Ned's own troopers. Ned recognized it at once, recognized it and didn't like it. The southrons weren't supposed to fight as dragoons, and weren't supposed to look as if they knew what they were doing when they did. Ned also recognized what Hard-Riding Jimmy's men were up to. If they could get close enough to Watson's engines to reach them with their crossbows, they could pick off the soldiers serving the engines. Yes, they knew what they were doing as dragoons, all right.

"Well, gods damn them, let's see how they like this," he growled, and spurred his unicorn toward them. If he killed a couple, the rest might run away. He'd seen that happen before.

He didn't see it this time. He didn't see the crossbow quarrels buzzing past his head, either. They were going too fast for that. He didn't see them, but he heard them. They sounded like a swarm of angry wasps. For a moment, he thought a big repeating crossbow had decided to open up on him alone, an honor he could have done without.

Then he realized it wasn't one big repeating crossbow, but a lot of quick-shooting weapons in the hands of southron troopers. They seemed to be crank- and lever-operated and to shoot ten-bolt clips, and they put more quarrels in the air than anything he'd ever imagined. One tugged at the brim of his hat. A couple of inches to one side and it would have hit him in the face.

Another bolt glanced off his blade, sending a shiver up his left arm. And another caught his unicorn in the neck. The beast's scream of pain turned to a gurgle. It staggered, stumbled, toppled.

Were this Ned's first unicorn lost in battle, he might have been badly hurt. But, having had so many mounts killed under him, he knew what to do. He kicked free of the stirrups even before the unicorn went down. When it did, he rolled away instead of getting crushed beneath its body. And then he was on his feet and running forward, shouting, "Come on, boys! Let's get 'em!"

On came his riders, all of them roaring like the Lion God: the fierce northern war cry that struck fear into southron souls. They shot as they advanced, too. Ned of the Forest didn't believe in closing with the sword as the be-all and end-all of battles. If crossbow quarrels would kill the foe, that was fine with him. That the southrons ended up dead mattered. How they ended up that way didn't.

Hard-Riding Jimmy's men were still shooting, too, shooting as if they'd brought all the bolts in the world with them. More quarrels hissed past Ned's head. One snipped a slice from his sleeve. It might have been a friend, pulling on his arm to urge him to go that way. It might have been, but it wasn't.

And he was one of the lucky ones. All around him, dismounted unicorn-riders in blue fell. The cries of the wounded echoed through Folly-free Gap. He wondered how the place had got that name. However that had happened, it was badly miscalled. Trying to force his way through was turning out to be nothing but folly.

"How many of those southron sons of bitches are there?" a trooper howled after two quarrels buried themselves in the dirt at his feet and a third snarled by his body.

"And how long can they keep shooting those gods-damned crossbows of theirs?" another soldier complained.

"Don't you know about that?" asked a third, who at

least wasn't disheartened. "They load 'em on the day they sacrifice to the Lion God and keep shooting 'em all week long."

Ned of the Forest laughed. He would have laughed harder if the soldier hadn't told too much of the truth in sour jest. The enemy's quick-shooting crossbows made him seem to have at least three times as many soldiers as he really did. Since he probably outnumbered Ned's men anyway, that just made matters worse.

To the hells with Lieutenant General Bell, too, Ned thought angrily. He might have had some chance in spite of those fancy crossbows if he'd had his whole force along. With only half of it? He shook his head. Barring a miracle, it wasn't going to happen, and the gods had been chary about handing the north miracles lately.

Then Ned shook his head again. There was a miracle, or what would do for one: Colonel Biffle remained on his unicorn and unwounded, though he was even closer to the enemy than Ned. He kept urging his men on. They would surge forward, whereupon a blizzard of bolts would knock them back till they could nerve themselves for another surge.

Ned looked for Major Marmaduke. Maybe magic would help. But Marmaduke was down with a quarrel in his shoulder; a soldier stooped beside him to bind up the wound. There would be no fancy wizardry today, even if Marmaduke had had such a thing in him, which was anything but obvious.

Spying Ned, Biffle called, "We can't do it, sir, not the way they're shooting."

Before Ned could answer, a bolt plucked the hat off his head. Calm as if no one were taking aim at him, he turned, stooped, picked it up, and set it back in place. "If we get in amongst 'em—"

"How?" Colonel Biffle asked bluntly.

Ned started to reply, but realized he had nothing to say. His men were *not* going to get in amongst the southrons, not with the enemy spraying so many quarrels all over the landscape. He'd been in a lot of hard fights in more than three years of war, but this was the first time he'd had to own himself whipped. Pain and wonder in his voice, he said, "What can we do, then, Biff?"

"I only see two things," Biffle said. "We can hang on here and keep getting shot to no purpose, or we can pull back, maybe see if we can outflank these sons of bitches, maybe just wait and see how Bell does back at Poor Richard and hope that makes them leave the gap on their own."

"Pull back." The words tasted foul in Ned's mouth. But they weren't going forward here, and they weren't going to outflank Hard-Riding Jimmy, either.

Folly-free Gap was the only way through the hills. Oh, Ned's unicorn-riders could filter past a few men at a time, but far too slowly to do them any good. "It's up to Bell, then," Ned said, hoping that wasn't so bad an omen as it seemed.

As Captain Gremio mustered the men of his company along with the rest of Colonel Florizel's regiment, along with the rest of the wing, Brigadier Patrick the Cleaver came riding up on his unicorn to look over the ground his men would have to cross before closing with the southrons entrenched outside of Poor Richard.

Seeing Patrick's face, Sergeant Thisbe whistled softly. "He doesn't look very happy, does he?" the underofficer said in a low voice.

"He sure doesn't," Gremio answered, also quietly. Patrick stared toward the waiting field fortifications sheltering John the Lister's men, then shook his head. His sigh was loud enough to make people thirty or forty paces from him turn and look his way.

Colonel Florizel rode his unicorn out toward Patrick. The young brigadier from the Sapphire Isle reined in. He managed a weary nod for Florizel. The two high-ranking officers spoke together not twenty feet in front of Gremio and Thisbe.

"We must be after doing it, Colonel." Patrick pointed toward the southrons' works. "Come what may, we have to take them. There's to be no shooting till the skirmishers amongst those southron spalpeens flee back to their line. So says the great and mighty Lieutenant General Bell, and he is to be obeyed."

"I shall so order my company officers, sir," Florizel said stiffly.

"You do that. They all must know. I'll not give Bell the least excuse to tell me I would not follow his orders in every particular." Yes, Patrick sounded weary and gloomy beyond his years.

Florizel also eyed the long, long stretch of ground the northern army would have to cross before closing with John the Lister's soldiers. He saluted Patrick the Cleaver, then remarked, "Well, sir, there will not be many of us that will get back to Palmetto Province."

Patrick nodded. He reached out and let his left hand rest for a moment on the regimental commander's shoulder. "Well, Florizel, if we are to die, let us die like men." His voice held sadness, but no fear. He flicked the unicorn's reins. The white beast slowly walked on down the line.

Florizel shook himself, as if awakening from a dream, a bad dream. He turned to Gremio, asking, "Did you hear that?"

"Yes, sir," Gremio replied. "It didn't sound good." He too stared across the expanse of ground he would have to cover before breaking into the southrons' lines. How bare it seemed! "If you'll forgive my saying so, it doesn't look good, either."

"No, it doesn't," Florizel agreed glumly. "Come what may, though, we can only do our duty. The gods, I trust, will favor our cause. The gods *must* favor our cause."

"They had better," Gremio said. "If they don't, we've got no chance at all."

He waited for the regimental commander to round on him for talking like a defeatist. But Baron Florizel only nodded. His gaze kept going back toward the southrons' entrenchments, there so far away. "We would stand a better chance if we were asked to storm almost any other position, I fear," he said.

Gremio also nodded. Florizel had always been a man who looked for the best, hoped for the best, expected the best. If he now thought the Army of Franklin would have a hard time managing what Lieutenant General Bell required of it . . . Gremio was used to drawing inferences from evidence. He didn't care for the inferences he couldn't help drawing here.

Otho the Troll commanded the brigade of which Florizel's regiment was a part. He came by now on foot. His broad, muscular shoulders slumped, as if he carried a sack full of rocks on his back. "No help for it," he muttered, again and again. "No help for it at all."

Sergeant Thisbe walked up to Gremio and spoke in a low voice: "I wish they'd send us, sir. All this waiting around and thinking about what we've got to try and do wears on the nerves."

"It does, doesn't it?" Gremio agreed. "Me, I'm scared green."

"You, sir?" Thisbe sounded astonished. "You never show it."

"That only proves I'm a better actor than I thought," Gremio said. "All barristers have to act some. It's part of the job. But I haven't been this frightened since Thraxton the Braggart's spell went awry at Proselytizers'

Ridge last year. That wasn't my fault. It was the spell. I see what we've got to do now, and I'm terrified. No magic today. Just me."

"I'm scared, too," Thisbe said. "I wouldn't admit it to anybody but you, but I am. They can massacre us, and we don't even get to shoot back at 'em till we're just about up to their trenches. If we get that far."

Before Gremio could answer, bugles sounded up and down the line. Without being told to, standard-bearers stepped out in front of their companies and regiments and flourished the flags. Officers—Gremio among them—drew their swords. The bugles cried out again, this time with an order officers and underofficers echoed: "Advance!"

Advance they did, at a steady, rapid pace. Once his feet sent him toward the enemy, Gremio found a lot of his fear falling away, as if he'd left it behind where he'd waited while Patrick's wing shook itself out into line of battle. Logically, that was madness. Every step took him closer to danger. But now he was *doing* something, not waiting and brooding. It helped.

His men came with him. Not a one hung back. In a way, that made him proud of them. In another way, he thought them all idiots. He thought himself an idiot, too. At some point, the men of the Army of Franklin would get close enough for the southrons to open up on them with everything they had. Every step he took brought that point closer. Who else but an idiot would deliberately march into deadly danger?

"Come on, men!" Thisbe called. "Let those bastards hear you! Let 'em know whose side the Lion God's on!"

They roared. Southron prisoners had told Gremio that that roar was worth regiments of men on the battlefield. The soldiers who fought for King Avram had no war cry to match it. Other companies and other regiments took up the great growl of the Lion God.

Soon, all of Patrick the Cleaver's men snarled out defiance at their foes.

Gremio hoped it made the southrons afraid. He looked back over his shoulder. His comrades and he had come more than halfway from their starting point toward the enemy's line. More than a mile. Before too much longer, the southrons' engines would bear on them. They would have to take whatever the men in gray dished out till they got close enough for revenge.

Thisbe said it—if we get that close, he thought, and wished he hadn't.

On came the northerners, roaring fiercely. On they came . . . and a firepot arced through the air toward them, smoke trailing from the oil-soaked rag that would ignite it when it hit and burst. It landed fifty yards in front of the advancing men in blue. The splash of fire was impressive, but harmed no one.

"See? They *are* afraid of us, if they start shooting that soon!" Thisbe said scornfully. Gremio hoped the sergeant was right, though he doubted it—both sides usually started trying their weapons beyond their true reach. Even if Thisbe was right, though, how much difference would it make in the end? Avram's men would have plenty of chances to do more and worse.

Another catapult let fly, this one hurling a thirty-pound stone ball. Instead of sticking where it landed, it bounded toward the men from the Army of Franklin. They scrambled to get out of its way. Once, a long time before, an incautious soldier had tried to stop a bounding catapult ball with his foot. It had looked easy, and safe enough—and had cost him a broken leg for his foolishness. People knew better now.

More firepots flew. So did more stones. Some of them smashed down among the northerners. Men crushed or burning shrieked and fell. The rest closed their ranks and kept on. Up on his unicorn, Florizel brandished his sword. "Forward!" he cried.

And then the enemy's repeating crossbows began their ratcheting clatter. Soldier after blue-clad soldier went down, some kicking, some screaming, some silent and still. Gremio watched a skirmisher out ahead of the main line take two or three staggering steps while clutching at his chest, then crumple bonelessly to the ground.

But the pits that held John the Lister's skirmishers were very close now. Men in gray scrambled up out of those pits and ran back toward their main line. "There's the sign, Colonel," Gremio called. "May we shoot now?"

"Yes!" Florizel answered. "Shoot! Send all those sons of bitches to the hells and gone!"

Behind Gremio, crossbows clicked and snapped. His men, those who still stood, took vengeance on the southrons for everything they'd endured. "Kill the bastards!" they shouted, and the pickets in gray died like flies, most of them perishing long before they reached their own entrenchments.

But they're only pickets, Gremio thought uneasily. A moment later, he once more wished he hadn't had a thought, for all the southrons in the first row of proper earthworks leaped up onto the shooting steps, leveled their crossbows on the parapet, and delivered a volley the likes of which Gremio had never seen for sheer destructive power. Horrible screams rose all along the line of Patrick the Cleaver's wing. Soldiers in blue toppled as if scythed.

Colonel Florizel's unicorn might have charged head-long into a stone wall. Pierced by half a dozen quarrels, it crashed to the ground. Gremio feared for Florizel, but the regimental commander twisted free from his mount's ruin and limped forward on his bad foot. "Bravely done, Colonel!" Gremio shouted. Florizel brandished his sword and went on.

So did Gremio. He had no idea why the gods had chosen to spare him. He knew that, had he had any sense, he would have run away. But his fear of looking bad in front of Thisbe and the ordinary soldiers of his company was worse than his fear of getting shot. By any logical standard, that was madness. Logic, though, died when battle beckoned. Fear of letting comrades down was the glue that held the Army of Franklin together—and probably all the armies on both sides.

Gremio almost stumbled over a body. The corpse wore blue, not gray: and not only blue, but also gold lace and stars and the other accouterments of rank. There lay Otho the Troll, shot once in the face, twice in the chest, and, for good measure, once in the leg. Gremio's stomach did a slow lurch. Battles when brigadiers fell like common soldiers did not bode well for the side that lost them.

Colonel Florizel needed to know, if he didn't already. "Colonel!" Gremio yelled. Florizel waved his sword again to show he'd heard. Gremio went on, "Brigadier Otho's down." That didn't say enough. "He's dead," Gremio added. He couldn't get much balder than that.

"Thank you, Captain," Florizel answered. He wasn't long on brains, but nobody could say he wasn't brave.

The only question was, would bravery be enough? Another volley tore into the northerners' ranks. More men crumpled. Behind Gremio, Sergeant Thisbe yelled, "Keep going! For gods' sake, keep going! When we get in amongst 'em, we can pay 'em back for everything they've done to us!"

Hearing Thisbe's voice, Gremio let out a sigh of relief. He'd been through too much with the sergeant to want to think about . . . He didn't have to think about it. There was the southrons' parapet, just ahead. He sprang onto it. A soldier in gray in the trench thrust up at him with a pike. He beat aside the spearhead with his sword. Shouting, "Provincial prerogative forever!" he leaped down into the trench.

He wasn't alone there for even a heartbeat. "Follow the captain!" Thisbe shouted. Yelling King Geoffrey's name, the northern soldiers did. Southrons rushed up to reinforce their men in the trench line. The soldiers thrust with pikes and slashed with swords and shot the bolts they had in their crossbows and then used the weapons to smash in their foes' heads. No one on either side gave an inch of ground. Both sides fed more men into the fight.

This wasn't war any more. This was madness. Soldiers were killed where they stood and had no room to fall down. Men clambered up on corpses to get at their foes. No one down in the trenches could hope to load a crossbow. Soldiers behind the line passed forward weapons already loaded and cocked. Whoever got them shot at the first man in the wrong-colored uniform he saw. The soldiers who got the loaded crossbows tried to shoot, anyhow. Sometimes they got shot or speared before they could. Then someone else would clamber up onto their bodies and shoot or thrust at the foe till he was wounded or killed. It went on and on and on.

Why am I still alive? Gremio wondered after perhaps half an hour went by. He had no idea, save that he was luckier than he deserved. Blood turned his blue tunic and pantaloons black, but it wasn't his blood. Most of it wasn't, anyhow. He had a couple of cuts and a crossbow graze that was actually a little more than a graze, but nothing he had to worry about except getting crushed to death in the press, which was anything but an idle fear.

Where was Thisbe? Gremio turned his head—at the moment, the only part of him that would move—but didn't see the sergeant. He managed to twist his right arm free, and slashed at a southron who couldn't hit back. It wasn't sporting. He didn't care. He just wanted to live, and killing southrons was the best way he knew how to do that.

After another time that might have been forever or fifteen minutes, the southrons ran out of men to throw into that part of the fight. Scrambling out of the trench over the bodies of the slain, Gremio dashed toward a farmhouse, the next southron strongpoint. And there, by the gods, came Thisbe, trotting along not ten feet away. Gremio ran harder. Maybe, in spite of everything, this was victory.

V

Rollant watched the Army of Franklin form its ranks. He watched it advance over the flat, gently rising ground that led to the earthworks John the Lister's army had thrown up outside of Poor Richard. As the northerners began to move, Smitty spoke with reluctant admiration: "They've got guts, don't they?"

"That they do," Rollant allowed. "And I want to see those guts scattered all over the landscape for the ravens and crows before the gods-damned sons of bitches get close enough to do me any harm."

He made Smitty laugh. "You're a funny fellow, your Corporalship, sir. Anybody who can tell a joke when the battle's about to start has to be a funny fellow."

Staring, Rollant asked, "What the hells makes you think I'm joking?"

He knew what the trouble was. Smitty didn't take any of this quite so seriously as he did himself. Smitty was a Detinan, and fought to reunite his kingdom. Rollant was a blond. He knew why he fought, too. He wanted to see every northern liege lord and would-be liege lord dead or maimed. He had no doubt the northerners felt the same way about him, too.

Here came Bell's men, proud banners flying before them. They were lean and fierce and terribly in earnest. If they hadn't been in earnest, would they have marched down from Dothan, close to two hundred miles, when so many of them had no shoes? That he respected them made him want to kill them no less. If anything, it made him want to kill them more. He understood how dangerous they were.

Standing on the shooting step, he listened to the traitors roar as they came on. They thought the Lion God favored them. Rollant had a different opinion.

Not far behind him, catapults began to buck and creak. Stone balls and firepots whistled over his head. The first few fell short. But, as the northerners kept coming, the engines began clawing holes in their line. Rollant whooped and cheered when a stone took out a whole file of traitors.

"How would you like to be on the receiving end of that?" Smitty asked.

"Wouldn't like it one gods-damned bit," Rollant answered without hesitation. "But I like giving it to the traitors just fine. You bet I do. I hope the engines wipe them all out. Then we won't have to do any fighting of our own."

"That'd be good," Smitty said. "I'm not what you'd call pleased when people try and kill me, either."

John the Lister's pickets shot a thin volley of their own at Bell's men, who kept on coming despite what the engines did to them. They *were* brave, think what you would of them. Repeating crossbows behind Rollant started clattering. More northerners fell. The ones who weren't hit leaned forward, as if into a heavy wind. Rollant had seen that before. He'd done it himself, when advancing into the teeth of a storm of bolts and stones and firepots.

"Be ready, men!" Lieutenant Griff called. "They'll come into range of our crossbows soon."

Rollant wished he had one of the quick-shooting weapons Hard-Riding Jimmy's unicorn-riders used. He wanted to be able to knock down as many Detinan liege lords as he could. He laughed. He was already living every northern blond's dream. Not only was he shooting at liege lords, he was getting paid to do it. If that wasn't right up there with living alongside the gods, he didn't know what was.

Only trouble was, the liege lords shot back.

They hadn't shot till the southron pickets pulled back. They'd just kept coming, taking whatever punishment they got for the sake of striking back when they jumped down into their foes' trenches. Rollant didn't want them jumping in there with him. He made sure his shortsword was loose in its scabbard.

"Looks like they're bunching toward the center," Smitty said.

"It does, doesn't it?" Rollant agreed. Their regiment was off to the left.

Not all of Bell's men moved toward the center, though. Only a few paces from Rollant and Smitty, a soldier in gray tunic and pantaloons fell dead, a quarrel in his forehead. He'd been looking out from the shooting step, exposing no more than the top of his head. That was all some traitor'd needed.

"Be ready!" Griff called again. "Take aim!" Rollant nestled the stock of the crossbow against his shoulder as the company commander cried, "Shoot!"

He pulled the trigger. The crossbow kicked. The bolt he shot was one of scores flying toward the northerners.

Several of them crumpled. He had no idea whether his bolt scored. The only way to improve his chances was to shoot again and again and again. Frenziedly, he loaded, cocked, aimed, and shot.

Northerners kept falling. But the ones who didn't fall didn't run, either. They called false King Geoffrey's name and their fighting slogans. They roared as if the Lion God dwelt in all their hearts. They came closer and closer to the entrenchment where Rollant shot yet again.

This time, he was pretty sure he saw the bolt go home. The black-bearded Detinan clutched at his midsection and slowly fell to the ground in front of the trenches. Rollant nodded to himself. A wound like that was mortal. If it didn't kill quickly, from loss of blood, it would in its own sweet time, from fever. Hardly anyone lived after getting shot in the belly. People said Ned of the Forest had, but people said all sorts of uncanny things about Ned. Thinking about Ned paralyzed Rollant, the way seeing a snake was supposed to paralyze a bird. A serfcatcher who'd turned into a first-rate general, and whose men had massacred blond soldiers? Yes, that was plenty to frighten him. He wasn't ashamed to admit it.

He shot again when the northerners were only fifty yards or so from the parapet. One of their bolts dug into the rampart and kicked dirt up into his face. As he rubbed his eyes, a repeating crossbow opened up behind him, hosing death into the men from the Army of Franklin at close range. They crumpled, one after another after another.

That was too much for flesh and blood to bear. Instead of swarming forward into the trenches, the men in blue in front of Rollant broke and ran. He couldn't imagine how they'd come as far as they had. John the Lister's soldiers and engineers had hit the traitors with everything they had as soon as they came into range. How many northerners were already down, dead or dying or—luckily—only wounded? Hundreds? No, surely thousands.

Beside Rollant, Smitty shouted, "See how much the Lion God loves you now, you bastards!" He shot a running man in the back, then turned to Rollant in surprise. "Why aren't you filling 'em full of holes, too?"

"I don't know," the blond answered. "Sometimes enough is enough, I guess." As he watched, the repeating crossbow cut down more men from behind. Even his blood lust was sated.

"Be ready to go after them if we get the order to pursue," Lieutenant Griff said.

"Pursue?" That startled Smitty and Rollant, who both echoed it. Rollant added, "I don't think we've got the men to chase them."

Colonel Nahath said, "Anyone who ordered us to pursue, given what we have and what Bell and the traitors have . . ." The regimental commander shook his gray-haired head. "He'd have to be crazy."

That hadn't always stopped officers on either side. Rollant knew as much. If someone wearing a brigadier's star on each epaulet saw the northerners fleeing and decided they needed a clout in the backside, he'd order a pursuit. And if it got the regiment slaughtered, how much would he care?

But the order didn't come. The din of battle got louder over to the right. "The sons of bitches are in the trenches there," Smitty said.

"They can go in, but let's see how many come out," Rollant said savagely. He'd already done his duty and more. He would have been perfectly content to stay right where he was. If Bell's men nerved themselves for another charge at this part of the line, he'd fight them off again. If they didn't . . .

If they didn't, as things turned out, he and his comrades would go to them. Colonel Nahath said, "Men, we're shifting to the right, to make sure the traitors don't break our line and cut us in half."

Rollant had plunged the butt end of the company standard's staff into the soft, damp dirt at the bottom of the trench. He snatched up the flag and carried it through the trenches toward the thicker fighting at the center of the southrons' line. As long as he carried it, he wouldn't be able to shoot at the traitors. He'd have to do his fighting with his shortsword. Sometimes, that meant he didn't do any fighting. He didn't think that would happen today.

Outside the parapet, a northern officer shouted, "For gods' sake, men, rally! We can whip them yet. For gods' sake, we can. All you have to do is fight hard, for—"

Smitty raised his crossbow to his shoulder and shot. No standard hampered *him*. The officer's exhortation ended in a shriek. "*Got* the preachy son of a bitch!" Smitty said exultantly.

The traitors cried out in dismay. "For Gods' Sake John is down!" one of them exclaimed.

"I think you just shot a brigadier," Rollant told Smitty.

His friend set another bolt in the groove of his crossbow and grunted with effort as he yanked back the bowstring. "Too bad the bastard wasn't a full general," he said. Detinans were seldom satisfied with anything, no matter how fine it was. Not for the first time, Rollant wondered whether that was their greatest strength or greatest weakness. Most blonds lacked that restless urge to change things. The lack made them have a harder time keeping up with their swarthy neighbors.

A southron officer still on his feet despite a bloody bandage on his head and another wrapped around his left arm waved a sword with his good hand. "Go on in there, boys, and give 'em hells!"

"Avram!" Rollant shouted. "Avram and freedom!" It was getting dark. Before long, nobody would be able to see anybody else, to see his gray uniform or his blond hair or which standard he bore. His own side would be almost as likely as the enemy to shoot him unless he kept yelling. "Avram and freedom!" he cried once more, louder than ever.

Some of the soldiers battling around the farmhouse shouted the same thing. Others called Geoffrey's name and cried out for provincial prerogative. Rollant's comrades poured a volley of crossbow quarrels into those men, then rushed at them, drawing shortswords as they charged. Pikemen came up with the crossbowmen in Colonel Nahath's regiment. They too stormed toward the northerners.

But more soldiers yelling for false King Geoffrey burst out of the trench line they'd overrun and reinforced their comrades already in the farmyard. If the southrons wanted to drive them back—indeed, if the southrons wanted to keep them from breaking through—they would have their work cut out for them.

"Avram!" Rollant shouted again. He shifted the company standard to his left hand and yanked out his shortsword. "Avram and freedom! Avram and victory!"

"Bugger Avram with a pine cone, you stinking southron son of a bitch!" a man in blue cried furiously. He too had a shortsword. He and Rollant hacked at each other. Rollant's sword bit flesh. The northerner groaned. Rollant slashed him again, this time across the face. He reeled back, hands clutched to the spurting wound.

Lightning smashed down out of a clear though quickly darkening sky. Southrons near Rollant screamed, their cries almost drowned in a thunderclap like the end of the world. The stink of charred flesh made the blond want to gag. A couple of minutes later, another lightning bolt smote Colonel Nahath's men. This one struck close enough to make every hair on Rollant's body stand erect. The sensation was extraordinarily distinct and extraordinarily unpleasant.

"Where are *our* wizards?" That cry had risen from southron armies ever since the war was new. Southron mages usually managed to do just enough to keep the traitors' wizards from destroying southron soldiers altogether. That was enough to have brought King Avram's armies to the edge of victory. It wasn't enough to keep a lot of men in gray tunics and pantaloons from dying unnecessarily. Rollant didn't want to be one of those unnecessarily dead men. He didn't even want to be a *necessarily* dead man. He wanted to live. How could he gloat at the beaten traitors if he didn't?

Yet another bolt of sorcerous lightning smashed into the battlefield, this one striking the two-story farmhouse where dozens of southrons sheltered and from which they shot at their foes. When nothing much seemed to happen, one more thunderbolt hit the farmhouse. Its roof caught fire. Some of the southrons inside fled. Others must have thought a burning farmhouse safer than the hellish battle all around, for they stayed where they were.

Rollant did his best to ignore the northerners' magics. If they slew him, they slew him, and he couldn't do much about it (he knew the protective amulet he wore around his neck was not proof against sorceries of that magnitude). And if he stood around gaping at them, some resolutely unsorcerous traitor would shoot him or spear him or run him through. All he could do was fight his own fight and hope John the Lister's wizards eventually realized they had something important to do here.

"Geoffrey!" someone nearby yelled. Without even thinking about it, Rollant lunged with his shortsword. His blade cleaved flesh. The traitor howled.

"Well done, Corporal!" Lieutenant Griff called. A crossbow quarrel or swordstroke had carried away the lobe of his left ear. Rollant wondered if he even knew it. Then he shrugged. With the sort of fight this was turning out to be, Griff was lucky to have got away so lightly—and he himself, so far, luckier still.

John the Lister had known he would have a fight on his hands at Poor Richard. Even he hadn't guessed the Army of Franklin would be able to make it as savage a fight as it was. A year and a half before, at Essoville down in the south, Duke Edward of Arlington had ordered the Army of Southern Parthenia to charge across open country against a fortified position. Most of the northern soldiers had given way under southron bombardment, and never reached the southrons' lines at all. The few who did were quickly killed or captured.

Here . . . Bell's men had to cross far more open ground than the Army of Southern Parthenia had. They had only a handful of engines of their own, where Duke Edward's catapults had pounded and pummeled the southron line before the charge. But they held part of John's position, refused to be dislodged, and still threatened to break through and cut his army in half. He had to admire them.

He also had to keep them from doing what they wanted. If he didn't, his whole army was liable to perish. He knew how badly his men had hurt them as they advanced into the fight. Now that they were in it, they were striking back with a fury at least half compounded of the lust for revenge. John ordered more men to move from the flanks, where the northerners hadn't been able to break into his entrenchments, to the center, where they had.

When lightning began striking in the center, John cursed and shouted, "Major Alva! Where in the hells is Major Alva?"

"I'm right here, sir," Alva said from beside him: from, in fact, almost inside the breast pocket of his tunic.

John the Lister glowered at him, and not because he hadn't noticed him, either. "What in the damnation are the traitors doing pounding us like that? Aren't you here to stop them from working this kind of wizardry?"

"No, sir," Alva answered. John glowered even more, but the mage ignored him, continuing, "I'm here to stop them from working any *really* big spells, and I've done that." John suddenly noticed how weary he sounded. After a sigh and a shrug, Alva went on, "If you knew what they *wanted* to do, and what they almost did . . . Well, they didn't manage it, and they gods-damned well won't now. This other stuff . . . This is fumbling in your pocket and and pulling out copper when you went looking for gold."

"Oh." John felt foolish. Not knowing exactly what to say, he tried, "I suppose I ought to thank you."

"That would be nice. Not a hells of a lot of people ever bother," Alva said. "But don't worry about it. I won't turn you into a red eft or anything like that if you don't."

"What in the name of the Lion God's tail tuft is a red eft?" John the Lister demanded.

"It's what you call a mostly water salamander—a newt—during the time it lives on land," Major Alva answered. Somehow, John was sure he would remember that utterly useless bit of information the rest of his life.

At the moment, though, he had more things to worry about than red efts. Pointing toward the center of his line, he said, "Look. That farmhouse is burning. It's a strongpoint for our men. If we get forced away from there, Bell's army will break thought and split us in half. If that happens, we'll all end up dead or captured. Stopping their lightning would make that a lot less likely, even if you don't think much of it as far as magic goes."

Alva very visibly paused to think it over. "Well, yes, I suppose you have a point," he said at last, as if it was one he hadn't thought of himself. Maybe he hadn't, for he went on, "We really do need to win this battle, don't we?"

"That would be nice, if you plan on living long enough to show how clever you are after this gods-damned war finally ends," John the Lister said dryly.

"I do." Now Alva sounded very determined. "Oh, yes. I certainly do." He pointed at the farmhouse, as imperiously as a king. He said one word, in a language John did not know and never wanted to learn. The fire ceased to be. It might have been a candle flame he'd blown out; the disappearance was as sudden and abrupt as that. "Now," the mage murmured, reminding himself, "the lightnings."

They struck again only moments after he spoke. He muttered something under his breath. Then he spoke aloud, again only one word. When the lightnings came down once more from the clear night sky, they struck off to one side of where they had been hitting.

"Is that still our position, or are they coming down on the traitors' heads now?" Alva asked. "Their mages are a little stronger than I thought. I wanted to stop that bolt, but all I could do was shift it."

John the Lister goggled. Alva was taking on several northern wizards at once . . . and winning? That sort of thing hadn't happened all through the war. John wasn't sorry to see it—he was anything but sorry to see it—but it took him by surprise. He needed a moment to remember the question Alva had asked. "I'll need to send a runner and find out," he said, several heartbeats slower than he should have.

"All right." Alva stretched and yawned. He still looked like an unmade bed. But John the Lister saw why Doubting George, a man who had confidence in no one, relied on Major Alva.

On John's command, a runner dashed toward the fighting. John hoped he wouldn't get killed up there. More lightning struck, in about the same place as the last bolt. Which side was it punishing? They would— John hoped they would—know soon.

He turned to Alva. "If you can do this now, what will you do in peacetime, when you get a little older and you come into your full power?"

"Do you think it will be greater than this?" Alva asked interestedly. "I've wondered about that myself. I suppose I'll just have to find out."

Back came the runner, going flat out, his face streaked with sweat in spite of the chilly night. "Sir," he panted, "those are still hitting our men, but not in such a bad spot."

"Thank you," John said, and turned to Alva. "What can you do about that, Major?"

"We'll see," the mage answered. "They're rallying against me, but they haven't got any one fellow who's really strong. A bunch of bricks doesn't make one rock, because they'll fall apart if the rock hits them the right way. Now I have to find it."

The northern wizards loosed another thunderbolt a couple of minutes later, in that same spot, while Alva stood there thinking hard. John the Lister wondered if the wizard's arrogance—which he unquestionably had, despite his shambling manner—had got the better of him.

Then Alva laughed out loud, a sound childish in its

sheer glee. He snapped his fingers and hopped up into the air. "*That's* what I'll do, by the Thunderer. Let's see how they like it."

This time, the charm he used wasn't just one word. He brought it out in a way that made it sound almost like one of the work chants blond serfs used. John found himself tapping his foot to the rollicking rhythm. Alva was tapping his foot, too. With a last little hop and a skip—and a pass as intricate as any John had ever seen—he sent the spell on its way.

"What will it do?" John the Lister asked when he judged it safe to jog the wizard's metaphorical elbow.

"Deflect the strike a little more," Alva answered absently. "We'll find out how they like that, and what they can do about it." By his manner, he didn't think they could do much. Yes, he had arrogance, all right. John waited to see if he deserved what he had.

When the lightnings didn't return for some little while, the commanding general began to wonder whether Alva had altogether stifled the northern wizards despite saying he couldn't. But then the thunderbolt crashed down once more. "Shall I send a runner to find out where that hit?" John asked. Later, he paused to wonder about the propriety of a brigadier's asking a major—and a major by courtesy, at that—what he required. That was later. At the time, it seemed the most natural thing in the world.

And Alva nodded as if it was the most natural thing in the world, too. "Yes, sir, thanks very much," he said. "I *think* I've done it, but I want to make sure."

Off dashed another runner. He came back panting even harder than his predecessor had, but with an enormous grin stretched across his face. "Sir, that came down on the traitors who were moving up to reinforce their position near the farmhouse, and it tore the hells out them."

At that news, John the Lister whooped and reached up to smack the taller wizard on the back. He almost knocked Alva over, and had to steady him to keep him from falling. "Well done, Major!" he exclaimed. "We're holding them everywhere else, so they're really stopped if we can stop them there."

"Good. That's good, uh, sir," Alva answered. "They'll try to break free of what I've done to them, you know. I don't think they can, but there is the off chance that I'm wrong."

"What then?" John asked. "Can they beat down your magic?"

"I don't think so, sir," the mage said. "But they might make me do some more work. You never can tell."

Even as he spoke, another thunderbolt smote the battlefield. Blinking against the greenish-purple afterimages, John the Lister said, "I think that came down on the same part of the field as the last one. If it did, it came down on the northerners' heads again, didn't it?"

"I think so, sir. I hope so, sir," Alva said. "We'd better find out, though, because I can't say for certain."

"All right." John sent forth yet another runner.

This one didn't even need to speak when he came sprinting back. The expression on his face said everything that needed saying. But he announced the news even so: "They dropped another one on their own men!"

John the Lister whooped and Major Alva hastily moved out of the way so he wouldn't get walloped again. "I've got the deflection where I want it, sure enough," he said once he was out of range of John's strong right arm. "Now the only question is, how stubborn are they? Will they keep pounding their own people, or will they give it up as a bad job?"

"Bell commands them," John said.

"Which means?" Alva asked. At John's expression, he explained, "I don't pay much heed to soldiers."

"Yes, I'd noticed that," John said, even more dryly than before. After a moment, he added, "You really should, you know. They're the opponents you're facing."

"I suppose so. I hadn't really looked at it that way. All a wizard usually worries about is other wizards." With the air of a man making a large concession, Alva went on, "Tell me about Bell, then."

"If he weren't a man who charges like a unicorn in heat and kicks like an ass, would he have attacked us here?" John asked.

"Hmm. Maybe not. We have hit him hard, haven't we?" Alva might have been noticing for the first time the carnage around him as carnage rather than as a problem—and not much more than an elementary problem, at that—in sorcery.

"If we hit him any harder . . ." John the Lister shook his head. "I don't see how we could have hit him any harder. He must have lost three or four times as many men as we have. We've had reports of several northern brigadiers falling when they fought right up at the front like common soldiers."

"That's brave of them," Alva said. "Isn't it kind of stupid, too?"

"Soldiers fight. If they didn't fight, they wouldn't be soldiers any more," John said, his voice clotted with disapproval.

"Sometimes, evidently, they aren't soldiers any more even if they do fight," Alva replied.

Before John had to worry about how to respond to that, lightning smashed down yet again in the same spot it had already struck twice. John didn't need to send a runner. What had happened was very obvious. "Do you see?" he asked Alva. "*Do* you see, by the gods?"

"Yes, sir. I see." The wizard sounded more respectful than he had up till now. "You were right, sir."

That's the key to it, John the Lister realized. *I was right. He takes people who are right seriously. If you happen to be wrong . . . gods help you if you're wrong around him. Maybe he'll be a little less heartless when he gets older. Maybe not, too.*

As if to prove how very right John was, one more bolt of lightning smote that same place. "He *is* a stubborn fool, isn't he?" Major Alva said. "His wizards are pretty stupid, too, to keep banging their heads against a wall they can't knock over. Well, that's their worry."

"Yes. It is." John allowed himself the luxury of a long sigh of relief. The northerners wouldn't break through in the middle now, and they'd never come close to breaking through on the wings. His army would live. Sooner or later, Bell's men would give up the attack and pull back. Then he could get his own force on the road south, get back into the works at Ramblerton.

I hope Doubting George thinks I've slowed Bell down enough, John the Lister thought. *He'd better, by the gods. No matter what happened to the Army of Franklin here, we've paid a heavy price, too.*

"I'm sorry, sir. I'm very sorry," one of the blue-robed mages told Lieutenant General Bell. "We've done everything we know how to do, but that gods-damned southron won't let us loose. It's like . . . like wrestling, sir. Sometimes you're pinned, and that's all there is to it."

"Sometimes you're useless, is what you mean," Bell snarled. "If you'd gone on pounding them there, we would have finished smashing them by now."

"Sir, they've got a stronger wizard than we do," the sorcerer replied. "I hate like hells to say that, since the son of a bitch is a southron. We ought to eat up southron mages the way we eat fried fish. We ought to, but we can't, not with this one."

"We were in amongst them," Bell said. "We *are* in amongst them. But how can we break through if this mage of theirs stifles your spells?"

"Well, sir," —the wizard picked his words with care— "if magic won't do it for us, pikes and swords and crossbows will have to."

"I told Patrick the Cleaver he dared not fail. I *told* him," Bell muttered. He shouted for a runner. "Go up to the front and tell Brigadier Patrick we require a breakthrough at all costs. At all costs, do you hear me?"

"Yes, sir. A breakthrough at all costs." The messenger hurried away. Bell might have sentenced him to death, sending him up to the part of the front where the fighting was hottest. The young man had to know that. So did Bell, though he didn't give it a second thought; he'd gone into plenty of hot fighting himself. Had the runner hesitated, he would have had something to say. This way, he took a pull at his little bottle of laudanum and waited.

He was just starting to feel the drug, just starting to feel the fire recede from his shoulder and his missing leg, when the runner returned, which meant something close to half an hour had gone by. "Well?" Bell barked.

"Sir, we haven't got the men in the center to break through," the runner said.

Laudanum or no laudanum, Bell's temper didn't merely kindle—it ignited. "Haven't got the men?" he shouted. "Who the hells told you that? Patrick the Cleaver? Patrick the coward? I'll cashier the white-livered son of a bitch, so help me gods I will."

But the messenger shook his head. "No, sir. Patrick's down. He's dead," he added, to make himself perfectly plain.

"Oh." Bell could hardly accuse a dead man of

dereliction of duty. "Who's in command there, then? Otho the Troll? Otho knows what we're supposed to do—what we have to do."

"No, sir. Brigadier Otho's shot, too—shot dead." Again, the runner didn't seem to want to leave Bell in any doubt.

"Oh," the general commanding repeated, this time on even more of a falling note. "Well, by the Lion God's fangs, who *is* in command in the center?"

"A colonel from Palmetto Province, sir—a man named Florizel," the runner answered. *Florizel?* Bell scratched his head. He'd heard the name—he was sure of that, but he could barely put a face to the man. He had no idea what sort of officer Florizel was. *A live one*, he thought. The runner, meanwhile, went on, "He says everything's all smashed to hells and gone up there. From what I saw, sir, he's right."

The news couldn't be good, not if a colonel was trying to command a wing. "Can we get help from the right or left, put the men where they'll do the most good?"

"For Gods' Sake John's been shot dead, too, over on our right," the runner said. "Florizel talked with men who saw him die."

"Oh." Bell was getting tired of saying that, but he didn't know what else he *could* say. "What about Benjamin the Heated Ham, then, over on our left?" That was the only straw he had left to grasp.

"I don't know, sir," the runner replied. "I wasn't over in that part of the field, and I can't tell you what happened there."

Bell didn't know, either, not in detail. He did know the men on the left wing hadn't broken into the southrons' trenches, which wasn't the best news in the world, or even anything close to it. With a sigh, he said, "I'd better find out, then."

"Will you send me again, sir?"

"No." Bell shook his head. "You've gone into danger once already." The runner didn't seem to know whether to look indignant or grateful. After two or three heartbeats, gratitude won. Lieutenant General Bell called for another runner.

"Yes, sir? What can I do for you?" This one sounded as eager as the last. The general commanding explained what he required. The runner saluted and hurried off toward the left wing.

Bell cocked his head, listening to the fighting ebb. He growled something his thick mustache and beard fortunately muffled. By the sound of things, his men had given everything they had in them. Even if the left had soldiers to shift to the center, could they revive the fight?

All he could do was wait till the runner came back. It seemed like forever, but this young man didn't take much longer than the other one had. "Well?" Bell demanded when the fellow reappeared. "Is Benjamin breathing?"

"Yes, sir," the messenger answered, "but John of Barsoom and Hiram the Cranberry are both dead, sir, so he's got two brigades commanded by colonels. And that whole wing's been shot to pieces."

Oh seemed inadequate: that was more bad news than it could bear. Instead, Bell said, "What the hells happened?"

"The way Benjamin tells it, sir, the southrons' right gradually sticks out. As the wing went forward, heading in toward the center, John the Lister's men enfiladed them. That put them in trouble even before the enemy started shooting at them from the front."

"Why didn't Benjamin suppress the enfilading shots before he went through with the rest of the right?" Bell asked.

"I can't tell you that, sir, not for sure. You'd have to ask him," the runner replied. "But I did see that part of the field, and I saw the bodies lying on it. I'd say he tried, but found out he couldn't."

He tried, but found out he couldn't. It sounded like something a priest would say before lighting a funeral pyre. And how great would the pyres be after this fight? For once, even Bell, who seldom counted the cost in a battle, shied away from thinking about that.

"Anything else for me, sir?" the runner asked.

"Eh?" Bell had to call himself back to the here-and-now. "No, never mind. You're dismissed."

"Thank you, sir." The youngster saluted again and left.

Bell stared after him like a man suddenly realizing he was trapped in nightmare. The commanding general shook his head, as if trying to wake. He opened his mouth, starting to say, "No!" but checked himself at the last instant.

Seeing the motion, the nearest runner asked, "What are your orders, sir?"

What are your orders? It was a good question. Bell wished he had a good answer for it, or any answer at all. With his right and left wings smashed, with his center thwarted, what *could* he do? What could the Army of Franklin do?

"Sir?" the runner asked when he didn't say anything.

He had to respond. The youngster was starting to stare. But all that came out was, "I have none."

"Oh," the runner said, in the same sort of tone Bell had used on hearing of disaster.

"I'll wait for more news to come in." Bell tried to put the best face on things he could. "Then I'll decide what we need to do next."

"Yes, sir." The runner sounded relieved, perhaps hoping the situation wasn't so black as he'd believed a moment before.

Maybe it wasn't. On the other hand, maybe it was. Lieutenant General Bell reached for the laudanum bottle again, longing for the haze the drug could put between him and the pain of reality.

Messengers from the front came back to him, some on foot, others on unicornback. Their news was all the same: the northerners were pulling back from the forwardmost positions they'd won, back to lines they might hold if John the Lister's men counterattacked. One of the runners said, "Some of the men on our left wing, sir, they'll building breastworks out of bodies."

"Are they?" Bell said tonelessly, and the soldier nodded. Bell muttered, then bestirred himself and waved to his own corps of runners. "Order my wing commanders here," he told them. "We will confer, and decide how to take up the attack in the morning." That the Army of Franklin *would* take up the attack in the morning he had no doubt.

Colonel Florizel was the first wing commander to arrive. He slid down off a unicorn and limped up to Bell. Saluting, he said, "Reporting as ordered, sir. We have done everything flesh and blood can do. You may rely on that."

"Very well, Colonel," Bell said. "Are you badly hurt there?"

"This is an old wound, sir," Florizel answered. "I went through everything today without a scratch, though I lost a mount. I aim to offer up a lamb to the Lion God for thanksgiving. I can't tell you *how* I got through—seemed like the crossbow bolts were thick enough to walk on."

"Can you go forward at sunrise?" Bell asked.

Florizel shrugged. "I don't have much to go forward *with*, sir. If you give the order, we'll try."

Before Bell could reply, Benjamin the Heated Ham came riding up from the left. Bell asked him the same question. Benjamin shook his head. "Go forward? Not a chance, sir. If the southrons strike *us*, I'm not sure we can hold our ground. We've been shot to pieces. I don't know how else to say it."

Last of all, Brigadier Stephen the Pickle, a sour-faced man not far from Bell's age, rode up from the right. He looked even more sour when Bell asked him if he could attack in the morning. But he answered, "I have a couple of brigades that haven't gone into the meat-grinder yet, sir. If you want to throw them at the southrons, they'll advance. But I don't know how many of them will come back again. Those lines are *solid*."

"Muster your men," Bell said. His wave encompassed the three wing commanders. "Muster your men, all of you. Care for the wounded. Pile up the dead and make them ready for the fires. We *will* go forward."

"Care for the wounded?" Benjamin the Heated Ham exclaimed. "Half the time, we can't even drag them back out of range. The southrons are too gods-damned alert and up too close for that. They shoot anybody who tries to save a comrade or a friend."

"They fight war as if it were nothing but murder," Bell said angrily. "They have been fighting that way ever since the Marthasville campaign. General Hesmucet's conduct during the siege was disgraceful."

"Yes, sir," Benjamin said.

"Yes, sir," Stephen the Pickle echoed. "But if that's the way they choose to fight, we have to fight the same way, or we'll go under."

"I know," Bell said. "That is one of the reasons I ordered this attack. We have to show the enemy we still have the spirit to fight it out with him man to man."

Colonel Florizel said, "But how much good does that do us, sir, if he stays in his entrenchments and shoots us down by the thousands before we can close with him? Wouldn't we be better served making him attack us and pay the bigger butcher's bill?"

Lieutenant General Bell glared at him. "That is what Joseph the Gamecock was doing in the Marthasville campaign before King Geoffrey relieved him and appointed me in his place. Geoffrey wants men who can fight, not soldiers who skulk in trenches."

"We fought, sir," Florizel said. "We fought as hard as flesh and blood can fight. I already told you that. When you're trying to carry a position like this one, it doesn't matter how hard you fight, though. You'll get chewed up any which way."

"I do not wish a defeatist to command a wing, Colonel," Bell said coldly. "Your tenure will be temporary."

"That suits me fine . . . sir," Florizel answered. "I'm not what you'd call eager to tell my men to go forward and get cut to pieces attacking a position they haven't got a chance in hells of taking."

"We *will* attack at first light tomorrow," Bell declared. "We *will* attack, and we *will* drive the southrons out of Poor Richard. Do you understand me? Do all of you understand me?"

"Yes, sir," the wing commanders chorused unhappily.

"Very well, then," Bell snapped. "You are dismissed. Go back to your men and ready them for the assault to come."

"Ready them to get their bums shot off," somebody muttered. Bell glowered at each wing commander in turn. All three of them glowered back. He gestured peremptorily. They turned to go. By then, it was well past midnight, the moon sinking low.

A runner dashed back toward the officers, shouting, "Lieutenant General Bell! Lieutenant General Bell!"

"What is it?" Bell braced for another disaster.

One of the wing commanders, braced for the same thing, growled, "Oh, gods, what now?"

"Sir, the southrons have pulled out of Poor Richard," the runner said. "Their fires are burning, but nobody's around 'em. They've gone. They've left."

"By the gods!" Bell said softly. "The field . . . the field is ours." He turned to the wing commanders. "Don't you see, men? This . . . this is *victory*!"

Colonel Andy pointed north to the outer defenses of Ramblerton. "Here they come, sir. Do you see them?"

"I can't very well *not* see them, now can I?" Doubting George asked, more than a little irritably. "There are enough of them out there, wouldn't you say?"

Hard-Riding Jimmy's troopers served as escorts and outriders for the rest of John the Lister's army. They would have held off Ned of the Forest's unicorn-riders had Ned tried to harry John's footsoldiers during the withdrawal from Poor Richard to Ramblerton. But, just as John had managed to knock Bell's footsoldiers back on their heels, so Hard-Riding Jimmy's men had warned Ned that hitting them again wouldn't be a good idea. No one had contested the withdrawal into Ramblerton.

George spurred his unicorn forward. Andy rode alongside him and yet not quite perfectly level with him: the perfect place for an adjutant. George saw John the Lister at the head of the long column of men in dirty, often bloodstained gray tunics and pantaloons. John saw him, too, and saluted.

Returning the salute, Doubting George made it into a courtesy not only for John but also for the soldiers he commanded. "Well done!" George shouted in a great voice. "*Well* done! You have given us time to prepare the defenses of Ramblerton, and to gather men from several provinces to hold those defenses. Now, when the time is ripe, we will drive the traitors far away!"

A few of John the Lister's soldiers raised a ragged cheer. Most of them just kept on marching. John pulled off the road and sat his unicorn in a field, watching them pass by. George—and Andy—rode over beside him. George saw what he knew he'd see: men who'd been through the mill; men with blank, stunned faces; men with bandages from wounds too minor to require them to take to the ambulance wagons. They'd seen too much, done too much, to be of much use yet.

"I had to leave a lot of the wounded behind," John said unhappily. "We didn't have room in the wagons for all of them. They're in Bell's hands now. So are our dead."

"He'll treat them with respect. I give him that much," George said. "We do the same for the northerners. This has been a pretty clean war, except now and again when it bumps up against the question of the blonds."

No sooner had he spoken than a blond corporal carrying a company standard tramped past. The fellow was as grimy and battered-looking as any of the Detinans around him. By his hollow-cheeked face, he'd seen as much hard fighting as they had, too. Looking at that face, George could wonder why there'd ever been a question about whether blonds were worth anything in war.

"I suppose he'll come after me now," John said. "I don't see what else he can do. It's less than twenty miles from Poor Richard down here to Ramblerton. He's not about to go around the city and strike for the Highlow, not now, not after the lick I gave him. Before he goes any farther south, he has to take Ramblerton."

"He's welcome to try." George's wave encompassed

the works John's men were entering. "I can't promise him a very hospitable reception, though."

John the Lister seemed to take a good long look at the fortifications for the first time. "You haven't been idle, I will say that. If Bell tries to storm *these* works, he won't take a man back to Dothan alive."

"That's the idea," George said. "And now I've got the men to fill them up, too, counting your soldiers and the ones I've scraped up from garrisons all over Franklin and Cloviston."

"Fill them up, hells," John said. "When Bell gets here, we ought to go out and trample the son of a bitch."

"We will," George replied. "Don't you doubt it for a minute. When the time is ripe, we will." He set a hand on John's shoulder. "Other thing is, I'll want you to get me the reports for your actions just as soon as you can. I'll send them on to Marshal Bart and to King Avram. If you don't get the rank amongst the regulars you deserve, there's even less justice in the world than I always thought."

"You'll have 'em, just as soon as I can write 'em up," John said. "A little real rank'd be welcome, and I won't tell you anything different. Right now, all I've got is a captain's prospects once the war is over . . . and if you look hard, you can see the end of the war from here."

"You can, and I can," Doubting George said. "I don't think Bell can yet. Well, we'll show him when the time comes, never you fear."

"Shouldn't be that tough, sir," John the Lister said. "I left him holding the ground at Poor Richard, but may the Lion God's claws rip out my guts if I didn't tear the heart from his army. He had to be mad, attacking me across a couple of miles of open country—mad, I tell you. Why didn't he just cut his own throat and save us the trouble?"

"He's not very smart. He proved that in the Marthasville campaign," George said. "Count Joseph the Gamecock didn't fight nearly so often, but he gave us a much harder time. Can you imagine Joseph charging you at Poor Richard?"

"Not a chance," John the Lister said positively. "Not a chance in the world. You're right—Count Joseph knows what he's doing."

"Come on into Ramblerton," Doubting George said. "Look at the works from the inside, not just the outside. You'll see we have some little suspicion about what we're doing, too."

"Let my men go in first," John said. "They bore the brunt of it. Lieutenant General Bell may be—hells, he *is*—a gods-damned idiot, but his soldiers still fight like sons of bitches. Next sign of quit I see in 'em'll be the first. No matter how stupid he was to attack us there, they almost carried the position."

"They're Detinans, too. They're as stubborn as we are," George said. "Sometimes even the stubbornest fellows get licked, though, and we'll lick 'em."

"Yes, sir." John nodded. He had heavy dark circles under his eyes. How much sleep had he had the night before? The night before that? Any at all? George had his doubts.

"We'll pour you a good, full mug of spirits," he said. "And we'll give you a nice, soft bed, and, by the gods, I don't care if Bell invests this place five minutes after you lie down—we won't wake you till you get up on your own. I expect we'll manage to keep Ramblerton out of that bastard's hands till then."

"I thank you very m . . ." John's voice trailed off into an enormous yawn. When at last he managed to close his mouth, he laughed ruefully. "I suppose I just proved I could use a long winter's nap, didn't I?"

"Let's say you gave me a pretty good hint." Doubting

George might have added more to that, but he noticed Major Alva riding by on an ass that looked almost as weary as John the Lister. Alva waved, but then remembered to salute. After returning the courtesy, George turned back to John. "How did that young whippersnapper serve you?"

"Whippersnapper's the word for him, all right. He kept going on and on about the gods-damned Inward Hypothesis till I wanted to kick him," John replied.

"I know. Makes me seasick just thinking about it," George said. "But he's a pretty fair mage, or I thought he was when I sent him to you."

John the Lister nodded. "He is. He is indeed. I wouldn't try to deny it. Last night, the traitors' wizards were punishing us in the center. Bell's men might've broken through. If they had, I wouldn't" — he yawned again— "be here now. But Alva stopped 'em. All by his lonesome, he stopped 'em cold. We held in the center, and we ended up giving Bell a thrashing."

"That's what I was hoping you would do," Doubting George said. John's wagons rattled past. The general commanding wished he didn't have to hear the groans from the wounded men inside them. He turned to John. "Shall we go in now?" Regardless of what he wished, he would listen to them all the way into Ramblerton.

"Yes, sir," John the Lister said.

He proved too worn to look very hard at the fortifications from the inside. George took him back to his headquarters, gave him the promised glass of spirits, and led him to a comfortable bed. John lay down without bothering to take off his boots. He fell asleep before George left the room.

A couple of hours later, after listening to preliminary reports from some of John's officers, George got in touch with Marshal Bart by scryer. "Good day, Lieutenant General," Bart said, peering out of the crystal ball at George. He was a stubby man, not very tall and not very wide, with a close-trimmed dark beard. "Haven't heard from you for a while. What's on your mind?"

"As of now, Marshal, John the Lister's a regular captain. After what he just did to Bell and the Army of Franklin, I believe he deserves better." George summed up what had happened at Poor Richard.

"Bell was fool enough to charge at him over open ground?" Bart said when he finished. George nodded. Marshal Bart shrugged. "Even so, you're right. That was well done, and no mistake. A disaster there would have hurt us badly. Tell John I'll recommend his promotion to brigadier of the regulars to King Avram."

What Marshal Bart recommended, King Avram would approve. Doubting George whistled softly. It wasn't that John the Lister didn't deserve to be a brigadier in Detina's regular army. He did; not even George could doubt that. But raising him to brigadier from captain in one fell swoop . . . George had expected Bart to make him a colonel, and then to promote him to brigadier's rank later if he continued to give good service.

"I'll tell him tomorrow, I think," George said.

Bart frowned. Most of the time, he looked like the most ordinary Detinan in the kingdom. Anybody who thought he *was* ordinary, though, did so at his peril. "Why not tell him now?" the marshal asked, in tones suggesting George had better have a good reason.

And George did: "Because he's liable to sleep till tomorrow, sir. He just got in to Ramblerton, and I don't think he's shut his eyes the last two days."

"Oh." Bart nodded. "All right. Yes, when you're that worn down, you don't care about anything. He'd probably strangle you if you woke him, and he might not remember anything you told him."

"True enough. And if he did strangle me, I couldn't very well tell him again."

"Er, right." Marshal Bart—the first marshal Detina had had in a long lifetime, the grandest soldier in the land—had no more idea what to do with Doubting George's foolishness than did Colonel Andy. Unlike Andy, Bart had the privilege of changing the subject: "Do you expect Bell to follow John up toward Ramblerton?"

"Yes, sir." George got down to business again. "I don't know what else he *can* do, sir. About the only other thing would be to turn around and march back up to Dothan, and I can't imagine Bell doing that. As long as he's got soldiers who will follow his orders, he'll take them into battle. If he attacked around Marthasville, if he attacked at Poor Richard, he'll attack anywhere."

Bart nodded again. "I think you're right. As soon as he gets up there, Lieutenant General, I want you to hit him with everything you've got."

"I will hit him, sir. You don't need to worry about that," George answered. "As soon as I'm ready, I will hit him a lick the likes of which he has never known before."

"Don't waste time," Bart told him. "Hit him just as soon as you can. Do not give him the chance to slip around you. Smash him. Send him back to Dothan with his tail between his legs. Send him back there whether he wants to go or not."

"Sir, I *will* strike him when I am ready. I will *not* let him get away," George promised. "The Army of Franklin will *not* slip by me. It will *not* get down into Cloviston. You may rely on that."

"Bell has the last northern army in the field that

can still maneuver and cause us trouble," Bart said worriedly. "I do not want us embarrassed, not when the war looks like being won."

He commanded all the southron armies. He had the right to say what he said. That made it no less galling to Doubting George. "Sir, when he comes here and I am ready, I will strike him," he repeated.

"I want him smashed like a bug under a boot," Marshal Bart said. "I want him . . . I want him *suppressed*, by the Thunderer's pizzle."

A couple of years earlier, Duke Edward of Arlington had used that contemptuous word in ordering the Army of Southern Parthenia forward to smash King Avram's soldiers at the second Battle of Cow Jog. John the Hierophant, who'd commanded Avram's men then, was off in the east these days with the equally luckless General Guildenstern, chasing blond savages. Bart took more than a little pleasure in applying the term to false King Geoffrey's Army of Franklin.

"Sir, when the time is ripe, I *will* suppress him," Doubting George said. "He won't beat me, and he won't get away."

"He'd better not." Bart still sounded fretful. George sighed. He feared the marshal would go right on nagging him even though a province and a half lay between them. *Gods damn crystal balls, anyhow*, George thought unhappily.

More times than Captain Gremio cared to remember, he'd seen a soldier hit square in the chest with a crossbow quarrel. Very often, the man would stagger on for a few paces and perhaps even fight a little before realizing he was dead and falling over.

Never, till now, had Gremio seen an army take a similar blow. But if, after the battle in front of Poor Richard, the Army of Franklin wasn't a dead man walking, then Gremio had never seen any such thing. He wished he hadn't. He wished he weren't seeing such a thing now. But he wasn't blind, and couldn't make himself so. He knew what his eyes told him.

Somehow, like one of those men shot in the chest, the Army of Franklin kept lurching forward. Gremio trudged south down a muddy road, south toward Ramblerton. Since the Battle of Poor Richard, he commanded not just his company but the whole regiment. That wasn't from any enormous virtue on his part. He was the senior captain left alive and not badly wounded, and Colonel Florizel, as the senior colonel alive and not badly wounded, was for the moment still leading the whole wing.

Commanding the regiment felt like a smaller promotion than it would have before the fight by Poor Richard, anyhow. Only a couple of companies' worth of men were still fit for duty.

Sergeant Thisbe led Gremio's old company. Thisbe wasn't the only sergeant in charge of a company in the Army of Franklin, either—far from it.

"Ask you something, sir?" Thisbe said now, coming up alongside of Gremio.

"If you're rash enough to think I know answers, go ahead," he replied.

"If you don't, sir, who does?" Thisbe asked. The answer to that, all too probably, was *no one*. Before Gremio could say as much, the underofficer went on, "Once we get down to Ramblerton, Captain, what are we going to *do* there?"

"Why, capture the town, of course. Storm the fortifications. Slay the southrons, and drive away the ones we don't slay. Go sweeping south into Cloviston. We'll see the Highlow River in a couple of weeks, don't you think?"

That was what Lieutenant General Bell had had in

mind when he left Dothan for Franklin. Maybe, if he'd crushed John the Lister at Summer Mountain instead of letting him get away, his dream might have come true. Now? It wasn't even a bitter joke, not any more.

Sergeant Thisbe sent Gremio a reproachful look. "That isn't even a little bit funny, sir. The way things turned out—" The underofficer stopped.

"Yes. The way things turned out." Gremio liked that. It let them talk about what they'd just been through without *really* talking about it. If Thisbe had called it *the catastrophe*, that would have been just as true and more descriptive, but they both would have had to remember the dreadful fighting in the trenches and their failure to dislodge the southrons from around that farmhouse. Even their mages had failed. If that wasn't catastrophe for the north, what was? But Gremio had to mention some of what had happened there, some of what had left him in charge of a regiment and Thisbe a company: "Half a dozen brigadiers dead, Sergeant. More wounded. Gods only know how many colonels and majors and captains and lieutenants."

"And soldiers, sir. Don't forget soldiers," Thisbe said.

"I'm not likely to," Gremio answered. "We lost one man in four in the fight by the River of Death. That's what kept Thraxton the Braggart from properly besieging Rising Rock—we'd got shot to pieces. Here we've lost a bigger portion than that. We must have. But Lieutenant General Bell is going on."

"Thraxton should have gone on," Thisbe pointed out.

"Yes. We had the enemy licked, and he held back," Gremio agreed. "Did we lick John the Lister? Bell says we did, but I doubt it. And speaking of doubting, how many more men has Doubting George got in Ramblerton? They aren't licked. Most of them haven't fought at all. They're just waiting for us."

Thisbe muttered something. It sounded like *licking*

their chops. Gremio thought about asking, then changed his mind. He didn't really want to know. *Licking their chops* seemed much too apt for comfort.

But then Thisbe spoke aloud: "Everything you said is true, sir, every word of it. So what *can* we do when we get to Ramblerton?"

"I don't know, Sergeant. I just don't know," Gremio replied. "I don't see anything. Lieutenant General Bell must, or we wouldn't be going forward."

Up till now, Gremio had always been a man who wanted to know answers. He'd wanted to learn what would happen next before it did. That way, he could try to wring the most advantage from whatever it was. Now . . . now he didn't want to know. All he wanted to do was go on putting one weary foot in front of the other. As long as he did that, he was doing his duty. No one could possibly complain about him. And whatever was going to happen—would happen.

Every so often, he marched past a wrecked wagon or a twisted corpse in gray: proof the Army of Franklin had hit hard as well as being hit hard. He needed the reminders. Whenever he thought back to the Battle of Poor Richard, he remembered nothing but northerners falling all around him.

Cold, clammy mud came in between the sole and upper of both shoes now. Still, he remained luckier than a lot of his men. Some of them had managed to take shoes from the bodies of southrons during the fight. Many more, though, were barefoot.

And I'm ever so much luckier than the ones who didn't come out of the fight. Gods damn Lieutenant General Bell. He yawned. He didn't really want to keep marching. He wanted to sleep, with luck for weeks. As happened so often in war, what he wanted and what he got weren't going to match.

One of those bodies by the side of the road was

neither southron nor, Gremio realized, dead. It was a northern soldier who'd fallen out of the column and fallen asleep because he couldn't take another step. Exhausted as Gremio was, he had a harder time blaming the soldier than he would have otherwise.

"Come on, men!" Thisbe's voice and demeanor didn't seem to have changed at all. "We can do it. We get where we're going, we'll rest then."

Where are we going? Gremio wondered. Oh, toward Ramblerton—he knew that full well. But what would the Army of Franklin do when it got there? What *could* it do when it got there? Gremio had had no answers for Sergeant Thisbe, and he had no answers for himself, either.

Here came Colonel Florizel, now mounted on yet another new unicorn. Since his sudden promotion from regimental to wing commander, maybe he knew more of what, if anything, was in Lieutenant General Bell's mind. Gremio waved to him and called out, "Colonel! Ask you something, sir?" *I sound the way Thisbe did asking me*, he thought.

"Oh, hello, Captain Gremio. Yes? What is it?" Florizel remained the picture of a northern gentleman.

"Sir, will we make Ramblerton today?"

"I don't think so, Captain," Florizel replied. "We are weary—I know how weary I am—and we have many walking wounded, *and* we got off to a late start this morning. I expect us to camp on the road when the sun goes down, and then reach the provincial capital tomorrow."

"Thank you, sir." Gremio supposed he really should have thanked Bell, not that he felt like it. He'd figured the commanding general would push on through the night regardless of the condition of his men. Why not? Bell had pushed ahead at Poor Richard, regardless of how many soldiers fell.

But Colonel Florizel hadn't finished yet. "There is something I want you to attend to most particularly tonight, Captain, you and all regimental commanders in my wing." He grimaced at that; had things gone better, neither his status nor Gremio's would have been so exalted.

"What is it, sir?" Gremio had rarely seen Florizel so serious.

"Post plenty of pickets. Post them well south of wherever we do encamp. If the southrons sally from Ramblerton, they must not—they *must* not—take us unawares. They will destroy us if they do. Destroy us, do you hear me?"

"Yes, sir. I agree completely. I'll attend to it," Gremio promised. He eyed his longtime superior, his new wing commander, with more than a little curiosity. Impelled by it, he risked a more abstract question: "What do you think our chances are, sir?"

Florizel had been hardly less eager to charge ahead than Bell himself. Bell hadn't learned much about restraint since taking command of the Army of Franklin. Had Florizel? Gremio waited to see.

The baron from Palmetto Province plucked at his white beard. "I think our chances are . . ." he began, and then rode away without finishing the sentence. That answered Gremio's question, too.

They did camp by the side of the road, about two thirds of the way down from Poor Richard to Ramblerton. Mindful of Colonel Florizel's orders, Gremio set an unusual number of pickets south of his regiment. That done, he wondered what he needed to take care of next. He'd commanded the regiment for less than two days now. As Florizel had, he went from one company to the next, making sure everything was in as good an order as it could be. He was sure Florizel had more to do than that: the colonel had surely kept records and talked with other regimental commanders. But no one was there to tell Gremio just what those other duties were. No one who knew was left alive and unwounded except for Florizel himself, and he was busy somewhere else.

Sergeant Thisbe had the same sort of trouble figuring out everything a company commander was supposed to do. The underofficer, though, could at least ask Gremio. After Gremio had answered the third or fourth question, he said, "You see, Sergeant? You should have let me make you a lieutenant after all. You would have known more about what you're doing now."

"I never wanted to be a lieutenant, and you know it . . . sir," Thisbe answered. "I don't want to do the job I'm doing, either, but I don't see that I've got much choice right now."

"I don't see that you do, either," Gremio said. "I'm proud to command the regiment, but this isn't how I wanted to do it. Too many men dead. Feels as though our hopes have been shot dead, too, doesn't it?"

"Yes, sir. I wouldn't have said that, but it's in my mind, too," Thisbe replied. The underofficer looked around to make sure nobody but Gremio was in earshot. "I wish we were marching back to Dothan, not down towards Ramblerton."

"Can't be helped, Sergeant," Gremio said, and Thisbe nodded. Gremio yawned. He went on, "The other thing is, we're both bone weary. This whole army is bone weary. Things may look brighter once we get a little rest."

"Maybe. I hope so, sir." Thisbe still sounded dubious. "Other question is, when will we ever get a little rest? We'll sleep tonight—we'll sleep tonight like so many dead men—but then we'll march again. And after that . . . after that, it's Ramblerton."

"I know. There's no help for it, not unless we'd want

to go back toward Dothan without orders or give up to the southrons the first chance we get."

"I'm no quitter, sir," Thisbe said. "I aim to stick as long as anybody else does, and then half an hour longer. But I wish I saw some kind of way of getting a happy ending to the story."

"After the war—" Gremio began.

"No, sir." The sergeant gave a shake of the head. "After the war is after the war. That's not what I'm talking about now. I'm talking about a happy ending to this campaign and to the whole fight."

"Oh." Gremio shrugged. "In that case, I don't know what to tell you."

He did sleep like a dead man that night, and woke the next morning still feeling like one. The nasty tea the cooks brewed up pried his eyelids apart and lent him a mournful interest in life.

"Come on, men!" Thisbe called when the soldiers moved out after a meager breakfast. "We'll go on to Ramblerton, and we'll whip the southrons there."

"That's right," Gremio said. "We'll chase the southrons all the way down to the Highlow River. We walloped 'em at Poor Richard. By the gods, we'll wallop 'em again." He did a barrister's best to mask his pessimism.

After every other fight in which he'd taken part, the men of his company—the men of the whole regiment—had always been ready for more, no matter how roughly the southrons had handled them. He'd expected them to raise a cheer now. They didn't. They got to their feet and they marched. They didn't complain. But something had gone out of them. Maybe it was hope.

Whatever it was, Gremio wished he could put it back into the soldiers. To be able to do that, though, he would have had to find hope, or something like it, within himself as well. Try as he would, he couldn't.

Hope or no hope, the Army of Franklin reached Ramblerton about noon the next day. The wan sun of late autumn, low in the north behind Lieutenant General Bell's men, sent their long shadows toward the capital of Franklin. At Bell's orders, relayed by trumpeters and runners, his blue-clad soldiers formed a line along a ridge not far north of the city.

As soon as Gremio's men reached their assigned place, they started digging trenches and throwing up breastworks in front of them. Bell, Gremio knew, looked down his nose at fieldworks. Gremio didn't care. He'd seen how many lives they saved, and urged the diggers on.

While they worked, he got his own first good look at Ramblerton's fortifications. Had he had much hope left, it would have died then.

VI

Ned of the Forest had been up close to Ramblerton before. He'd never had so many men at his back as he did now. All the same, he'd never felt less cheerful about his army's chances.

"What's Bell going to do, Biff?" he demanded, pointing south. "What *can* Bell do, going up against . . . *that*?"

"Gods damn me if I know, Lord Ned," his regimental commander replied. "Those aren't just fieldworks. That's real fortcraft on display there: real castles, real stone walls, engines everywhere, ditches out in front of everything so we can't even get at it, let alone over it."

"I know." Ned scowled and kicked at the muddy ground under his feet. "When I joined up with the Army of Franklin, I reckoned it was pretty good-sized. I figured it could do something worth doing. But it's just asking to kill itself if it goes up against works like those there."

"Other side of that copper is, the Army of Franklin's a deal smaller now than it was before it got out of Poor Richard," Colonel Biffle said. "What the hells was Bell thinking, going at that place that way?"

"I told him I could flank the southrons out," Ned said. "I told him and told him. He didn't want to listen—fools never do want to listen. He stole half our men, too, the son of a bitch. He thought he could smash right on through, and look what it got him."

"Me, I don't much fancy the way the footsoldiers look right about now," Biffle said. "They haven't got a hells of a lot of spunk in 'em. If the southrons were to sally from those forts . . ." He didn't go on. He didn't need to go on.

"We've got to keep 'em too busy to even think of it," Ned said. "I hope we can bring it off, I truly do."

Colonel Biffle noticed his unhappy tones. "You . . . hope, sir?" he said. "As long as I can remember, you've *made* things happen. Now you just *hope* they do?"

Gloomily, Ned nodded. "You saw what happened when we bumped up against those southron unicorn-riders. They've got crossbows we can't hope to match. Only ones we can get are the ones we take from their dead. We don't make anything of the sort our ownselves. We ought to, but we don't."

"We can only use the bolts we get from dead southrons, too," Biffle said.

"I know." Another, even gloomier, nod from Ned. "They're clever bastards, no two ways about it. These crossbows have a skinnier groove than the regular sort, so our standard quarrels won't fit. Takes a sneaky son of a bitch to think of that."

"Sure does," Biffle agreed, and sighed. "Well, the southrons have folks like that, and that's the truth. We could use some of our own right about now, and that's the truth, too."

"We could use . . . a lot of things right about now." Ned of the Forest went no further. Saying anything more wouldn't do any good. Lieutenant General Bell had courage and to spare. Asking the gods to equip him with a real working set of brains to go with it was a prayer unlikely to be answered. People had been asking for that for a long time, with no luck.

"You know what worries me most, Lord Ned?" the regimental commander said.

"Tell me." Ned hoped it would be the same thing he worried about most himself. That way, no new worries would go on his stack.

Biffle said, "What worries me is, Bell still thinks we *won* the fight at Poor Richard. We advanced afterwards, and the southrons left behind a lot of their wounded, and that makes it a triumph to him. He doesn't look at the state the army's in."

That came close to matching Ned's concern about Bell, but didn't quite. He looked toward Ramblerton's formidable works once more. "You don't reckon he wants to try and storm this town, do you?" Very few things had ever frightened Ned of the Forest. The idea of hurling the Army of Franklin at Ramblerton's fortifications came closer than anything that had happened lately.

"He'd better not!" Biffle exclaimed. "If he does, you have to talk him out of it—that or bang him over the head with a rock, one."

"I will," Ned said grimly. "By the Lion God's tail tuft, I don't know how he can do *anything* for a little while. We've got a colonel commanding a wing, captains in charge of regiments, sergeants leading companies. . . . Nobody knows what the devils he's supposed to be doing." He eyed the scraggly ranks of Bell's army, then laughed a bitter laugh. "He likely figures we're laying siege to Ramblerton."

"I wish we were," Biffle said. "I wish we could."

"So do I, both way," Ned replied. "But I know we're *not*. I hope Bell does, too. I better go find out, I reckon."

He swung up onto his unicorn and rode off to find Bell's headquarters. The general commanding had set himself up in a farmhouse a little behind the line. As Ned rode up, Bell was talking to a young major: "You should think yourself a made man, heading up a brigade at your tender age."

"Thank you, sir," the junior officer said. "If it's all the same to you, though, I wish I were still second-in-command in my old regiment. I'd know what I was doing there—and we wouldn't have so many men above me dead."

"We go on," Lieutenant General Bell said. "We have to go on. What else can we do? Turn around and run back up to Dothan? Not likely!" Pride rang in his voice. When he tossed his head to show his scorn for the southrons, he caught sight of Ned of the Forest. "You may go, Major. I have business to talk with Lieutenant General Ned here."

The major saluted and hurried away. Ned saluted, too. As usual, he wasted no time on small talk. "What are we going to do now that we're here?" he demanded. Very much as an afterthought, he added, "Sir?"

"I aim to give John the Lister and Doubting George another whipping of the same sort as they had at Poor Richard," Bell declared grandly.

"One more 'whipping' like that and *you* won't have any army left yourself," Ned said, his voice harsh and blunt.

Instead of answering right away, Bell took out his little bottle of laudanum, pulled the stopper with his teeth, and swigged. "Ahh!" he said. "That makes the world seem a better place."

"No matter what it seems like, it isn't," Ned said, even more bluntly than before. "I'm going to ask you again, sir, and this time I expect a straight answer: what do you aim to do next?"

Something seemed to leach out of Bell. He tried to gather himself, to hold on to the force of will that Ned had seen failing him, and succeeded . . . to a degree. "Lieutenant General, I am going to make the southrons come out of their works if they intend to fight us. If they come out, things can go wrong for them. I don't intend to storm the entrenchments around Ramblerton. I can see we would be unlikely to carry them, the men feeling as they do about attacking forts."

Ned of the Forest considered. If he were a foot-soldier, he wouldn't have cared to try to storm Rambler-ton's fortifications, either. Who in his right mind wanted to get killed to no purpose? But Bell's plan, if that was what it was, struck him as being about as good as any-one could want for in the Army of Franklin's present battered state.

"All right, sir," he said. "Don't reckon we've got much hope trying anything else. But I want to warn you about something."

"And what's that?" Bell rumbled. "How do you have any business warning your commanding officer?"

"Somebody'd better," Ned said. "You have to listen, too. Don't go splitting things up. We haven't got the men for it. We haven't got room to make any mistakes. Not any at all. You understand what I'm saying?"

"I have led us south for two hundred miles now," Bell replied. "I have had plenty of underlings make mistakes—and no, I am not speaking of you, so you need not take offense. I do not believe *I* have made any substantial blunders in this campaign."

"You took half my men away from me when I was trying to outflank the southrons," Ned exclaimed. "If I'd had those men, I might've broken through and made John the Lister fall back without any need for a fight at Poor Richard."

"I needed those men no less than you did," Bell said. "The battle was long and hard enough even with their aid. Without it, our arms might not have triumphed."

"What makes you reckon they did?" Ned asked.

Bell looked at him as if he'd started speaking the language of one of the blond tribes instead of plain and simple Detinan. "We held the field when the fight was done," the commanding general said; Ned might have been an idiot child to doubt him. "We advanced afterwards. We took charge of the wounded men the southrons abandoned in their retreat. If that is not victory, what would you call it?"

By all the rules they taught in the officers' collegium at Annasville, Bell was right. Ned of the Forest knew about those rules, and all other formalities of the military art, only by hearsay. But he knew what he saw with his own eyes. He had no doubt at all there. "If this here is a victory . . . sir . . . then we'd better not see another one. And that's all I've got to say about that."

He saluted with as much precision as he could muster, then turned on his heel and strode away from Lieutenant General Bell. "Here, now!" the general commanding called after him. "You come back at once—at once, I say—and explain yourself. Do you say we failed to win a victory at Poor Richard? Do you? How dare you?"

Ned pretended not to hear. Bell couldn't very well run after him, after all. As he neared his unicorn, Bell's complaints grew fainter. He mounted and rode off. Once in the saddle, he didn't have to listen any more.

But the army's still stuck with Bell, he thought

unhappily. Then, even more unhappily, he shrugged. *If you were in charge of things now, what would you do different?* he asked himself. He found no answer. Too late to worry about that. The damage had long since been done.

"Well?" Colonel Biffle asked when Ned got back among his unicorn-riders.

"Well, Biff, the good news is, we don't have to try and take Ramblerton all by our lonesome," Ned replied. "The bad news is—or maybe it's good news, too; to the hells with me if I know—we wait here outside of Ramblerton till the southrons decide they're good and ready to hit us."

"What do we do then?" Biffle asked dubiously.

"Hope we can lick 'em," Ned said.

"Think we can?" the regimental commander inquired, even more dubiously.

"Don't know," Ned of the Forest answered. "What I think is, we'd better. Are you going to tell me I'm wrong? If we're in our trenches and they're trying to come at us . . . well, we've maybe got some kind of chance, anyways."

"Maybe." Biffle didn't sound as if he believed it. Then he shrugged. "Odds *are* better than us going up against those forts, I expect. Odds of anything'd be better than that."

"Don't I know it!" Ned said. "It could work, I suppose. If John the Lister and Doubting George figure we've got no fight left in us, it *could* work. But by the Lion God's claws, I hate laying my hopes on the off chance that the sons of bitches I'm up against don't know what they're doing."

"Why?" Colonel Biffle said. "Been plain for a goodish while now that *we* don't. Why should they be any different?"

Ned laughed. Biffle's words held altogether too

much truth. "Long odds, Biff," he said. "Long odds indeed."

"Well, we've had long odds before, and licked the southrons anyways," Biffle said. "This past summer, down in Great River Province . . ."

"I know. I know. And maybe we can do it again," Ned said. "Somehow or other, we've got to do it again. You reckon we can?"

He waited. For a long time, Colonel Biffle stood there without saying a word. Ned of the Forest coughed, telling him he *would* have an answer. Reluctantly, the regimental commander replied, "You had it right, Lord Ned. We've got to lick 'em. Anything we've got to do, we will."

"How?" Ned neither minced nor wasted words.

All he got by way of a reply this time was a shrug. He coughed again, louder. Even more reluctantly, Colonel Biffle said, "Gods damn me if I know. Maybe the southrons really will make a mistake."

"They'd better." Ned of the Forest sounded as if he held his regimental commander responsible for it. Both men looked toward the works in front of Ramblerton. Even at this distance, Ned could see southrons in gray moving back and forth in those works. Even at this distance, he seemed to see a whole great swarm of southrons moving back and forth. "How many of those bastards are there?" he grumbled.

"Too many," Biffle replied, which startled another laugh out of Ned. The colonel continued, "You put any southrons—*any* southrons, mind you—in a province that's sworn loyalty to good King Geoffrey and that's too fornicating many."

"True enough," Ned said. "It'll take a good deal of pounding to be rid of 'em, though."

Now his gaze went to Captain Watson, who was attacking a broken-down dart-thrower with a hammer and a set of wrenches. The young officer in charge of Ned's engines was as much a mechanic as a leader of fighting men, as much a mechanic as any southron. That made him all the more valuable to the northern cause. Had Geoffrey had more men like Watson loyal to him, the north would have been in better shape. Ned saw that. After a little while, though, he also saw the north would not have been the land he knew were that so. How to win, though? Try as he would, Ned could not see that.

Once again, Rollant looked out at the northern army from the security of strong fortifications. Up at Poor Richard, Bell's men had done everything they could to overwhelm the southrons' works. Here . . . Rollant turned to Smitty. "Do you suppose Bell'd be dumb enough to try and attack us again?"

"I hope so," Smitty answered at once. "If he does, we'll kill every last one of the bastards he's got left. We won't get hurt doing it, either."

"That's how it looks to me, too," the blond said. "I was wondering if maybe I was wrong."

"Not this time," Smitty said with a grin.

Rollant glared. "Funny. You and your smart mouth. I ought to set you chopping extra firewood for that." Even as he spoke, he knew he wouldn't.

By Smitty's impudent grin, he must have known the same thing. "Have mercy, your Corporalship!" he exclaimed. "I'll be good! I really will. I won't give you any more trouble, not ever!"

Rollant laughed. "Do you know what you remind me of?"

"No, your illustrious Corporalship, but I expect you're going to tell me, so that's all right."

With a snort, Rollant said, "You remind me of a fast-talking serf trying to flimflam his way out of trouble with his liege lord. I always used to wish I could talk that way when I got in trouble on Baron Ormerod's estate. It never used to work for me, though."

From behind them, Sergeant Joram growled, "It shouldn't work for this fast-talking son of a bitch, either." Rollant and Smitty both jumped; they hadn't heard Joram come up. The sergeant went on, "Smitty, go chop firewood. Go chop lots of it. I want to see your hands bleeding when you bring it back. Go on, get out of here."

Smitty disappeared as if made to vanish by magecraft. He knew there were times when he could argue with Sergeant Joram and times when he couldn't. He also knew which was which, and that this was plainly one of the latter.

Joram folded massive arms across his broad chest. He eyed Rollant. "Flimflam, is it?" he said.

"Sergeant?" Rollant asked.

"You've made a good underofficer," Joram said. "Truth to tell, you've made a better one than anybody figured you would. But you can't be soft on somebody just because you like him and he's a funny fellow."

"I haven't meant to be soft on anybody, Sergeant," Rollant said. By his own standards, that was true. By Joram's, it probably wasn't. Joram was fair. He treated everybody under him the same way—miserably.

"Maybe not," he said now, "but I think you go too easy on Smitty, and I know the two of you were pals before you made corporal."

"Pals?" Not for the first time, Rollant wondered about that. Could a blond and an ordinary Detinan be pals? Didn't too much history stand in the way? Rollant still thought so. That he wasn't quite sure any more said something about Smitty—and something about how long he'd lived in the south.

"Ask you something, Sergeant?" he said.

"Go ahead," Joram growled.

"When are we going to get out there and smash the traitors?"

"To the hells with me if I know. Whenever Doubting George gives the order." The sergeant leered. "When he does, I promise you'll hear about it."

"Yes, Sergeant. I know that. But . . . even when we just had the little army John the Lister led, we put the fear of the gods in Bell's men. Now we've got a lot more soldiers." Rollant waved back toward Ramblerton. "We've got all these extra men, but Bell doesn't even have what he hit us with before, because we chewed him up. So now maybe we ought to do some hitting of our own."

"It's not up to me," Joram said. "It's up to Doubting George. When he tells us to march, we march. When he tells us to stay where we are, we stay. When he tells you you can complain, go ahead and complain. Until he tells you you can complain—shut up, gods damn it."

"What do free Detinans ever do but complain?" Rollant returned. "And if I'm not a free Detinan, what am I?"

That, of course, was *the* question of the War Between the Provinces. If a blond wasn't a free Detinan, what was he? Northerners insisted he was a serf, and could never be anything else. King Avram disagreed with that, and had the southrons on his side. But even Avram didn't seem convinced blonds would become ordinary Detinans the instant the north gave up the fight.

Joram's heavy-featured face—the gods might have made him on purpose to be a sergeant—clouded up. But he had an answer that applied to Rollant, even if it didn't to blonds in general: "What are you? By the Thunderer's balls, you're a corporal—and I'm a sergeant. If I tell you to swallow your bellyaching, you'd better swallow it, on account of I've got the right to tell you to. Have you got that?"

"Yes, Sergeant," Rollant said—the only answer he could give. Joram recognized his right to be a corporal. As soon as that right was recognized, as soon as a blond's right to pick up a crossbow or a pike and go fight the northerners was recognized, everything else would follow. And if Grand Duke Geoffrey wanted to deny it and call himself king in the north . . . too bad for him. He had left only the Army of Southern Parthenia and the Army of Franklin. Marshal Bart had one by the throat, while the other waited here for whatever Doubting George would do to it.

"When we *do* whip Lieutenant General Bell, what will Geoffrey have left here in the east?" Rollant wondered aloud. "Nothing I can see."

"That's the idea," Joram said. "The son of a bitch is a traitor. When he's done losing, he ought to go up on a cross. The buzzards can peck out his eyes, for all I care. We're going to smash those bastards, smash 'em good. Don't you worry about that, not even a little bit. It'll happen. Nobody knows when yet, but it will." He thumped Rollant on the back, hard enough to stagger him, then trudged on down the trench line.

"Boy," Smitty said, "if I gave him half that hard a time, he'd have my guts for garters."

"And you'd deserve it, too," Rollant said. "I thought you went off to cut firewood."

"So did Joram," Smitty answered. "I just went into the little jog in the trench where we ease ourselves. That's one good thing about cold weather, anyhow— the little jog doesn't stink the way it would in summer. Hardly any flies, either."

"Button yours," Rollant said.

Smitty looked down. Rollant snickered. That was the sort of joke schoolboys played on each other—not that he'd ever been a schoolboy. "Think you're pretty gods-damned funny, don't you?" Smitty said indignantly.

"What I think is, you'd better go cut that wood before Joram sees you're still around," Rollant said. "He's right—I let you get away with all kinds of things. But he won't, and you know it."

Nodding gloomily, Smitty went off to do his work. Rollant looked out at the northerners' lines again. They weren't within crossbow range, or even within range of the stone- and dart-throwers that could outshoot any hand-held weapon. They had their own fortified positions on the hills in front of Ramblerton, a couple of miles north of Doubting George's outworks.

All right. They're there. Now what the hells do they do? Rollant wondered. *What would I do, if I were Bell?* One answer to that question immediately came to mind: *I'd go somewhere high and jump off.* Could Bell jump with only one leg? One more thing Rollant didn't know. But he wouldn't have wanted to go around leaving pieces of himself on different battlefields, as the northern general commanding had done.

Tiny as ants in the distance, blue-clad traitors went about their business. As soldiers, they weren't much different from their southron counterparts. As men . . . as men, they were welcome to the hottest firepits in the seven hells, as far as Rollant was concerned. He knew they wished him the same, and would do their best to send him there. If he'd cared about what northern Detinans thought, he never would have run away from Baron Ormerod's plantation.

Night fell early this time of year. Before long, all Rollant could see of the enemy was the light from his campfires. Over there, common soldiers were also grumbling because their underofficers made them chop firewood. One thing was different over there, though. None of the northerners' underofficers was a blond.

Lieutenant Griff came up the line. "Everything all right, Corporal?" he asked. He spoke thickly; up at Poor Richard, a shortsword had laid one cheek open. The black stitches the healers had put in to close the wound made him look like an outlaw or a pirate instead of the mild-mannered fellow he'd seemed before. Even when they came out, he'd be scarred for the rest of his days.

"Everything's fine, sir," Rollant answered. "How are you?" He hadn't expected to sound so anxious. Griff had made a better company commander than most of his men thought he would after Captain Cephas got killed. His voice still broke now and again, but he had plenty of nerve, and he looked out for his soldiers the way a good officer would.

Now he managed a mostly one-sided grin. "I'll do," he said. "No sign of fever in the wound—it's healing, not festering. That was my biggest worry. I'm not what you'd call fond of soaking a rag in spirits and pressing it on the cut—"

"Ow!" Rollant said sympathetically. "Does that really do any good? Seems like a lot of hurt for not much help."

"Some of them say it does, so I'm doing it," Griff replied. "I asked one of them if he'd do it himself, and he showed me a clean scar and said he *had* done it. Not much I could say to that."

Rollant thought of raw spirits on raw flesh. "I don't know, sir. I think I'd almost rather have the fever."

Lieutenant Griff shook his head. "No. That can kill. This just hurts. I'll get through it." Unlike a lot of Detinans, he didn't brag or bluster about his bravery. He just displayed it. Pointing to the fires north of Ramblerton, he said, "I wish Lieutenant General George would turn us loose against the traitors."

"I've been saying the same thing. Why won't he, do you think?" Rollant asked.

Griff shrugged. "How can I say? I'm not Doubting George. I'm not going to go back into Ramblerton and ask him. Not even Colonel Nahath could get away with that. George would throw him out on his ear. Maybe he's waiting for more men—I hear another wing may be coming from the far side of the Great River."

"Why does he need them?" Rollant asked. "We stopped the Army of Franklin all by ourselves, and George has a lot of soldiers here who didn't go north with John the Lister. We ought to be able to ride roughshod over the traitors."

Smiling—again, lopsidedly—Griff said, "Well, Rollant, no one who listened to you would ever get the idea that blonds are shy about mixing it up."

He means that for praise, Rollant reminded himself. *And he's my company commander. If I bop him over the head with something, it will only land me in trouble.*

"You do have to remember, though, attacking a position is a lot harder than defending one," Griff went on, cheerfully oblivious to the way he'd angered Rollant. "We would have to pay the price of winkling the northerners out of their trenches."

"Mm, yes, sir, that's true." Even if Rollant was annoyed with Griff, he couldn't deny the officer made sense. "Still and all, we've *already* got a whole lot more men than the traitors do."

"Corporal, if you want to go petition the general commanding for an immediate attack, you have my permission to do so," Griff said.

Rollant tried to imagine himself marching into Doubting George's headquarters and doing just that. It wasn't that George didn't know who he was. George did: he was the man who'd ultimately approved Rollant's promotion to corporal up in Peachtree Province. But that made things worse, not better. It was only likely to mean he'd come down on Rollant harder than he would have otherwise.

"No, thank you, sir," Rollant said hastily.

Lieutenant Griff nodded as if he'd expected no different response. Odds were he hadn't. And yet . . . now that Rollant thought about it, more than a few Detinans would have taken Griff up on his offer. Detinans were convinced they were all just as good, all just as smart, as anybody else. To a common soldier, only a little luck separated himself from Doubting George. Why *wouldn't* the commanding general want to listen to him?

I sometimes wonder what besides my hair and my blue eyes separates me from Detinans, Rollant thought. *There it is. I think George knows more about fighting a war than I do, and down deep a lot of them don't believe any such thing. Do I have good sense, or do they?* His shoulders went up and down in a shrug of his own. Considering some of the things generals on both sides had done during this war, the answer wasn't altogether clear.

"Any which way," Griff said, "I don't think you'll have to wait very long."

Rollant looked north toward the traitors' campfires once more. *Do I really want to try to storm those lines?* he wondered, and nodded to himself. *By the gods, I really do.* To Lieutenant Griff, he said one word: "Good."

Lieutenant General Bell stared south toward Ramblerton. The stare was hungry and frustrated, the stare of a hound eyeing a big, juicy chunk of meat hung too high for it to reach.

Here and there, Bell could see gray-clad southrons marching along the works that defended the capital of Franklin. In the distance, the enemy soldiers might have been so many gray lice crawling along the back of some huge, hairless animal. Getting rid of lice in the field was never easy. Bell knew that all too well. He'd been lousy himself, a time or two. Getting rid of the southrons in Ramblerton looked harder yet.

He'd told Ned of the Forest he wouldn't try to storm the place. He didn't see how he could, not when Doubting George's men outnumbered his and had the advantage of those redoubtable redoubts. (Such things hadn't stopped him at Poor Richard, of course, but these were in a different class altogether.) He'd expected George to try to take advantage of southron numbers and attack *him*, but that hadn't happened yet. Bell was beginning to wonder if it would. Waiting seemed an anticlimax, and a squalid one at that.

His right leg itched. He settled his crutch in his armpit and reached down to scratch. Only when his good hand met nothing but air did he remember he had no right leg, though itching was the least of what it did.

For once, though, apparent sensation from his missing member didn't appall him, didn't send him grabbing for the tiny bottle of laudanum. Given what he'd been thinking, he'd wondered if he was lousy again. Realizing he wasn't came as no small relief.

A messenger saluted and waited to be noticed. When Bell nodded, the man said, "Sir, Brigadier Benjamin would like to speak to you."

"Oh, he would, would he?" Bell considered. He didn't care to be lectured or harangued, as wing and brigade commanders had been in the habit of doing since this campaign began. On the other hand, Benjamin the Heated Ham hadn't bothered him so much as several other officers, most of them now dead. As if Bell were a god, he inclined his head in acquiescence. "He may come forward."

Benjamin saluted with all due courtesy. He was politeness personified when he inquired, "Sir, may I ask you a question?"

"Go ahead," Bell replied. "I don't necessarily know that I'll answer it."

"Oh, I hope you do, sir," Benjamin said earnestly. "You see, it's important." He paused for dramatic effect. He'd got his nickname for bad acting, and he still lived up to it. Bell half expected him to clasp his hands together in front of his chest. He didn't, but he did send Bell an imploring look.

"Well, ask." Bell knew he sounded gruff. He didn't care. He had no patience for melodrama now.

Benjamin the Heated Ham at last came to the point: "All right, sir. What I want to know is, now that we've come this far, what are we going to do? What *can* we do, facing *those* works?" He pointed toward Ramblerton.

Ned of the Forest had wanted to know the same thing. *Have they no confidence in me?* Bell wondered. As he had to Ned, he said, "We'll wait here for Doubting George to assail our lines. When he does, we'll beat him back."

"Sir, if what the spies and prisoners say is true, the southrons have a hells of a lot more men than we do," Benjamin observed.

Bell glowered. He knew that, but didn't care to be reminded of it. He said, "Everyone keeps telling me this army doesn't care to fight away from the protection of entrenchments. Do you claim the men will not fight even when they enjoy that protection?"

"No, sir. I never said any such thing." Benjamin the Heated Ham backtracked in a hurry.

"What precisely *did* you say, then?" Bell inquired with icy courtesy.

"Sir, this army will fight like a pack of mad bastards.

The men will do what you tell them to do, or they'll die trying. If Poor Richard didn't teach you that, nothing ever will," Benjamin said. Bell realized that wasn't exactly praise for his ordering the army to fight at Poor Richard, but his wing commander hurried on before he could show his displeasure: "It all depends on what you order them to do. If too many gods-damned southrons come at them, they're not going to win regardless of whether they're in entrenchments or not."

"Do you believe Doubting George has *that* many men, Brigadier?" Lieutenant General Bell said. "I, for one, do not."

"I don't know for certain, sir," Benjamin answered. "All I know for certain is, like I said, he's got a lot more than we do."

"Regardless of which, I still maintain the southrons are a cowardly lot," Bell said. Now Benjamin the Heated Ham stirred, but the commanding general overrode him: "Consider, Brigadier. The southrons have outnumbered us all along, yet we have advanced about two hundred miles against them, and they have yet to dare stand against us. Whenever we have faced them in the field, we have defeated them." Benjamin stirred again. Again, Bell refused to notice. "We whipped them at Poor Richard. They yielded not only the battlefield but also prisoners and wounded. If that doesn't prove them cowards, I don't know what would."

"Sir, you weren't up at the front at Poor Richard," Benjamin said. "No offense to you; with your wounds, you couldn't be. But the southrons aren't cowards. If you don't believe me, ask Patrick the Cleaver or For Gods' Sake John or John of Barsoom or Provincial Prerogative or Otho the Troll or—"

"How *can* I ask them? They are dead. Have you a crystal ball that will reach to Mount Panamgam, beyond the fields we know?" Bell asked.

"No, sir. That's my point. They wouldn't *be* dead if the southrons were cowards. Cowards don't kill half a dozen brigadiers in one fight."

"If that's your point, it's a feeble one," Bell said. "It wasn't the enemy's courage that killed our officers. It was their own. They closed with the foe, and gloriously fell in service to their kingdom."

"Have it however you like," Benjamin the Heated Ham said. "But I wouldn't be doing my duty if I didn't warn you you'd be making a mistake by counting on the southrons to play the craven."

"Thank you, Brigadier." Bell sounded—and felt—anything but grateful. "You have passed on your warning. I shall bear it in mind. Now that you have performed this duty, you are dismissed."

"Yes, sir." Benjamin saluted and strode off, stiff-backed and proud.

Lieutenant General Bell muttered something pungent under his breath. He was sick to death of officers stalking away from him. He'd seen altogether too much of it on this campaign. Some of the brigadiers who'd neglected military courtesy had paid for their bad manners with their lives. But Ned of the Forest and Benjamin the Heated Ham were still very much around. Bell couldn't even punish them for their insolence. After the fight at Poor Richard, the Army of Franklin had lost so many commanders, he couldn't afford to sack any more. Things creaked bad enough as they were.

The general commanding remembered the losses. He conveniently forgot that his orders at Poor Richard had led to them. He also forgot that those orders might have had something to do with the surviving officers' lack of confidence in him. As far as he was concerned, they had no business behaving any way but respectfully. King Geoffrey had put him in charge of

the Army of Franklin, and he had every intention of
leading it to glory . . . somehow.

He shifted his weight on his crutches. That proved
a mistake—his ruined left shoulder and arm screamed
at him. He took out the little bottle of laudanum,
yanked the stopper with his teeth, and gulped down
the drug that helped keep him going. Glory didn't
concern itself with ruined shoulders and missing legs.
A man who stopped to think about the cost would
never find the true magnificence of battle. Whether
such a man might find victory was another question
that never occurred to Bell.

Little by little, as the laudanum took hold, he floated
away from his pain-wracked body. As long as that
wrecked arm and missing leg didn't torment him, he
could forget all about them, just as he forgot about
other inconveniences on the way to the victory that
surely lay ahead.

One of those inconveniences was Doubting George's
army. He couldn't very well attack it if it stayed in the
works of Ramblerton. Oh, he *could*, but even he
doubted that that would have a happy ending. He
needed to lure that army out of those works if he was
to have any chance of beating it. There he and his
subordinate commanders agreed.

But how? He'd hoped simply sitting in front of the
city and making his army a tempting target would
suffice. Evidently not. He needed some new stratagem
to make sure the southrons came forth. What, though?
What could he do that he wasn't already doing?

Suddenly, he snapped his fingers. His right hand had
not forgotten its cunning—and he chuckled at the
cunning his brains showed, too, despite (*or perhaps*,
he thought, *even because of*) all the laudanum he had
to take.

"Runner!" he called.

"Yes, sir?" the closest messenger said.

"I need to speak to Ned of the Forest just as soon as you can bring him here," Bell replied.

"Yes, sir," the messenger said again, but then, in a puzzled voice, "Wasn't he here not too long ago?"

"What if he was?" Bell demanded. "I am the commanding general, and I am entitled to summon the officers of my army if I need to confer with them. Would you care to quarrel with that, Corporal?"

"Uh, no, sir," the messenger said hastily. Bell fixed upon him the stare that had led to his being compared to the Lion God. The messenger left in a hurry.

Bell had to wait a while before Ned of the Forest returned. For one thing, the unicorn-riders camped at some little distance from the rest of the men in the Army of Franklin. For another, Bell suspected Ned of being slow to obey orders on purpose. Ned was still fuming because the general commanding had pulled back some of his riders to fight with the rest of the army at Poor Richard.

"Well, too bad for Ned," Lieutenant General Bell said. A couple of the runners standing not far away sent him curious looks, but none of them had the nerve to ask a question. As far as Bell was concerned, that was as it should be.

In due course, Ned of the Forest did ride up. Slowly and deliberately, he dismounted from his unicorn. He made a small production of tethering the animal to a tree. Only after he'd done that did he nod to Bell. "What can I do for you . . . sir?" His tone and manner made it plain he tacked on the title of respect very much as an afterthought. He didn't bother saluting.

"I have had an idea," Bell announced.

"Have you? Congratulations," the commander of unicorn-riders said.

"Thank you." Only after the words were out of his

mouth did Bell realized Ned might not have meant that as a compliment. He gave the other officer the same glare as he'd used against the luckless runner. Ned, though, was made of sterner stuff. He stared back, as intent on intimidating Bell as Bell was on intimidating him.

The silent, angry tableau could have lasted even longer than it did, but Ned's unicorn tried to jerk free from the tree to which he'd tied it. It failed, but the motion distracted both men. When Ned of the Forest looked back, some of the cold fury had left his face. "What is your idea, sir?" he asked.

"I aim to send some of your unicorn-riders against Reillyburgh, to harass the southrons there and to draw Doubting George out of Ramblerton," Bell said.

"Didn't I tell you before, you'd better not divide your forces? Didn't you have enough of splitting up my men when we were down at Poor Richard?" Ned said. "Look what you got there."

"You are insubordinate," Bell said.

"And you are a gods-damned fool," Ned retorted. "By the Thunderer's thumbs, you haven't got enough men now to stretch from one bank of the Cumbersome River to the other. There's gaps on both sides. And now you want to take soldiers *away* from this scrawny little army? You must be clean out of your tree."

"Can you think of anything likelier to lure the southrons away from Ramblerton than a threat to one of their outlying garrisons?" Bell said. "We cannot fight them while they are in there. They must come forth."

"Be careful what you ask for, on account of you're liable to get it," Ned of the Forest said.

"And what, pray tell, does that mean?"

"If they come out . . . sir, do you really reckon we can handle 'em?" Ned asked.

"Of course we can. Of course we will. Would I have come all this way if I expected my campaign to fail?"

"I don't know anything about what you expect," Ned answered. "All I know is, I expect you're going to be sorry for splitting up your army the way you're doing. You haven't got enough men to fight Doubting George as is, let alone if you go detaching a piece of your force here and another piece there."

"I am the commanding general," Bell declared in a voice like frozen iron. "Obey my orders, Lieutenant General." Ned snarled something that sounded more like a wildcat's hiss than real words. But he did salute as he stormed off. Bell thought that meant he would obey. If it didn't, the Army of Franklin could probably scrape up a new commander of unicorn-riders, too. Somewhere.

"Sir?" A gray-robed mage stuck his head into Doubting George's office and waited to be noticed.

George made him wait for quite a while. At last, though, the southrons' commander had no choice but to acknowledge the fellow's existence. "Yes, Lieutenant? What do you want?"

"It isn't me, sir." The wizard made a point of distancing himself from the message he had to deliver. "It isn't me," he repeated, "but Marshal Bart is on the crystal ball, and he needs to talk to you."

"Ah, but do I need to talk to Marshal Bart?" Doubting George replied. "I wonder. I truly do wonder."

"Sir," the young wizard said desperately, "sir, Marshal Bart *orders* you to come and talk with him."

"Oh, he does, does he?" George said. The scryer nodded. George sighed and got heavily to his feet. "Well, I suppose I'd better do it then, eh?"

"Yes, sir. I think that would be a very, a *very* good

thing to do, sir." The mage was all but babbling in his relief.

George didn't think it would be anything of the sort. Only three men in all Detina were in a position to make him do anything he didn't think would be very good: King Avram, General Hesmucet . . . and Marshal Bart. Avram had always let him alone. Hesmucet, marching toward Veldt and the Western Ocean, was otherwise occupied. Bart, off in front of Pierreville laying siege to Duke Edward of Arlington and the Army of Southern Parthenia, should have been otherwise occupied, too. But, as commander of *all* of Avram's armies, he insisted on poking his nose into what should have been Doubting George's business.

Although George made the walk to the chamber where the scryers hunched over their crystal balls as slow as he could, he did eventually get there. The lieutenant dogged his heels like a puppy. Several other scryers in the room beamed when George did at last appear.

He sat down on a stool in front of a crystal ball from whose depths Marshal Bart's blunt, weathered features stared. "Reporting as ordered, sir," George said blandly. "How are things over in Parthenia?"

"Tolerable," Bart answered. "We've got Edward by the neck. Sooner or later, we'll throttle him. But I don't want to talk about Parthenia. I want to talk about Franklin, about Ramblerton."

"You're the marshal." George sounded cheerier than he felt. "Whatever you want, that's what happens."

That was a mistake. Doubting George realized as much as soon as the words were out of his mouth— which was, of course, too late. Bart said, "I'll tell you what I want. I want what I told you I wanted a week ago. I want you to go out there and smash the Army of Franklin.

"I intend to do exactly that, sir," George answered. "As soon as I am ready, I *will* do it."

"And just when do you expect to be ready, Lieutenant General?" Marshal Bart asked pointedly. "You've already dithered too long."

"I am not dithering, sir," George replied with dignity. "I am waiting for a couple of good brigades to come in from the far side of the Great River. As soon as they're here, I will land on Bell like a ton of barristers."

"I am of the opinion—and King Avram is also of the opinion—that you have enough men to do the job without these footsoldiers from beyond the Great River," Bart said. "I want you to get on with it, George."

"Sir, I will attack when I am ready," Doubting George said stiffly. "Until I am sure I can do the job as it should be done, I don't see how I can—or why I should—launch an attack."

"Lieutenant General, if you stay in Ramblerton much longer *without* attacking, you put your command in jeopardy," Marshal Bart said. "Do I make myself plain?"

"Odiously so," George answered. "If you want to replace me, you have the right to do just that. You are the marshal, after all."

"Confound it, George, I don't *want* to replace you," Bart said irritably. "I want you to go out there and fight and win. The longer you sit there and don't fight, though, the worse you look, and the louder people scream for your head."

"Tell those people to go scream about something else," George said. "Have I ever let you down? Have I ever let the kingdom down?"

"No, but they say there's a first time for everything. I'm beginning to wonder myself," Bart said. "I tell you that frankly, as one soldier to another. You outnumber Bell. He is there in front of you. Go strike him."

"You outnumber Duke Edward. He is there in front of *you*. Go strike him," Doubting George said.

"You are not so funny as you may think. If you saw the works of Pierreville, you would be more sparing of your advice."

"Sir, it could be," George allowed. "I do not understand the situation there. I admit it. And you do not understand the situation here—only you refuse to admit it."

"I understand that I am the commanding general of all the armies of the Kingdom of Detina," Marshal Bart said. "I understand that I have ordered you to attack. I understand that you are not attacking. What more do I need to understand about Ramblerton?"

"That ordering me to attack when my army is not ready is about as bad a mistake as you can make . . . sir," Doubting George said. "That you are flabbling over nothing. Bell will not get away, and I will whip him."

"You are a stubborn man, Lieutenant General," Bart said. "I warn you once more, though: you are trifling with your career."

"I will take the chance, sir," George replied. "Let history—and you—judge by the result."

"If you don't get moving before too long, history would judge me if I didn't remove you from your command," the marshal said. "You had better bear that in mind if you mean to sit around with a superior force."

"You will do what you think best," Doubting George said stolidly, not showing any of the outrage that boiled up in him at Bart's threat. "I wish you would credit me with doing the same, though."

"I believe you are doing what you think best," Marshal Bart said. "But if I do not also happen to think that is the best thing to do, I would be remiss in my duty if I did not take steps to see what I want done, done."

"You want a victory. I will give you a victory. If I don't give you a victory, send me out to the trackless east and let me chase the blond savages along with Guildenstern and John the Hierophant."

"I want a victory *now*, Lieutenant General. You have it in your power to give me what I want," Bart said. "If you don't give me what I want, I will get it from someone else. That is the long and short of it." Bart turned to the scryer dealing with his end of the mystic connection between crystal balls. The scryer broke it. Bart's image vanished from the crystal ball in front of Doubting George.

George's scryer asked, "Do you want to send any messages of your own, sir?"

"Eh? No." George shook his head. "Not only that, I didn't want to hear the one I just got."

"I don't blame you a bit," the scryer said. Then, remembering such conversations were supposed to be confidential, he turned red. "Not that I was paying much attention to it."

"No, of course not." George's irony was strong enough to make the scryer flinch. "Just keep that convenient forgetfulness in mind when you're talking with anybody else, eh?" The wizard nodded quick and, George thought, sincere agreement. It wasn't so much that he had George's interests uppermost in his mind. But he had to know the general commanding could make his life amazingly miserable if he let his mouth run away with him.

Doubting George stalked away from the room full of crystal balls. *Miserable invention*, he thought. *They let distant commanders inflict their stupidity on someone on the spot. If the ignorant bastards off in the west actually knew what they were doing and what things were like here . . .* He shook his head. As he'd seen, that was too much to ask for.

He went out onto the streets of Ramblerton. He hoped he wouldn't have anyone asking him questions out there. No such luck. Colonel Andy emerged a couple of minutes later. Someone must have tipped him off that George had been summoned to talk on a crystal ball. "Well?" George's adjutant asked.

"No, as a matter of fact, it's not so well," George answered. "Bart wants everything to start yesterday."

"And if it doesn't?" Andy asked.

"He'll throw me out on my ear," George answered. "Then he'll go and pull somebody else's strings."

Andy scowled like an irate chipmunk. "That's a hells of a thing for him to go and do. Fat lot of gratitude he shows for all *you've* done. If you hadn't saved things by the River of Death, we might really be worrying about how to hold on to Cloviston now."

"Nothing I can do about it," Doubting George said. "Anyone who puts his faith in a superior's gratitude is like the fellow who said he believed in no gods at all till the Thunderer hit him with a lightning bolt: you can try it, but chances are it won't do you much good."

He'd heard that story since he was a little boy. For the first time, he paused to wonder if it was so. From some of the things Alva had said, the wizard believed the gods were a lot less powerful than most people thought. A solid conservative, George doubted that, but the Thunderer hadn't smitten Alva with any lightning bolts. And, if the Inward Hypothesis somehow turned out to be true, how much room did it leave for the action of the gods in the world? Less than George would have wanted, plainly.

To his relief, Colonel Andy brought him back to the mundane world of battles: "Could you make Marshal Bart happy and attack the traitors now?"

"I suppose I *could*," George replied, "but we'd have more of a chance of coming away with a bloody nose if I did. When I hit them, I want to hit them with everything we can get our hands on. For that, I need those last two brigades from the east side of the Great River to get here."

"What if Bart replaces you before they do?" Andy asked nervously.

"Why, then I suppose they send me off to hunt blonds out on the steppe. I already told Bart I'd go." George spoke with equanimity. In fact, he doubted anything so dreadful would happen. He was a brigadier in the regulars, and he wouldn't have lost a battle like Guildenstern or John the Hierophant. Odds were he'd just spend the rest of his career in Georgetown counting crossbow quarrels or something equally useful.

Andy . . . *If I remember rightly, Andy is a captain of regulars*, George thought. His adjutant probably would get sent to the steppe, and to one of the less prepossessing forts there. No wonder he seemed nervous.

"Don't fret," George told him. "If you let anything but what you need to do prey on your mind, you're in trouble. I know what's going on here. Marshal Bart doesn't, regardless of whether he thinks he does."

"But he's the one who can give the orders," Andy said.

"Well, yes, he can," Doubting George admitted. "But he'd be wrong if he did."

"By the gods!" Colonel Andy burst out. "When in the hells has that ever stopped one of our generals, or even slowed the stupid son of a bitch down?"

"Do bear in mind, Colonel, that you are presently talking to one of those stupid sons of bitches," George said. Andy had the grace to look embarrassed, though George suspected he wasn't, or not very. The general commanding continued, "And I don't happen to think I'm wrong in delaying. If I did, I wouldn't." He listened to himself to make sure he'd said what he meant there. After a bit of thought, he decided he had.

Andy, however, still looked unhappy. "Maybe we ought to move forward now, sir. If Bell gets reinforcements—"

"Where?" George broke in, shaking his head. "What are the odds of that? Whatever he can scrape up, he's got."

"*I* don't know where he'd get them," Andy said petulantly. "I just think we ought to hit him as hard as we can as soon as we can."

"And we will," George said. "But that isn't quite yet, in my opinion. And mine is the opinion that counts."

"Not if Marshal Bart removes you," his adjutant said.

"He won't." Doubting George sounded more confident than he felt.

"What if, while you're waiting for your brigades, Bell comes up with a new strong wizard?" Andy asked.

"From where?" George asked again. "If the northerners have any decent mages who aren't already wearing blue robes, you can bet your last piece of silver it's news to Bell and Geoffrey both. Besides, even if Bell does come up with one, Alva will handle him." He patted Andy on the shoulder. "Cheer up. Everything will be fine."

"I doubt it," Andy said, in exactly the tone George would have used. George found himself with no reply.

Brigadier of the regulars. The words—and what they betokened—sang within John the Lister. Up till he could use those words about himself, he'd almost dreaded the end of the War Between the Provinces. He enjoyed being a brigadier, and he thought he'd proved he did a good job at that rank. To drop down to a captain's meager command would have been hard.

To drop down to a captain's meager pay would have been even harder.

He didn't have to worry about that any more. He would hold brigadier's rank till he died or retired. He wouldn't have to go out to some steppe castle in the middle of nowhere and listen to wild wolves and wilder blonds howling outside the walls. Doubting George had said he would recommend him for promotion, and he'd kept his promise. Marshal Bart and King Avram had recognized what John did at Poor Richard. Now all the southrons had left to do was finish squashing Lieutenant General Bell and the Army of Franklin.

For some reason John couldn't fathom, Doubting George didn't seem to want to do that. There the traitors *were*, out on ridges in plain sight of Ramblerton. They didn't even have enough men to stretch their line all the way across the neck of the loop of the Cumbersome River in which the capital of Franklin laid. As far as John the Lister could see, outflanking them and rolling them up would be the easiest thing in the world.

Why didn't George want to move?

John knew he wasn't the only one who had trouble finding an answer. Most of the officers inside Ramblerton kept scratching their heads, wondering what George was doing—or rather, why he wasn't doing it. And the rumors that came out of the scryers' hall . . .

Rumors like that came out all the time. More often than not, soldiers had the sense to ignore them. This time . . . John the Lister shook his head. How could you ignore rumors that Bart was threatening to sack Doubting George? How could you ignore rumors that Bart was threatening to leave the siege of Pierreville and come east, either taking command in Ramblerton himself or appointing George's replacement?

You couldn't. It was that simple. Whenever two

officers—hells, whenever two soldiers—got together, the gossip started up afresh. Some people started saying John the Lister ought to take Doubting George's place. When a colonel did it in John's hearing, he rounded on the man. "I am not going to replace Lieutenant General George," he growled. "I don't think George needs replacing. Do you understand me?"

"Uh, yes, sir," the man answered, his eyes wide with surprise.

"You'd better, Colonel," John said. "If I hear you've been spouting more of this disruptive gossip, I won't be the only one who hears about it. I hope I make myself plain enough?"

"Uh, yes, sir," the unhappy colonel said again, and retreated faster than General Guildenstern had fallen back from the River of Death.

That wasn't enough to satisfy John the Lister. He went and told Doubting George what had happened, though he named no names. He finished, "Sir, I don't want you to think I'm intriguing against you."

"I'm glad to hear it," George replied. "Now the question is, do you want me not to think that because you're not doing it or because you really are intriguing against me but you want to keep me in the dark?"

"What?" John the Lister needed several heartbeats to work through that. When he did, he stared at the commanding general with something approaching horror. "That's the most twisted bit of thinking I do believe I've ever run into, sir."

"Thank you," Doubting George replied, which only flummoxed John further. George continued, "Now answer the question, if you'd be so kind."

"Sir, I am not intriguing against you, and that is the truth," John said stiffly. "If you don't believe me, go fetch Major Alva and let him find out by magic."

He didn't fear what might happen if Doubting

George did that. He'd told the general commanding the truth: he'd shown no disloyalty in word, deed, or manner. On the contrary. That didn't mean he would have been unhappy if Marshal Bart booted George out of the command and set him in George's place. Again, on the contrary. Ambition, he told himself, was different from disloyalty.

He didn't care for the smile that played on what he could see of George's lips behind the other officer's thick beard and mustache. Still smiling that unpleasant smile, George said, "I won't sic Major Alva on you if I think you're scheming against me, Brigadier. I'll just dismiss you. Have you got that?"

"Yes, sir," John replied. "You leave me no room for, er, doubt." Doubting George laughed out loud. John went on, "But may I ask you one different question?"

"Go right ahead." George was the picture of northern hospitality.

"Sir, why the hells *won't* you attack Bell?" John the Lister blurted.

"Why? Because the son of a bitch isn't going anywhere, and I'm not quite ready to give him what-for yet. I want those last couple of brigades from the far side of the Great River here before I do," George answered. "I tell this over and over to anybody who'll listen, but nobody seems to want to. Is it so godsdamned hard to grasp?" He sounded as plaintive as a commanding general was ever likely to.

"Sir, he's right in front of us. He's just waiting to be hit. If we can't whip him with what we've got here . . ."

"If we can't, we'd be stupid to try, especially when those brigades are almost here," Doubting George said.

"But I think we can!" John the Lister said.

"That's nice." George sounded placid. Whether he was . . . Well, now John was the doubting one. The commanding general went on, "If Marshal Bart bounces me and names you in my place, you can go charging forth just as though you'd borrowed Bell's brains, such as they are. Meanwhile, you'd better do what I tell you. We'll both be unhappy if you don't, but you'll end up unhappier. I promise you that, Brigadier."

"Yes, sir," John the Lister said. "If you'll excuse me, sir . . ." He waited for Doubting George's affable nod, then left George's headquarters at something just this side of a run.

Still steaming, he hurried up the muddy, puddle-splashed streets of Ramblerton till brick buildings gave way to log huts and log huts gave way to bare-branched broad-leafed trees and brooding, dark green pines. The southrons' line of fortifications abridged the forest along the ridges north of Ramblerton. John ascended to a sentry tower in the nearest fort. The sentry in the tower was so startled to have a brigadier appear at his elbow, he almost fell out of his observation chamber coming to attention when John did.

"Give me your spyglass," John barked.

"Sir?" The sentry gaped.

"Give me your gods-damned spyglass," John the Lister said again.

Numbly, the sentry handed over the long, gleaming brass tube. John raised it to his eye and swept it over the traitors' lines. Lieutenant General Bell's soldiers seemed to leap toward him. Mages insisted spyglasses weren't sorcery: only a clever use of the mechanic arts. No matter what the mages said, the effect always seemed magical to John.

Now, almost as if he were standing in front of its parapets, he could see the Army of Franklin in action, and in inaction. Scrawny men in tattered blue tunics and pantaloons, many of the poor bastards barefoot, lined up in front of kettles to get their midday meals.

They looked more like the survivors of some disaster than an army that probably imagined it was laying siege to Ramblerton. The earthworks they'd thrown up were very fresh and new, but they didn't have many soldiers in them.

John scanned the northerners' position, trying to spy out how many unicorn-riders they had with them. Fewer than he'd expected. He wondered if some of them had gone off to raid somewhere else. *He* wouldn't have divided his forces in the face of an enemy that outnumbered him. What Bell would do, though, was liable to be known only unto the gods.

Back swung John's narrow circle of vision. Suddenly, the spyglass stopped. There was some northern sentry or officer looking straight back at him out of a spyglass of his own. The traitor's glass had stopped moving, too. Had he spotted John watching him? By way of experiment, John raised his left hand, the one that wasn't holding the spyglass, and waved.

Sure as hells, the soldier in the Army of Franklin waved back. John laughed and lowered the spyglass. The southron sentry's face was a mask of perplexity. "What's so funny, sir?" he asked.

John the Lister told him. The sentry nodded. "Oh, yes, I've seen that son of a bitch. I don't know that he's ever seen me, but I've seen him. He's got the very same kind of spyglass as mine."

"Well, of course," John said. "We all have the same kind of stuff. The traitors took whatever was in their provinces when they declared for false King Geoffrey, and they've been using it ever since."

Yet even though he'd said *of course* to the sentry, it wasn't something about which he'd thought much before. It was worth remembering. The two branches of the Detinan trunk had spent the past three and a half years showing each other how different they were.

Yet they were without question branches from the same trunk. Even if the northerners wanted to hold on to their serfs and their great estates while manufactories and glideways spread across the south, both sides still spoke the same language, worshiped the same gods— and even used the same tactical manual for training their soldiers. Roast-Beef William, who'd written it, fought for Geoffrey these days, and had the unlucky assignment of trying to stop General Hesmucet's march across Peachtree Province toward the Western Ocean. If he could have scraped up even a quarter as many men as Hesmucet commanded, he might have had a chance. As things were . . .

"As things are, he's in just as much trouble as Bell and the gods-damned Army of Franklin," John the Lister said.

"Who is, sir?" the sentry asked.

"Never you mind." John descended from the observation tower as abruptly as he'd climbed to the top of it. Looking over the traitors' position had only gone further to convince him that they were ready for the taking now. Maybe if he dragged Doubting George up here and made him look with his own eyes . . .

And if that doesn't work, John thought, *to the seven hells with me if I wouldn't be tempted to take that spyglass and shove it up his . . .* A subordinate wasn't supposed to have such ideas about his superior. Whether John was supposed to or not, he did.

He was just coming back to the outskirts of Ramblerton when a young officer on unicornback waved to him. "Brigadier John!" the other man called. "Congratulations on your promotion in the ranks of the regulars."

"Thank you kindly, Jimmy," John the Lister said, and then, "Do you mind if I ask you a question?"

"Ask away," Hard-Riding Jimmy answered. "After

what we went through around Poor Richard, we'd better be able to talk to each other, eh?"

"Do you think we can whip the traitors with the men we've got here already?"

"Me, sir? Hells, yes! I'm within shouting distance of being able to do it all by myself," Jimmy said. "I've picked up a ton of reinforcements, and they've all got quick-shooting crossbows. Send me around their flank and into their rear and I'll rip 'em to shreds."

"Would you tell that to Doubting George?" John asked eagerly.

"I already have," the commander of unicorn-riders answered.

"And?" John said.

Hard-Riding Jimmy shrugged. "And he wants to wait a bit."

"Why?" John the Lister asked in something not far from desperation. "Why does George want to wait, in the name of the Thunderer's great right fist? Why does he *need* to wait?"

"He's the general commanding." Jimmy shrugged again. "Officers who're in charge do whatever they please, no matter how silly it is." He tipped his hat to John. "Meaning no disrespect, of course."

"Of course." John's voice was sour. What had *he* done that Hard-Riding Jimmy thought silly? He decided not to ask. The younger man was too likely to tell him. Instead, he said, "You do agree George is making a mistake by not attacking the Army of Franklin?"

"I don't know if it's a mistake or not," Jimmy said. "He says he can whip Bell whenever he pleases. Maybe he's right; maybe he's wrong. If he's wrong, waiting is a mistake. If he's right, what the hells difference does it make? I will say this much, though: if I were in charge here, I'd've hit the traitors a couple-three days ago. I already told you that."

"Yes. You did. I'm glad to hear it again, though. Now, the next question is, what can we do either to get George moving or to get a commanding general who *will* move?"

Hard-Riding Jimmy studied him. John the Lister didn't care for that sober scrutiny. The commander of unicorn-riders likely suspected him of wanting that command for himself. He'd told George he wouldn't intrigue for it, and here he was, intriguing. *I wouldn't, if only George would move*, he thought. At last, Hard-Riding Jimmy said, "*We* can't do anything, sir. But Marshal Bart *can*."

VII

Papers in Ramblerton could not print everything they chose. Most of them, had they had a choice, would have backed the cause of false King Geoffrey. As a southron army had held Ramblerton for more than two and a half years, they didn't have that choice. Doubting George had several officers deciding what the papers could and couldn't say. Editors screamed of tyranny. But they printed what George wanted them to print— or else, as had happened, they abruptly stopped doing business.

The *Ramblerton Record* was not conspicuously better or worse than any of the other surviving dailies. Because the army kept an eye on them (and, when necessary, a thumb as well), they all tended to sound alike. Doubting George preferred the *Record* because its type was a little larger than those of its rivals. He could read it without bothering to put on spectacles.

As its chief story this morning, it carried a speech King Avram had made to his council of ministers a few days before. Would it have done that without . . . encouragement from those southron officers? "I doubt it," George murmured, and peered at the paper.

Avram said, *The most remarkable feature in the military operations of the year is General Hesmucet's attempted march of three hundred miles, directly through the insurgent region. It tends to show a great increase of our relative strength that our Marshal should feel able to confront and hold in check every active force of the enemy, and yet to detach a well-appointed large army to move on such an expedition.*

Doubting George made a sour face. The King of Detina thought—or said he thought—the traitors were stopped all over the map. Why didn't Marshal Bart think the same way? George feared he knew—Bart was trying to drive him out of his mind. The marshal was doing a pretty good job of it, too.

And am I trying to drive Marshal Bart out of his mind? George shook his big head. He wasn't *trying* to do anything of the sort. He was trying to get rid of the Army of Franklin, and to make sure he didn't get rid of his own army instead. If Bart couldn't see that . . . then, gods damn him, he'd give the army to someone else.

Muttering—he'd distracted himself—Doubting George returned to the *Ramblerton Record*. King Avram continued, *On careful consideration of all the evidence accessible it seems to me that no attempt at negotiation with the insurgent leader could result in any good. He would accept nothing short of severance of the Kingdom—precisely what we will not and cannot give. He does not attempt to deceive us. He affords us no excuse to deceive ourselves. He cannot voluntarily reaccept the unity of Detina; we cannot voluntarily yield it. It is an issue which can only be tried by war, and decided by victory. If we yield, we are beaten; if the northern people fail him, he is beaten.*

The more George studied Avram's speeches, the more he became convinced the rightful King of Detina was a very clever man. He hadn't thought so when Avram took the throne. The new king's uncompromising attitude on serfdom had prejudiced him. He saw that now.

He had to open the *Record* to an inside page to find out the rest of what Avram had told his ministers. *What is true, however, of him who heads the insurgent cause, is not necessarily true of those who follow. Although he cannot accept the united Kingdom of Detina, they can. Some of them, we know, already desire peace and reunion. They can, at any moment, have peace simply by laying down their arms and submitting to the royal authority. A year ago general pardon and amnesty, upon specified terms, were offered to all, except certain designated classes; and, it was, at the same time, made known that the excepted classes were still within contemplation of special clemency. During the year many availed themselves of the general provision. During the same time also special pardons have been granted to individuals of the excepted classes, and no voluntary application has been denied.*

Doubting George had to read that twice. He hadn't realized King Avram was so reasonable, so merciful. Was the king softening on serfdom, too?

He got his answer right away, for Avram finished, *In presenting the abandonment of armed resistance to the royal authority on the part of the insurgents, as the only indispensable condition to ending the war on the part of the Kingdom, I retract nothing heretofore said as to serfdom. In stating a single condition of peace, I mean simply to say that the war will cease on the part of the Kingdom, whenever it shall have ceased on the part of those who began it.*

No, Avram hadn't softened. As well as more wit, there was also more iron in the King of Detina than anyone would have suspected when the Thunderer's chief hierophant first set the crown on his head. A few days afterwards, another hierophant of the Thunderer had put a different crown, hastily made for the occasion, on Grand Duke Geoffrey's head up in the north. Not much later, Avram and Geoffrey had stopped talking and started fighting. They'd been fighting ever since.

"Matter of fact, Avram makes a pretty fair King of Detina," Doubting George murmured. He'd sided with Avram when he hadn't believed that at all, out of loyalty to the notion of a united Detina rather than from any particular loyalty to or admiration of the sovereign. A lot of people, in the north and even in the south, had expected Avram to make a dreadful hash of things. But he hadn't, and it didn't look as if he would.

Colonel Andy knocked on George's door, which was open. When George waved for him to come in, he said, "Sir, there's a scryer here who wants to talk with you. Do you want to talk with him?"

Scryers, lately, had brought little but bad news. Even so, George shrugged and nodded. "I'd better, don't you think?"

"Who knows?" Andy turned away and spoke to a man in the antechamber: "Go ahead, but don't you waste the general's time."

"I won't, sir." The scryer, a captain, wore a gray mage's robe, his epaulets of rank, a sorcerer's badge, and a gold—in fact, probably polished brass—crystal ball to show his specialization. He shut the door on Andy after he came inside. Doubting George's adjutant let out a squawk, but the scryer ignored him. To George, he said, "This is for your ears alone."

The commanding general reached up and tugged at one of the organs in question. "Seems to be in tolerable working order," he observed. "Say your say, Captain—?"

"I'm called Bartram, sir. Bartram the Traveler." Bartram was somewhere in his thirties, with a long, lean, mournful face and sad, clever, hound-dog eyes. He gave off a feeling of reliability. Some people did. Some of those people also let you down, as George was painfully well aware. The scryer coughed a couple of times, then said, "My hobby, sir, is looking for ways to read crystal balls that ought to be out of range."

"Some people grow roses. Some people raise snakes. You never can tell," George said.

"Er—well—yes," Captain Bartram said. "But I wouldn't be here now if I did those things."

"I suppose not. You'd probably be happier if you weren't, too," Doubting George said, though he wondered whether Bartram could be happy anywhere. His face denied the possibility. The commanding general went on, "Since you *are* here, suppose you go ahead and tell me why."

"Yes, sir. I'm here because of some of the things I heard when I was fooling around with my crystal ball late last night. They stretch farther then. I don't know why, but they do."

"And what you heard was—?" George tried to project an air of expectant waiting.

"Sir, what I heard was orders for Baron Logan the Black to hop on a glideway carpet and head east to take command of this army. And what I heard was Marshal Bart saying he'd come east, too, to take charge of Logan."

"Did you, now?" George said slowly, as if he came from the Sapphire Isle. Now he tried not to show the anger he felt. Logan the Black wasn't a regular at all.

Hesmucet had declined to let him keep command of a wing when he took it over after James the Bird's Eye was killed outside Marthasville. And now Marshal Bart wanted to hand him command of a whole army? Of *this* whole army? If that wasn't an insult, Doubting George had never run into one.

"What will you do, sir?" Bartram the Traveler asked. "I thought you ought to know."

"I will do just what I am doing," George replied. "I don't see what else I can do. If Bart wants to show me the door for doing what I think is right, then that's what he will do. I don't intend to lose any sleep over it."

That sounded very pretty. George wished it were true. When he saw Captain Bartram's expression, he wished it were convincing; he would have traded truth for that. *Of course, in war, sometimes we can turn what's convincing into what's true, as long as the bastards on the other side don't see behind it.*

Since he obviously wasn't being convincing here, though, that didn't apply. Bartram said, "Sir, maybe you really ought to attack now."

"Even you, Bartram?" George said. Then he surprised even himself by starting to laugh.

"What the hells is funny, sir?" the scryer blurted. He started to apologize.

Doubting George held up a hand. "Don't worry about that, Captain. It's one of the most honest things I've heard lately. And I'll even give you the answer. John the Lister is another one who's been nagging me to do what I don't care to do just yet. He has to have wondered if he'd take over this army once Marshal Bart gave me the boot. Now we know—he wouldn't. He can't like the idea of serving under Logan the Black. So I suspect he'll stay loyal as loyal can be for as long as I keep command."

"You've still got two or three days, sir," Bartram the Traveler said. "Maybe even four. Baron Logan will come east to Cloviston, then north from there to here. Marshal Bart will have to sail from Pierreville down to Georgetown, and then he'll hop on the glideway, too. He's a few days behind Logan."

"I see. Thank you for putting everything so precisely," George said. "One more thing I need to ask you: how reliable is all this? When you're playing with your crystal ball there, you're not just imagining you're hearing what you're hearing, are you?"

"No, sir," Bartram replied. "I'm doing the same sorts of things we do when we try to read the northerners' crystal balls, except I'm doing them to our own side. And I have some tricks not every scryer knows. Quite a few tricks not every scryer knows, if I do say so myself." He drew himself up with pride.

Doubting George wondered whether to congratulate him or clap him in the brig. Finding out what you wanted to know regardless of whether you were supposed to know it was a very Detinan thing to do. If the individual was altogether free and untrammeled, the kingdom would surely be free, too, wouldn't it? *I don't know. Would it?* As usual, George had his doubts. The kingdom might go down the drain instead.

He said, "Since no one has bothered telling *me* Logan the Black is on the way to steal my command, do me the courtesy of keeping this under your hat till it *is* official, if you'd be so kind."

"Yes, sir." Bartram touched the brim of that hat with a forefinger in what wasn't quite a salute. "You can count on me."

"Thank you, Captain." George nodded. The scryer left. George sighed. If he'd been Guildenstern, he would have reached for a bottle of brandy. Being who he was, he just sighed again. Before long, the news *would* get out: if not from Bartram the Traveler, then rushing ahead of Baron Logan. *Gods damn his thieving soul*, Doubting George thought. That wasn't fair. He didn't care. Bart wasn't being fair to him, either.

He wanted to rush to the scryers' room and find out exactly how far away those two brigades of foot-soldiers from the east were. He wanted to, but he didn't. If he showed worry, people would start wondering why. If they started wondering, they would find out before long. And a lot of his authority would fly right out the window if they found out.

He went outside, shaking off Colonel Andy's questions. *Maybe I ought to attack the Army of Franklin without those two brigades.* George shook his head. He still felt—he strongly felt—he would do better to wait. What happened to his career was one thing. What happened to his men was something else again, something much more important.

If Baron Logan the Black took over this army, of course, *he* would attack regardless of whether those brigades had come. Doubting George understood that. Logan would be taking over for the purpose of immediate attack. As long as he got a victory out of it, would he care what happened to the army? George shook his head. "Not fornicating likely," he muttered.

"Hey, General!" a soldier called. George's head came up. The man went on, "Do you doubt we can lick those stinking traitors? Turn us loose! We'll do it!" Without waiting for an answer, he tipped his cap and went on his way.

Doubting George laughed in something not far from despair. How many times in the War Between the Provinces had generals from both sides sent their men out to do things flesh and blood simply could not do? More times than anyone could hope to count; George doubted that not at all. But how many times had generals held back from an attack their soldiers actually wanted to make? If this wasn't the first, he would have been astonished.

Does that mean I'm wrong? he wondered. When he shook his head, it was at first with the air of a man bedeviled by bees, or at least by doubts. But then his resolve stiffened. He earned his pay because he allegedly knew more about what he was doing than the men he commanded.

"Allegedly," he said. Much of the soldier's art was obvious. Advancing crossbowmen and pikemen usually had a pretty good notion of whether they would prevail even before bolts started flying. *Maybe I am wrong here*, George thought. *Maybe I am—but I still doubt it.*

"Logan the Black?" John the Lister stared as if he'd never heard the name in all his born days. "Baron Logan the Black? Bart's sending *him* to take over this army? He's not even an Annasville man!"

Colonel Nahath shrugged. "That's what I heard, sir. A couple of blonds who serve the scryers were gossiping about it, and one of my men, a corporal, listened to 'em. They didn't shut up because he's a blond himself. I thought you ought to know."

"Thanks—I think," John told the regimental commander from New Eborac.

"I understand how you must feel, sir," Nahath said sympathetically. "If Doubting George doesn't use this army . . ."

He stopped right there: that was the place where another word would go too far. *If George doesn't use this army, you ought to*, might get back to Baron Logan if he did oust Doubting George. If Logan ever heard that, he was likely to make both John and Nahath sorry for it.

"Nothing we can do, is there?" Colonel Nahath said, changing course.

"Doesn't seem to be," John answered. "If the enemy gives us a hard time, we can always go out and fight him. I know Doubting George doesn't seem to want to, but we *can*. But who's going to protect us from the people on the same side as we are? No one ever has. No one ever will."

"I suppose not." Nahath sighed. "Seems a pity, doesn't it? George has done so much good here in the east—and so have you, sir. You ripped the guts out of Bell's army at Poor Richard, same way a tiger will rip the guts out of a sheep with his hind claws. They're a sorry lot now. Have you seen them?"

"Seen them? I've even been up in an observation tower with a spyglass. They're close enough for a man with a decent glass to see how many of 'em are barefoot."

"I know." Colonel Nahath nodded. "But they've still got pikes and crossbows and some engines. And they still don't like us. When we do attack them, they'll fight hard." He sighed again. "I've never yet seen those bastards *not* fight hard. The first time would be nice. I don't suppose I'd better hold my breath."

"No, I don't think you should, Colonel," John the Lister said. "They'll always fight hard. But if we can beat 'em once more, beat 'em the way they should be beaten, what'll they have left to fight with after that?"

"Teeth. Fingernails. Ghosts," Nahath answered. "That might be enough to scare some blonds—though that corporal I was telling you about would be angry if he heard me say so—but it doesn't frighten me. If we beat 'em once more, sir, I think you're right. I think they fall to pieces." He tipped his hat. "I think we *can* give 'em that beating, too. If it's not under Doubting

George, I also think it's a gods-damned shame you don't get the chance to do it." There. He'd come out and said it.

"That's very kind of you, Colonel. I do appreciate it, believe me."

The regimental commander shrugged. "I'm telling you what I think, sir. I'm just as much a free Detinan as Baron Logan the Black, even if he's got a fancier pedigree than I do. He's a brave man. He's a good soldier, for a man who's not a regular. But we've been through this whole campaign, and he hasn't. A man who has ought to be in charge when it all pays off. That's how I look at things, anyhow." Nahath shrugged again. "Marshal Bart's liable to look at it differently."

"Looks like he does," John said. Nahath nodded, saluted, and went on his way.

John strode down the board sidewalks and muddy streets of Ramblerton. Here was a town unusual in the Kingdom of Detina: a town with plenty of men of fighting age on the streets and going about their ordinary, everyday business. In most places, south and north, a large number of them would have been called to serve the gold dragon or the red. Not here. The southrons who occupied Ramblerton didn't trust the locals to fight on their side, and they'd done their best to keep those men from slipping out of town and fighting for King Geoffrey. And so, in between one side and the other, the Ramblertonians had what neither side enjoyed: peace.

Having it, they refused to enjoy it. One of them jeered at John as he went by: "You southron bastards are scared to fight General Bell. You've never been anything but a pack of stinking cowards."

John smiled his politest smile. "We're winning," he said, and kept walking.

"Blond-lover!" the Ramblertonian shouted.

Smiling still, John answered, "Well, most of the blonds I've thought of loving are a lot prettier than your sister."

The man thought about that for two or three heartbeats. Then, bellowing like an aurochs in the mating season, he lowered his head and charged. No matter how furious he was, though, he'd never really learned anything about fighting. That was what the occupation of Ramblerton had done to the men who lived there: it had deprived them of the chance to become efficient killers.

John the Lister sidestepped and hit the local in the pit of the stomach with his left fist. "Oof!" the man said: a sound more of surprise and outgushing air than of pain. Pain or no, though, he folded up like a concertina. John straightened him with an uppercut to the point of the chin.

His foe was made of solid stuff. He stayed on his feet after that shot to the jaw, though his eyes went glassy. John the Lister's sword hissed from its scabbard. Far more often than not, a brigadier's sword was a parade weapon, nothing more.

High-ranking officers seldom came close enough to enemies in the field to use steel against them. Half a dozen of Bell's brigadiers had died fighting in the front ranks at Poor Richard, but that was as unusual as everything else about the battle there.

But even though John seldom used the blade, he kept it sharp. Its point caressed the Ramblertonian's throat just below the edge of his beard. Wan late-autumn sunshine glittered off the bright blade.

"You were just leaving, weren't you?" John inquired in honeyed tones.

Blinking—and swaying more than a little—the local stood there with his mouth hanging open, trying to make his wits work enough to answer. A small trickle of blood ran from the corner of his mouth down into his beard. "Yes," he said at last. "I reckon maybe I was."

To make sure he was, his friends grabbed him and hauled him away from John the Lister. "He'd better be careful," John called after them. "He might run into another southron coward and not live through it."

None of them answered, which he thought mean-spirited.

If one southron can whip one northerner, how many southrons do we need to whip all the northerners in the Army of Franklin? John wondered. *Fewer than we've already got, I think.*

Most of the other southron officers in Ramblerton came up with the same answer. Doubting George had a different one. He was in command, and so his answer was the one that counted.

But how long would he stay in command? What sort of answer would Logan the Black come up with when he got here from the west? John the Lister had no trouble figuring that out. Logan would attack. He would probably win, too. And whatever glory there was would go to him.

If it doesn't go to George, it ought to go to me. John had thought that before. It did him exactly no good. He wasn't the one who got to apportion such things. Marshal Bart was, and Bart had chosen Baron Logan.

He can give out glory, John thought wonderingly. *If that doesn't make a man a god on earth, what would?*

Then he shook his head. Bart could give out the chance for glory. There was no guarantee Logan the Black could seize it. But after John looked north toward the Army of Franklin's curtailed lines, he let out a long sigh. If Logan couldn't whip Lieutenant General Bell— if *anybody* couldn't whip Lieutenant General Bell—now, he didn't *deserve* glory.

A man in a gray robe came out of a building on the

far side of the street: a tall, skinny, graceless man who looked as if he would fall over in a strong breeze. John the Lister waved to him. "Major Alva!" he called.

After a moment of blinking and staring and obviously trying to recall who this person wanting his attention was, Alva waved back. "Hello, sir," he said, and trotted across the street toward John. An ass-drawn wagon full of barrels bore down on him. The teamster aboard the wagon jerked the reins hard. Braying resentfully, the asses stopped less than a yard from Alva. The teamster cursed like . . . *like a teamster*, thought John, who was too horrified at the sight of the best southron wizard east of the Green Ridge Mountains—and very possibly west of them, too—barely escaping destruction to indulge himself with fancy literary figures.

What was even more horrifying was that Alva himself had no idea he'd just escaped destruction. The braying jackasses and cursing teamster? The rattling wagon full of barrels? As far as he was concerned, they might have been in New Eborac City or on the far side of the moon. That meant he was liable to do something else just as idiotic this afternoon or day after tomorrow, and luck and a foul-mouthed teamster might not be enough to keep him safe then.

"Is something wrong, sir?" he asked, which meant that John the Lister's horror must have been even more obvious than he thought.

"You should be more careful when you cross the street, Major," John got out after considerable effort.

"You're right," Alva said gravely. That cheered John till the mage went on, "I almost stepped in a couple of mud puddles there. Only fool luck I didn't, I suppose."

"Mud puddles," John muttered. He shook his head. "The gods must watch over you, because you certainly don't seem to be able to take care of it for yourself."

"What do you mean, sir?" Alva asked. John spread his hands. It wasn't that he couldn't explain. But he could see explaining would be as useless as explaining the facts of life to a bullfrog. Then Alva brightened. "Whatever it is, I hope it can wait. I've been meaning to congratulate you on your promotion, and this is the first chance I've had."

"Er—thank you." John wouldn't have bet that Alva knew the difference between a captain and a brigadier. His attitude toward subordination argued against it.

But the wizard said, "You're welcome. Making brigadier in the regulars will set you up for after the war."

He'd already shown he was thinking about what he would do once the War Between the Provinces finally ended. Maybe he was thinking about what everyone would do once the war ended. John nodded and said, "I hope so, anyhow. Are the traitors up to anything sorcerous that's strange or out of the ordinary?"

"What an interesting question, sir," Major Alva said. "As a matter of fact, I was checking on them yesterday afternoon. You never can tell about those people."

"Well, no," John the Lister said. "We are fighting a war with them, if you recall. What did your check show?"

"Nothing," Alva replied. "Oh, not a great big glow-in-the-dark Nothing, the kind that can only mean somebody's hiding a great big ugly, nasty Something behind it. But as far as I can tell, Bell's mages are just doing the usual kinds of things mages in an army do—healing, scrying, investigating for a what-do-you-call-it. . . ."

He didn't explain. "A what-do-you-call-it?" John asked.

"You know, where they try to find out whether a son of a bitch really is a son of a bitch," Alva said helpfully.

However helpful he meant to be, he wasn't. And then, all of a sudden, a light went on inside John's head. "A court-martial!" he exclaimed.

"Yes, one of those." It was, plainly, all the same to Alva. The wizard went on, "Anyhow, uh, sir, they're doing that kind of thing, but I don't see them doing anything much else: nothing that they're showing, anyhow."

"Could they hide it from you?" John the Lister asked.

Alva looked indignant. No—Alva looked offended. "The bunglers Bell's got with him? They couldn't hide their prongs when they pull up their pantaloons . . . sir," he said scornfully.

John the Lister had never heard a southron wizard talk that way about his northern opposite numbers. Most southron sorcerers viewed the northerners with fearful respect. Most of them needed to. Not Alva, and he didn't.

The thump of drums, the skirl of horns, and the wail of pipes came from the south, from the banks of the Cumbersome. Alva peered. "Look!" he said in childish delight. "A parade!"

And so it was. Their musicians leading the way, flags flying, regiment after regiment of tough-looking southron soldiers in gray tunics and pantaloons marched from the river north toward the encampments by Doubting George's field fortifications. For a little while, John the Lister simply watched them, as Major Alva did. Then, realizing who those soldiers had to be, he muttered, "By the gods!"

"What is it, sir?" Alva asked.

"Curse me if those aren't the two brigades from the far side of the Great River."

"That's nice," the wizard said agreeably. "What about 'em?"

"What about 'em?" John echoed. "This about 'em: they're the men Doubting George has been waiting for the past two weeks. He's said he couldn't attack Bell without 'em. Now they're here. I wonder if he really will attack now that they are."

"Why wouldn't he?" Alva asked. "I mean, if he did say that—"

"People can come up with all sorts of excuses for not doing what they don't want to do," John answered. "I don't know whether George has done that. By the Lion God's fangs, I hope he hasn't. But we're going to find out, because he hasn't got any other excuses left."

Lieutenant Griff looked up and down the trench. His larynx, big as an apple, bobbed up and down in his throat. He called, "Are you men ready to do all you can for good King Avram and for Detina?"

"Yes, sir!" Corporal Rollant shouted. He gripped the staff of the company standard hard enough to whiten his knuckles. His voice wasn't the only one eagerly raised, either. He hoped Bell's men were too far away to hear the southrons yelling. He thought they were, but he wasn't sure. His comrades all along the line were making a lot of noise.

"We've waited a long time for this now," Griff said. "Some people will tell you we've waited *too* long. There's all sorts of stupid talk going about. You'll have heard it. Some folks say a new commander for us is coming from the west. Some folks say Marshal Bart is on his way here. Some even say a new commander *and* Bart are heading this way. In a few days, maybe all that would have mattered. But it won't now. And do you know why?"

"Why?" the men called.

Lieutenant Griff, who'd cupped a hand in back of

his ear waiting for just that call, grinned at them. "I'll tell you why. Because we're going to lick the hells out of the gods-damned traitors before *anybody* can get here from the west. *That's* why!"

A great cheer erupted, as if the southrons had already gone and won their battle. Rollant gripped the flagpole harder than ever. Were they all deaf over there in Bell's lines? Well, it wouldn't matter for long, because the southrons were going to come forth from the line of forts they'd held for the past couple of weeks. When they did, the northerners would no longer have any possible doubt about what they intended.

Rollant's regiment, along with the rest of the wing John the Lister commanded, was stationed on the right of Doubting George's line. John's men were, in fact, the rightmost footsoldiers in the line. Out beyond them were only Hard-Riding Jimmy's unicorn-riders.

Horns screamed, all along the southrons' front. "Forward!" Colonel Nahath shouted in a great voice. "Forward for good King Avram! Forward for freedom! Forward because smashing this army of traitors into the dust at last takes a long step toward winning the war!"

"Forward!" Lieutenant Griff yelled. "Avram and victory!" His voice would never be very deep, but it didn't crack. He was, bit by bit, growing up.

"Forward!" Sergeant Joram boomed. "We'll whip the stinking traitors out of their boots, or I'll know the reason why." Like any sergeant worth his silver, he wanted his men to fear him more than the enemy.

"Forward!" Rollant yelled. He was an underofficer; he wanted to, and had the right to, make his voice heard. "Forward for freedom!" For him, no other war cry mattered. In the north, he wouldn't have been allowed to wear a sword on his hip, let alone a corporal's stripes on his sleeve.

Beside him, Smitty said, "I'm confused, your high and mighty Corporalship, sir. Which direction should we go in?"

Laughing, Rollant answered, "You can go to hells, Smitty—but take some traitors with you before you do. Come on!"

His breath smoked as he scrambled out of the trench. The day was clear but cold, the sun low in the northeast. He waved the company standard back and forth. More and more southrons came out of the works in front of Ramblerton. They formed their lines and advanced.

Off to the right, Hard-Riding Jimmy's troopers swept out on what looked to be a looping path around the far left of the Army of Franklin. Rollant saw that much, and then stopped worrying about the riders. They still had to beat Ned of the Forest. He knew all about Ned—and when had southrons ever come close to matching what he'd done? Rollant knew the answer to that only too well: never.

He looked to the left. The standard he carried was one of scores—hundreds—sweeping forward at the same time. The right was a little in front of the center, where the banners seemed a little farther apart. Off to the left, he thought the standards were tightly bunched once more. He wasn't so sure of that, though, as the left was a long way off.

Here and there, stones and firepots arced through the air toward the oncoming southrons from behind the northerners' lines. The first ones fell short. Then they began clawing holes in the ranks of the men in gray. Repeating crossbows clattered into action, too. Engineers were pushing the southrons' own catapults and repeating crossbows forward as fast as they could. They soon started shooting back.

Lieutenant Griff brandished his sword. He said, "It

must be true what they say about Bell's army—they haven't got a whole lot of engines left."

"A good thing, too, sir, if anyone wants to know what I think," Rollant answered. "They'd hack us to pieces if they did."

Bell's men had dug shooting pits in front of their first line of trenches, as John the Lister's army had done in front of Poor Richard. Men in blue popped up out of those pits and started sending crossbow quarrels toward the advancing southrons. One hummed past Rollant's ear. Another—*thock!*—punched a hole in the standard he carried. It would have punched a hole in him, too, had it happened to fly a few feet lower.

Behind him, crossbowmen began to shoot at Bell's men. *Zip! Zip!* More bolts flew past, too close for comfort. Every so often, a standard-bearer or an officer got shot in the back "by accident" when someone in the ranks who didn't care for him let fly. As a blond, Rollant knew plenty of people didn't care for him. He couldn't do anything about it now, and tried not to think about it.

Motion ahead and to his right caught his eye. It wasn't, as he'd hoped, Hard-Riding Jimmy's men sweeping down on the traitors' flank. Instead, it was Ned of the Forest's unicorn-riders, red dragon on gold flying from their standards, maneuvering to block Hard-Riding Jimmy and keep him from doing whatever he'd set out to do.

Well, who ever saw a dead unicorn-rider? Rollant thought, not without bitterness. If a footsoldier said that out loud to a unicorn-rider, it was guaranteed to start a fight. That didn't mean Rollant and his comrades didn't think such things, though.

Unicorn-riders lent a touch of style to what would otherwise be vulgar brawls. Past that, on the southron side at least, they'd never been good for much. Maybe Hard-Riding Jimmy could change that. Rollant would believe it when he saw it.

The northerners in the shooting pits ran back toward their own line. "Provincial prerogative!" they shouted, and, "King Geoffrey!"

"Freedom!" Rollant yelled back. "King Avram and freedom!" He took one hand off the flagpole to shake a fist at Bell's men.

Still waving his sword, Lieutenant Griff ran ahead of his men toward the earthen breastwork in front of the northerners' forward trench. "King Avram and one Detina forever!" Griff shouted. Rollant hustled forward to keep up with the company commander. Griff swung the sword again. "Avram and free—"

A crossbow quarrel caught him in the throat. He made a horrible gobbling noise and threw up both hands to clutch at the wound. The sword fell forgotten to the ground. Blood, dreadfully red, fountained out between Griff's fingers. Seeing so much blood, Rollant knew the wound had to be mortal. Griff couldn't have bled much more or much faster if a stone had struck off his head. He staggered on for another couple of steps. Then his knees gave out, and he crumpled to the ground.

Rollant stooped to snatch up the sword he had dropped. An officer's blade, it was half again as long as the stubby weapon the blond carried on his hip. As he bent to take it—shifting the company standard from right hand to left at the same time—another bolt hissed malevolently over his head. If he hadn't bent down, it might have caught him in the face. "Thank you, Thunderer," he muttered. "I'll do something nice for you if you let me live through this fight."

When he straightened, he waved the standard and swung the sword. A standard-bearer, he'd found, had to have some ham in him, or the rest of the men wouldn't follow him the way they should.

And now he had the perfect war cry to make his comrades give all they could. "For Lieutenant Griff!" he shouted, and ran on, past the company commander's body.

"For Lieutenant Griff!" the men behind him roared. Griff's fall meant Sergeant Joram was in charge of the company for the time being. He ran up alongside of Rollant. Joram had his own way of getting the most out of his men. Pointing to Rollant, he bellowed, "Are you sons of bitches going to let this fellow do it all by himself?"

"Sergeant—" Rollant began, and then let it go. He'd already seen that Joram didn't have too much against blonds. The sergeant was also trying to get the men to fight hard. Later might be the time to talk about it. Now wasn't.

"*Avraaaam!*" Joram yelled as he sprang up onto the parapet. He shot one traitor, threw his crossbow in the face of another, drew his shortsword, and leaped down into the trench.

"*Avraaaam!*" Rollant echoed. He jumped down into the trench, too, and spitted a northerner before the man in blue could shoot him.

Another northerner rushed forward, grappling with him to wrestle away the company standard. Struggling and cursing, Rollant couldn't get his arm free enough to stab the enemy soldier. He hit him in the face with the pommel of Lieutenant Griff's sword. Something—probably the northerner's nose—flattened under the impact. The man howled but hung on and tried to trip him. Rollant smashed him again with the weighted pommel. The second blow persuaded the traitor he wasn't going to get what he wanted. He lurched down the trench, his face dripping blood.

More and more southrons jumped into the trench. Northern pikemen rushed up to drive them back. That was bad—pikes had far more reach than shortswords. But southron pikemen joined the fight moments later, thrusting and parrying against their foes. Rollant was too busy trying to stay alive to pay much attention to the details. He did know that southron reinforcements eased the pressure on his comrades. The southrons were into the Army of Franklin's trenches, and it didn't look as if Bell's men could throw them out again.

There was Colonel Nahath, scrambling up out of the first trench and pointing to the next one with his sword. "Come on, boys!" he cried. "Are you going to let a pack of dirty, stinking traitors slow us down?"

"No!" the soldiers shouted. They hurried after the regimental commander. The northerners they fought *were* dirty and stinking. Rollant and his comrades weren't, or not so badly; they'd spent the past couple of weeks in far better quarters than their foes had. A few days in the field, though, and nobody civilized would want to get anywhere near them, either.

"Let's go! Let's go! Let's go!" That was Sergeant Joram, urging his men on. Rollant waved the company standard again. Then he too fought his way up onto the high ground between the trenches. He waved the standard yet again. Joram nodded. "That's the way to do it, Corporal!"

"King Avram!" Rollant yelled, and sprang down into the melee in the second trench. A bolt lifted his hat from his head and carried it away. He didn't even have time to shudder at his narrow escape. He was a standard-bearer, and so a target. He was a blond in a gray uniform, and so a target. He was a blond in a gray uniform who'd had the presumption to fool his superiors into thinking he deserved to be a corporal and bear a standard—so northerners would think of it, anyhow—and so doubly or triply or quadruply a target. He was glad he'd picked up luckless Lieutenant Griff's sword. It gave him more reach than most of his foes had. It wouldn't do anything against crossbow quarrels, of course, but by now the trench was so packed with battling men, hardly anybody could raise a crossbow, let alone aim one.

Again, Bell's men tried to drive the southrons out of the trench. Again, gray-clad reinforcements swamped them. Rollant climbed up over dead bodies—he hoped they were all dead—wearing blue and gained the next stretch of open ground between entrenchments.

"Fancy meeting you here," Smitty said, panting.

Rollant looked him up and down. "You mean they haven't killed you *yet*?" he demanded.

"I don't think so." The other soldier patted himself, as if looking for bolts or a pike or two that might have pierced him when he was busy with something else. He shook his head. "Nope. I still seem to be more or less alive. How about you?"

"About the same, I think. Come on, let's get back to it," Rollant said. "We've pushed 'em pretty hard so far."

"Haven't broken through yet, though." Smitty spoke with a connoisseur's knowledge of what he wanted. "But who knows? We just might."

"Yes." Rollant nodded. "We just might." That was as much of a breather as he allowed himself. He waved the standard and rushed forward into the fight. If the southrons *did* break through at last, he wanted to be part of it. After so much hard struggle, he thought he'd earned the right.

Later that day, a crossbow quarrel nicked his left ear. He bled all over his tunic, but it wasn't even close to a serious wound. A healer put a stitch in it and said, "I don't even think you'll have a scar."

"Oh." Rollant almost felt cheated—with the little wound, and with the battle. The northerners gave ground, but they didn't break. He wanted them ruined, not just driven back. He could see that that smashing victory ought to be there. He could see it, but he couldn't—Doubting George didn't seem able to—find a way to reach out and grab hold of it.

Captain Gremio's regiment, along with the rest of what remained Colonel Florizel's wing, was posted at the far right end of the Army of Franklin's line. "Lieutenant General Bell expects the southrons to concentrate their attack against this wing," Gremio told his company commanders—three captains, four lieutenants, and three sergeants. "You've got to let your men know they'd better fight hard. A lot is liable to depend on them when the southrons move. And I think the southrons are going to move today." As if to underscore his words, the sun rose in the northeast and spilled blood-colored light over their lines and over the works in front of Ramblerton to the south.

Sergeant Thisbe raised a hand. When Gremio nodded, Thisbe asked, "How does Bell know this is where Doubting George aims to hit hardest?"

"I can't tell you that, because Colonel Florizel didn't tell me," Gremio answered. "I don't know whether Bell told his wing commanders how he knows—or why he suspects, I should say." As usual, he spoke with a barrister's relentless precision.

One of the other company commanders—Gremio didn't see who—muttered, "I hope Bell's not right the way he was when he sent us at the southrons' trenches by Poor Richard."

"That will be enough of that," Gremio said sharply. He wished the other man hadn't done such a good job of voicing his own fear. He'd lost faith in the commanding general. That did him exactly no good, as Bell was going to keep right on giving orders regardless of whether Gremio had faith in him. The regimental commander continued, "We ought to get the men fed early, too, in case we do have to fight today."

None of the company commanders quarreled with that. They got the cooks working earlier than usual, and grumbling more than usual on account of it. Even so, only about half the men got breakfast before warning cries from the sentries in the shooting pits out in front of the main line announced that the southrons were indeed coming forth. Gremio got nothing to eat himself. His belly growled in disappointed resentment when he rushed out of the breakfast line and up toward the parapets.

When he looked to the south, his jaw dropped. That wasn't hunger. It was shock. He'd known Avram's soldiers would be moving against the Army of Franklin. He'd known, yes, but he'd never dreamt the move would look like . . . this. From one end of the line to the other, miles of southrons swarmed forward under what looked like thousands of company and regimental standards. The attack might not succeed. Whether it did or not, though, it was the most awe-inspiring thing Gremio had ever seen.

"Forward!" he shouted to his own soldiers. "By the Thunderer's lightning bolt, come forward! We have to beat them back!"

Up came the men, some eating, others complaining they'd got no breakfast. Thisbe's light, clear voice put paid to that: "Will you be happy if you get killed with full bellies?"

Gremio half expected some stubborn soldier to answer *yes*. No one did, or no one he heard. The men filed into the trenches, baggy wool pantaloons flapping as they ran. They loaded their crossbows. Some of them thrust quarrels into the dirt in front of them so they could reload faster.

On came the southrons. It was a couple of miles from their line to the one the Army of Franklin held. *We came that far over open country at Poor Richard,* Gremio thought, *and then they tore hells out of us. Maybe we can do the same to them.*

But it wouldn't be easy. Even the part of the southron army that had fought at Poor Richard had had far more engines than the Army of Franklin boasted. Gremio shook his head. *How can you boast about something you* don't *have?*

Not only that, unicorns were hauling the southrons' catapults and repeating crossbows right along with the rest of the army. Yes, Gremio's side started shooting first, but Doubting George's men wasted no time replying in kind. A stone thudded into the front of the parapet. It didn't plow through, but dirt flew out and hit Gremio in the face.

Farther down the line, a firepot came down on top of the parapet, sending up a great gout of flame and smoke. Another one landed in the trenches. Burning men shrieked, some not for long. With the sulfurous reek of the firepots came the stink of charred flesh.

A soldier on the shooting step suddenly toppled, shot through the head by a long, thick bolt from a repeating crossbow. The scouts in the shooting pits in front of the main line came out and dashed back toward the entrenchments. More than a few of them fell, shot in the back, before they made it. Some of them were shot by their own comrades in the trenches, too. The southrons had made the same mistake at Poor Richard. *Why didn't we learn from them?* Gremio wondered.

Southrons were falling, too. A stone knocked down three men before losing its momentum. Repeating crossbows cut down more. And firepots burst among the soldiers in gray.

"Shoot!" Gremio shouted when he judged the southrons were in range of his men's weapons. Up and down the entrenchment, crossbows clacked and snapped. Men reloaded with frantic haste. Someone not far from Gremio cursed horribly when his bowstring broke. He fit a replacement to the crossbow and went back to the business of slaughter.

Gremio didn't need long to see that the southrons assailing his end of the line were veterans. In the face of what the northern soldiers flung at them, they went to the earth and started shooting back from their bellies. Some of them began to dig in; Gremio watched the dirt fly. Raw troops would have charged home in spite of everything, not knowing any better. They would have paid for it, too, paid gruesomely. The Army of Franklin punished the southrons here, but less than Gremio would have hoped.

Sergeant Thisbe said, "They don't have orders to take our trenches no matter what, the way we did a couple of weeks ago with theirs." The underofficer—now the company commander—sounded bitter. Gremio had a hard time blaming Thisbe for that, not when he was bitter himself.

"We're holding 'em here." Gremio peered off toward the left. "Anybody know how we're doing along the rest of the line?"

He didn't, even after peering. A swell of ground just a little to the east kept him from seeing much. All he could do was wonder—and worry. Even here, where the Army of Franklin seemed to be doing fine, a hells of a lot of southrons were attacking. If Lieutenant General Bell happened to be wrong, if this *wasn't* the stretch where Doubting George's army was pushing hardest, what was happening off to the left, out of

Gremio's sight but, with luck, not out of the commanding general's?

Lieutenant General Bell? Wrong? Gremio laughed. How could anyone possibly imagine Bell making a mistake? The idea was absurd, wasn't it? Of course it was. Up till now, Bell had conducted a perfect campaign, hadn't he? Of course he had. The Army of Franklin had smashed John the Lister at Summer Mountain, hadn't it? And then gone on to destroy John's remnants at Poor Richard?

He shook his head. Some of those things could have happened. Some of those things *should* have happened. But they hadn't. That was at least partly Bell's fault. Could he make another mistake? Gremio knew too well that he could.

Thinking along with him—as the underofficer so often did—Sergeant Thisbe asked, "What if they're hammering us at the far end of the line?"

"Then they are," Captain Gremio replied with a fatalistic shrug. "I don't know what we can do about it except either send reinforcements or run away."

Off to the south, something *roared*. The chill that ran through Gremio had nothing to do with the weather. A roar like that touched him deep in his brain, deep in his belly. A roar like that meant, *Whatever is making this noise wants to eat you—and it can.* Another roar resounded, and another, and another.

The dragons looked old as time, deadly as murder, and graceful enough to make an eagle blush. Their great bat wings effortlessly propelled them toward the northerners' trenches. They took no notice of the southrons out in the open below them. It was as if they'd decided to feast on pork, and didn't care whether mutton was out there waiting for them.

Several northerners didn't wait to be eaten. They

jumped out of the trenches and ran away, as fast as they could go. "Hold!" Gremio shouted, though he wanted nothing more than to run, too.

"Why?" somebody yelled back, fleeing faster than ever.

For a couple of heartbeats, Gremio found himself altogether without an answer. Then the rational part of his mind reasserted itself. "Because they're magical!" he exclaimed. "They aren't real. They *can't* be real. When was the last time anybody saw a dragon that isn't on a flag west of the Great River? Over in the Stony Mountains, out past the eastern steppes, yes. But here? Not a chance!"

"They sure *look* real," someone else said.

And they did. The fire that burst from their jaws looked real, too. More men, not willing to take the chance, scrambled out of the fieldworks and started running away. The southrons shot several of them when they broke cover.

Colonel Florizel limped past. "Don't panic, boys!" he shouted. "It's just the gods-damned southrons telling lies again. What else are they good for?" He nodded to Gremio. "And a fine day to you, Captain. We're doing pretty well here, aren't we?"

"We're holding them, sir, sure enough," Gremio answered. Florizel had limits—anything requiring imagination was beyond his ken. Within those limits, though, he made a pretty good soldier—exactly how good, Gremio had come to understand more slowly than he should have. The captain asked, "How are we doing off to the left? I can't tell from here."

Florizel's face clouded. "Not so well. They've forced back the line there. We may—we likely will—have to fall back here, too, just to keep things straight. I don't think any counterattack at that end will push the southrons out of our works."

Gremio looked over his shoulder. Another ridge line stood a mile or two north of the one the Army of Franklin presently held. He jerked a thumb towards it. "I suppose we'll make another stand there."

"Yes, I suppose we will, too." Florizel nodded. "We've hurt the southrons. They've hurt us, but we've hurt them more than a little. If we can hold off the next attack—if they can even manage another attack, tomorrow or the next day—I'd say we'll have won ourselves a victory . . . and I don't mean the kind Bell says we won at Poor Richard, either." He made a sour face.

"You . . . may be right, your Excellency." Gremio still reckoned Florizel an optimist, but he couldn't say for certain his superior was wrong. Florizel knew more about what was going on than he did. And even an optimist could be right some of the time—Gremio supposed. He said, "Funny how we've held them here, where they were supposed to be pushing hardest, but we had to give ground at the other end of the line."

"Yes, this is a mite strange," Colonel Florizel agreed. "Still and all, though, battle's a funny business. What you figure will happen doesn't, and what you don't does."

"That's true. I wish it weren't, but it is," Gremio said.

"Has my regiment fought well, Captain?" Florizel asked.

"Yes, sir," Gremio answered truthfully.

"Good. It's a funny business of a different sort, you know—needing to ask about the soldiers I commanded for so long."

"You still command us, Colonel."

"Yes, but not *that* way. How about your old company? That will give you some notion of what I mean."

"My old company is doing just fine, sir, even if it does have a sergeant in charge of it," Gremio answered.

"Good. That's good. You know, if you'd ever wanted to promote that Thisbe to lieutenant's rank, I'd have done it in a heartbeat. He's a hells of an underofficer. I saw that right away."

"Sir, I suggested promotion more than once. Whenever I did, Sergeant Thisbe said no."

"Ah, well. There are some like that. It's too bad. I think he would have made a pretty fair officer, and I don't say that about every sergeant in the regiment."

"I know, sir. I agree. But" —Gremio shrugged— "Thisbe didn't. Doesn't."

"Nothing to be done about it in that case," Florizel said. "A pity, though."

A panting runner came up to him from the left. "Sir, you are ordered to withdraw to the ridge line to the rear," the messenger said. "We've been forced back to it on the left, and we haven't got the men to stretch from one ridge to the other. We have to keep our line as short as we can."

"Is that what Lieutenant General Bell says?" Gremio asked. The runner nodded.

"I can't say he's wrong," Florizel observed. Gremio couldn't say the commanding general was wrong, either. He wasn't sure Bell was right, but, as with Florizel before, that was a different story. Florizel went on, "Prepare my regiment—I'm sorry, Captain: *your* regiment—for withdrawal. Make sure it can still fight while pulling back. The rest of the wing will accompany it."

"Yes, sir," Gremio said. "Up till now, the southrons haven't pressed us hard. I don't suppose they will here, either." *But why haven't they?* he wondered, and found no answer that satisfied him.

Ned of the Forest had gone up against Hard-Riding Jimmy's unicorn-riders pushing south, trying to flank John the Lister out of Poor Richard. He hadn't been able to shift them. It was the first time in the whole course of the war that he'd tried to make a move and had the southrons completely thwart him. He hadn't cared for the experience one bit.

Now Hard-Riding Jimmy's troopers were the ones moving forward, and Ned had to stop them. He was discovering he liked that even less.

For one thing, he was again operating without his own full force of riders. Bell, in his infinite wisdom, had sent some of them off to raid Reillyburgh. He'd claimed the raid would help draw Doubting George out of Ramblerton and make him attack the Army of Franklin's entrenched positions. He'd been right, too. Ned wondered how happy Bell was now about being right.

For another, between the fight near Poor Richard and this one, Jimmy had been massively reinforced. Every single one of his unicorn-riders seemed to be using a newfangled, quick-shooting crossbow. He would have badly outnumbered Ned of the Forest even had Ned had all his own riders. This way . . . this way, it was like trying to hold back an avalanche with his hands.

Every inch of ground between the left end of Lieutenant General Bell's line and the Cumbersome River seemed to have a southron unicorn-rider galloping forward over it. And all of them were putting so many crossbow quarrels in the air, a man might almost have walked across the battlefield on them.

"What the hells do we do, Lord Ned?" Colonel Biffle wailed after Jimmy's men made him give up a knoll he'd badly needed to hold. It was either give up the knoll or wait to get flanked out of the position . . . or wait a little longer and get surrounded and destroyed. "What the hells *can* we do?"

"Fight the bastards," Ned snarled. He'd been living

up to his own advice; his saber had blood on it. He laid it across his knees for a moment while he snapped off a shot at a gray-clad southron. He missed, and cursed, and reloaded as fast as he could. A southron could have got off three or four shots with his fancy weapon in the time Ned needed to shoot once.

When he shot again, though, a southron unicorn-rider crumpled in the saddle. "That's the way!" Biffle exclaimed.

But Ned remained gloomy even as he set yet another bolt in the groove of his crossbow and yanked the string back with a jerk of his powerful arms. "They've got four or five times the men we do, and a lot more than that when it comes to shooting power," he said. "How the *hells* are we supposed to whip 'em with odds like that?"

"If we had all the men we're supposed to—" his regimental commander began.

"It might help a little," Ned broke in. "I hated Bell's guts when he stole 'em from me. I hated his guts, and I hated his empty head. But you know what, Biff? Right this minute, I'm not sure how much difference they'd make."

Colonel Biffle stared at him. "I've never heard you talk this way before, Lord Ned. Sounds like you're giving up."

Before Ned could answer, a crossbow quarrel hummed past between the two men. "I'm not quitting. There's no quit in me. I'll fight till those sons of bitches kill me. Even after I'm dead, I want my ghost to haunt 'em. But by the Lion God's claws, Biff, how am I supposed to win when I've got to fight everything the southrons can throw at me?"

"I don't know, sir. I wish I did. You always have, up till now."

"But up till now I've been operating on my own.

If too many southrons came after me, I could always ride off and hit 'em again somewhere else. Here, though, here I'm stuck. I can't pull away from this fight, on account of if I do, Hard-Riding Jimmy gets around the footsoldiers' flank and eats 'em for supper. So I've got to stand here and take it—take it right on the chin."

Another hillock fell, the southrons shooting at the men on it from the front, right, and left at the same time. Ned's troopers barely escaped. If they'd waited much longer, they would have been cut off and surrounded. Watching them fall back, Colonel Biffle said, "That's what happened to me, too."

"I understood you," Ned said. Yet another bolt thrummed past, wickedly close. He went on, "If it's just a shooting match, they're going to whip us. I don't know of anything in the whole wide world plainer'n that." If the southrons did push aside or beat back his unicorn-riders, they *would* outflank the Army of Franklin's footsoldiers, and then . . . That was all too plain to Ned, too.

Biffle said, "What else can it be but a shooting match?"

"Let's close with 'em," Ned said savagely. This wasn't the kind of fight he usually made, or usually wanted to make. He knew how expensive it would be. But he also knew how disastrous continuing the fight as it was going would be. "They're tough enough with the crossbow, all right. How are they with sabers in their hands?"

"I don't know, sir," Biffle said in wondering tones.

Ned of the Forest wondered, too: he wondered if he'd lost his mind. But when you were desperate, you had to do desperate things. He stood tall in the saddle, brandishing his blood-streaked saber. Pointing it toward the southrons, he roared out a command: *"Chaaarge!"* He set spurs to his unicorn and thundered at Hard-Riding Jimmy's men.

if a southron wizard hadn't thwarted the northerners' sorcerous assaults.

Now it looked to be happening again. What did that say? Probably that Bell's wizards hadn't learned anything new since the fight at Poor Richard, which surprised Ned not a bit. Bell hadn't learned anything much since then, so why should his mages prove any different?

Again the futile lightnings crashed. Ned of the Forest forgot about them. They wouldn't change anything, and he had to stay alive. He traded swordstrokes with a southron who knew what he was doing with a blade in his hand. Battle swept them apart before either could wound the other.

Colonel Biffle's shout resounded in his ears: "Lord Ned, we've got to pull back!"

"Hells with that," Ned ground out. "We're still giving 'em a hard time."

"But they're giving us worse," Biffle said, "and besides, sir, the footsoldiers are falling back."

"What's that?" Engrossed in his own fight, Ned of the Forest had paid scant attention to what was going on off to his right. But the regimental commander had told the truth. Pressed by swarms of pikemen and crossbowmen in gray, Bell's left wing was pulling back toward the rise a mile or two north of the position in which it had started the day.

The retreat was orderly, the men in blue giving a good account of themselves as they withdrew. No signs of panic showed. But a retreat it unquestionably was.

And Biffle had also told the truth about Ned's charge. Not many of his unicorn-riders remained on their mounts. Like the footsoldiers, they'd done all they could. But they'd come up against too many men and too many quick-shooting crossbows. They'd slowed the southrons, yes. The price they'd paid for slowing them . . .

"All right. All right, gods damn it," Ned said. "Now we *can* pull back without everything going to hells and gone. And we can anchor our new line on the one the footsoldiers are setting up."

That sounded good. But the farther north from Ramblerton they fell back, the wider the loop of the Cumbersome River became. Ned knew he could keep Hard-Riding Jimmy off the footsoldiers' flank. But who was going to keep the southrons from getting around *his* flank and into the Army of Franklin's rear?

Nobody. Nobody at all. That was the only answer he could see. He glanced toward the west, where the sun had slid far down the sky. Things hadn't gone too badly today. Darkness would force the fighting to stop before long. If the southrons had enough left to push again tomorrow, though . . .

"They'd better not, gods damn it," Ned muttered.

His men, the survivors, broke off their hand-to-hand struggle with Jimmy's unicorn-riders. Another volley of crossbow quarrels helped speed them back toward their comrades. But the riders in gray didn't try to close with them. That charge might not have done—hells, hadn't done—everything Ned wanted, but it had knocked the southrons back on their heels. Better than nothing.

And *better than nothing* was about as much as the north could hope for these days. Ned knew that all too well. His own years of campaigning in Dothan and Great River Province, in Franklin and even down in Cloviston, had driven it home. He'd needed one desperate makeshift after another to keep his unicorn-riders in the field. Had he had any lingering doubts, Bell's all but hopeless lunge down into Franklin would have murdered the last of them.

"One more day, and we're still here fighting," Colonel Biffle said.

"That's right. That's just right, gods damn it," Ned

said. "And we gave the southrons all they wanted, and then a little more, too." He spoke loudly, to make sure his men listened. He wanted their spirits as high as possible. He feared they would need to do more hard fighting when the sun came up tomorrow.

He'd succeeded in heartening Biffle, anyhow. The regimental commander nodded. "After the botch the footsoldiers made of the fight at Poor Richard, I was afraid they'd fold up and run when the southrons hit 'em. But they didn't. They fought like mad bastards, and no mistake."

"Like mad bastards, yes." Ned of the Forest didn't echo that *and no mistake*. Too many people had already made too many mistakes in this campaign. Far too many of those people wore northern generals' uniforms. Some of them were now dead. Some . . . weren't.

With the darkness, quiet settled over the battlefield, quiet punctuated by occasional challenges and flurries of fighting, and by the groans of the wounded. What were Hard-Riding Jimmy's men doing in the darkness? Ned sent out scouts, but they couldn't learn much. The southrons' patrols were very aggressive, very alert. *We'll find out tomorrow*, Ned thought, and tried to fight down worry.

VIII

Lieutenant General Bell hadn't just listened to the moans of wounded men on the battlefield. At Essoville in the west and at the River of Death, he'd added his own moans to the mix. Better than most of his subordinates, he knew what the wounded were going through, for he'd gone through it himself. He'd given up trying to escape the laudanum bottle. It was as much a part of him now as his ruined left arm.

All things considered, though, he was more pleased than not with the day's fighting. He wished the Army of Franklin could have held its original line, but it hadn't had to fall back too far. The army remained in good order. It hadn't been routed. It *had* hurt Doubting George's men as they came forth to attack. If things hadn't gone exactly as Bell hoped, they hadn't missed by much, either.

He levered himself off a stool and made his slow

way across the pine boards flooring the shack that was, for the moment, Army of Franklin headquarters. Runners waited on the front porch, shivering against the chill of evening. They came to attention and saluted when he stuck his head out.

"Fetch me my wing commanders and my commander of unicorn-riders," he told them. "We have to plan tomorrow's fighting."

"Yes, sir," they said as one. After briefly putting their heads together to see who went to get which officer, they hurried away.

Benjamin the Heated Ham reached the farmhouse first. That didn't surprise Bell. Benjamin commanded the center, and Bell's headquarters lay in his part of the field. He saluted. "Good evening, sir," he said. "We've weathered the first day. That's something, anyhow."

"That's not all we'll do, either," the commanding general declared. "Let them throw themselves at our works again tomorrow. Let them bleed to death charging field fortifications."

"Yes, sir," Brigadier Benjamin replied. "I hope they do. It's a pity you didn't feel that way when we assaulted John the Lister at Poor Richard, sir."

Before Bell could do anything more than glare, Colonel Florizel limped into the farmhouse. "Reporting as ordered, sir," he said.

"Hello, Colonel," Bell said discontentedly. He still wanted to replace Florizel, but surviving brigadiers were so thin on the ground in the Army of Franklin, he hadn't been able to do it. He couldn't complain about the way the colonel's wing had fought today. "I congratulate you, your Excellency, for withstanding the southrons' hardest thrusts."

"I'm no wench, sir. They'd better not go thrusting at me," Florizel said. Bell had seldom laughed since the wounds that mutilated him, but he did then.

Benjamin the Heated Ham threw back his head and let out a long, high, shrill guffaw. Colonel Florizel went on, "Sir, I'm not sure the gods-damned southrons *did* strike us harder than they did anywhere else."

"What? Don't be silly. Of course they did," Bell said. "Everything our spies could learn in Ramblerton plainly shows Doubting George planned to throw the main weight of his army against our right. You had the key assignment, and you did a beautiful job of carrying it out."

"I hope so, sir," was all Florizel said.

Again, Bell didn't get the chance he would have liked to argue the point further. A couple of more men on unicorns rode up to the farmhouse together. Ned of the Forest and Brigadier Stephen the Pickle, who commanded the left wing of Bell's footsoldiers, came in side by side. Ned looked grim; Stephen looked sour enough to show how he'd come by his nickname.

Without preamble, Stephen said, "We're in trouble."

Ned of the Forest nodded. "We're in *big* trouble," he said.

"I'm not surprised you feel that way," Bell said. "You, sir" —he pointed at Stephen the Pickle— "you were the one whose line gave way. You were the one whose men retreated. If they'd held their ground—"

"They'd all be dead, every gods-damned one of them," Stephen snarled. "It was a gods-damned avalanche coming down on us. You ought to sacrifice a lamb to the Lion God they didn't go to pieces and run like hells. After what they went through today, I'd have trouble blaming 'em if they had."

Lieutenant General Bell took another pull from his little bottle of laudanum. He hurt no worse than usual, but maybe the drug would help calm him—and he needed calming. He glared toward Ned of the Forest. "You don't say much."

"No, I don't," Ned said. "I already told you we're in trouble. I'd be angrier at having half my men off by Reillyburgh if I reckoned getting 'em back would have made much difference. I don't, so I'm not. But Hard-Riding Jimmy's outflanked us, and gods only know how much that'll cost us in the morning."

"Why didn't you stop him?" Bell yelped.

"On account of I couldn't," Ned said bluntly. "Too many riders, too many quick-shooters."

"You mean they're loose? You mean you let them get loose?" Bell demanded.

"I thought I just said that." Ned aimed a cold glower at the commanding general. "I might have had a better chance with all my men. I told you about that and told you about that, but did you want to listen? Not likely." But then he softened a little. "Of course, like I said, I might have got licked any which way. Hard-Riding Jimmy's got more riders than you can shake a stick at."

"What are we going to do?" Benjamin the Heated Ham said. "If they have turned our flank, we'd be nailing ourselves to the cross giving battle tomorrow."

"If they have turned our flank, how are we supposed to retreat?" Bell asked in turn. "Head right on past them? Do you suppose they'd be kind enough to give us a Summer Mountain, the way we did for them? I'm afraid I don't think it's likely."

A poisonous silence followed. Benjamin, the only one who'd commanded a wing then, broke it by saying, "That was your fault . . . sir."

"It was *not!*" Bell thundered.

More silence, even more poisonous. At last, Colonel Florizel said, "It's a little too late to worry about what we did or didn't do then. We can't change that. We've still got some say over what we do or don't do tomorrow, though."

"That makes good sense, Colonel," Ned of the

Forest said. "Odds are we won't pay any attention to it, but it makes good sense anyways."

"All right. What can we do?" Bell said. "If we fall back, we fall into the southrons' hands. Does any man here say otherwise?" He waited. No one spoke. He nodded. "Well, then, what does that leave? As far as I can see, it leaves only one thing—fighting and doing our best. Does any man here say no to *that*?"

His wing commanders and commander of unicorn-riders stirred, but none of them claimed he was wrong. Stephen the Pickle did say, "They're going to pound on us in the morning, and my wing'll get it worse than anybody else's, on account of we're the ones who're flanked."

"Do you think we would do better trying to sneak past Doubting George's men and skulking off toward the north?" Bell asked.

The other officers stirred once more. Even so, they didn't—couldn't—ask to retreat. "All right, gods damn it," Benjamin the Heated Ham said savagely. "We'll fight 'em. I don't think it'll do us much good, though."

"Nothing's going to do us much good now," Ned said. "We'll have to see what sort of scraps and pieces we can save, that's all."

Lieutenant General Bell had demoted men for talk far less defeatist than that. Now he watched his wing commanders somberly nod. He felt like nodding himself. He felt like it, but he didn't. He said, "We fought hard today, and we stopped most of them. We can do it again. We *will* do it again."

He tried to put his own heart into his subordinate commanders. He tried—and felt himself failing. "They're going to hammer on us tomorrow no matter how hard we fight," Stephen the Pickle said.

"We'll do our best. It may keep a few more of us alive," Benjamin the Heated Ham said. He saluted and strode out of the farmhouse without so much as a by-your-leave. Ned, Stephen, and Florizel followed, leaving Lieutenant General Bell all alone.

No one had ever accused Bell of being a reflective man. There were good and cogent reasons why no one had ever leveled such a charge at him, chief among them being that he *wasn't* a reflective man. Here tonight, though, he wished his officers hadn't left so abruptly. He would rather have argued with them than had to face his own thoughts with no one for company.

He'd got what he wanted. Doubting George would have been impossible to beat—impossible even to confront—inside the works of Ramblerton. Now the southrons had come forth. They'd carried the fight to the entrenched Army of Franklin, as Bell had hoped they would. The only trouble was, they'd done a better job of it than Bell had thought they could. The way things stood, none of his subordinate commanders believed they could stand up under another day of attacks.

We can't fall back, Bell told himself. Not even the wing commanders had argued about that. *If we can't fall back, we have to fight. If we fight, we have to find some way to win.* All that seemed obvious. What didn't seem obvious was what the way to win might be.

He snapped his fingers. He might have one throw of the dice left. He struggled to his feet again and hitched across the floor to the doorway. The runners on the porch came to attention. Bell pointed to the closest one. "Order my chief wizards here."

"Yes, sir." The runner hurried off into the night.

The wizards came before Bell's temper frayed too badly. They didn't look like happy men. Bell, anything but a happy man himself, would have been furious if they had. Without preamble, he said, "The southrons will likely hit us again tomorrow."

"Yes, sir," the wizards agreed: a mournful chorus.

"My wing commanders fear the soldiers won't be able to hold them back," Bell went on.

"Yes, sir," the wizards chorused again.

Bell scowled at them. "If the soldiers can't, you'll have to," he declared. "What can you do to beat Doubting George's men and his mages?"

No chorus this time. No answer at all, in fact. Only silence. At last, one of the wizards replied, "Sir, I don't know that we *can* do anything. Everything we've tried today has gone wrong. We did our best to hold back the southron unicorn-riders with our lightnings. We did our best—but the lightnings went awry."

"Gods damn it, you're supposed to be better than those southron mages!" Bell burst out.

"Once upon a time, we were," the wizard said. "But the southrons have had three and a half years of war to learn what we knew going in. And Doubting George has at least one very fine mage under his command." He shivered. "We found that out at Poor Richard, if you'll recall."

"I found you that failed me there," Bell snarled. "Now I find you failing me again. What are you good for except telling me what you can't do?"

"Sir," the wizard said stiffly, "if we weren't holding off a lot of what the southrons have tried to do to us, things would be worse yet."

"How?" Bell asked. "How could they be?"

"Would you like to have gone up in flames?" the wizard asked. "Would you like to have seen a pit open under our left? One nearly did."

"All that is easy enough for you to claim," Bell said. "It makes you sound impressive. It even makes you sound *useful*, by the Thunderer's prong. But such claims are all the better for proof."

"Oh, you can have your proof, sir. You can have it as easily as you please," the mage told him.

"Eh? And how do you propose to give it to me?" Bell asked.

The wizard bowed like a courtier. "Nothing easier, sir. All you have to do is send us away. Then, when the fighting starts again and the southron mages start flinging their spells, you'll see if we've done your army any good."

For a moment—for more than a moment, in fact—Lieutenant General Bell was tempted to call his bluff. He started to fling up his arms and order all the mages to be gone, to head straight for the hottest of the seven hells. He started to . . . but he didn't. He growled, "You haven't got the right attitude."

"Generals always say such things," the wizard replied imperturbably. "They say them until they remember they need us after all."

"You are dismissed. You are all dismissed," Bell said. "You are *not* discharged from your service to King Geoffrey. I intend to fight to the end. I intend for every man in the Army of Franklin to do the same. And if I had any women in this army, I would expect nothing different of them."

The wizards stirred. One of them began, "As a matter of—" Another one poked him in the ribs. He subsided. The wizards saluted in ragged unison. Bell sneered. Out went the wizards, noses in the air.

"Good riddance," Bell muttered. "Gods-damned good riddance. They can't help me. They don't think anybody can help me. Well, to hells with what they think. We'll lick the southrons yet, wizards or no wizards."

He took a large, blissful swig from the laudanum bottle. Already well drugged, he felt no particular pain except pain of the spirit. After a while, thanks to the potent medicament, he stopped caring about that. He stopped caring about anything. No matter what, tomorrow would come. Doubting George would attack, or else he wouldn't. If he did, the Army of Franklin would fight. They would win. Or they would lose. Whatever would happen, would happen.

Oh, by the gods, laudanum was marvelous stuff!

Slowly, ever so slowly, so very slowly as to seem to be tormenting Doubting George, the sun rose over the battlefield. Black faded to gray; gray took on colors. It all happened an inch at a time, though, so that from one glance across the field to the next nothing seemed to have changed.

George was less happy than he wished he would have been after the first day's fighting. He'd driven Bell's men back, yes, but he hadn't routed them as he'd hoped to do. They remained in front of him, still ready to fight some more. He hadn't wanted that to happen. He hadn't expected it to happen.

Yawning, Colonel Andy came up beside him. "What do we do now, sir?" George's adjutant asked. "Do we renew the attack, or . . . ?"

"Well, Colonel, I'll tell you," Doubting George began. Before he could say more, though, Hard-Riding Jimmy rode up on a hard-ridden unicorn. George waved to show just where he was. Jimmy brought his unicorn—his indubitably hard-ridden unicorn—to a halt. George nodded to him. "Hello, there. Lovely day, isn't it?"

"For a coot, maybe," the commander of unicorn-riders answered. Sure enough, it could have been better. No sooner had the sun risen than gray clouds rolled towards it. Along with the stinks of the battle-field, the wet-dust smell of impending rain filled George's nostrils. Hard-Riding Jimmy went on, "Sir, have you got a spyglass?"

"On my person? No," Doubting George replied. "Can I rustle one up if I need to? I expect I can."

"Would you please, sir?" Hard-Riding Jimmy quivered with urgency. George hadn't seen the like since the last time he'd watched Major Alva incanting.

More than anything else, that excited quiver convinced him not to tease Hard-Riding Jimmy—too much. He shouted for a spyglass, and got one in short order. Raising it to his eye, he said, "And where shall I train this little toy?"

"North, sir," Jimmy said. "North past the traitors' line."

"They're bent back into a kind of fishhook on their left here, I see," George remarked. "Trying to keep us from outflanking them, no doubt. Clever."

"No doubt." Hard-Riding Jimmy quivered even more. "They've tried, but they haven't done it. Do you see, sir? Do you *see*?"

Doubting George scanned with the spyglass. "I see . . . I see standards with the gold dragon on red."

"Yes!" Jimmy said. "*Yes!* Those are *my* men, sir, and we're square in the enemy's rear. If you don't take advantage of that, sir, it'd be . . . it'd be criminal, that's what it'd be. Order us to the attack! Order your footsoldiers to the attack! We've got the gods-damned traitors in a vise. All we have to do is close it on them."

"Well . . ." George scanned some more. He opened his other eye. Hard-Riding Jimmy looked about ready to jump out of his skin, or perhaps to throttle the commanding general. Letting him do that would have been bad for discipline. It wouldn't have been very good for Doubting George himself, either. He lowered the spyglass and beckoned for a runner.

"Yes, sir?" the young man said.

Regretfully, George decided he'd pushed Hard-Riding Jimmy as far as he could. "Order a general attack, all along the line," he said. The messenger saluted and dashed off. Doubting George turned to the commander of unicorn-riders. "And your men may attack, too."

"Thank you, sir. *Thank you*, sir!" Hard-Riding Jimmy said. For an awkward moment, George thought Jimmy was going to kiss him. The young brigadier didn't. He dashed back to his unicorn, adding over his shoulder, "You won't regret this, sir. You won't, but the traitors will."

"That's the idea," George answered. He wasn't sure his commander of unicorn-riders heard him. Jimmy roweled the unicorn with his spurs. George, a fine rider himself, wouldn't have treated a mount so harshly. But the unicorn sprang away as if it had wings on its heels. That was the point of the exercise. George signaled for another runner. When the soldier came up, George said, "Tell John the Lister to press the enemy especially hard. Between him and Jimmy, I want Bell's left broken. *Broken*—have you got that?"

"Yes, sir. Broken." By the way the messenger dashed off, he might have had Hard-Riding Jimmy on his heels.

"What do you think happens now, sir?" Colonel Andy asked.

Doubting George eyed his adjutant. "Now, Colonel," he replied, "I think we're going to break those traitorous sons of bitches."

Things didn't go quite so smoothly as he'd hoped. He'd thought John the Lister, whose force greatly outnumbered the northerners facing it, would lap around the end of their line and eat them up. But the spur their wing commander had dropped back from the end of his line to the north hampered John, so that, instead of outflanking the foe, his advancing southrons met them face to face. It was a pretty piece of tactics. George would have admired it much more if it hadn't been aimed at him.

He shouted for the spyglass again. As he raised it

to his right eye, he asked Andy, "What the hells is Bell using to try to hold off Jimmy's unicorn-riders?"

"How do I know?" Andy replied with more than a little annoyance. "You're the one with the gods-damned glass, and I haven't had the chance to look through it."

"Oh. Yes. That's right." Doubting George felt considerable embarrassment. Having considered it, he dismissed it. He wasn't about to let his adjutant get his hands on the spyglass till he'd had a good long look himself.

Bell had put together some kind of a line to withstand the onslaught of Hard-Riding Jimmy's troopers, a line with its back to the rest of the Army of Franklin. Even as George watched, more northerners slipped out of the line facing his footsoldiers and hurried north to try to stop the unicorn-riders. Doubting George cackled like a laying hen.

"What's so funny, sir?" Andy asked irritably.

Thrusting the spyglass at him, George said, "Here. See for yourself."

Colonel Andy swept the glass across Bell's position. Before long, he was cackling, too. "They're robbing the painter to pay the potter," he said. "Pretty soon, it'll be the piper they're paying."

"Yes. That did occur to me," George said. "That surely did occur to me. They're— Now *you're* squawking. What's going on?"

"Hard-Riding Jimmy's men just swamped a section of that makeshift line Bell managed to cobble together," his adjutant replied. "They're pouring through the gap. To the hells with me if I know what Bell can do to stop 'em."

"As a matter of fact, he's doing about as well as he can, considering what he's up against," Doubting George said. "He's in worse shape than we were on Merkle's Hill, there by the River of Death. We outnumber him worse than the traitors outnumbered us then. I didn't think he'd even be able to slow down Hard-Riding Jimmy's troopers, but he did."

"And a whole fat lot of good it did him." Andy pointed. He looked like nothing so much as an excited chipmunk sitting up at the mouth of its burrow. "Look, sir! Just look at that! Now the line he's holding against our footsoldiers is starting to break up, too! And there go our men, right on through."

"I told Marshal Bart I could whip Bell," George said. "I told him so—and I was right, by the Thunderer's great right hand."

"Yes, sir." His adjutant's voice held awe. "I thought we could beat them, too, but I never thought we'd manage—this."

"I told Bart I would wait till I was ready, and then I'd hit hard," George replied. "I did what I said I was going to do—no more, no less—and this is what we got. I don't know about you, Colonel, but I've seen men do more and get less." Even as he spoke, another chunk of Bell's line dissolved and disappeared like a lump of sugar in hot tea.

Colonel Andy also noted that. He said, "Sir, for this victory I don't see how they can help promoting you to lieutenant general of the regulars."

"Do you know what, Colonel?" Doubting George said. "As a matter of fact, I don't care if you know or not, since I'm going to tell you. And what I'm going to tell you is, I don't give a good gods-damn. They should have made me a lieutenant general of the regulars for what I did by the River of Death. They didn't do it then, and I have a hells of a time caring now."

A column of muddy, disheveled northern prisoners came stumbling by, the hale helping the wounded along. Grinning soldiers in gray carrying crossbows and pikes herded the captives toward the south. One of the northerners, spotting Doubting George called, "By the gods, General, why didn't you go and drop an anvil on us, too?"

"What's that?" George boomed. "What's that you say? Don't you think I already went and did it?" The northerner didn't answer. He just lowered his head and trudged on into captivity.

Before long, more prisoners followed that first column. This time, one of the guards called out to Doubting George: "We're capturing a hells of a lot of their catapults, too, sir."

"Good. Good. I like to hear that." The commanding general turned back to his adjutant. "Let's see Baron Logan the Black come one inch—one godsdamned inch, do you hear me?—past Cloviston now. By the Lion God's claws, I swear I'll clap him in irons if he has the gall to try it."

"Yes, *sir*!" Colonel Andy said enthusiastically. "We don't need anybody but you here in the east."

"Well, I don't know about *that*," Doubting George said. "Having a good many thousands of soldiers who know what they're doing makes my life a lot easier."

No sooner had those words crossed his lips when a messenger came tearing back to him, shouting, "Sir! Sir! The enemy's breaking up and running. What do we do, sir?"

Somehow, being confronted by one of his soldiers who didn't know what he was supposed to do bothered George not in the least, not when the man brought news like that. The general commanding answered, "Chase the sons of bitches! Chase 'em hard. Don't slow down for anything. Don't let 'em regroup. Keep pushing 'em till you run the legs right off 'em. Have you got that?"

"Yes, sir. We are to pursue vigorously." Saluting, the messenger dashed back toward the north.

"Pursue vigorously." The words tasted bad in George's mouth. The man had squeezed all the juice from the order. But he'd got it right, or right enough.

More prisoners came back. Each time a new column stumbled and staggered past, the guards wore bigger smiles. They understood what was happening, how the battle was going. "We've got 'em whipped!" one of them shouted to Doubting George. "They can take provincial prerogative and put it on the pyre, because it's dead."

Some of the captured northerners still had spirit left. They jeered and hooted and called out false King Geoffrey's name. More, though, tramped along with their heads down, glum and dejected and weary. One fellow said, "To the hells with provincial prerogative. Fill my belly full and you can have King Avram, for all of me."

Doubting George hadn't heard that very often. He hoped he would hear more of it. Colonel Andy said, "Sir, I really think we've broken them." He sounded as if he couldn't believe it.

That irritated George. "You don't need to seem so surprised, Colonel. Did you think this war would go on forever?"

Andy looked startled. "Do you know, sir, I think I almost did."

"Well, by the gods, it won't," George declared. "It is going to end, and we are going to help end it. We are going to take the Army of Franklin and grind it to dust. And when we do, what does Geoffrey, that son of a bitch, have left east of the mountains? Not bloody much, that's what."

Even as he spoke, another stretch of Bell's line, assailed from the front and both flanks, collapsed into a chaos of men running away as fast as they could go or throwing down crossbows and pikes, throwing up their hands, and surrendering. The northern soldiers had done everything a general could reasonably ask of his men. They had, very likely, done more than a general could reasonably ask of his men. In asking a small number of weary, hungry soldiers to beat more than twice as many well-fed, well-rested, well-armed ones, though, Lieutenant General Bell had wanted altogether too much. Now he was—or rather, his men were—paying the price for his asking that of them.

Colonel Andy watched that stretch of line go to pieces, too. "This is . . . this is what victory feels like, isn't it? I don't mean victory in a battle. I mean . . . victory." He sounded disbelieving, but he said the word.

Doubting George nodded. "That's what I've been telling you, Colonel. That's what I've been telling anybody who'd listen. Up till now, nobody's much felt like listening. Not Bart, by the Thunderer's beard. Some people you've just got to show. We'll, we've shown 'em, all right."

"We have. We really have." Yes, Andy sounded dazed.

Having shown the world, Doubting George wanted to see for himself, too. He shouted for his unicorn. When an orderly brought it, he swung up into the saddle and rode north so he *could* see it for himself.

"What will you do if an enemy attacks you, sir?" Colonel Andy called after him.

"What'll I do? I'll kill the bastard," George answered. His adjutant stared. Doubting George laughed. Didn't victory make the world seem fine?

Back when Rollant was a serf, he'd had to harvest rice and indigo on Baron Ormerod's estate in Palmetto Province. Every year, the job looked enormous, far too large for the serfs on the estate to finish in time.

Pitching in to do it only strengthened that feeling. But then, one day, you realized it was almost done. Usually, you realized that with something approaching astonishment. Where had all the work gone?

Rollant had something of the same feeling now. Where had all the war gone? No one in his regiment despised the northerners more than he did. No one had better reason to despise them, though some of the other blonds had reasons just as good. But, however much he loathed the traitors, he'd always known them as men who fought hard. Had anyone anywhere ever fought better for a worse cause? He didn't think so.

Yesterday, Bell's men had gone right on fighting hard. Yes, the southrons had driven them back, but they hadn't had an easy time of it. The Army of Franklin had retreated to this second ridge line in good order, and they'd seemed ready enough to offer battle again today.

And the northerners had even fought hard in the early hours of the morning, though they'd had foot-soldiers coming at them from the south while Hard-Riding Jimmy's unicorn-riders pressed them from the north. Before too long, though, they seemed to realize they simply did not have the men to hold off all their foes. Here, being unable to hold off all their foes meant about the same thing as being unable to hold off any of those foes. They seemed to realize that, too. The Army of Franklin's battle was lost, lost irretrievably.

Once Bell's men figured that out, once it sank in, they did something Rollant had never seen them do before: they went to pieces. Rollant had northerners surrender to him without even complaining about yielding to a blond. Others, instead of taking a shot they were all too likely to make at a standard-bearer, threw away their crossbows and ran.

That didn't always do them any good. Rollant and his comrades pursued, and pursued hard. Not only that, Hard-Riding Jimmy's troopers still lay between the northerners and escape. Some of Bell's men surrendered to them. Others never got the chance. Troopers with quick-shooting crossbows put a lot of bolts in the air. More than a few of them struck home.

"Keep on! Keep on, gods damn it!" Colonel Nahath shouted, his voice cracking with excitement. "Push 'em hard! Keep pushing! Drive 'em! We've got 'em where we want 'em! Now we finish 'em off!"

In all his time in King Avram's army, Rollant had never heard orders like that. No one on the southron side had ever had an excuse for giving orders like that. Now people did—they had that excuse and made the most of it.

"Come on!" Sergeant Joram bellowed. "They haven't got much fight left in 'em. Let's kick 'em while they're down. The harder we pile on this time, the easier the next battle gets—if there is a next battle."

If there is a next battle. No, Rollant hadn't heard anything like that before, either. But he didn't think Joram was wrong. Waving the company standard, he charged past blue-uniformed northerners crumpled in death, past blue-uniformed northerners writhing in the torment of their wounds, and past blue-uniformed northerners throwing up their hands and hoping they could yield before someone killed them.

Here and there, by ones and twos and small groups, some few of Bell's soldiers still showed fight. But even when a whole company held together under a stubborn officer, how long could it hold back the southrons? Not long, as Rollant and his comrades proved again and again and again. Even the bravest northern soldiers found that, when attacked from three sides at once, as they were repeatedly, they could fall back or die. Those were the only choices they had. They could not stem the southron tide.

"Keep after 'em!" Sergeant Joram yelled. "Don't let 'em get away!" One more order whose like Rollant had never heard. He liked it. Joram looked around. "Where's the company standard?"

"Here, Sergeant!" Rollant waved the banner.

"Good. That's good." Joram looked around again. "Come on, you lugs! Don't get lazy on me now, gods damn it!"

They didn't. They tasted triumph as surely as the northerners tasted disaster. This was what they'd waited for ever since they'd joined King Avram's army. Many of them, no doubt, had wondered if it would ever come. Rollant knew he had. Now that it was here at last, they intended to make the most of it.

Waving the standard, Rollant trotted past a pair of repeating crossbows the men of the Army of Franklin had abandoned in their desperate retreat. He eyed the engines with the respect they deserved. How many southrons had they slain? Now his own side would use them against their former owners. He'd never understood the phrase *poetic justice*. Suddenly, he did.

The soldiers of the Army of Franklin were falling back to the west and then to the north, trying to wriggle out of the trap whose jaws were Doubting George's footsoldiers and Hard-Riding Jimmy's unicornriders with their quick-shooting crossbows. Some of the traitors got away. More didn't, or so it seemed to Rollant.

However much the southrons pushed, their officers never seemed satisfied. Colonel Nahath kept right on shouting for the men of his regiment to press the pursuit. Joram, a company commander now but still not an officer, did the same for his soldiers. Rollant, not an officer and certain never to become one, did his share of shouting, too. Why not? The stripes on his sleeve gave him the right.

His regiment, along with the rest of John the Lister's wing, followed Bell's men west and north. Although Rollant would never make an officer, he could see what John wanted: to bring the Army of Franklin to battle one last time, to roll over it, and to wipe it off the face of the earth. If they could make the northerners stop and fight, they *would* wipe them off the face of the earth. Rollant could see that, too.

Much as John wanted it, it didn't quite happen. There was a time in the middle of the afternoon when Rollant thought it would. One of the southrons' columns was moving faster than the shattered force of traitors it pursued. If it could swing in, hit Bell's men from the flank while the rest of the southrons assailed them from the rear . . .

Rollant always believed the southrons waited a little too long to try. Before they could, a regiment of Ned of the Forest's unicorn-riders pitched into the head of that flanking column. The unicorn-riders couldn't hope to beat the southrons. But they could slow them down, and they did. Meanwhile, the remnant of the Army of Franklin got over a bridge across a rain-swollen stream. The southrons, once they drove off Ned's men, looked for another bridge or, that failing, a ford. They didn't find one.

Southron soldiers around Rollant cursed furiously when their comrades came up short. No less than he, they understood what a successful attack then would have meant. "War'll go on a while longer now," Smitty said in disgust.

"I'm afraid so," Rollant agreed. "But it's going our way. By the gods, it really is. How far do you suppose we've come today?"

"Hells with me if I know." Smitty looked back

toward Ramblerton. Rollant had no idea what good that did; several rows of ridges hid the town from sight. But maybe it helped Smitty make whatever arcane calculations he required, for he went on, "Has to be six, eight miles, easy."

Rollant thought it over, then nodded. "Yes, that feels about right. My feet are that tired, I'd say."

"Not just my gods-damned feet—all of me. What I wouldn't give for a nice, soft featherbed and a nice, soft . . . girl to keep me company there."

He'd probably been on the point of saying *blond girl* when he remembered Rollant was a blond himself. Blond women had a reputation for being easy even among southrons who'd never seen a blond, woman or man, in all their lives. Rollant knew why his people had that reputation: Detinans in the north, especially but not only nobles, took blond women whenever they wanted to. If the women already had husbands . . . well, so what? Either they could keep their mouths shut or they could end up dead—and so could those husbands. Blonds died easily in the north. No one asked a lot of questions when they did.

"I'll take the featherbed. You can have the girl," Rollant said. "If this miserable war really is somewhere close to getting done, I'll go home to my wife before too long. I hope so, by the gods. I miss her."

"You could grab whatever you find, the way most married men do out in the field," Smitty said. "She'd never know."

"I would," Rollant answered. Smitty shrugged and scratched his head. Rollant's fidelity to Norina never failed to bemuse him.

"Forward!" Sergeant Joram yelled. His voice was raw and hoarse from all the shouting he'd done the past couple of days. He pointed to the bridge Bell's men had used to get over the stream. "If we can cross there ourselves, we'll keep the heat on those northern sons of bitches. They don't have much in front of the bridge, and they've been running all day. They'll run some more if we push 'em. We can do it. *King Avram!*"

"Avram!" Rollant shouted. "Avram and freedom!" He didn't know whether the men from the Army of Franklin would run. He didn't much care, either. If they tried to make a stand, the southrons would roll over them. Only as he trotted toward the soldiers in blue did he blink. Even yesterday morning, he wouldn't have assumed victory would come so easy.

Run the northerners did. They ran like rabbits, in fact, before the southrons even got within crossbow range. They scampered over the bridge to jeers from John the Lister's soldiers: "Cowards!" "Yellow-bellies!" "Come back here and take your whipping, you nasty, naughty little boys!"

That last, shouted out by Smitty, made Rollant laugh so hard he got a stitch in his side and had to slow down. He was still short of the bridge when lightning crashed down on it and set it ablaze. The northerners hadn't had much luck smiting southron soldiers with thunderbolts. But nothing, no spell, seemed to keep them from calling down lightning on a place where no soldiers stood.

Balked, Rollant and the rest of the southrons stared from the southern branch of the stream at the escaping northern soldiers. A few northerners took shots at them before retreating. Most didn't bother. They'd had enough.

"Engineers!" Colonel Nahath shouted and waved. "We need pontoons here! By the gods, we need 'em fast, too. The traitors are getting away."

The engineers did eventually come forward. They did eventually bridge the stream. By then, though, more than an hour of precious daylight on one of the shortest days of the year had been lost. The soldiers who would go after the Army of Franklin understood as much, too. Even though the pursuit would have taken them into new danger, they cursed and fumed at the delay. They knew a shattering victory when they saw one, and they wanted to finish off Bell's army and crush it altogether.

It didn't quite happen. Bell and Ned left behind crossbowmen and unicorn-riders who fought a series of stubborn rear-guard actions and kept the southrons from overwhelming what was left of the Army of Franklin. As twilight spread over the land, Rollant realized his comrades and he weren't—quite—going to destroy the Army of Franklin that day.

A lone unicorn-rider came up to Sergeant Joram's company. For a moment, Rollant thought the fellow was a messenger. Then he took a longer look and joined the cheers ringing out: it was Doubting George himself.

"Gods damn it to hells, boys," the commanding general said, waving his hat at the southron soldiers, "didn't I tell you we'd lick 'em? Didn't I tell you?"

"Yes, *sir!*" Rollant roared along with everybody else.

"And we'll finish the job, too," George said. "I aim to run the legs right off the traitors. Any of 'em who get away from us'll be some of the fastest men nobody's crucified yet. Isn't that right?"

"Yes, *sir!*" the men cried, even more excitedly than before.

Doubting George rode past them, as if he intended to capture singlehanded not only Bell but also all the men the enemy general still commanded. Rollant turned to Smitty, who stood not far away. "You know something?"

"What's that, your Corporalship, sir?" Smitty asked.

"George was the rock in the River of Death, but he's the hammer at Ramblerton."

"The Hammer." Smitty paused, tasting the words. "You're right, by the Thunderer's lightning bolt."

"I don't want to stop here tonight," Rollant said. "I want to go on, the way Doubting George went on. I want to stomp the traitors into the ground. I want them *beaten*, gods damn it. How about you, Smitty?"

"Me?" Smitty shrugged. "Right now, what I want is supper."

Thus reminded of the flesh and blood of which he was made, Rollant realized he wanted supper, too. In fact, he was ravenous. He remembered gulping down a hasty breakfast. Had he had anything after that? He didn't think so, and he'd come a long way since then.

A cook handed him a hard cracker and a chunk of raw, dripping meat. He roasted the gobbet on a stick over a fire without asking what it was. Beef? Dead donkey? Unicorn? He didn't much care, not right now. It helped fill the hole in his belly. Next to that, nothing else mattered.

Picking his teeth with a twig, Smitty gave his own opinion of what supper had been: "I don't know for sure, mind you, but I think I just ate Great-Aunt Hilda."

"That's disgusting!" Rollant exclaimed.

"I didn't know you'd met the old battle-axe," Smitty answered. Rollant grimaced. Blithely, Smitty continued, "We should've turned Great-Aunt Hilda loose against the traitors. She'd've nagged 'em back into the kingdom in about five minutes, tops."

"You're ridiculous," Rollant said, "and I'm sure your Great-Aunt Hilda is, too. After all, she's related to you. But the way things are going, I think we can handle the traitors without her." Smitty didn't argue. Evidently he thought so, too.

❖   ❖   ❖

Marching down to Ramblerton, Captain Gremio had thought of the Army of Franklin as a dead man walking. On the second day of the battle in front of the town, the dead man stopped walking. He fell over.

That was true only in the metaphorical sense. Literally speaking, the Army of Franklin, or those parts of it that managed to escape Doubting George's men, spent most of that second day in headlong retreat. Only when night fell at last could the survivors begin to take stock and figure out how enormous the disaster truly was.

But that came later. When the second day of fighting started, Gremio, whose regiment remained on the far right of Lieutenant General Bell's line, again thought the southrons weren't pushing so hard as they might. Every attack they made, his men and the rest of Colonel Florizel's wing pushed back without much trouble.

Sergeant Thisbe said, "I don't much care what Bell thinks, sir. It doesn't look to me like Doubting George is putting all his weight into the fight here."

"I'd say you're right, Sergeant," Gremio replied. "I wish you were wrong, but I'd say you're right. Which makes me wonder . . . If he's not putting his weight into the fight *here*, where *is* he putting it?"

He got his answer within an hour. A horde of northern soldiers came running over from the left, with southrons on their heels and even in their midst. "Surrounded!" the men from the Army of Franklin cried. "Footsoldiers!" some of them yelled. "Unicorn-riders!" others shouted. "Trapped! Outflanked!" They all seemed pretty sure about that.

From behind them came other shouts, the kind Gremio least wanted to hear: "King Avram!" "Freedom!" "Hurrah for Doubting George!"

"What do we do, sir?" Thisbe asked urgently. The

underofficer commanding a company didn't sound afraid. Gremio never remembered hearing Thisbe sound afraid. But Gremio could hardly blame the sergeant for that urgency.

He also wished he had a better response than, "Try to hold them back. What else can we do?"

"Them who?" Thisbe said. "Them the enemy, or them our own men?"

That was another excellent question. Gremio had no idea whether anything could stop the retreat—he didn't want to think *rout*—sweeping down on his regiment. "You soldiers!" he shouted, doing his best. "Get into line with us. Face the southrons! Maybe we can stop them."

A few of the retreating—he didn't want to think *fleeing*, either—soldiers obeyed him. He pulled some of his own men out of the south-facing trenches to join them. But more men from the Army of Franklin kept right on going. They'd had all the war they wanted. And the southrons who hadn't been pushing hard now saw their foes in disarray and stepped things up.

More and more shouts of "Avram! King Avram!" came from what had been the left but was rapidly turning into another front. More and more crossbow quarrels came from that direction, too. The southrons were putting more bolts in the air than Gremio would have imagined possible from their numbers. Then he realized that when people talked about the quick-shooting crossbows the southron unicorn-riders used, they weren't joking.

He also realized his makeshift line facing east wasn't going to hold. At almost the same time, he realized what had been the real line, the line facing south, was liable not to hold, either.

"Captain, they're going to break through!" Sergeant Thisbe exclaimed in dismay. What was obvious to Gremio was also obvious to other people, then.

"Hold fast! By the gods, men hold fast!" Colonel Florizel shouted, diligently whipping a dead unicorn: the soldiers on the right weren't going to stop the southrons even if they died in place to the last man. But Florizel made more sense when he went on, "They'll just shoot you down from behind if you run away."

"Pikemen!" Gremio yelled, looking around for some. "We need more pikemen to hold the enemy off our crossbows!"

Not far away, another officer was roaring, "Crossbowmen! Gods damn it, where can I get some crossbowmen? The southrons are shooting down my pikemen, and I can't answer back!"

Not enough crossbowmen, Gremio thought glumly. *Not enough pikemen, either. We can put them together and have not enough of both—which is about what the north has everywhere these days.* Even so, he sent a runner to the officer who commanded pikemen. They did join forces . . . just as the southrons rolled down on them.

And they did prove not to have enough of both. More than a little to Gremio's surprise, they beat back the southrons' first charge, leaving dead and wounded men lying in front of their improvised line. The pikemen did vicious work against the southrons who leaped down among them, while the crossbowmen shot down Avram's gray-clad soldiers in droves.

Gremio was proud of the detachment he'd patched together—proud for about five minutes. Then a mournful cry rose from his left: "We're flanked!" As if to underscore that, crossbow quarrels zipped up the line, cutting down one northerner after another. The southrons there on the left whooped with glee. They knew what they'd done.

So did Gremio. He looked around, wondering if making a stand here and selling his regiment as dearly as he could would let the rest of the Army of Franklin escape. He was willing to sacrifice the men, but only for something worthwhile.

He didn't see the point, not here, not now. Even Colonel Florizel had stopped shouting about holding fast. Florizel was a stubborn man, but he wasn't altogether an idiot. "Retreat!" Gremio shouted. He didn't like it, but he didn't like getting destroyed, either. "Fall back! Form a new line as you can!"

If you can, he should have said. A lot of his men had already started falling back without permission. Once they got it, they fell back faster. The Army of Franklin had some order left as the southrons drove its remnants north, but only some. Gremio had heard of routs before. Up till now, he'd never been part of one. Today, he was. He felt like a man staggered after a blow to the head with a club.

Because his regiment, along with the rest of Colonel Florizel's wing, kept more cohesion than the rest of the Army of Franklin, he went on trying to form new lines and hold back the southrons while the rest of Bell's men pelted off toward the north. Sometimes the enemy disrupted his efforts before they were well begun. Sometimes he did manage to hold them off for a while. But then, as they had before, Doubting George's soldiers would outflank the line he'd pieced together. Then it was retreat again, retreat or stand and be massacred.

One of his men asked, "Why have the gods turned their backs on us, Captain?" He sounded not far from despair.

Gremio felt not far from despair himself, and had no time for anyone else's. "Ask a priest," he snapped. "Maybe he'd know, or tell you he knows. All *I* know is, we've still got to try to come out of this in one piece."

The soldier sent him a wounded look. He had no

time for those, either. Too many men were really wounded; their groans filled his ears. He looked back over his shoulders. A couple of hundred yards to the rear stood a woodlot, the trees bare-branched and skeletal now that winter was at hand. He didn't much care about the branches. The trunks? The trunks were a different story.

Pointing to the trees, he said, "We'll get in among them and use the trunks for cover. We haven't got time to dig trenches, and the tree trunks will be better than nothing. When the southrons get close, we'll give 'em a volley they'll remember for a long time."

His men did, too. The southrons recoiled, as much from surprise—here were northerners still showing fight—as because of the damage the volley did. But the surprise didn't last long. Neither did the recoil. The men in gray started sliding around the woodlot to the east and west. They also brought engines forward with what was, to Gremio, truly damnable speed.

Firepots flew through the air. Some of them smashed on bare ground. Those were harmless, or near enough. But the ones that hit trees set them afire. Before long, the whole woodlot would burn. Not only that, Gremio saw the southrons' outflanking move.

"Fall back!" he yelled once more, coughing from the lungful of smoke he'd inhaled.

"Fall back!" Sergeant Thisbe echoed. "We'll make another stand soon. They can't drive us like this forever." Gremio wondered why not. What was going to stop the southrons? Not the Army of Franklin, not by what had happened today. But Thisbe had never been one to give up a fight as long as one last crossbow quarrel remained in the quiver.

Before long, Gremio began to wonder whether that last bolt was gone. Doubting George's men were pressing him from the front and both flanks, and they'd got so far ahead of his regiment that even retreat would be like running the gauntlet. He thought about throwing aside his officer's sword and raising his hands in the air. The war would be over for him, and he would have lived through it.

But he knew Thisbe wouldn't surrender; Thisbe, of all people, would think it impossible, and had good reasons to think so. Gremio couldn't stand to give up while the sergeant was watching. And then, quite suddenly, he didn't have to. A detachment of Ned of the Forest's unicorn-riders came galloping up from the east and pitched into the southrons assailing Gremio's flank. The men in gray, taken by surprise, scattered in wild disorder. Had they had any notion Ned's riders were close by, they surely would have put up a better fight. As things were? No.

"Thank you kindly, Colonel," Gremio called to the rider who looked to be in charge of the detachment.

"You're welcome," the other officer answered, touching the brim of his hat. "Nice to know not quite everything's gone to hells in a handbasket, isn't it?"

"*Not quite* is about the size of it, I'm afraid," Gremio said. "Do you knew where, or even if, the army is going to make some real stand?"

The colonel of unicorn-riders shook his head. "Sorry, Captain. Wish I did."

"Colonel Biffle! Colonel Biffle, sir!" A rider hurried up to the officer, and reined in. He pointed off to the west. "More footsoldiers in trouble over there, sir."

With a weary sigh, Colonel Biffle nodded. "Well, let's see if we can't get 'em out of it, then." He tipped his hat to Gremio again. "Nice talking with you, Captain. Sorry I can't stay longer. Good luck." He rode off, followed by his men.

Colonel Florizel limped over to Gremio. "Still here, I see."

"Same to you, sir," Gremio replied.

"Oh, yes. Still here." Florizel shrugged wearily. "For how much longer, though, who knows? They've whipped us right and proper this time."

"Yes, sir." Gremio admitted what he could hardly deny. "How do we go on after . . . this? How *can* we go on after . . . this?"

"I have no idea," Florizel answered. "All I know is, nobody's ordered me to throw down my sword. Till someone does, I'm still in the fight. Until King Geoffrey has to give up, if he ever does, *he's* still in the fight. So we've got to keep grinding away, see what happens next, and hope it's something good."

He's a simple man, Gremio thought, not for the first time. Here, though, Florizel's simplicity amounted to strength. The wing commander didn't worry about what he couldn't help. He kept his mind on his own job, and did that as well as he could. Anything else? Anything else was—simply—beyond his ken, and he didn't dwell on it. Gremio wished he could ignore the world falling to pieces around him as well as his superior managed the trick.

"If we can use a couple of more rear-guard actions to get some separation between our main force—" Florizel began.

"You mean, the biggest mob of soldiers running away," Gremio broke in.

Florizel only nodded. He didn't even bother quarreling about the way Gremio put it. "If we can get some separation," he went on, "we can salvage *something* from the ruins, anyhow: an army that can keep Doubting George from marching all the way through Dothan to Shell Bay the way Hesmucet's marching through Peachtree."

"Maybe," Gremio said, though he wasn't sure the Army of Franklin could have done that even before the southrons smashed it to bits. It certainly would have had a better chance then; he couldn't deny that, either.

"Gods damn it, we're free Detinans," Florizel said, as if Gremio had claimed they were blond serfs. "I'd sooner die on my feet than live on my knees."

"Yes, sir," Gremio said. "But I'd sooner *live* on my feet, if I possibly can."

Florizel considered that. By the startled look on his face, it hadn't occurred to him up till now. After more than a little thought, he nodded. "Yes, that *would* be best, wouldn't it? It would if we could manage it, I mean. I don't know how we're going to."

"We have to get away from the southrons." Gremio preferred not to mention that only a little while before he'd almost surrendered to Doubting George's men. Florizel didn't need to know that. It hadn't happened, and now—maybe—it wouldn't. Gremio dared hope, anyhow.

But even if they did get back up to Dothan or Great River Province, what could they do then? Precious little, not after the losses they'd taken. For years, the Army of Franklin had been the heart of King Geoffrey's power here in the east. Now it was broken, and so was that power. How could it be revived? *Could* it be revived? Gremio didn't know. He shook his head. No, that wasn't true. He *did* know. He just didn't care to think about what he knew.

For as long as Lieutenant General Bell could, he looked on the second day's fighting in front of Ramblerton much as he had on the first day's: the southrons had pushed his men hard, but he'd held his lines together even if he had had to give some ground.

The night before, though, his wing commanders and Ned of the Forest had agreed with him, or at least not disagreed too loudly. None of them had quarreled with his intention of inviting the second day of battle. None of them had seen any better choices available to the Army of Franklin. Tonight, though . . . tonight, the wing commanders and Ned didn't wait to be summoned. They sought Bell out in the pavilion he'd run up when he couldn't find a farmhouse as night fell.

One word came from all the officers: *disaster*. "Sir, my wing was attacked from front, rear, and flank all at the same time," Stephen the Pickle said. "Those gods-damned southron unicorn-riders with their quick-shooting crossbows . . ." He shuddered. "We didn't break, not in any ordinary sense of the word. They tore us to shreds. Not much of what is the left is left."

"Or of the center," Benjamin the Heated Ham said. "The southrons tore us to pieces, too, from the front and then from the flank when the left retreated." He nodded to Stephen. "Seeing what happened to it, I don't know how it could have done anything but retreat."

Bell turned to Florizel. "And you, Colonel? What have you got to say?" He'd expected the least from Florizel. He'd got the most. A fair part of Florizel's wing remained in good fighting trim—or as good as any in the Army of Franklin.

"Well, sir," Florizel answered, "we thought the hardest blows would fall on us, and I'd say we got the softest. That's why we're not in such dreadful shape—compared to the other wings, I mean."

Even there, a knife. He'd expected to take the hardest blows because Bell had said they would fall on the right. But Bell had been mistaken. Did Florizel also think he'd been mistaken elsewhere in the campaign? The general commanding bristled. *He* didn't believe that, regardless of whether anyone else did.

"Question now is, how do we pick up the pieces? If we can, I mean," Ned of the Forest said.

"What have we got to pick up?" Stephen the Pickle asked sourly. "We left most of the pieces on the field."

"That is not so," Bell declared. "The Army of Franklin remains in being. It remains a fighting force."

No one contradicted him. He found himself wishing somebody would have. The chilling silence from Ned of the Forest and the wing commanders hurt worse than any argument could have done. The officers just stood in poses of weary dismay. They didn't bother quarreling with him. It was as if they were beyond quarreling, as if the catastrophe was too obvious to need any more quarrels.

In what was, for him, an unwontedly small voice, Lieutenant General Bell asked, "What do we do tomorrow?"

"Fall back." Two wing commanders and Ned said the same thing at the same time. Ned added, "The southrons will be coming after us with everything they've got. With all those unicorn-riders and their quick-shooting crossbows and with their swarm of footsoldiers, they've got a lot. They're going to want to finish us off. Unless we scoot, they'll do it, too."

"Can't we stop them?" Bell said in dismay. "If we take a strong defensive position and force them to come at us—"

"They'll roll right over us," Benjamin the Heated Ham broke in. All the other officers nodded somber agreement.

Ned added, "That 'pick a good place and make 'em come at us'—that'll do for rear-guard actions. We'll have to fight a lot of 'em, I reckon, to keep the southrons off our main body. If we can."

More nods from the wing commanders. Stephen the Pickle said, "If we can get away, that's a victory. That's about as much as we can hope for, too."

"If you men abandon the idea of victory, you condemn this army to irrelevance," Bell said, horrified.

Benjamin the Heated Ham replied, "If you try to win a victory now, sir, you condemn this army to extinction."

Once more, the rest of the officers in the pavilion solemnly nodded. Bell started to ask what they would do if he ordered them to attack, or even to stand and fight. He started to, but he didn't. The answer was entirely too obvious: they would disobey him. Even he could see he was better off not giving some orders. With a long sigh, he said, "You are dismissed, gentlemen. In the morning, we will . . . see what we can do."

They ducked out of the pavilion, one after another. Left all alone again, Bell eased himself down into a folding chair, then leaned his crutches against the chair's wooden arm. "Gods damn it," he said softly. "Gods damn it to all seven hells."

He wished he were whole. A whole man had choices a cripple didn't. Had he been whole, he could have hurled himself into the fighting when things went wrong. He could have killed several of Doubting George's men on his own. He could have made them kill him. He wouldn't have had to live through the disastrous battle, wouldn't have had to suffer this humiliation. And, once dead, he could have looked the Thunderer and the Lion God in the eye and assured them he'd been as gallant as it was given to a mortal man to be.

Instead . . . here he sat, with the Army of Franklin as mutilated as he was.

He pulled out the little bottle of laudanum and stared at it. Then he pulled the stopper off with his teeth. If he gulped the whole bottle instead of his usual swig, maybe that would be enough to stop his heart. On the other hand, maybe it wouldn't. He'd got used to ever bigger doses of the drug. He'd had to, to come even close to holding his unending pain at bay.

A small gulp sufficed him. He put the bottle back into the pouch on his belt. In a little while, some of the pain from his wounds would ease. In a little while, some of the pain from the lost battle would recede, too. Yes, laudanum was marvelous stuff.

Relief had just started to sparkle along his veins when a scryer came into the pavilion and said, "Sir, King Geoffrey would speak to you by crystal ball."

"Would he?" Bell said grandly. "And what if I would not speak to him?"

Instead of answering that, the scryer stood there with his mouth hanging open in surprise. Maybe that was lucky for Bell. He reached for his crutches. Unfreezing, the scryer said, "I'll tell him you're on the way."

"Yes, do that," Bell said. But, as the scryer turned to go, he added, "Wait. What does the king want to talk about?"

"Why, how the fight went, sir," the scryer replied. "What else?"

"Yes, what else?" the commanding general agreed gloomily. The laudanum hadn't done nearly enough to shield him from what was bound to be King Geoffrey's wrath. "Go on. Go on. Tell his Majesty I'm coming as fast as I can."

The scryer disappeared. Lieutenant General Bell wished he could do the same. He'd led the Army of Franklin south. He'd fought hard. And he'd lost. He'd lost disastrously, in fact. Had he won, he would have been a hero. He hadn't. He wasn't. Instead of the credit, he would get the blame. That was how things worked.

Bell couldn't have moved fast even if he'd wanted to. He wanted anything but. This camp seemed much too small to house the Army of Franklin. Up till tonight, it would have been. But this was what remained of the army. Bell scowled and shook his head. Wounded men groaned as healers and mages did their best to help them. A cricket too stupid to realize how cold it was let out a few lethargic chirps. An owl hooted. A unicorn whickered. Soldiers snored.

Only a few hitching steps to the scryers' pavilion. A guard outside held the tent flap wide so Bell could go in. He could have done without the courtesy.

There was the king's face, in one of the crystal balls. The others were mercifully dark. Bell wished this one would have been, too. As usual, folding himself so his fundament came down on a stool was an adventure, but he managed. "Your Majesty," he said, nodding to the image in the crystal ball.

"Lieutenant General." King Geoffrey favored him with a single curt nod. Geoffrey had a lean, almost ascetic countenance, with burning eyes, a long, thin blade of a nose, and a disconcerting beard: it grew under his chin but not on the front of it. Bell, who sported a particularly luxuriant growth of face foliage, had never understood why his sovereign chose to trim his whiskers that way.

"How may I serve you, your Majesty?" Bell asked.

"Tell me how things stand in the east," the king replied. "Have you won the victory over the southrons our cause so badly needs?"

"Well . . . no. Not yet," Bell said, looking down at the dirt under his foot.

King Geoffrey frowned. He looked unhappy even at his most cheerful. When he *was* unhappy, a man could watch the end of the world on his face. And he'd been a soldier, so he knew what questions to ask to determine the exact situation. "Tell me your present position," he said crisply.

"We are . . . about fourteen miles north of Rambler-ton," Lieutenant General Bell replied, wishing he had the nerve to come right out and lie to his sovereign.

Geoffrey's eyebrows leaped like startled stags. "*Four-teen miles!*" he burst out. "Did I hear you correctly, Lieutenant General?" He sounded as if he hoped he hadn't—not for his own sake, but for Bell's.

But he had. "Yes, your Majesty," the commanding general said unhappily.

"What *happened*?" King Geoffrey demanded. "You lost . . . twelve miles of ground today?"

"More like ten miles," Bell said. "We lost a couple of miles in yesterday's fighting, but we took a strong defensive position at the end of it."

Geoffrey rolled his eyes. The motion, shown in perfect miniature inside the crystal ball, seemed even more painfully scornful than it would have face to face. "Oh, yes, Lieutenant General, it must have been a wonderfully strong defensive position." His sarcasm flayed. "By the Thunderer's thumbs, you probably would have run all the way up to Dothan by now if the gods-damned southrons had forced you out of a *weak* position."

Bell hung his head. "We held their footsoldiers— most of them, anyhow—for quite a while," he said. "But Hard-Riding Jimmy's unicorn-riders got into our rear with their quick-shooting crossbows, and . . . and . . . and we broke." There. He'd said it. He waited for the King to do or say whatever he would.

"You . . . broke." Geoffrey's voice was eerily flat.

"Yes, your Majesty. We were assailed from front, rear, and flank by an army more than twice our size. We fought hard, we fought bravely, for a very long time. But in the end . . . In the end, we couldn't take the pounding any more. The men did what men will do: they tried to save themselves."

"Assailed from front, rear, and flank by an army more than twice your size," King Geoffrey echoed, still in that tone that showed nothing of what he was thinking. "And how, pray tell, did you manage to put the Army of Franklin in such an enviable strategic position?"

"Your Majesty!" Bell said reproachfully.

"Answer me, gods damn you!" Geoffrey screamed, loud enough to make every scryer in the tent whip his head toward the crystal ball from which that anguished cry had come. "You went south to whip Avram's men, not to . . . to throw your own army down the latrine."

"This result is not what I intended, your Majesty."

"A man who walks in front of a runaway unicorn doesn't intend to get gored, either, which does him no good at all," King Geoffrey ground out. "My army, Lieutenant General Bell! Give me back my army!"

"I would like nothing better, your Majesty," Bell whispered.

"How many men have you got left?" the king asked. "Any at all? Or is it just you and some gods-damned scryer wandering in the dark?"

"No, sir. Not just me," Bell said with such dignity as he could muster. "After the . . . the initial collapse" —he had to keep hesitating— "we retired in . . . fairly good order. We could fight again tomorrow if we had to." *We'd get slaughtered, but we could fight.*

By the way King Geoffrey's eyebrows twitched, he was thinking the same thing. But he didn't say anything about that. What he did say was, "You did not answer my question, Lieutenant General. How many men have you got left?"

"Sir, I have not tried to make a count," Bell answered. "My best guess would be about half of those who went into today's fight."

"*Half?*" Geoffrey yelped painfully. "That's even worse

than I thought, and I thought I'd thought things were as bad as they could be." Now he paused, perhaps wondering whether he'd said what he meant to say. Apparently deciding he had, he continued, "What happened to the rest of them? Shot? Speared?"

"Not . . . not all, your Majesty," Bell said; the king seemed intent on embarrassing him every way he could. "Some unknown but, I fear, fairly large number of men were captured by Doubting George's footsoldiers and unicorn-riders."

"And probably glad to come out of it alive," Geoffrey commented, yet more acid in his voice. "What do you aim to do now? Whatever it is, do you think it will matter? Or will the southrons smash you to pieces, come what may?"

"I don't think so, your Majesty," Bell said. "We still can resist." King Geoffrey hadn't asked him how many engines he'd lost. That was likely just as well. If the king heard that Doubting George's men had captured more than fifty, he'd burst like a firepot, except with even more heat. And Bell couldn't blame him, however much he wanted to. He almost blamed himself— almost, but not quite. The disaster had to be *someone* else's fault. Didn't it?

IX

Had General Guildenstern won a victory, he would have got drunk to celebrate. John the Lister was sure of it. He saw Doubting George drunk, too, but drunk on triumph rather than spirits.

"I told you so," George cackled. "Gods damn it, I told you so. I told you, and I told Marshal Bart, too. And do you know what else? I was *right*, that's what else. We didn't just lick 'em. We fornicating *wrecked* 'em."

"Yes, sir," John said dutifully.

He would rather have won a victory under Doubting George than under Baron Logan the Black, who would have been promoted over his head. The more George carried on, though, the more John wondered if listening to the general commanding was worth the triumph.

It was. Of course it was. He couldn't remember ever

making such an astounding, amazing, fantastic advance against the traitors, and wondered if it had an analog anywhere in the War Between the Provinces. Prisoners by the thousands, their war over at last, shambling off into captivity. More northerners dead on the field, and in the long retreat north from the field. More captured catapults and repeating crossbows than he'd ever seen before.

"*Wrecked* 'em," Doubting George repeated, and John the Lister could only nod. The commanding general went on, "I'm going off to the scryers' tent. Marshal Bart and Baron Logan need to know what we've done today, and so does King Avram. Yes, sir, so does King Avram." Away he went, a procession of one.

John the Lister nodded again. No one doubted Doubting George now. He'd said he needed to wait, and would win once he was done waiting. And what he'd said, he'd done. Could he have won without waiting? John still thought so, but it didn't matter any more.

And John, still a new brigadier of the regulars, knew this victory was better for *his* career than any Baron Logan the Black could have won. He was George's reliable second-in-command. He would have been Logan's second-in-command, too, but he would have been passed over for the main prize. Now nobody could say that about him. *And a good thing, too,* he thought.

Colonel Nahath came up to him. After the salutes and the congratulations, Nahath said, "I've got a little problem I'd like to talk over with you, sir."

"Go ahead," John said expansively. "Nobody has big problems, not after today. What's your little one?"

"Well, sir, one of my company commanders, Lieutenant Griff, got killed in yesterday's fighting," Nahath said. "Sergeant Joram took over the company and did well with it. I'd like to promote him to lieutenant."

"Go ahead," John repeated. "That's your problem? We should all have such little worries."

But Colonel Nahath shook his head. "No, sir. That's not my problem. The problem is, I'd like to promote my standard-bearer, a corporal, into the sergeant's slot Joram's leaving open. He's carried the banner well and he's fought bravely. He should get another stripe."

"If he's as good as all that, go ahead and promote him, by the gods," John the Lister said. "Why are you flabbling about it, anyway?"

"Because the corporal's a blond, sir."

"Oh." Sure enough, that got John's attention. He snapped his fingers. "I remember. This is the fellow who grabbed the flagstaff when your standard-bearer got killed over in Peachtree, isn't it? The one you said deserved a chance to fail as a corporal."

"Yes, sir. His name is Rollant. And he hasn't failed as a corporal. He's had to win a fight or two to hold the rank, which an ordinary Detinan wouldn't have, but he's done it. From what poor Griff told me, Rollant told him he didn't dare lose," the colonel from New Eborac said. "If he can do a corporal's job, why not a sergeant's? He's earned the chance to fail again, but this time I don't think he will."

"A blond sergeant," John the Lister said musingly. "Who would have imagined *that* when the war started?"

"King Avram would have, I think," Nahath answered.

John pursed his lips. When Avram announced his intention of freeing the blond serfs from the land and from their ancient ties to their liege lords, who had taken him seriously? (Well, Grand Duke Geoffrey and the northern nobles had, but that was a different story.) People in the south hadn't dreamt blonds could ever amount to much even if they did have the right to leave the land. From a southron point of view, the war, at first, had been much more about holding Detina together than it had been about removing the serfs from bondage to the land.

But maybe Avram really *had* seen something in the blonds that almost everyone else missed. "You may be right, Colonel," John said solemnly. "Yes, you may be right."

"You don't object if I promote this fellow, then?" Nahath asked. "I wanted to make sure before I went and did it."

"If he's been a good corporal, odds are he'll make a good sergeant," John said. "Go ahead and do it. The other thing to remember is, it likely won't matter as much as it would have a year ago. I don't see how the war can last a whole lot longer, not after what we've done the past couple of days."

"I hope you're right, sir. I'd like to go home, get back to the life I left when the fighting started," Nahath said. He was a colonel of volunteers, not a regular at all. When the war ended, he would take off his gray uniform and go back to running his farm or putting up manufactories or practicing law or whatever he did.

John didn't know what that was. He'd never asked. He would be glad to go on soldiering, even if he'd never again lead another army the size of the one he'd commanded here. He didn't see how he could; the only enemies in his lifetime who'd truly challenged Detina were other Detinans.

He said, "I've seen regular officers who didn't do their jobs as well as you do, Colonel." He spoke the truth; Nahath was everything anyone could want as a regimental commander, though he might have been out of his depth trying to lead a brigade or a division.

Nahath touched the brim of his gray felt hat now. "I thank you very much, sir. I've done my best, but this isn't my proper trade." He looked north, toward what was left of the Army of Franklin. "What will we do tomorrow?"

"I don't know, not for a fact. I spoke with Doubting George a little while ago, but he didn't say," John the Lister replied. "Still, my guess would be that we'll go on driving them as hard as we can. I don't think the general commanding will be content to let the traitors' remnant get away. If we can take that army off the board altogether . . ."

"Yes, sir. That would be a heavy blow to whatever hopes the north has left." Nahath nodded. "Good. I hoped you'd say something along those lines." Saluting, he did a smart about-face and marched off.

Whatever he does back in New Eborac, I'll bet he's a success at it, John thought. Then he started to laugh. It wasn't necessarily so. Marshal Bart, the one southron officer who'd won victory after victory even in the dark days when few others did, had failed at everything he tried away from the army. Only after he redonned his gray tunic and pantaloons did he show what he could do.

Shouts and cheers rang out not far away. John hurried over to find out what was going on. Picking his way past the campfires came Hard-Riding Jimmy. Every man who saw the young commander of unicorn-riders tried to clasp his hand or pound his back or give him a flask. By the way he swayed, he'd already swigged from quite a few flasks.

John came forward to congratulate Jimmy, too. "Well done!" he said. "Without you, we couldn't have broken them the way we did."

Jimmy's answering grin was wide and foolish; yes, he'd done some celebrating before he got this far. "Thank you kindly, sir," he said. "You didn't do too bad yourself, by the Lion God's holy fangs."

"Every day another step," John said. On a night where Hard-Riding Jimmy and even Doubting George were sounding like the great Detinan conquerors of days gone by, the men who'd subjected the blonds, he could afford to be, or at least to sound like, the voice of reason. He added, "We took a big step today."

"None bigger," Hard-Riding Jimmy said. "No, sir, none bigger. I've never seen the traitors go to pieces like this before." He flashed that grin again. "I hope I see it some more."

"Do you expect anything different from now on?" John asked.

Jimmy shook his head. "Not me. They're ruined. It'd take a miracle—no, by the Thunderer's balls, it'd take a miracle and a *half*—for them to rally after this. Bell's got to be fit to be tied from what we did to him."

"He's still got Ned of the Forest," John remarked, curious to see what the mention of one leading commander of unicorn-riders would do to the other.

"Ned's a fine officer," Hard-Riding Jimmy said with the owlish sincerity of a man who'd had a little too much to drink. "A *fine* officer, don't get me wrong. But we whipped his men, and we'll whip 'em again next time we bump into 'em, too. They're plenty brave. Never braver—don't get me wrong." If he hadn't had too much to drink, he wouldn't have repeated the phrase. "But he hasn't got enough troopers and he hasn't got enough proper weapons to give us a real fight."

"Those quick-shooting crossbows make that much difference?" John asked.

"Hells, yes! I should say so!" Hard-Riding Jimmy exclaimed. "Sir, inside of five years the ordinary cross-bow will be gone from the Detinan army. Gone, I tell you! It makes a decent hunting weapon, but that's all. With quick-shooters, we'll sweep the blond savages off the eastern steppe like that." He snapped his fingers, but without a sound. He tried again. This time, it worked. "*That*, gods damn it."

"Well, after what you've done the past two days, I can't very well tell you you don't know your business," John the Lister said. He clapped Hard-Riding Jimmy on the back again. Grinning still, the commander of unicorn-riders lurched off.

"Brigadier John!" a runner called. John turned and waved to show he'd heard. The messenger hurried over to him. "I'm glad I caught up with you, sir. Doubting George's compliments, and the orders for the morning for your wing are hard pursuit. You are to take an eastern route, as best you can, and try to get ahead of the traitors. That way, with luck, we can surround them and wipe them out."

"Hard pursuit by an eastern route," John repeated. "I'm to get out in front of the Army of Franklin if I can. My compliments to the commanding general in return. I understand the orders, and I'll obey them." With another salute, the runner trotted away.

George had brought engineers forward to put more bridges across the stream that had slowed pursuit the evening before. As soon as they got near the far bank, northern snipers started shooting at them. The southrons pushed repeating crossbows up to the edge of the stream and hosed down the brush on the north bank of the stream with quarrels. They sent men in gray in there after the northerners, too. All that slowed but did not stop the sniping. Slowing it let the bridges reach the north bank and let the southrons cross with ease. After that, the snipers fell back.

Riding at the front of his column of footsoldiers, John the Lister pushed ahead as hard as the tired men would go. Every once in a while, off to the west, he got a glimpse of the remnants of the Army of Franklin, which was also moving north at something close to double time. The traitors had to be even more weary than his own men. How long could they continue that headlong withdrawal? John grinned. Not long enough, or so he hoped.

He was about to order his men to swing in on the fleeing northerners when a crossbow quarrel zipped past his head. If he could see Bell's men, they could see him, too. And even Bell, no great general—as he'd proved again and again—could see what the southrons had in mind.

Bell's rear guard came from Ned of the Forest's troopers. They were, as every southron who'd ever met them had reason to know, a stubborn bunch. Here they were fighting mostly dismounted from a stand of trees that gave them good cover.

John the Lister wanted to roll over them even so. He wanted to, but discovered he couldn't. They knocked his first attack back on its heels. Cursing, he shouted, "Deploy! We'll flank them out, by the Lion God's mane!"

And his men did exactly that, with some help from Hard-Riding Jimmy's unicorn-riders. They did it, yes, but doing it took them an hour and a half. They didn't damage Ned's force very much, either. Instead of waiting to be surrounded and slaughtered, the northern troopers went back to their unicorns and rode off when their position grew difficult. They wouldn't have any trouble catching up with Bell's retreating column of footsoldiers.

They wouldn't—but John the Lister's men would. While the southrons were fighting that rear-guard action, the main body of their foes marched several miles. John did some more cursing. "Step it up, boys!" he called.

The soldiers tried. He'd feared he was asking more

of them than flesh and blood could give. Toward evening, they came close to catching up with the northerners again. Again, though, a detachment of Ned's troopers, this time backed up by footsoldiers in blue, delayed them long enough to let Bell's main force get away.

"We'll keep after them," John declared. He wondered if they would be able to make the traitors stand and fight, though.

Ned of the Forest supposed he might have been more disgusted, but he had trouble seeing how. One thing that might have let him show more disgust would have been less to worry about. He was as busy as a one-armed juggler with the itch. The southrons knew they had the Army of Franklin on the run. For once, that didn't satisfy them. They wanted the army dead—no, not just dead; extinct.

They were liable to get what they wanted, too. Bell had given Ned the dubious honor of commanding the rear guard against Doubting George's onrushing army. Ned didn't want the job. The only reason he'd taken it was that he couldn't see anyone else who had even a chance of bringing it off.

"They're going to hound us all the way out of Franklin, Biff," he said at the end of the first day's retreat.

"Yes, sir." Colonel Biffle nodded. "Gods damn me to all the hells if I see how we can stop 'em, either."

"Stop 'em?" Ned started. He didn't know whether he felt more like laughing or crying. Since both would have made Colonel Biffle worry, he contented himself with a growl that could have come from the throat of a tiger in the far northern jungle. "By the Thunderer's belly button, Biff, we're not going to stop those stinking sons of bitches. If we can slow 'em down enough so

they don't eat all of Bell's army, King Geoffrey ought
to pin a medal on us just for that."

"Yes, sir," Biffle said, and then, after a long, long
pause, "If we can't stop 'em, though, Lord Ned, the
war's as good as lost."

Ned of the Forest only grunted in response, as he'd
tried not to show pain whenever he was wounded. He
didn't think his regimental commander was wrong—
which only made the words hurt worse.

"What do we do, sir?" Biffle asked. "What do we
do if . . . if King Avram's bastards really can lick us?"

"The best we can our ownselves," Ned answered
firmly. "They haven't done it yet, and I aim to make
it as hard for them as I can. As long as we keep fighting, we've got a chance. If we throw up our hands and
quit, we really *are* licked."

"Yes, sir." Colonel Biffle sounded a little happier—
but only a little.

When Ned of the Forest got a good look at his own
troopers after their latest encounter with John the
Lister's footsoldiers, he understood why. Their heads
were down; their shoulders slumped. For the first time,
they looked like beaten men. They kept on, yes, but
they plainly had no faith in what they were doing.

"Come on, boys," Ned called. "We'll hang a few
more bruises on those southron bastards, and after a
while they'll give up and go home. We can do it. We
always have. What's one more time?"

A few of the unicorn-riders smiled and perked up.
Most of them, though, kept that . . . trampled look
they'd been wearing. When they compared what they
heard to what they saw, they realized the two didn't
match. And what they saw, what everyone in the east
who followed King Geoffrey couldn't help seeing, was
a great tide of disaster rising up to roll over them and
drown them.

Captain Watson rode up to Ned. The young officer in charge of his siege engines said, "Sir, the catapults are about played out. We've done so much shooting with 'em, the sinew skeins are stretched to death. Our range is down, and our accuracy is worse. Where can we get more sinew?"

"Hamstring some southrons," Ned answered.

Watson started to chuckle, but then broke off, as if unsure whether Ned was kidding. Ned wasn't sure he was kidding, either. But he didn't contradict when Watson said, "I can't do that, sir."

"Well, to the hells with me if I know where you'll come up with any sinew," Ned said. "Sinners, yes—sinners we've got swarms of. But sinew?" He shook his head. "What else can you use?"

"Next best thing is hair: long, coarse hair," Watson answered.

"Then shave the unicorns," Ned said at once. "Cut off their manes, trim their tails, do whatever you need to do. Start with my beast. Can troopers twist hair into skeins?"

"Uh, yes, sir. I'd think so," Watson said dazedly. "It's not hard to do, once you know how."

"All right. Get started on it, then. Show 'em what they need to do. Don't waste any time," Ned said. "We're going to need those engines—you can bet on that."

Captain Watson nodded. "Oh, yes, sir. I know. I do believe I would have come up with that notion myself, but I know I wouldn't have done it so fast." He laughed. "After all, I *didn't* do it so fast, did I?"

"Never mind," Ned of the Forest said. "Just get on with it. Where it comes from doesn't matter, long as you can make it work."

"Do you know, sir, there are men—more than a few of them, too—who would want a promotion for coming up with an idea like that," Watson said. "You don't even seem to care."

"I don't, much," Ned said. "Nobody's going to promote me now. I'm already a lieutenant general, and King Geoffrey isn't going to fancy up my epaulets any more. Besides, the mess we're in now, the idea counts more than whoever had it."

Some of his troopers didn't care for the scheme at all. It wasn't that they minded twisting unicorn hair into skeins for the catapults and repeating crossbows; they didn't. But they hated the way the unicorns looked once shorn of shaggy manes and tails. In piteous tones, one of them said, "Lord Ned, those gods-damned southrons're going to laugh at us when they see us riding such sorry beasts."

"Too bad," Ned answered heartlessly. "If they do laugh, Watson'll shoot 'em out of the saddle with the hair he's taken. That counts for more."

Because he was who he was, he bullied them into going along with him with a minimum of fuss and feathers. That Captain Watson had trimmed his unicorn first helped. And the unicorn did look sorry after it was trimmed: more like an overgrown white rat with a horn on its nose than one of the beautiful, noble beasts that added a touch of style and old-time glory to modern battlefields, most of which, taken all in all, were anything but glorious. But if their leader was willing to go into a fight on a unicorn that looked like that, the troopers couldn't very well cavil.

And Ned, for his part, didn't care what his mount looked like. He felt none of what northern officers of higher blood called "the romance of the unicorn." As far as he was concerned, a unicorn was for getting from one place to another faster than he could walk or run. He'd had plenty of mounts killed under him. If this

one, shorn or not, lasted to the end of the war, he
would be astonished.

Watson's engine crews spent the wee small hours
threading the roughly made skeins of unicorn hair into
the engines. Their thumping and banging and clattering
kept Ned awake. Those weren't the usual noises he
heard in the field, and they bothered him on account
of that.

He poured honey into a cup of nasty tea the next
morning, trying to make it palatable. It stayed nasty,
but at least was sweeter. There not ten feet away stood
Captain Watson doing the same thing. "Well, Captain?"
Ned called.

"Pretty well, sir," Watson answered, sipping from his
tin cup and making an unhappy face. "How about you?"

"Hells with me," Ned said. "How are the engines?"

"In working order," Watson said. "Better than they
were before we reskeined 'em. Thank you, sir."

"Never mind me," Ned told him. "Long as we can
give the southrons grief."

They got a fair amount of grief themselves later that
morning, beating back an attack from some of Hard-
Riding Jimmy's troopers. The two disastrous days of
fighting in front of Ramblerton had made Ned of the
Forest despise the southron unicorn-riders. They would
have made any normal man fear those troopers, but
Ned reserved fear for the gods, and doled it out spar-
ingly even to them.

The southrons had too many men and could put too
many bolts in the air to make it any kind of fair fight.
That being so, Ned didn't try to make it one, either.
Instead, he used a feigned retreat to lead the eager
southrons—who did jeer at his men's funny-looking
unicorns—straight up to Captain Watson's engines,
which sat cunningly concealed at the edge of a thicket.

Watson had been right—the engines worked the way

they were supposed to. A barrage of firepots and stones greeted the southrons. So did the nasty, mechanical *clack-clack-clack* of the repeating crossbows. Southrons tumbled out of the saddle. Unicorns crashed to the ground as if they'd run headlong into a wall. The survivors galloped away from the trap a lot faster than they'd galloped towards it.

"There's a proper job of licking them," Watson said, beaming.

Colonel Biffle remained gloomy. "They'll be back, the stinking sons of bitches."

"Oh, yes. They'll be back," Ned of the Forest agreed. "But they won't be back for a while. The time they spend figuring out how they stuck their peckers in the meat grinder, our footsoldiers can use to get away. That's what the game we're playing is all about right now."

"They won't be so easy to trick next time," Biffle said.

That was also true, without a doubt. Hard-Riding Jimmy had shown himself to be no fool. But Ned said, "Other side of the copper is, from now on they'll look before they leap. That'll slow them down. We want them slow. We don't want 'em charging all over the landscape."

Captain Watson nodded. He understood. Colonel Biffle had a harder time. He still wanted to beat the southrons here, even if he knew how unlikely that was to change the course of the war. Ned had stopped worrying about beating them, at least in the sense he would have used for the word before setting out on this campaign. Delaying them counted as a victory, for it let the battered fragments of the Army of Franklin put more distance between themselves and Doubting George's disgustingly numerous, revoltingly well-fed, and alarmingly well-armed soldiers.

It isn't fair, Ned thought. *It isn't even close to fair. If we had that many men and could give them the food and gear they need . . .*

He laughed, though it wasn't really funny. If the north could have raised and supported armies like that, of *course* it would have broken away from King Avram's rule. But it couldn't. It couldn't come close. And nobody had ever said war was the least bit fair, Ned included. He'd used every trick he knew, and invented several fresh tricks on the spur of the moment. Expecting the southrons not to use their advantages of wealth and manpower was like wishing for the moon. You could do it, but that didn't mean you'd get what you wished for.

A rider came up and pointed to the northeast. "The southrons are trying to slip around our flank again, Lord Ned," he said.

"Well, we'd better try and stop the bastards, then, eh?" Ned said.

"Yes, sir," the messenger said, and then, "Er—how, sir?"

"You leave that to me." Ned handled the problem with unfussy competence. It wasn't as if he hadn't dealt with such situations before. Detaching men from the right, he shifted them around behind the center to extend the left. General Hesmucet had made the same sort of flanking maneuver again and again for King Avram's army in Peachtree Province the year before as Hard-Riding Jimmy was using now, and Count Joseph the Gamecock had matched it time after time.

Joseph had traded space for time, again and again. Not Bell, not after he took command of the Army of Franklin. He'd gone right out and slugged toe to toe with Hesmucet's bigger army . . . which went a long way toward putting the Army of Franklin in its present unhappy predicament.

Ned shifted Captain Watson's engines along with the men from the right. They were the only things that could give his riders a decent chance against the quick-shooting crossbows Hard-Riding Jimmy's men used. By the shouts of dismay from the southrons when the repeating crossbows clattered into action, Jimmy's troopers knew it, too.

Of course, had Ned's unicorn-riders already been under attack on the right when Hard-Riding Jimmy's men hit them on the left, he wouldn't have been able to shift troopers and engines like that. All through the war, the southrons had had a certain trouble coordinating their blows. *A good thing, too*, Ned thought. *They'd've whipped us a long time ago if they really knew what they were doing.*

Northern magecraft had also helped hold King Avram's armies at bay. That made it all the more disconcerting when lightning crashed down from a clear sky and wrecked one of Captain Watson's precious, newly reskeined catapults. A few minutes later, another deadly accurate thunderbolt set a second siege engine afire.

"Major Marmaduke!" Ned of the Forest roared furiously. "Where in the godsdamnation are you, you worthless excuse for a mage?"

The wizard in the blue robe came over at a fast trot. "I'm . . . sorry, sir," he quavered. "I'll do my best, but he's too quick and strong for me."

"He'd better not be," Ned ground out. "Without those engines, my troopers are dead men. If they lose them, Major, *you're* a dead man."

Marmaduke went even paler than he was already. He did not make the mistake of thinking Ned was joking. When the commander of unicorn-riders spoke in such tones, joking was the furthest thing from his mind.

And, perhaps more inspired by fear than he'd ever been by patriotism, Major Marmaduke succeeded in deflecting the next strokes from the southron sorcerer. The lightnings smote, yes, but not where the engines were. The invaluable repeating crossbows survived, and kept spitting death at Hard-Riding Jimmy's men. Eventually, the southron unicorn-riders drew back in discouragement.

Made it through another day, Ned of the Forest thought. *How many more?*

Rollant wasn't much with needle and thread. His wife would have laughed if she'd seen the clumsy botches he'd made of some repairs to his uniform. But Norina was back in New Eborac City, so he had to do what he could for himself. And sewing a third stripe on his sleeve wasn't a duty. It was a pleasure.

He'd never expected to make sergeant's rank. Come to that, he'd never expected to make corporal's rank, either. If the south hadn't needed bodies to throw at false King Geoffrey's men, he might never have got into the army at all.

Bodies . . . His mouth twisted at that. If two Detinan soldiers hadn't suddenly become no more than bodies, he wouldn't have been promoted once, let alone twice, and he knew it. Snatching up the company standard when the standard-bearer went down won him his corporal's stripes—that, of course, and staying alive once he did it. And now Lieutenant Griff was dead, too, Sergeant Joram was Lieutenant Joram . . . and Corporal Rollant became Sergeant Rollant.

Ordinary Detinans could get promoted without having someone die to open a slot for them. Blonds? It didn't look that way. But ordinary Detinans could also get promoted when someone did die. Sitting crosslegged in front of the fire by Rollant was Smitty, who was making heavy weather of sewing a corporal's two stripes onto the sleeve of his gray tunic.

He pricked himself, yelped, and looked up from what he was doing. "This whole business of being an underofficer seems like more trouble than it's worth," he said.

"No." Rollant shook his head. "Oh, no. Not even a little bit. This is as good as it gets—it says the army likes what you're doing, what kind of a man you are."

To him, that meant a great deal—meant everything, in fact. Respect always came grudgingly to blonds . . . when it came at all. But Smitty, a Detinan born, took his status for granted. "I know what kind of man I am, gods damn it. I'm a man who's sick of getting shot at, who's sick of sleeping on the ground, and who's ready to pack this whole stinking war in and go home."

"Can't do that. Not yet. Not till it's over," Rollant said.

"Don't remind me," Smitty said mournfully. He raised his voice to call out to a couple of common soldiers to gather up water bottles and fill them at a nearby creek.

"See what happens?" one of them said: a Detinan speaking his mind, as Detinans did. "You haven't even got the stripes on your sleeve yet, and already you're treating people like you were a liege lord." Off he went, still grumbling.

Smitty turned to Rollant. "Thunderer's ballocks, Sergeant, but we're getting a poor sort of common soldier these days." His voice brimmed with righteous indignation.

Rollant gaped at him, then started to laugh. "When you were a common soldier and I was a corporal, didn't you bray like a whipped ass whenever I asked you to do the least little thing? If that wasn't you, it sure looked a lot like you."

"Oh, but I didn't understand then," Smitty said. "Now I do."

"I know what you understand," Rollant told him. "You understand you'd rather get somebody else to do something for you than do it yourself."

"Well, what else is there *to* understand?" Smitty said.

Although the blond thought Smitty was joking, he wasn't sure. He answered, "I'll say this, Smitty: the liege lords up here think the same way. It's great for them, but not for their serfs."

"Fine," Smitty said. "You can do as much work as a common soldier and still keep your stripes. Or you could—I don't see you *doing* it."

"It's different in the army," Rollant insisted.

"How?"

"Because . . ." Rollant grimaced. Spelling out what he meant wasn't so easy. He did his best: "Because the army tells me what I'm supposed to do, and what all sergeants and corporals are supposed to do. And it doesn't have one set of rules for ordinary Detinans and a different set for blonds—now that blonds get paid the same as ordinary Detinans it doesn't, anyway."

"That never was fair," Smitty allowed.

"Gods-damned right it wasn't," Rollant growled. "If they send us out to get killed the same as anybody else, we'd better make the same silver as anybody else, too. And Sergeant Joram—when he was a sergeant, I mean—did the same things as I'm doing. So if you don't like it, take it up with him."

"No, thanks," Smitty said, in a way implying that that subject wasn't open to discussion. Whether he liked the rules or not, he didn't like Joram, regardless of rank.

He went back to sewing the stripes onto his sleeve. Rollant returned to adding the sergeant's stripe. Joram came up to the fire with a shiny new lieutenant's epaulet on the left shoulder of his old, faded gray tunic. The only place the tunic still displayed its original color was where the underofficer's chevrons he'd just cut off had protected the wool from sun and rain.

When Rollant and Smitty jumped to their feet and saluted, Joram grimaced. "As you were," he said, and then, "I'm not used to this—not even close. I never wanted to be an officer."

"I never wanted to be a corporal, either," Smitty muttered.

"Shall I tear those stripes off before you finish putting 'em on, then?" Joram asked. Smitty hastily shook his head. Lieutenant Joram nodded in something approaching satisfaction.

Rollant couldn't say he hadn't wanted his promotion. He hadn't counted on it; he hadn't even particularly expected it. But he'd craved it, just as he'd craved corporal's rank after giving himself the chance to earn it. Rank meant the Detinans had to recognize what he'd done. It would vanish at the end of the war, but what it meant would remain inside him forever.

"Is all well here?" Joram asked, plainly serious about meeting his new responsibilities.

"Yes, sir," Rollant and Smitty chorused.

"Good." The new company commander went off to another campfire.

The troopers Smitty had sent out came back with the water bottles. They started to dump them at the new corporal's feet. Rollant shook his head. "You know that's not how you do it. Take each one to the man it belongs to and give it to him. To begin with, you can give me mine."

He took it from one of the soldiers. He'd delivered plenty of water bottles before he got promoted. Now that was someone else's worry. Rollant didn't miss it, or cutting firewood, or digging latrine trenches, or any of the other duties common soldiers got stuck with because they were so common.

Smitty unrolled his blanket and started wrapping himself in it. "We ought to grab whatever shuteye we can," he said. "Come morning, they'll try and march the legs off us again."

He wasn't wrong, as Rollant knew too well. His own legs were weary, too; he could feel just how much marching he'd done. But he said, "As long as we've got the traitors on the run, I'll keep going. I'd chase that serfcatching son of a bitch of a Ned of the Forest all the way up into Shell Bay if I could."

"He came after you when you ran away?" Smitty asked, a strange blend of sympathy and curiosity in his voice.

"Not him—he's always worked here in the east," Rollant answered. "But there are plenty more like him over by the Western Ocean. I hate 'em all. I know every trick there is for shaking hounds off a trail, and I needed most of them, too."

"And you did all that so you could come down to New Eborac and get yourself three stripes?" Smitty said. "You ask me, it was more trouble than it was worth."

Rollant also spread out his blanket. He knew Smitty was pulling his leg. Some jokes were easier to take than others, though. "Maybe it looks that way to you," the blond said. "To me, though, these three stripes mean a hells of a lot. They mean I can give orders—I don't have to take 'em my whole life long."

Smitty eyed him as he cocooned himself in the thick wool blanket. "You may be a blond, your Sergeantly Magnificence," he said, "but I swear by all the gods you talk more like a Detinan every day."

"It's rubbed off on me—like the itch," Rollant answered, and fell asleep.

"Up! Up! Up!" Lieutenant Joram shouted at some ungodly hour of the morning. All Rollant knew when his eyes came open was that it was still dark. He groaned and unwrapped himself and relieved his own misery by booting out of their bedrolls the men who'd managed to ignore the racket Joram was making.

After hot, strong tea and oatmeal thick and sweet and sticky with molasses, the soldiers started after the Army of Franklin again. Rollant had had to get used to the idea of eating oatmeal when he came down to New Eborac. In Palmetto Province, oats fed asses and unicorns, not people. Right now, though, he would have eaten anything that didn't eat him. Marching and fighting took fuel, and lots of it.

The northerners had also abandoned their encampments, a few miles north of those of Doubting George's army. But they'd left Ned of the Forest's unicorn-riders and a small force of footsoldiers behind to slow down the retreating southrons. The troopers and crossbowmen would take cover, fight till they were on the point of being outflanked, and then fall back to do it again somewhere else. They weren't fighting to win, only to delay their foes. That, they managed to do.

Even though the rear guard kept the southrons from falling on the Army of Franklin one last time and destroying it, Bell's army kept falling to pieces on its own from the hard pursuit. More and more men in blue tunics and pantaloons gave up, stopped running, and raised their hands when King Avram's soldiers came upon them. Most went off into captivity. A few—those who came out of hiding too suddenly, or those who just ran into southrons with grudges—met unfortunate and untimely ends. Such things weren't supposed to happen. They did, all the time, on both sides.

Even after surrendering, northerners stared at

Rollant. "What is this world coming to, when blonds can lord it over Detinans?" one of them exclaimed.

"It's simple," Rollant said. "I wasn't stupid enough to pick the losing side. You were. Now get moving."

The prisoner looked from one ordinary Detinan in gray to the next. "You fellows going to let him talk to me like that?" he demanded indignantly.

"We have to," Smitty answered, his voice grave.

"What do you mean, you have to?" the prisoner said. "He's a blond. *You're* supposed to tell *him* what to do."

"Can't," Smitty said. "He's the sergeant. We tell him off, he gives us the nastiest duty he can find, just like a regular Detinan would."

"I think you people have all gone crazy," said the man from the Army of Franklin, setting his hands on his hips.

"Maybe we *are* crazy," Rollant said. "But we're winning. If we can win while we're crazy, what does that make you traitors?"

"*I'm* not a traitor." The northerner got irate all over again. "It's you people who let blonds do things the gods didn't mean to have 'em do—*you're* the traitors, you and that gods-damned son of a bitch of a King Avram."

"If the gods didn't want me to do something, they'd keep me from doing it, wouldn't they?" Rollant said. "If they *don't* keep me from doing it, that must mean they know I *can* do it, right? And since you traitors are losing the war, that means the gods don't want you to win it, right?"

His comrades in gray laughed and whooped. "Listen to him!" Smitty said. "He ought to be a priest, not a sergeant."

And Rollant saw he'd troubled the captured northerner. The man said nothing more, but he looked worried. He hadn't before. He'd looked angry that the southrons had taken him prisoner, and at the same time relieved that he wouldn't be killed. Now, his brow furrowed, he seemed to be examining the reasons for which he'd gone to war in the first place.

Rollant jerked a thumb toward the south. "Take him away. I'd like to give him just what I think he deserves, but I have to follow orders, too."

Off went the prisoner, still looking worried. From not far away, Lieutenant Joram boomed out an order Rollant had heard a great many times since joining the army, but one he'd come to enjoy the past few days: "Forward!"

"Forward!" Rollant echoed, and waved the company standard. And forward the company went. Sooner or later, Ned of the Forest's troopers would try to slow them down again. Even if the northerners managed to do it, they wouldn't delay King Avram's men for long.

If something happens to Joram—not that I want it to, but if—will they make me a lieutenant? Rollant wondered. It wasn't *quite* impossible; there were a handful of blond officers, though most of them were healers. But it also wasn't even close to likely, and he had enough sense to understand as much. He'd been lucky to get two stripes on his sleeve, amazingly lucky to get three.

For that matter, considering the fighting he'd seen, he'd been amazingly lucky to come through alive, and with no serious wounds. He wanted that luck to go on, especially with the war all but won. Next to staying in one piece, what was rank? If they'd offered to make him a lieutenant general like Bell, but with Bell's missing leg and ruined arm, would he have taken them up on it? Of course not.

The war couldn't last too much longer . . . could it? He wanted to live through it and go home to Norina. Getting killed—even getting hurt—now would be doubly unfair. He'd done everything any man could do to win the fight. Didn't he deserve to enjoy the fruits of victory?

He snorted. He was a standard-bearer. He had no guarantee of staying alive for the next five minutes. "Forward!" he shouted again. If anything *did* happen to him, he would be facing the foe when it did. And if *that* wasn't a quintessentially Detinan thought, when would he ever have one?

Lieutenant General Bell sat in a carriage as the Army of Franklin tramped over a wood bridge to the northern bank of the Smew River. The Smew ran through rough, heavily wooded country in northern Franklin. Bell wished he were on a unicorn, but days of riding had left his stump too sore for him to stay in the saddle. If he didn't travel by carriage, he would have been unable to travel at all. No matter how obvious that truth, it was also humiliating. He felt like a civilian. He might have been going to a temple on a feast day, like any prosperous merchant.

To his relief, the men didn't seem bothered about how he got from one place to another. They waved to him as they trudged past. Some of them lifted their hats in lieu of a more formal salute. Bell waved back with his good arm.

"We'll lick 'em yet, General!" a soldier called.

"By the gods, we *will*!" Bell answered. "Let's see them try to drive us off the line of the Smew!"

He wanted to make a stand while he still remained here in Franklin. Even if the Ramblerton campaign had accomplished less than he would have liked—that was how he looked at it, through the most rose-colored of mental spectacles—he didn't want to have to fall back into Dothan or Great River Province. Staying in Franklin would show the doubters (he didn't pause to think about Doubting George) both in his own army and in King Geoffrey's court back at Nonesuch that he was still in charge of things, that these battered regiments still responded to his will.

Boots thudded on the planks of the bridge. More men, though, had none. *Their* feet, bare as those of any blond savage, made next to no sound. Some of them left bloody marks on those gray and faded planks. The weather was not far above freezing, and the road up from the south an ocean of mud. How many of the surviving soldiers had frostbitten feet? More than a few, surely. More than Bell cared to think about, even more surely.

Here came Ned of the Forest's unicorn-riders and the rest of the rear guard. The unicorns' hooves drummed as they rode over to the north bank of the Smew. "Come on, sir!" Ned yelled to Bell. "Nobody left between you and Avram's bastards."

I wish I could fight them all singlehanded, Bell thought. Had he been whole, he would have, and gladly. Things being as they were, though . . . Things being as they were, Bell muttered to his driver. The man flicked the reins. The unicorn started forward. Each jolt as the wheels rattled across the bridge hurt. Bell wondered when he would get used to pain. He'd lived in so much for so long, but it still hurt. He suspected it always would.

As soon as he'd crossed, wizards called down lightning. This time, the cursed southron sorcerers didn't interfere with the spells. The lightnings smote. The bridge crashed in ruins into the Smew.

Bell hoped to find a farmhouse in which to make his headquarters. He had no luck. Most of the country was woodland and scrub, with farms few and far between— so far that none of them made a convenient place from which to lead the Army of Franklin. Up went the pavilion. Even with three braziers burning inside it, it made a cold and cheerless place to spend a night.

After a meager supper, Bell summoned his wing commanders and Ned of the Forest. When they arrived, he said, "We have to hold this line. We have to keep the southrons out of Dothan and Great River Province."

Stephen the Pickle looked as steeped in vinegar as his namesakes. "How do you propose to do that, sir?" he said. "We haven't got the men for it, not any more we haven't." He looked as if he wanted to say more, but checked himself at the last minute.

What Stephen didn't say, Benjamin the Heated Ham did: "We've thrown away more men than we've got left. If we can make it to Great River Province or Dothan with the pieces of this army we've got left, that'd be the gods' own miracle all by itself. Anything more? Forget it." He shook his head.

"Where is your fighting spirit?" Bell cried.

"Dead," Colonel Florizel said.

"Murdered," Ned of the Forest added.

Glaring from one of them to the next, the commanding general said, "We need a great stroke of sorcery to remind the southrons they can't afford to take us for granted, and to show them we are not yet beaten." Stephen, Benjamin, Florizel, and Ned all stirred at that. Bell ignored them. "I aim to fight by every means I have at my disposal till I can fight no more. I expect every man who follows me to do the same."

"Trouble is, sir, we don't have enough men left *to* fight," Benjamin the Heated Ham said. "We don't have enough wizards, either." The other wing commanders and the commander of unicorn-riders all nodded at last.

"Gods damn it, we have to do *something!*" Bell burst out. "Do you want to keep running till we run out of land and go swimming in the Gulf?"

"No, sir," Benjamin said stolidly. "But I don't want to get massacred trying to do what I can't, either."

Ned of the Forest said, "Sir, while we're trying to hold this stretch of the Smew, what's to keep the southrons from crossing the river east or west of us and flanking us out of our position or surrounding us?"

"Patrols from your troopers, among other things," Lieutenant General Bell replied, acid in his voice.

"I can watch," Ned said. "I can slow the southrons down—some. Stop 'em? No way in hells."

"If you fight here, sir, you doom us," Stephen the Pickle said.

"I don't want to fight here. I want to form some kind of line we can defend," Bell said.

No one seemed to believe he could do it. Silent resentment rose in waves from his subordinate commanders. They had no hope, none at all. Bell waved with his good arm. Stephen, Benjamin, Florizel, and Ned filed out of the pavilion.

I could use their heads in a rock garden, Bell thought, never once imagining they might feel the same way about him—or that they might have reason to feel that way. He called for a runner. What went through his mind was, *Half the men in this army are runners. They've proved that.* The young soldier who reported, though, was still doing his duty. Bell said, "Fetch me our mages. I want to see what we can expect from them."

"Yes, sir." Saluting, the runner hurried away.

In due course, the wizards came. They looked worn and miserable. Bell wondered why—it wasn't as if they'd done anything useful. He said, "I propose holding the line of the Smew. I know I'll need magical help to do it. What can you give me?"

The magicians looked at one another. Their expressions grew even more unhappy. At last, one of them said, "Sir, I don't see how we can promise you much, not when the southrons have handled us so roughly all through this campaign."

"But we need everything you can give us now," Bell said, and then brightened. He pointed from one wizard to the next. "I know what we need! By the gods, gentlemen, I do. Give us a dragon!"

"Illusion?" a mage said doubtfully. "I think we're too far gone for illusion to do us much good."

"Not illusion." Bell shook his big, leonine head. "I know that won't serve us. They'll penetrate it and disperse it. Conjure up a *real* dragon and loose it on the gods-damned southrons."

The wizards stared at one another again, this time in something approaching horror. "Sir," one of them said, "there *are* no dragons any more, not west of the Great River. Not west of the Stony Mountains, come to that. You know there aren't. Everybody knows there aren't."

"Then conjure one here *from* the Stony Mountains," Bell said impatiently. "I don't care how you do it. Just do it. Let's see Doubting George and his pet mage handle a real, live, fire-breathing dragon."

"Do you expect us to seize one out of the air in the Stonies, bring it here, and turn it loose?" a mage demanded.

"Yes, that's exactly what I expect, by the Lion God's mane," the general commanding said. "That's what we need, that's what we have to have, and that's what we'd better get."

"But *how*?" The sorcerers made a ragged chorus.

"*How* is your worry," Lieutenant General Bell said grandly. "I want it done, and it *shall* be done, or I'll know the reason why—and you'll be sorry. Have you got that? A dragon—a real dragon, not one of the stupid illusions the southrons threw at us a few times in front of Ramblerton—by day after tomorrow. Any more questions?" He didn't gave them time to answer, but gestured peremptorily. "Dismissed."

Out went the wizards. If anything, they looked even more put-upon than Bell's subordinate commanders had a little while earlier. Bell didn't care. He'd given them an order. All they had to do was obey.

Bell stretched himself out on his iron-framed cot. He didn't sleep long, though. When his eyes first came open, there in the darkness inside the pavilion, he couldn't imagine what had roused him. It wasn't a noise; no bright lights blazed outside the big tent; he didn't need to ease himself. What *was* the trouble, then?

Sentries in front of the pavilion murmured to one another. A single word dominated those murmurs: "Magic."

Grunting with effort, Bell sat up, pushing himself up with his good arm. Then he used his crutches and surviving leg to get to his foot. He made his slow way into the chilly night. The sentries exclaimed in surprise. Bell ignored them. Now he knew why he was awake. Like the sentries, he'd felt the power of the wizardry the sorcerers were brewing.

He couldn't see it. He couldn't hear it. But it was there. He could feel it, feel it in his fingertips, feel it in his beard, feel it in his belly and the roots of his teeth. The power was strong enough to distract him both from his constant pain and from the laudanum haze he used as a shield against it.

He stood there in the darkness, his breath smoking, and waited to see what that power would bring when it was finally unleashed. *Something* great, surely. What he wanted? *It had better be*, he thought.

The marvel didn't wear off. More and more soldiers came out of their tents to stare at the wizards' pavilion. Like Bell, they stood there and stood there, careless of sleep, careless of anything, waiting, waiting, waiting.

Dawn had begun painting the eastern horizon with pink and gold when the building bubble of power finally burst. High overhead, the sky opened, or so it seemed to a yawning, half-freezing Bell. The sky opened, and a dragon burst forth out of thin air, a great winged worm where *nothing* had been before. Had it stooped on the Army of Franklin . . . But it didn't. The wizards held it under so much control, at least. Roaring with fury, it flew off toward the Smew River, off toward the southrons.

Doubting George had a habit of rising early so he could prowl about his army and see what was what. Major Alva had a habit of staying up very late on nights when he wasn't likely to be needed the next day. Every so often, the two of them would run into each other a little before sunrise.

So it chanced this particular morning. The commanding general nodded to the wizard. Alva remembered to salute. Doubting George beamed. Alva would never make a proper soldier, but he was doing a better and better impersonation of one.

"How are things?" George asked. He expected nothing much from the wizard's reply. As far as he could see, things were fine. Bell's army was on the run. He hadn't managed to crush it altogether, and realized he probably wouldn't, but he was driving it out of the province from which it drew its name, driving it to the point where it would do false King Geoffrey no good.

Waving to the north, Alva answered, "The mages over there are up to something, sir." He was a beat slow using the title, but he did.

"What is it this time?" Doubting George was amazed

at how scornful he sounded. Before finding Alva, he would have been worried. Northern magecraft had plagued the southron cause all through the war. Now? Now, in this weedy young wizard, he had its measure.

Or so he thought, till Alva's head came up sharply, like that of a deer all at once taking a scent. "It's . . . something big," the sorcerer said slowly. "Something very big."

"Can you stop it?" George asked. "Whatever it is, you can keep it from hitting us, right?"

"It's not aimed at us," Alva answered. "It's aimed . . . somewhere far away."

"Then why worry about it?" the commanding general asked.

Alva didn't answer him this time, not right away. The wizard stared north, his face tense and drawn. Much more to himself than to Doubting George, he said, "I didn't think they could still manage anything like that." He sounded both astonished and admiring.

"Can you stop it?" George asked again, his voice sharp this time.

"I . . . don't know." Alva didn't look at him; the mage's attention still aimed toward the north, as a compass needle did toward the south. "Maybe I could . . ." He raised his hands, as if about to make a string of passes, but then let them fall to his sides once more. "Too late . . . sir. Whatever they were trying to do, they've just gone and done it. Can't you feel that?"

Doubting George shook his head. "You know how Marshal Bart is tone-deaf and doesn't know one tune from another? I'm like that with wizardry. A lot of soldiers are. Most of the time, it's an advantage. Unless magic bumps right up against me, I don't have to worry about it."

Shouts from the pickets and the forwardmost encampments said somebody was alarmed about something. Soldiers in gray tunics and pantaloons pointed up into the sky. "A dragon!" they shouted. "A gods-damned dragon!"

"A gods-damned dragon?" Doubting George threw back his head and laughed. "Is that all the traitors could cook up? An illusion? It's a stale illusion at that, because we aimed the seemings of dragons at them in the fights in front of Ramblerton. Good for little scares, maybe, but not for big ones."

Quietly, Major Alva said, "Sir, that is not the illusion of a dragon. That is . . . a dragon, conjured here from wherever it lives. My hat is off to Bell's sorcerers." He suited action to word. "No matter how desperate I was, I would not have cared to try the spell that brought it here."

"A real dragon?" George, who'd served in the east, had seen them before, flying among the peaks of the Stony Mountains. "What can your magic do against a real dragon, now that the beast is here?"

"I don't know, sir," Alva answered. "Not much, I don't think. Magic isn't what drove dragons out to the steppe and then to the mountains. Hunting is."

Stooping like an outsized hawk, the dragon dove towards a knot of tents. Flame burst from its great jaws. The southron soldiers hadn't panicked till that moment, thinking it an illusion similar to those Alva and their other wizards had also used. Then the tents—and several soldiers—burst into flame. Some of the screams that rang out were anguish. More were terror, as the men realized the beast was real—real, angry, and hungry.

They were good soldiers. As soon as they realized that, they started shooting at the dragon. Ordinary crossbow bolts, though, slowed it about as much as mosquitoes slowed a man.

The dragon roared, a noise like the end of the world.

It didn't like ordinary crossbow quarrels, any more than a man liked mosquitoes. As a man will pause to swat, the dragon paused to flame. As mosquitoes will get smashed, so a couple of squads of soldiers suddenly went up in smoke.

"Do *something*, gods damn it!" Doubting George shook Major Alva. He didn't even realize he was doing it till he noticed the wizard's teeth clicking together. Then, not without a certain regret, he stopped.

Once Alva had stopped clicking, he said, "I'm sorry, sir. I still don't know what to do. Dragons aren't a wizard's worry."

"This one is," George snapped.

Before Alva could either protest or start working magic, the repeating crossbows opened up on the dragon along with the ordinary footsoldiers' weapons. Those big crossbows shot longer, thicker quarrels and flung them faster and farther than a bow that a man might carry could manage.

This time, the dragon's roars were louder yet, louder and more sincere. Now it might have had wasps tormenting it, not mosquitoes. But however annoying they are, wasps rarely kill. The dragon remained determined to lash out at everything that was bothering it and everything it saw that it could eat. As far as Doubting George could tell, between them those two categories encompassed his whole army.

Thuk! Thuk! Thuk! Crossbow bolts tearing through the membrane of the dragon's wings sounded like knitting needles thrust through taut cotton cloth. Cotton, though, didn't bleed. The dragon did. Drops of its blood smoked when they hit the ground. Soldiers that blood touched cried out in pain. But even if the dragon did bleed, that made it no less fierce, no less furious. On the contrary.

It flew towards a battery of repeating crossbows that

hosed darts at it. Again, the fang-filled jaws spread wide.
Again, fire shot from them. The flames engulfed the
repeating crossbows. Some of the crews managed to flee.
Others kept working the windlasses till the very last
moment, and went up in flames with the engines they
served.

The dragon landed then. Its tremendous tail lashed
about, obliterating repeating crossbows its fire had
spared. Doubting George cursed. Those engines
would have been useful against the Army of Franklin.
Now . . . now they might as well never have been built.

But, with the dragon on the ground, the soldiers
serving catapults started flinging firepots at it. Some
of them had already let fly while the dragon was still
in the air. That was not the smartest thing they could
have done. Their missiles missed, and came down on
the heads of southron soldiers still in their tents or in
the trenches or rushing about.

They aimed better with the beast on the ground.
When a firepot burst on its armored back, the dragon
remained grounded no more. It sprang into the air with
a scream like all damnation boiled down into a pint.
No mosquitoes here, and no wasps, either. Not even
a dragon could ignore a bursting firepot.

Screaming again, the terrible beast flew off . . .
toward the west. That set Doubting George to cursing once more. He'd hoped the dragon would visit
vengeance on the northern sorcerers who'd summoned
it, but no such luck. *Have to take care of that ourselves*,
he thought.

Major Alva was staring in the direction the dragon
had gone. "How much harm will it do before people
finally manage to kill it?" he wondered.

"I don't know. Probably quite a bit." Even
Doubting George was surprised at how heartless he
sounded.

Alva looked more appalled than surprised. "Don't you care?"

Shrugging, the commanding general said, "Not a whole hells of a lot. For one thing, the dragon won't be doing it to us. For another, most of the people it *will* harm would rather see Geoffrey over them than Avram. Since Geoffrey's wizards summoned it here, you could say they're getting what they deserve."

"Oh." The wizard considered. "You make a nasty sort of sense."

"We're fighting a war, Major. There's not much room for any other kind." George stabbed a finger at the mage. "What are the odds the traitors will try flinging another dragon at us?"

"Thunderer smite me with boils if I know . . . sir," Alva answered. "I'll tell you this, though: *I* wouldn't have tried bringing one, let alone two. Anybody who works that kind of spell has to be as close to crazy as makes no difference."

"You say that?" George asked in amazement. "After the great sorceries you've brought off, *you* say that?"

"Hells, yes, I say that," the wizard told him. "What I do is dangerous to the enemy. It's not particularly dangerous to me. If something goes wrong with one of my spells, well, then, it doesn't work, that's all. If something went wrong with the spells those northern wizards cast to snare that dragon, it would have eaten them or flamed them or something even worse, if there is anything worse. Anybody who risks bringing that down on his own head has got to be a few bolts short of a full sheaf, don't you think?"

"When you put it that way, I suppose so," George said. "But you're the one who knows about magecraft. I don't, and I don't pretend to."

Alva let out a barely audible sniff, as if to say that anybody who didn't know much about wizardry had no business commanding an army. In this day and age, he might well have been right. But George was the fellow with the fancy epaulets on his shoulders. He had the responsibility. He had to live up to it.

Part of that responsibility, at the moment, involved finishing the destruction of the Army of Franklin. He pointed to Alva. "Can you make it seem to the traitors that the dragon hurt us worse than it really did?"

"I suppose so, sir. But why?" Puzzlement filled Alva's voice.

Doubting George let out a more than barely audible sniff, as if to say that anybody who didn't know much about soldiering had no business putting on a uniform, or even a gray robe. Then he condescended to explain: "If they see us here in dreadful shape, maybe they won't be looking for us to outflank them and cut them off."

"Oh!" Alva wasn't stupid. He could see things once you pointed them out to him. "Deception! Now I understand!"

"Good," George said. "Now that you understand, can you do it?"

"I don't see why not," the sorcerer replied. "It's an elementary problem, thaumaturgically speaking."

"You'll be able to fool the traitors and their mages?"

"I think so," Alva answered. "I don't see why I wouldn't be. The wizards on the other side of the Screw—"

"It's called the Smew," Doubting George said diplomatically.

Alva waved the correction away. "Whatever it's called, those fellows aren't very bright," he said. "Like I told you, they have to be pretty stupid, in fact, if they go and yank a real dragon out of the air. So, yes, I ought to be able to fool them."

That the northern wizards had *succeeded* in yanking

the dragon out of the air impressed Alva not at all, not in this context. He didn't waste time talking more about what he was going to do. He set about doing it instead. As far as Doubting George was concerned, taking care of what needed doing was one of Alva's best traits.

Apologetically, the wizard warned, "You won't be able to see the full effects of the spell, sir. You'd need to be looking from the other side of the river to do that, because it's directional. So don't worry about it. To the traitors, it'll look just the way it's supposed to."

"All right," the commanding general said. "Thanks for letting me know."

He wasn't even sure Alva heard him. The wizard had dropped back into his incantation. His skinny face showed how intensely he was concentrating. He muttered spells in Detinan and in a language George had never heard before. His bony, long-fingered hands thrashed through passes as if they had separate lives of their own. Sooner than George had expected him to, he finished the enchantment, shouting, "Transform! Transform! Transform!"

Transform things did. The wizard had been right to warn Doubting George about the directional nature of the spell. George saw the result, but as if it were made from fog: everything seemed half transparent, and ragged around the edges. He might almost have been watching the memory of a dream. Smoke, or the wraithlike semblance of smoke, poured up from the encampment. The ghosts of flames sprang from tents that weren't really burning. Shadowy figures that might have been men ran in all directions, as if in terror.

"Bell's wizards are seeing this sharply?" George asked.

"Not just the wizards, sir," Alva told him. "Anybody peering across the, uh, Smew will think the dragon has wrecked everything in sight."

"All right, then," the general commanding said. "Hold the illusion for as long as you can, and I'll get Hard-Riding Jimmy's troopers and some engineers moving. If they can cross the river and hit Bell in the flank when he thinks I'm all messed up here . . ."

"Deception," Major Alva said happily. "Yes, sir. I get it."

"Good." Doubting George shouted for a messenger. When the young man appeared, came to attention, and saluted, George gave him his orders. The youngster saluted again. He trotted off.

Before long, the unicorn-riders and the engineers hurried up the Smew. Ghostly smoke between them and the river should conceal them from prying eyes on the other side, assuming it seemed as solid as it was supposed to from the north. Doubting George had no cause to doubt that; another reason he approved of Alva as a mage was that the man delivered.

A messenger came back and reported, "We're over the Smew, sir."

"Good," George said. "Can I send a column of foot-soldiers after you? Have you got a ford or a bridge safe and ready to use?"

"Yes, sir," the messenger answered. "But Brigadier Jimmy says to warn you that if you're looking to surprise the traitors, you're going to be disappointed. They already know we're moving against them."

"Gods damn it!" George exclaimed in disgust. "What went wrong?"

"We hadn't been on the north bank of the river more than a couple of minutes before Ned of the Forest's unicorn-riders found us," the messenger replied.

"Well, to hells with Ned of the Forest, too," the commanding general said. "All right—we're discovered. Can Jimmy's riders get in front of Bell's men and hold them until the rest of us come north and finish them off?"

"Sir, I don't think so," the young man on unicornback said. "Bell's men are scooting north as fast as they can go, and Ned's unicorn-riders are slowing our troopers down so we can't reach Bell's main force. I'm sorry, sir."

"So am I," Doubting George said wearily. "We did everything right here—after that gods-damned dragon, anyhow—but it didn't quite work. Well, we'll go after them anyhow. Maybe Bell will make a mistake. It wouldn't be the first one he's made on this campaign, by the Lion God's tail tuft."

He said that, but he didn't really believe it. It wasn't that he didn't believe Bell could make more mistakes; he was sure Bell could. But prisoners had told him Ned of the Forest commanded the northern rear guard. Doubting George had seen that Ned made a very solid soldier. George wished *he* had more officers of Ned's ability. He was just glad the war looked nearly won. Even Ned didn't matter—too much—any more.

Captain Gremio had never particularly wanted to command a regiment. For that matter, Gremio had never particularly wanted to command a company; had his previous captain not been killed at Proselytizers' Rise, he would have been more than content to remain a lieutenant, with but a single epaulet on his shoulder.

But he had the whole regiment in his hands now, like it or not, and had it in the worst possible circumstances: a grinding retreat after a disastrous battle. And his men could hardly have had a harder time. They were worn and ragged and hungry, as was he. His shoes, what was left of them, leaked mud onto his toes at every stride. Too many of them had no shoes at all.

"What the hells am I supposed to do, sir?" one of the soldiers asked. "My feet are so gods-damned cold, how long will it be before my toes start turning black?"

"Well, we're in camp now, Jamy," Gremio answered,

"camp" being a few small, smoky fires in a clearing in the woods. "Get as close to the flames as you can. That'll keep you from frostbitten toes."

"Yes, sir, we're in camp *now*," Jamy said. "But what am I supposed to do about tomorrow morning, when I start tramping through half-frozen muck again?"

"Find some rags. Wrap your feet in them." Gremio helplessly spread his hands wide. "I don't know what else to tell you." Jamy muttered something under his breath. It sounded like, *If I let myself get captured, I don't have to worry about it any more.* Gremio turned away, pretending not to hear. If Jamy did hang back, how could Gremio stop him? More than a few men had already given themselves up to the southrons.

Also muttering, Gremio went off to stand in line and get something to eat. Half a hard biscuit and some smoked meat that was rancid because it hadn't been smoked long enough weren't going to fill his belly. He asked the cooks, "What else have you got?"

They looked at him as if he'd lost his mind. "You're gods-damned lucky we've got this here . . . sir," one of them said. "Plenty of folks in this here army, they get a big fat nothing for supper tonight."

"Oh." Gremio sighed and nodded. "I suppose you're right. But how long can we go on with this kind of food?"

In unison, the cooks shrugged. "Hells of a lot longer than we can go on with nothing," replied the one who'd spoken before.

The worst of it was, Gremio couldn't even argue with him. He was incontestably, incontrovertibly, right. "Scrounge whatever you can," Gremio told him. "I'm not fussy about how you do it—just do it. I won't ask you any questions. We've got to keep moving, one way or another."

One by one, the cooks nodded. "We'll take care of it, Captain. Don't you worry," said the one who liked to talk. "Pretty good, a regimental commander who tells us we can forage however we want." The rest of the cooks nodded again.

One of them added, "Sergeant Thisbe already said the same thing."

"That's a sergeant. This here is a captain. Them's two different breeds, you bet, like unicorns and asses," the mouthy cook said.

Gremio wondered whether officers were supposed to be unicorns or asses. He didn't ask. The cook was all too likely to tell him. What he did say was, "If Sergeant Thisbe told you it's all right, it is. You can bet on that."

"Oh, yes, sir," the talkative cook agreed. "Thisbe, he's got his head screwed on tight. Probably why he never made lieutenant." He didn't look a bit abashed at smearing officers. With the Army of Franklin falling to ruins, what was Gremio going to do to him? What *could* Gremio do that the southrons hadn't done already?

"Sergeant Thisbe has been offered promotion to officer's rank more than once, but has always declined," Gremio said stiffly.

The cooks looked at one another. None of them said a thing, not even the mouthy one. Gremio turned away in dull embarrassment. *They* hadn't embarrassed him; he'd done it to himself. If Thisbe was a good soldier (and Thisbe was) and if Thisbe didn't want to become an officer (and Thisbe didn't, as Gremio had admitted), what did that say about officers?

It says officers are asses, Gremio thought. Feeling very much an ass, he went off to eat his meager and unappetizing supper.

He was cleaning his mess tin when Thisbe came

over to the creek to do the same thing. Scrupulous as always, Thisbe saluted. Gremio answered with an impatient wave. "Never mind that nonsense," he said. "Nobody's going to worry about it now."

"All right, sir," Thisbe said equably.

"What's this I hear about your saying it was all right for the cooks to gather food any which way they could?" Gremio inquired.

With an anxious look, Thisbe asked, "Was I wrong, sir?"

"Not so far as I'm concerned," Gremio answered. "I told them the same thing."

"We've got to keep eating," Thisbe said. "If we don't eat, we can't march and we can't fight. We might as well lay down our crossbows and shortswords and give up, and I'm not ready to do that."

"Neither am I." But Gremio thought of Jamy. How long could his men keep marching without shoes? Not forever; he knew that too well. Remembering Jamy made him ask, "How are *your* feet, Sergeant?"

"Not bad at all, as a matter of fact." Sure enough, shoes much newer than Gremio's covered and protected Thisbe's feet. The underofficer explained, "I found this dead southron, a little short fellow. His shoes were some too big on me even so, but I stuffed some rags into the toes, and they're all right now—a lot better than the ones I had."

"Good. That's good. Nice somebody's taken care of, one way or another," Captain Gremio said. "I wish all our men were that lucky." His laugh held nothing but bitterness. "I wish a lot more of our men were lucky enough to still be here."

"Yes, sir." Sergeant Thisbe nodded. "Sir, *can* we fight another battle now? If we have to, I mean?"

"Depends on what you mean by a battle—and on what Lieutenant General Bell wants us to do," Gremio answered. "We can fight plenty of these rear-guard actions—and we've got to, to keep the southrons from running over us like a brewery wagon on a downgrade. But if the Army of Franklin lines up against everything Doubting George has got . . . if that happens, we're all dead."

Thisbe nodded once more. "That's about the way I look at things, too. I just wondered whether you were thinking along with me again."

That *again* warmed Gremio. "When we get back to Palmetto Province, Sergeant . . ."

"Who knows what will happen, sir?" Thisbe said. "We have to worry about getting home first of all, and about whether home will even be worth getting back to if. . . ." Now the sergeant's voice trailed away.

"If?" Gremio prompted. But that wasn't fair; that was making Thisbe say something Gremio didn't want to say himself. With an effort of will, he forced it out: "If we lose the war."

No one but Thisbe could have heard the words. Gremio made sure of that. Even so, mentioning defeat came hard, despite all the disasters the Army of Franklin had already seen. Just imagining the north could lose, imagining King Avram could rule all of Detina, felt uncommonly like treason.

So Gremio thought, at any rate. But when he said so, Thisbe faced the idea without flinching. "We'll pick up the pieces and go on, that's all," the sergeant replied. "What else can we do?"

Win. Gremio wanted to say it, but found he couldn't. With the Army of Franklin broken, with Duke Edward of Arlington penned up inside Pierreville north of Nonesuch, what did his side have with which to resist the oncoming southron armies? Not enough, not from what he could see.

"Sergeant—" he began.

Thisbe held up a hand. "This isn't the right time, is it, sir?"

"If it's not, when would be?"

"After the war is over." Thisbe looked around, too, before adding, "I don't reckon it'll be too much longer." Another pause, and then the sergeant said, "I'd kind of hate to get killed now, when dying won't make the least bit of difference one way or the other." A laugh, of sorts. "That's probably treason, too."

"If it is, they'll have to crucify me next to you," Gremio said. They smiled at each other. With a grimace, Gremio went on, "Sometimes dying can make a difference even now. Not about who wins and loses— I think that's pretty much over and done with. But if you can help some of your friends get away safe . . . Well, what else is a rear guard for?"

Sergeant Thisbe looked as unhappy as Gremio felt. "You're right, sir. You usually are." Gremio shook his head. He felt as empty—as *emptied*—of good answers as of everything else. Thisbe ignored him. "But even though you are right, I still think it'd be a shame."

"Oh, so do I. I don't want to get killed. I've never been what you'd call eager for that." From somewhere, Gremio dredged up a wry smile. "I've known a few men who were, or seemed to be." *Bell, gods damn him. Getting mutilated—getting mutilated twice—didn't satisfy him. No, not even close. He had to cut off his army's leg, too.*

By the way Thisbe nodded, the underofficer was also thinking of the commanding general. Thisbe went back by the fires, got out a blanket, and made a cocoon of it. Around a yawn, the sergeant said, "Maybe it'll look better in the morning."

Following Thisbe toward what warmth they had, Gremio doubted that. He doubted it would ever look better for King Geoffrey's cause. But he was also too

weary to see straight. He rolled himself in his own
blanket, using his hat for a pillow. "Good night, Sergeant. Maybe it will. It can't look much worse, can it?"

With the winter solstice close at hand, nights were
long and cold. Gremio woke well before sunrise. He
wasn't much surprised to find Thisbe already up and
gone. He also wasn't much surprised to find Ned of
the Forest prowling around on foot. Ned's eyes threw
back the dim red light of the campfires like a cat's.
Men's eyes weren't supposed to be able to do that, but
Ned's did.

"Who's in charge of this here regiment?" he
demanded of Gremio.

"As a matter of fact, I am." Gremio gave his name
and rank, adding, "At your service, sir."

"I don't want service. I want to kill some of those
southron bastards. Are your men up to it?"

Such straightforward bloodthirstiness appealed to
Gremio. "Tell us what to do, sir. If we can, we will.
If we can't, we'll try anyway."

That won him a thin smile from the commander of
the rear guard. "All right, Captain. That'll do. Can't ask
for anything more, in fact. Here's what I've got in
mind. . . ."

An hour or so later, Gremio found himself behind
a tree trunk, waiting as Ned of the Forest's unicorn-
riders galloped past to the north. It looked as if even
the rear guard of the Army of Franklin were breaking up in ruin, as so much of the rest of the army
already had. It looked that way, but it wasn't true.
Gremio hoped it wasn't, anyhow.

After a brief pause, riders in King Avram's gray
pounded after Ned's troopers. The southrons weren't
worried about their flanks. They weren't worried about
anything. Why should they worry? Bell's men were on
the run.

Gremio remembered Ned of the Forest's instructions. *Don't shoot too soon*, the commander of unicorn-riders had said. *I'll rip the head off any fool who starts shooting too soon.* Gremio didn't think he'd meant it metaphorically. He didn't think Ned would have known a metaphor if it walked up and tried to buy him a brandy (and, for that matter, he probably would have turned it down if it did—he was famous for his abstemiousness with spirits).

And so Gremio and his crossbowmen waited till the southrons were well into the trap. They were veterans. They could all figure out when that was. And they all raised their crossbows to their shoulders and started shooting at almost exactly the same moment.

Unicorns screamed like women in anguish. Unicorn-riders screamed, too, some in pain, others in fury. Unicorns crashed to the ground. Unicorn-riders crouched behind them. Those who could started shooting back.

Frantically reloading and shooting, Gremio discovered how many bolts the enemy put into the air with their quick-shooting crossbows. It was as if each of them had five or six pairs of arms, each pair busy with its own crossbow. Without the advantage of surprise, Gremio's regiment would have been mad to attack them.

But it had that advantage, and made the most of it. And Ned's unicorn-riders came hurrying back—on foot, as dragoons—as soon as the trap was sprung. Not only that, but Ned's commander of engines, a captain named Watson who seemed improbably young, got a couple of repeating crossbows placed in the roadway where they bore on the southrons. Those weapons put out even more quarrels, and quarrels that flew farther, than the southrons could manage with their quick-shooters.

Beset from front and flanks, the southrons did just

what Gremio would have done in their boots: they fell back. And as they fell back, hungry, barefoot northerners dashed forward—not to push them back farther still, but to plunder the corpses they'd had to leave behind.

Gremio was no slower than anybody else. He pulled a pair of shoes—solid, well-made shoes, shoes that would last a while—about his size off the feet of a southron trooper who wouldn't need them any more. He stole the trooper's tea and hard biscuits and smoked meat, too. If he could have got his hands on some indigo dye, he would have also taken the man's tunic; it was thick wool, better suited to this cold, nasty weather than his own. But he didn't, and didn't want to get shot for wearing gray. Even after knocking the southrons back on their heels, he knew he was all too likely to get shot for wearing blue.

Ned of the Forest was as happy as he could be in his present circumstances, which is to say, not very. Everything had gone perfectly when the rear guard he led taught Hard-Riding Jimmy's troopers a sharp lesson: no matter how good they were, they couldn't have everything their own way. Everything had gone perfectly, and what had it accomplished? It made the Army of Franklin's retreat a little more secure, and that was all.

"Huzzah," Ned said sourly. That meant Bell's force might make it back to Dothan or Great River Province, and not be altogether destroyed in northern Franklin. An improvement, without a doubt, but how large an improvement? Not large enough, and Ned knew it.

Colonel Biffle rode up to him in the dismal winter woods. "We've driven them back, sir." He sounded pleased and excited.

"Well, so we have, Biff." Ned sounded anything but. "Next question is, how much good will that do us?"

Biffle's long face corrugated into a frown. After a moment's thought, he said, "It'll do us a lot more good than if they'd busted through."

Ned of the Forest had to laugh at that. "I can't even tell you you're wrong," he admitted. "But are we going to win the war because we gave Hard-Riding Jimmy a black eye? Are we going to win anything that's worth having?"

He watched Colonel Biffle's eyes cross as the regimental commander worked on that. Biffle wasn't used to thinking in such terms. He was a man you pointed at the enemy and loosed, as if he were a crossbow quarrel. Again, he paused before answering. At last, he said, "Well, we're still here to try again."

"I can't say you're wrong about that, either." Ned looked south. "And, unless I miss my guess, we're going to have to if we hang around here much longer. Jimmy won't like getting poked. He'll send more men forward, and we won't have such an easy time suckering them into an ambush. I'd say it's about time to leave. We've bought the army a few hours, anyways. That's the most we can hope for these days."

"Yes, sir." Colonel Biffle suddenly blinked several times. He frowned again, though this time for a different reason. "Gods damn it! It's starting to rain. Got me right in the eye."

He was right. It *was* starting to rain and, with scarcely any warning, to rain hard. "Good thing this held off till we drove the southrons back," Ned said. "We'd have looked a proper set of fools, wouldn't we, if we'd tried shooting at those bastards with wet bowstrings? Good thing we didn't."

Before he'd got out of the woods, his unicorn was squelching through mud. Big, fat, heavy raindrops poured down. With all the trees bare in winter, nothing slowed down the drops. Ned pulled his broad-brimmed felt hat down low on this face to keep the rain out of his eyes. That helped, a little.

The regiment of footsoldiers who'd helped in the ambush came out of their cover and retreated along with his unicorn-riders. Ned waved to their commander, who nodded back. The fellow was only a captain, but he'd done his job well, and without fuss or feathers. "Get your boys moving," Ned called to him. "We'll keep the southrons off your back." He had the more mobile troops, and owed the footsoldiers that much.

"Thank you kindly." The captain touched the brim of his own hat, which was also pulled down low. He handled the withdrawal with the same unfussy precision he'd used against the southrons. One of his company commanders, a sergeant who'd managed to shave amazingly well considering the sorry state the Army of Franklin was in, also proved very competent. By the way the captain and the sergeant sassed each other without heat, they'd served together a long time. They might almost have been married. Ned hid his amusement. He'd seen such things before.

At the moment, he had business of his own to attend to. "Captain Watson!" he called. "Come here, if you please."

"What do you need, sir?" the young man in charge of his engines asked.

"I need you to trundle your repeating crossbows south down the road a little ways and give Hard-Riding Jimmy's men a proper hello when they start coming after us again," Ned answered.

Watson frowned. "I would, sir, but . . ."

"But what?" Ned of the Forest asked ominously. He wasn't used to having Captain Watson tell him no. Watson was the fellow who did whatever needed doing. But then Ned thumped himself in the head with the heel of his hand, a gesture of absolute disgust. "Oh. The rain."

"Yes, sir. The gods-damned rain," Watson agreed. "It's not as hard on the skeins of a repeating crossbow as it is on an ordinary bowstring, but they do lose their . . . their *pop*, you might say, when they get wet."

"I knew that. I *know* that. I just wasn't thinking straight." Ned still sounded—still *was*—angry at himself for forgetting. "Never mind moving 'em, then. It won't work. Have to try something else instead." He thought for a little while, then nodded to himself. "*That* might do it, by the Lion God's tail tuft."

"You've got something, sir. I can see it in your eyes," Watson said, a certain gleam coming into his own.

"Trip lines," Ned said. "We string a few of them between the trees on either side of the road, the southrons come swarming up to get their revenge on us, and then they go flying. Unicorns break their legs, maybe some riders break their necks. And a good driving rain makes trip lines work better, not worse, on account of they're harder to spot."

"Yes, sir!" The gleam in Captain Watson's eyes grew brighter. "I'll take care of it, sir."

"You don't need to do that," Ned said. "It's got nothing to do with engines."

"Oh, sir, it'll be my pleasure," Watson said with a jaunty grin. "And you know I've got plenty of ropes. I need 'em to pull the engines and wagons. I can set up the trip lines, and I'll enjoy doing it, too."

"All right. See to it, then." Ned of the Forest nodded decisively.

He himself rode north, leaving Watson to do what he'd said he would. At the edge of the woods, he waited. Before too long, Watson came out with the last of the engines, unicorn teams straining to haul them up the increasingly soupy road. Catching sight of Ned, Watson waved and nodded. Ned waved back.

The long retreat went on. After trying and failing to make a stand at the Smew River, Lieutenant General Bell seemed to have abandoned all hope of holding the southrons. All he could think to do was fall back as fast as he could and stay ahead of Doubting George's men. Ned of the Forest would have reckoned that more contemptible if he'd had more hope himself. Since he didn't, he found it harder to quarrel with the commanding general.

Hard-Riding Jimmy's men didn't come bursting out of the woods to harry the retreating northerners. Ned didn't run into them at all for the next couple of days, in fact. He concluded that Captain Watson had not only enjoyed putting down trip lines, he'd also done a good job of it. Watson might be a puppy, but he was a puppy who'd grown some sharp teeth.

Bell's army stumbled through the town of Warsaw on the way up to the Franklin River. Ned of the Forest remembered crossing the river heading south a couple of months before. He'd still had hope then, hope and the confidence that, whatever happened, he would figure out some way to whip the southrons. That wasn't going to happen now. All he could hope to do was figure out some way to keep the southrons from destroying the Army of Franklin.

In Warsaw, the townsfolk stared glumly at the retreating northerners. "What are we going to do now?" one of them called to Ned of the Forest, as if all too well aware the town would see King Geoffrey's soldiers no more, and would have to make what peace it could with King Avram.

"Do the best you can," Ned told him, unable to find any better answer. By the look the local sent him, that wasn't what the fellow had wanted to hear. It wasn't what Ned had wanted to say, either. But he had a very clear sense of what was real and what wasn't. He hoped the other man did, too.

North of Warsaw, Ned loaded a lot of the men in the rear guard who were barefoot into unicorn-drawn wagons. That kept them from getting their feet frostbitten. If they had to fight, they could deploy from the wagons. "Pretty sneaky, Lord Ned," Colonel Biffle said admiringly.

"Oh, yes, I'm clever as next week," Ned said. "Think how smart I'd be if I only had something to work with."

They went up into the province of Dothan just before they came back to the Franklin River. The weather was no better there than it had been in the province of Franklin. The river, swollen by the cold, hard rain, ran almost out of its banks. No one would find an easy way to ford it, as Doubting George had at the Smew.

Bell's engineers and wizards didn't have an easy time creating a pontoon bridge across the Franklin. For one thing, pontoons were hard to come by. For another, the river kept doing its best to carry them away before the engineers and mages could secure them one to another. And, for a third, precious few engineers and wizards were left to do the work; they'd suffered no less than the rest of Bell's army.

At last, though, the job was done. Bell's weary, footsore soldiers began crossing to the northern bank of the river. By then, the southrons were very close behind Ned of the Forest's rear guard. Ned told his troopers, and the footsoldiers with them, "Well, boys, we're going to have to wallop the sons of bitches one more time. Reckon you're up to it?"

"Yes, sir!" they shouted, and "Hells, yes!" and, "You bet, Lord Ned!"

And they did. Roaring as if the Lion God had taken possession of them body and soul, they hit the advancing southrons a savage blow that sent them reeling back toward Warsaw in surprise, dismay, and no little disorder. Ned of the Forest didn't think he'd ever been prouder of men he led than he was on that frozen field. They had to know they weren't going to win the war with this fight. They couldn't even turn the campaign into anything but a disaster. They struck like an avalanche all the same.

Captain Gremio came up to Ned. Saluting, he said, "Sir, I beg leave to report that my men have captured one of the southrons' siege engines. Doesn't begin to make up for all the army lost, of course, but now that we've got it, what should we do with it?"

"Well done!" Ned said, and then, "Captain Watson will take charge of it, Captain."

"He's welcome to it, then," Gremio said. "I'll have my men drag it over to him. I expect he'll have unicorns to haul it off toward the north?"

"I expect he will," Ned agreed. "And once you've done that, Captain, order your regiment ready to get moving again. You know we can't stay around here and enjoy the victory we've won."

"I understand, sir," the other man said. "I sure as hells wish we could, though, because this is the only victory we've won in this whole gods-damned campaign, and the only one we're likely to." Bitterness came off him in waves.

"Can't be helped," Ned said. Captain Gremio nodded, sketched a salute, and then went off to carry out Ned's orders.

The footsoldiers went off toward the Franklin first, with Ned's unicorn-riders screening them. Again, the southrons held off on their pursuit for some little while; the ferocious attack Ned had put in persuaded them they would do better to wait. That being so, Ned retired as slowly as he could.

To his surprise, though, a courier came riding down from the north, from Lieutenant General Bell's main force, urging him to move faster. "By the Thunderer's iron fist, what's the trouble now?" he growled.

"The southrons have galleys carrying catapults in the Franklin River, sir," the rider answered. "They're heading toward the bridge. If they land a couple of firepots on it before you get across, you'll be stuck on this side of the river."

Ned of the Forest had never yet reckoned himself stuck. He was confident he could handle whatever trouble the southrons gave him, if he had to by ordering his men to disperse and to reassemble somewhere else. He said, "Doesn't Bell have his own engines up near the bridge to keep it safe?"

"Yes, sir," the courier told him. "But you never can tell."

That was altogether too true. You never could tell. And, where Bell was concerned, you might worry not just about whether things could go wrong, but about *how* they could go wrong. With an angry mutter, Ned said, "All right, then. Don't fret yourself, sonny boy. We'll step lively."

He came to the southern bank of the Franklin a day and a half later, making better time than even he'd expected. Looking up the river, he saw no sign of southron war galleys. He did see, on the far bank, engines lined up wheel to wheel. Here, Bell hadn't blundered.

"Get moving!" he called to the men under his command. "Let's put the river between us and the bastards on our heels."

Those bastards were starting to nip close again— but not close enough. Ned was sure they wouldn't catch him. Gremio's footsoldiers crossed over to the north bank of the Franklin. Wheels rumbling on the planks laid over the pontoons to pave the bridge, Watson's engines and the supply wagons followed. Last came Lieutenant General Ned's troopers, and last of all came Ned of the Forest himself.

As soon as he reached the northern bank of the river, a couple of Bell's men set a firepot on the bridge. The pot began to burn. A moment later, so did the bridge. The Army of Franklin, or what remained of it, wended its way north and east, into Great River Province.

John the Lister saw the great column of black smoke rising into the sky from a couple of miles away. He knew what it had to mean. Cursing, he spurred his unicorn forward, toward the Franklin River.

He got to the river too late. He'd known he would be too late even as he set spurs to the flanks of his mount. He would have been too late even if he hadn't had to delay because columns of footsoldiers and unicorn-riders and prisoners wouldn't get out of his way as fast as he wanted them to. Having to squeeze through them did nothing to make his curses any less sulfurous, though.

Sure enough, the pontoon bridge by which the Army of Franklin had crossed was engulfed in flames, far beyond the hope of any man's quenching it. Not even an opportune storm would save it now. And the Franklin was a formidable river, wide and swift and, now, swollen like so many other streams by the winter rains. On the far bank, most of the northerners had gone their way, but a few, tiny in the distance, still moved about on foot and on unicornback. One of them, a mounted officer, waved mockingly to the southrons on the opposite side of the river.

Fury made John the Lister grab for the hilt of his sword. Half a heartbeat later, he checked the motion, knowing he'd been foolish. Even the bolt from a repeating crossbow right on the riverbank would have splashed harmlessly into the Franklin, less than halfway on the journey to that northern unicorn-rider.

Hard-Riding Jimmy came up beside John. On his face was the same frustration as John felt. "We'll be a while bridging this stream, and longer if their troopers give us a hard time while we're working at it," Jimmy said.

"I know," John answered unhappily. He shook his head toward the traitors on the far bank. "They're going to get away, gods damn them."

Jimmy tempered that as best he could: "Some of them will get away. But an awful lot of them godsdamned well won't."

"Well, I can't tell you you're wrong," John the Lister said. "Still, I wanted more. I wanted this whole army destroyed, not just wrecked. So did Doubting George."

The southrons' commander of unicorn-riders laughed. "If all our officers were so bloodthirsty, we'd've won this war two years ago."

"We're supposed to be bloodthirsty," John said. "We've spent too much time putting up with men who aren't. And d'you think Bell and Ned of the Forest didn't want to drink our gore? They knew what they wanted to do to us, all right; they just couldn't bring it off."

"I admire Ned. I hate to admit it, but I do," Jimmy said. "Wasn't that a lovely spoiling attack his men put in a couple of days ago? As pretty as anything I've ever seen, especially considering how worn they had to be."

"Yes. They're still bastards, though," John said. "He's a bastard, too, but he's a bastard who's monstrous good at war."

"That he is," Jimmy said. "And now, sir, if you'll excuse me . . ." He rode off.

Out in the Franklin River, a galley flying King

Avram's flag drew near. John scowled at it. Why couldn't it have come sooner, to attack the now burning pontoon bridge before Bell's soldiers crossed it? A moment later, he got his answer to that. Cunningly hidden catapults on the northern side of the river opened up on the galley. Stones and firepots splashed into the Franklin all around it. It hastily pulled back out of range.

John the Lister shook his fist at the northerners again. But then, suddenly, he started to laugh. In the end, how much difference did it make that a few of them had managed to escape? For all practical purposes, the war here in the east was won.

Before long, the soldiers in Doubting George's army would go elsewhere—maybe after Lieutenant General Bell's men, maybe off to the west to help finish off the armies there that remained in the field for false King Geoffrey. Either way, how likely was it that Geoffrey's rule would ever be seen in this part of the kingdom again? Not very, and John knew it.

From now on, if the locals wanted to send a letter, they would have to send it through a postmaster loyal to King Avram. If they wanted to go to law against each other, they would have to do it in one of Avram's lawcourts. If one of the local barons wanted to keep on being a baron, he would have to swear allegiance to Avram. If he didn't, if he refused, he wouldn't be a baron any more. He would be an outlaw, and hunted down by Avram's soldiers.

And, from now on, all the blonds in this part of the kingdom would be free men, no longer bound to their liege lords' lands as they had been for so many hundreds of years. Ever since the invaders from the far side of the Western Ocean overwhelmed the blonds' kingdoms they'd found in the north of what became Detina, they'd looked on the people they'd conquered as little more than domestic animals that happened to walk on two legs. That had changed—changed some— in the south, where blonds had been fewer and the land itself poorer, and where serfdom never really had paid for itself. Now, no matter how little the northerners liked it—and John the Lister knew how little that was—it was going to change here, too.

King Avram had always been determined about that. He'd made his views plain long before succeeding old King Buchan. He'd made them so plain, Grand Duke Geoffrey had rebelled the instant the royal crown landed on Avram's homely head, and he'd taken all the northern provinces with him, even if some of them hadn't actually abandoned Avram till after the fighting started. Geoffrey's war was going on four years old now. It wouldn't—couldn't—last much longer. After the spilling of endless blood and endless treasure, King Avram would get his way.

John the Lister wondered how well things would work once peace finally returned to the kingdom. Like a lot of southrons (and almost all northerners), he remained unconvinced that the average blond was as good a man, as smart a man, as brave a man, as the average Detinan. He'd needed the war to convince him that *some* blonds could match *some* Detinans in any of those things. He knew one of his regiments had a blond sergeant in it, thanks to the promotion from Colonel Nahath. That a blond could rise so high, could give orders to Detinans and get away with it, still surprised him. That a Detinan with such abilities who'd started as a common soldier would probably be a captain or a major by now never once crossed John's mind.

One other thing of which John was convinced was that the Detinans in the north weren't about to accept blonds as their equals, no matter what King Avram had to say about it and even if they did lose the War Between the Provinces. The brigadier wondered how that would play out in the years to come. How many soldiers would Avram need to garrison the northern provinces to make sure his will was carried out? Would he keep them there to make sure it was? He was a stubborn man; John knew as much. But the northerners, like any Detinans, were stubborn, too.

Gods be praised, it isn't my worry, John the Lister thought. All he had to do was carry out commands. King Avram was the one who had to give them, and to figure out what they ought to be. Most of the time, Brigadier John had the same schoolboy fancies as flowered in the heart of any other man. *What if I were King of Detina? Wouldn't it be wonderful, for me and for everybody else?*

Looking at what lay ahead for the kingdom, at what King Avram would have to do if he wanted to knit things back together for south and north yet at the same time cling to his principles, John decided the current king was welcome to the job. *After he's straightened things out—then, maybe . . .*

John got so lost in his reverie, he didn't notice another unicorn coming up beside his. A dry voice snapped him back to the here-and-now: "Well, Brigadier, it hasn't turned out *too* bad the past couple of weeks, has it? No matter what those bastards over in Georgetown say, I mean."

Snapping to attention on unicornback wasn't practical. John the Lister did salute. "No, sir. Not too bad at all."

"Glad you agree," Doubting George said. "Of course, Baron Logan the Black would have done everything a hells of a lot better. He's sure of it even now, I bet, and so is Marshal Bart."

Sarcasm like that flayed. John said, "Sir, I don't see

how anybody could have done anything better on this campaign." Maybe his words held some flattery. He knew they also held a lot of truth.

Doubting George muttered something into his beard, something distinctly *un*flattering to the Marshal of Detina. Part of John the Lister hoped the general commanding would go into more detail; he liked gossip no less than anyone else in King Avram's gossip-loving armies. But all George said after that was, "Well, by the Thunderer's prick, we've done every single thing we were supposed to do with the Army of Franklin. We've done every single gods-damned thing we were supposed to do *to* the Army of Franklin, too."

That wasn't altogether true. The Army of Franklin still existed, at least after a fashion. George had wanted to expunge it from the field altogether. Thanks more to Ned of the Forest than anyone else, he hadn't quite managed to do it, though Bell's force wouldn't endanger Cloviston, or even Franklin, again. "What now, sir?" John the Lister asked. "Do we go up and down the river till we find a place where we can get our own pontoon bridge across? Do we keep on chasing Bell and whatever he's got left of an army?"

With a certain amount of regret—more than a certain amount, in fact—George shook his head. "Those aren't my orders, however much I wish they were. My orders are to hold the line of the Franklin and to garrison the northern part of Franklin against possible further attacks by the traitors." A chuckle rumbled, down deep in his chest. "I don't expect that last'll be too gods-damned hard. A weasel doesn't come out and bite a bear in the arse."

"They'd better not, by the Lion God's talons!" John exclaimed. "Not even Bell could be crazy enough to want to go back to the fight."

"Ha!" Doubting George said. "You never can tell

what that son of a bitch'd be crazy enough to do. I'm sure he *wants* to fight us some more. He just doesn't have any army left to do it with, that's all, at least not so far as I can see. Our job now is to make sure we send him back with his tail between his legs if he *is* daft enough to try it." He paused and frowned, dissatisfied with the figure of speech. "How the hells can we send him back with his tail between his legs if he's only got one leg?"

"If that's your biggest worry, sir, this campaign is well and truly won," John said.

"I expect it is." Doubting George still sounded imperfectly ecstatic. "Did I tell you? I had a call on the crystal ball from his Imperial Bartness the other day, telling me what a clever fellow I was, and how I'd been a good little boy after all."

"No, you didn't mention that," John the Lister replied. He couldn't help echoing, "His Imperial Bartness?"

"What would you call him?" George said. "We have Kings of Detina all the time—we've got too godsdamned many Kings of Detina right this minute, but there's always at least one. But till Bart, we hadn't had a Marshal of Detina for seventy or eighty years. If that doesn't make a Marshal of Detina fancier and more important than a King of Detina, to the hells with me if I know what would. And don't you suppose a fancy, important rank deserves a fancy, important-sounding title to go with it?"

"To tell you the truth, sir, I hadn't really thought about it." John wondered if anyone *but* Doubting George would have thought of such a thing.

"Well, anyway, like I say, he told me I was a good little boy, and he patted me on the head and said I'd get a bonbon or two for singing my song so nice, even over and above making me lieutenant general of the regulars," the general commanding went on, not bothering to hide his disdain. "And I rolled on my back and showed him the white fur on my belly and kicked my legs in the air and gods-damned near piddled on his shoe to show him how happy I was about the bonbons."

John the Lister had an alarmingly vivid mental image of Doubting George acting like a happy, bearded puppy and Marshal Bart beaming benignly out of a crystal ball. John had to shake his head to drive the picture out of it. "You always have such an . . . interesting way of putting things, sir," he managed at last.

"You think I'm out of my mind, too," George said equably. "Well, hells, maybe I am. Who knows for sure, especially these days? But crazy or not, I *won*. That's what counts."

It *was* what counted. For a soldier, nothing else really did. John nodded and said, "This kingdom's going to be a different place when the fighting finally stops. I've been thinking about that a lot lately."

"I've been thinking about it myself, as a matter of fact," Doubting George replied. "I doubt I'm going to be very happy with all the changes, either. But it'll still be *one* kingdom, and *that's* what counts, too."

He was right again. That *was* what counted, too, for King Avram's side. John the Lister nodded. "Yes, sir."

What was left of the Army of Franklin straggled into the town of Honey, in the southwestern part of Great River Province. The southrons had given up their pursuit after failing to bag the army in front of the Franklin River. Now Lieutenant General Bell wanted to salvage whatever he could from the ruins of his campaign up toward Ramblerton. He even hoped to salvage what was left of his own career.

That last hope died a miserable death when he

recognized the officer sitting his unicorn in the middle of Honey's muddy main street and waiting for him. Saluting, Bell spoke in a voice like ashes: "Good day, General Peegeetee. How . . . very fine to see you, your Grace."

Marquis Peegeetee of Goodlook punctiliously returned Bell's salute. "It is good to see you, too, Lieutenant General, as always," he replied, reminding Bell which of them held the higher rank. He was a short, ferret-faced man, a very fine and precise commander who would have been of more use to King Geoffrey if he hadn't been in the unfortunate habit of making plans more elaborate than his men, most of whom were anything but professional soldiers, could carry out . . . and if he weren't at least as touchy as Count Joseph the Gamecock. He went on, "We shall have a good deal to talk about, you and I."

Bell liked the sound of that not a bit. He would even rather have seen Count Thraxton the Braggart; he and the luckless Count Thraxton, at least, both despised Joseph the Gamecock. But what he liked wasn't going to matter here. With a grim nod, he said, "I am entirely at your service, your Grace." If he could be brave facing the enemy, he could be brave facing his own side, too.

Even on this chilly day, a bee buzzed by Bell's ear. He shook his head and the bee flew off. The hives around the town had helped give it its name. General Peegeetee's expression, though, could have curdled honey. He said, "Where is the rest of your army, Lieutenant General?"

There it was. Bell had known it was coming. He said what he had to say: "What I have, sir, is what you see."

Peegeetee's expression grew more sour, more forbidding, still. Bell hadn't imagined it could. The marquis blurted, "But what happened to the rest of them? I knew it was bad, but . . ."

"Sir, the ones who survive and were not captured are with me," Bell said.

"By the Thunderer's big brass balls!" Marquis Peegeetee muttered. "You cannot have left more than one man out of four from among those who set out from Dothan in the fall. It is a ruin, a disaster, a catastrophe." When it came to catastrophes, he knew exactly what he was talking about. He'd been in command at Karlsburg harbor, where the war between Geoffrey and Avram began. He and Joseph had led the northern forces at Cow Jog, the first great battle of the war, down in southern Parthenia, which had proved that neither north nor south yet knew how to fight but both had plenty of brave men. And he'd taken over for Sidney the War Unicorn after Sidney bled to death on the field at the Battle of Sheol, a hellsish conflict if ever there was one.

"We made the southrons pay a most heavy price, your Grace," Bell said stiffly.

"They paid—and they can afford to go on paying," Peegeetee said. "But what of this army?" He shook his head. "This army is not an army any more."

"We can still fight, sir," Bell insisted. "All we need to do is refit and reorganize, and we'll soon be ready to take the field again."

"No doubt." This time, General Peegeetee's politeness was positively chilling. "I am sure your host—your *small* host, your *diminished* host—can defeat any enemy army of equal or lesser size." He did not sound sure of even so much, but continued before Bell could call him on it: "Unfortunately, my good Lieutenant General, Doubting George's force is now about five times the size of yours. You will correct me if I chance to be mistaken, of course."

He waited. Bell thought about protesting that the southrons surely could not have more than four times as many men as he did. He might even have been right to claim that. But what difference would it make? Four times as many men or five, Doubting George had far too many soldiers for the Army of Franklin to hope to withstand.

When Bell kept silent, Peegeetee nodded to himself. As calmly and dispassionately as if talking about the weather, he remarked, "King Geoffrey is most unhappy —most vocally unhappy, you understand—about the manner in which this campaign was conducted."

Again, a hot retort came to the tip of Lieutenant General Bell's tongue—came there and went no further. He was unhappy about a whole great raft of things Geoffrey had done, too. Once more, though, what difference did it make? Geoffrey was the king. Bell wasn't. All he said was, "By the gods, General, we tried as hard as mortal men could."

"Have I tried to deny it?" Peegeetee replied. "No one denies your valor, Lieutenant General, or the valor of the men you lead—those of them who survive. Unfortunately, no one doubts your lack of success, either." He steepled his fingertips and looked past Bell's right shoulder. "This now leaves you with a certain choice."

"A choice?" Bell echoed, frowning in incomprehension. "What kind of choice?"

Marquis Peegeetee still didn't seem to want to meet his eyes. "You may pay a call on the headsman, or you may fall on your own sword. This, I fear me, is the only choice remaining to you at the moment. A pity, no doubt, but such is life."

For a moment, Bell thought he meant the words literally. Figurative language had always been a closed book to the man who led the Army of Franklin. Here, though, he found the key. "You mean his Majesty will sack me if I don't lay down my command?"

"But of course," Peegeetee told him. "As I say, I regret this, but I can do nothing about it save convey the choice to you."

Bell thought about making Geoffrey dismiss him. That would show the world he thought he'd done nothing wrong. But what counted except results? Nothing. And what had come from this campaign? Also nothing, worse luck. Shrugging—the motion sent a wave of agony through his ruined left shoulder, making him long for laudanum—he said, "You may convey to his Majesty my resignation, and my readiness to serve him in any capacity in which he believes I may be of use."

Peegeetee bowed in the saddle. "Your sentiments do you credit."

"I want no credit, your Grace. What I wanted was to beat our enemies. Since that was denied me . . ." Bell shrugged again, not so much careless of the pain as embracing it. Once it had washed over him, he asked, "And who will succeed me in command of this army?"

To his surprise, Marquis Peegeetee looked past him again. "I am afraid, Lieutenant General, that that is not such an easy question to answer."

"Why not?" Bell demanded. "Someone has to, surely."

"Well . . . no. Not necessarily," Peegeetee replied. "King Geoffrey plans to send part of your army to Count Joseph the Gamecock, who is gathering forces in Palmetto Province to try to hold off the southrons. Veldt, you know, fell to General Hesmucet a couple of weeks ago. His Majesty fears Hesmucet will turn south, aiming to join Marshal Bart in an assault against Nonesuch. The rest of your force here . . ." He shrugged, too, a dapper little shrug. " . . . will be able to carry on without the formal name of the Army of Franklin."

Rage ripped through Lieutenant General Bell.

"What?" he growled. "You'd gut *my* army to feed soldiers to that useless son of a bitch of a Joseph?"

With icy courtesy, Peegeetee replied, "It seems to me, Lieutenant General, that you are the one who has gutted your army."

Bell ignored him. "Gods damn it, if I'd known Geoffrey was going to do that, I never would have resigned. As a matter of fact, I withdraw my resignation!"

"I am going to pretend I did not hear that," the marquis said. "Believe me when I say you are lucky I am going to pretend I did not hear it. I told you his Majesty was disappointed in the Army of Franklin's performance. I did not tell you *how* disappointed, and how . . . how wrathful, he was. If you fail to resign, he *will* sack you, Lieutenant General. And he will do worse than that. 'Lieutenant General Bell, give me back my army!' he cried when word of your sad, piteous overthrow before Ramblerton reached him. If he sacks you, you will go before a court-martial, one with membership of his choosing. Perhaps you will only see the inside of a prison. Perhaps, on the other hand, you will see a cross."

"A . . . cross?" Bell said hoarsely. "He would do that to me, for fighting a campaign the best way I knew how? By the Thunderer's strong right hand, where is the justice in this world?"

"A cross not for the fight, I would say." General Peegeetee judiciously pursed his lips as he paused to find just the right words. "A cross for throwing away Geoffrey's last hope east of the mountains—his last hope, really, of ruling a kingdom that amounts to anything."

A tiny flicker of disdain, gone from his face almost— but not quite—before Bell was sure he saw it, said Peegeetee shared King Geoffrey's opinion of Bell and of what he had—and hadn't—done. That scorn hurt him worse than either his missing leg or his ruined arm.

"Excuse me," he said thickly, and fumbled for his little bottle of laudanum. He gulped, careless of the dose. Poppies and fire chased each other down his throat.

"I regret the necessity of bringing you such unfortunate news when your wounds trouble you so," Peegeetee murmured.

Bell doubted he regretted it. If he had to guess, he would have said Peegeetee derived a sneaking pleasure from his pain. And, for once, the wounds weren't what troubled the general commanding—no, the general formerly commanding—the Army of Franklin. Could laudanum also dull torment of the spirit? If it couldn't, nothing could. That possibility sent a cold wind of terror howling through Bell's soul.

"Have you now reconsidered your reconsideration?" the marquis inquired.

"I have," Bell replied in a voice heavy as lead. "But, your Grace, no matter what you say, I aim to go to Nonesuch to put my case before his Majesty."

"I would not dream of standing in your way," Peegeetee said. "I do offer two bits of advice, however, for whatever you may think they are worth. First, do not get your hopes up. King Geoffrey has always been touchy, and he is all the touchier now that the war is going . . . less well than he would have liked."

"And whose fault is that?" Bell said, meaning it was Geoffrey's.

But General Peegeetee answered, "In his opinion, yours. I also note that Nonesuch is not the place you think it to be."

"I am familiar with Nonesuch," Bell said. "It is less than a year and a half ago that I last passed through it. Surely it cannot have changed much in so short a time."

"It can. It has," General Peegeetee told him. "With Marshal Bart's army clinging to the siege of Pierreville as a bulldog clings to a thief's leg, the shadow of the gibbet and the cross falls ever darker on the city. It is not without its gaiety even yet, but that gaiety has a desperate edge."

"I care nothing for gaiety," Bell snapped. "I care only for victory, and for vindication."

"Both of which, I fear, are in moderately short supply in Nonesuch these days." Peegeetee shrugged. "This is not my concern, however. I, like you, wish it were otherwise. And please believe me when I tell you I wish you good fortune in your quest. As I say, though, do please also be realistic in your expectations."

Bell had never been realistic, either in the field or in his maneuverings with and against other officers serving King Geoffrey. His headlong fighting style had made him a hero. It had also left him a twice-mutilated man. He had risen to command the Army of Franklin—and, in commanding it, had destroyed it. When he told Marquis Peegeetee, "I shall, of course, take your advice, most seriously," he meant, *I shall, of course, pay no attention whatsoever to you.*

With another bow in the saddle, Peegeetee replied, "I am most glad to hear it," by which he meant, *I don't believe a word of it.*

"Which men will be sent to Palmetto Province?" Bell asked. By putting it that way, he didn't have to mention, or even have to think of, Count Joseph the Gamecock. The less he thought of Joseph, the better he liked it. That Joseph might not care to think of him, either, had never once entered his mind.

Marquis Peegeetee pulled a sheet of paper from the breast pocket of his gold-buttoned blue tunic. "You are ordered to send the wing commanded by Colonel Florizel . . ." He paused and raised an eyebrow. "A wing, commanded by a colonel?"

"Senior surviving officer," Bell said. "When we fight, your Grace, we fight *hard.*"

"Fighting *well* would be even better," Peegeetee murmured, and Bell glared furiously. Ignoring him, the nobleman continued, "You are also ordered to detach half the brigades from the wing commanded by Brigadier Benjamin, called the Heated Ham—how picturesque. The said brigadier is to accompany the attached brigades. Have you any questions?"

"No, sir, but do please note you are taking half the army's strength," Bell said.

"Not I, Lieutenant General. I am but delivering his Majesty's orders. And the Army of Franklin—the former Army of Franklin, I should say—is from this moment on no longer your official concern."

"I understand that . . . your Grace." Bell held his temper with no small effort. "Even so, its fate, and the fate of the kingdom, still interest me mightily, as they should interest any man with a drop of patriotic blood in his veins. I have, you know, spent more than a drop of my blood on King Geoffrey's behalf." He glanced down toward the stump of his right leg.

Peegeetee's gaze followed his own—but only for a moment. Then the marquis looked away, an expression of distaste crossing his narrow, clever features. Still not meeting Bell's gaze, he muttered, "No one has ever faulted your courage." He gathered himself. "But would you not agree it is now time to let other men shed their blood for the land we all hold dear?"

"I am still ready—still more than ready—to fight, sir," Bell said.

"That, I regret to repeat, you must take up with his Majesty in Nonesuch," General Peegeetee replied. Bell nodded. To Nonesuch he would go. He had scant hope, but he would go. His good hand folded into a fist. By all he could see, Geoffrey's kingdom had scant hope, either. Righteously, Bell thought, *I did all I could.*

❖   ❖   ❖

"Come on," Captain Gremio called to his regiment. "Get aboard the glideway carpets. Fill 'em up good and tight, too. We don't have as many as we need."

Beside him, Sergeant Thisbe murmured, "When have we ever had as much of anything as we need? Men? Food? Clothes? Siege engines? Glideway carpets?"

That was so obviously unanswerable, Gremio didn't even try. He said, "What I'm wondering is, how the hells are we going to get to Palmetto Province? We ought to go through Marthasville—just about all the glideways from the coast out here to the east pass through Marthasville. But the southrons have held the place since last summer."

He felt foolish as soon as he'd spoken. Thisbe knew that as well as he did. The Army of Franklin—the army now breaking up like rotting ice—had done all it could to keep Hesmucet and the southrons out of Marthasville. All it could do hadn't been enough. Gremio didn't think the attack orders Lieutenant General Bell had given after taking command from Joseph the Gamecock had helped the northern cause, but he wasn't sure Marthasville would have held even absent those orders. Any which way, it was much too late to worry about them now.

One after another, soldiers in blue stepped up onto mounting benches and from them up onto the carpets. From time out of mind, men had told stories of magic carpets, of carpets that flew through the air like birds, like dragons, like dreams. But, up until about the time Gremio was born, they'd been only stories. Even now, glideway carpets didn't rise far above the ground. They traveled at no more than the speed of a galloping unicorn, though they could hold their pace far longer than a unicorn. And they could only follow paths sorcerously prepared in advance: glideways. As so often happened, practical magecraft proved very different from the romance of myth and legend.

Colonel Florizel limped toward Gremio, who came to attention and saluted. "As you were, Captain," Florizel said.

"Thank you, sir." Gremio relaxed. "We're heading back towards our home province, eh? Been a long time."

"Yes." A frown showed behind Florizel's bushy beard. "Under the circumstances, I worry about desertion. Can you blame me?"

"No, sir. I understand completely," Gremio answered. "I wouldn't worry so much if the war were going better. As things are . . ." He didn't go on.

Florizel nodded heavily. "Yes. As things are." It wasn't a complete sentence, but what difference did that make? Gremio understood him again. Florizel continued, "What makes it so bad for my regiment— excuse me, Captain: for *your* regiment—is that we are ordered back to our homes in the middle of a war that is . . . not going well. If our men think, *to hells with it*, what is to stop them from throwing down their crossbows and heading back to their farms or wherever they happen to live?"

"Not much, sir, I'm afraid. Maybe things will go better, or at least seem better, once we get to Palmetto Province. If they do, the men will be less likely to want to run away, don't you think?"

"Maybe. I hope so." Colonel Florizel still sounded profoundly dubious. Shaking his head, he went on down the line of glideway carpets. Gremio wondered whether he doubted things would go better in Palmetto Province or that it would make any difference to the men if they did—or maybe both.

Gremio could have given Florizel even more to worry about. Being convinced the war was lost and not just going badly, he'd begun to think about deserting himself. No one in Karlsburg would have anything much to say if he returned before the fighting formally finished. He was sure of that. He could resume his career as a barrister easily enough.

He felt Sergeant Thisbe's eyes on his back. Sure enough, when he turned he found the underofficer looking at him. Thisbe quickly turned away, as if embarrassed at getting caught.

Gremio quietly cursed. He wasn't cursing Thisbe—far from it. He was cursing himself. He knew he wasn't going to desert as long as the sergeant kept fighting for King Geoffrey. He couldn't stand the idea of losing Thisbe's good opinion of him.

And if Hesmucet storms up through Palmetto Province with every southron in the world at his back? Gremio shrugged. *If you get killed because you're too stupid or too gods-damned stubborn to leave while you still have the chance?* He shrugged again. *Even then.*

It wasn't anything he hadn't already known, and known for months. Now, though, he'd spelled it out to himself. He felt none of the fear he'd thought he might. He simply liked having everything in order in his own mind.

"Well, Sergeant, our men seem to be aboard the carpets," he said to Thisbe. "Shall we get on ourselves?"

"Yes, sir," Thisbe said. "After you, sir."

"No, after you," Gremio answered. "I'm still the captain of this ship: last on, last off."

Thisbe tried to argue, but Gremio had both rank and tradition on his side. Clucking, the sergeant climbed up onto the closest carpet and sat crosslegged at the edge. Gremio followed. He found a place by Thisbe; soldiers crowded together to make a little more room for them.

A man in a glideway conductor's black uniform came

by. "No feet over the edges of the carpet," he warned. "Bad things will happen if you break that rule."

The men all knew that. Most of them also probably knew, or knew of, someone who'd broken a foot or an ankle or a leg against a rock or a tree trunk that happened to lie too close to a glideway line. Detinans were stubborn people who delighted in flouting rules, no matter how sensible those rules might be.

Silently, smoothly, the carpets slid west along the glideway. The silence persisted. The smoothness? No. The spells on the glideway line badly needed refurbishing. No mages seemed to have bothered doing that essential work. The wizards the north had were all busy doing even more essential work: trying to keep the southrons from pushing deeper into King Geoffrey's tottering realm. They weren't doing any too well at that, but they were trying.

Great River Province and Dothan had suffered relatively little from the war. Even in those provinces, though, everything had a shabby, rundown look to it, as if no one had bothered taking care of anything that wasn't vital since the war began. Gremio saw a lot of women working in the fields, sometimes alongside blond serfs, sometimes by themselves. No Detinan men who didn't have white beards were there to help them. If they didn't take care of things themselves, who would? Nobody.

A measure of how little the war had touched Great River Province and Dothan was that serfs *were* working in the fields. Down in Franklin, most of the blonds had fled their liege lords' holdings, choosing with their feet liberation from feudal ties. Northern nobles had long proclaimed that blonds preferred the security of being tied to the land. The evidence looked to be against them.

Here and there, the path the soldiers detached from

the Army of Franklin took twisted like a drunken
earthworm. Even here, so far north, southron raiders
had sometimes penetrated. Their wizards had dethaum-
atized stretches of the glideway. On those stretches,
the carpets might as well have lain on the floor of some
duke's dining hall, for all the inclination toward flight
they displayed. The soldiers had to roll them up and
carry them along till they reached a working stretch
of glideway once more.

And then, more slowly than they should have, the
glideway carpets reached Peachtree Province. They had
to skirt Marthasville, which had been the hub of all
glideway routes. It still lay in the southrons' hands, and
the garrison there was far too strong for this ragtag
force to hope to overcome. Instead, Florizel's men and
those led by Benjamin the Heated Ham went west and
then north. They passed through the swath of destruction Hesmucet's army had left a couple of months
before, marching west from Marthasville to the Western
Ocean.

That swath was a good forty miles wide. The southrons had ruined the glideways along with everything
else. The men who'd set out from Honey had to march
across it, and they got hungry on the way. Hesmucet's
men had burned every farm and castle they came upon.
They'd ravaged fields, cut down fruit trees, and slaughtered every animal they caught. Skeletons with bits of
hide and flesh still clinging to them dotted the landscape. Vultures still rose from the bones, though
the carrion birds had long since battened on most
of the bounty presented them. The stench of death
lingered.

No blonds remained here. They'd run off with the
southrons by the thousands.

"How could Hesmucet's men do such a thing?"
Thisbe wondered.

"How? Simple," Gremio answered grimly. "They were strong enough, and we couldn't stop them."

Everyone was grim by the time the detachment reached the far edge of that strip of devastation torn across Peachtree Province. It had to run all the way from Marthasville to the ocean. Had Geoffrey's kingdom been strong, Hesmucet's men never could have done such a thing. Since they had . . .

Colonel Florizel wasn't far from despair by the time his men got to unravaged soil. He came up to Gremio, asking, "How can I ask even the bravest soldiers to give their lives for King Geoffrey's realm when everything is falling into ruin here at the heart of it?"

"I don't know, sir," Gremio answered. "How much more can we take before . . . before we go under?" Before the disaster in front of Ramblerton, he wouldn't have dared ask his superior such a question. Florizel would have called him a defeatist, maybe even a traitor. Now not even Florizel could believe the north's prospects were good.

He looked at Gremio for a long time before he shook his head and said, "I don't know, either, Captain. By the Thunderer's strong right arm, though, we'd better find out soon." He stumped away without waiting for a reply.

Later that evening, Gremio and Thisbe sprawled wearily in front of a campfire. Gremio said, "I think even the colonel is losing hope." He told Thisbe what had passed between Florizel and him.

"What do *you* think, sir?" Thisbe asked, staring into the yellow flames as if they were a crystal ball. "Is it all over? Shall we go home when we get to Palmetto Province, or do we still have a chance if we still keep fighting?"

"I'll fight as long as you will, Sergeant." Gremio had

thought that before, but now he amplified it: "If you decide you've had enough, I won't say a word."

Thisbe swung around to face him. "That's not fair, sir—putting it all on me, I mean."

"I'm sorry, Sergeant," Gremio said. "I just thought—"

"You didn't think, sir," Thisbe said with a shake of the head. "You're the officer, so it's really up to you. You said so yourself, when we were getting on the glideway carpet at Honey."

"I do believe I've just been hoist with my own petard." Gremio mimed taking a deadly wound.

Although Thisbe laughed, the underofficer's face remained serious. "If it is up to you, sir, what will you do?"

"I'll see how things look when we get into Palmetto Province, and I'll make up my mind then," Gremio answered. "What will *you* do?"

"Follow you," Thisbe said without hesitation. "I know you'll come up with the right thing to do. You always have."

"Thank you. I only wish it were true."

Before they could say any more, a rider came up from the southwest. "Are you the men coming to the aid of Joseph the Gamecock?" he asked tensely, looking ready to gallop away in a hurry if the answer were no.

But Gremio said, "That's right. How are things in Palmetto Province these days? A lot of us are from there."

"Been a lot of rain," the unicorn-rider answered. "Plenty of what would be roads most of the year are underwater now. That ought to slow down the gods-damned southrons. If it doesn't, we're in a hells of a lot of trouble, on account of those fornicating bastards outnumber us about five to one."

Gremio and Sergeant Thisbe looked at each other.

That was what had happened to Lieutenant General Bell. Once you came to a certain point, bravery stopped mattering much. No matter how brave you were, you'd get hammered if you were outnumbered badly enough.

One of Gremio's soldiers said, "Well, it ain't so bad any more, on account of now you've got us."

The unicorn-rider managed a nod, but the look on his face was pained. Gremio didn't, couldn't, blame him for that. A good many farmers who put on Geoffrey's blue tunic and pantaloons had hardly more education than blond serfs. The men who'd come from Bell's shattered army to the one Joseph the Gamecock was trying to build might mean his force was outnumbered only four to one. How much would that help him when he tried to hold back Hesmucet? The answer seemed obvious to Gremio, if not to the common soldier.

"What do we do now, sir?" Thisbe asked.

It wasn't a question about how they should proceed on the next day's travel. Gremio knew it wasn't, and wished it were. It would have been much easier to deal with as that sort of question. He sighed and shook his head. "I don't know, Sergeant. I just don't know."

XI

Sergeant Rollant looked across the Franklin River. On the north bank, Ned of the Forest's unicorn-riders trotted up and down on endless patrol. Rollant reached for his crossbow, but arrested the motion before it got very far. What was the point? The Franklin was a lot more than a bowshot wide.

Beside Rollant, Smitty—Corporal Smitty—also eyed the unicorn-riders, who were tiny in the distance. Smitty said, "If we could push some men across, we could smash up all those sons of bitches."

"I know. I've been thinking the same thing." Rollant let out a small noise full of longing, the sort of noise a cat on the ground might make at seeing a plump thrush high in a treetop. "The other thing I've been thinking is, it wouldn't be very hard."

"That's right. That's just exactly right. It wouldn't be hard at all." Smitty practically quivered with eagerness.

"We could head straight on up to the Gulf, and how could the traitors stop us, or even slow us down?"

"They couldn't. Not a chance." Rollant was as sure of it as he was of his own name. "We'd be heroes."

"We're already heroes. I've had a bellyful of being a hero," Smitty said. "What I want to do is win the gods-damned war and go home."

"Home." Rollant spoke the word with enormous longing. For the first time since he'd taken King Avram's silver and put on the kingdom's gray tunic and pantaloons, the idea that he would be going home before too long began to seem real. "*Why* doesn't Doubting George turn us loose on them?"

"Beats me." Smitty shrugged. "But you know what? I don't much care one way or the other." He waved across the river. "I mean, look at those poor sorry sons of bitches. We've *licked* 'em." His voice held absolute conviction, absolute certainty. In fact, he said it again: "We've *licked* 'em. They aren't going to come back and give us trouble, the way they did in Peachtree Province. We could all go home tomorrow, and Ramblerton still wouldn't have a thing to worry about. You going to tell me I'm wrong?" He looked a challenge at Rollant.

"No," the blond admitted. "No, I don't suppose you are."

"Gods-damned right I'm not," Smitty said. "And since they *are* licked, what the hells difference does it make whether we go after 'em hard or not?"

What difference did it make? Any at all? Rollant hadn't looked at things like that. Now he did. Again, he couldn't say Smitty was wrong. "What do you think we'll do, then?" he asked. "Wait here by the river till the war ends in the west? Just stay here and make sure Ned of the Forest doesn't get loose and make trouble?"

Like most blonds, he had a respect and dread for

Ned that amounted almost to superstitious awe. A man who was both a serfcatcher and a first-rate—better than first-rate: brilliant—commander of unicorn-riders, and whose men had been known to slaughter blonds fighting for Avram? No wonder he roused such feelings in the soldiers who had the most reason to oppose him.

Smitty, on the other hand, was an ordinary Detinan. If anything impressed him, he wasn't inclined to admit it, even to himself. He said, "To the hells with Ned of the Forest, too. He tries getting cute, Hard-Riding Jimmy'll take care of him." Smitty spoke with the blithe confidence most ordinary Detinans showed, the blithe confidence that baffled Rollant and other blonds. And, as if to say he didn't think Ned or the rest of the northerners were worth worrying about, he turned his back on the unicorn-riders and the Franklin River and strode off, whistling.

"Licked." Rollant tasted the word in his mouth. Could it really be true? He'd thought so during the pursuit, but now that seemed over. Was it still true with him standing here in cold blood? "By the gods, maybe it is," he murmured. Where Smitty had turned his back on the river, Rollant stared avidly across it. "Licked." What a lovely word!

He was recalled to his side of the Franklin when somebody spoke to him in a tongue he didn't understand. Several blond laborers, all plainly escaped serfs, stood there gaping at him in open-mouthed admiration. Some wore the undyed wool tunics and pantaloons Avram's army issued to such men, others the rags in which they'd run away from their liege lords' estates.

Such things had happened to him before. Blonds in the north had used a swarm of languages before the Detinan conquerors came. Many still survived, if precariously, and a lot of them had added words to the Detinan spoken in the north. But the speech whose fragments Rollant had learned as a child on Baron Ormerod's estate in Palmetto Province sounded nothing like this one.

"Talk Detinan," he told them in that language. It was the conquerors' tongue, but the only one they had in common. "What do you want?"

They looked disappointed he couldn't follow them. He'd expected that. One of them, visibly plucking up his courage, asked, "You are really a sergeant, sir?"

"Yes, I'm a sergeant," Rollant answered. "And you don't call me *sir*. You call officers *sir*. They're the ones with epaulets." He saw the blond laborers didn't know what epaulets were, so he tapped his shoulder. "The fancy ornaments they wear here. You men haven't been with the army long, have you?"

"No, sir," another of them said. The laborer who'd spoken first poked him with an elbow. He tried again: "Uh, no, Sergeant."

Yet another blond asked, "How did you get to be a sergeant, sir?" Force of habit died hard in them. The man added, "How did they let you be a sergeant?"

"They made me a corporal when I took the company standard after the standard-bearer got killed," Rollant replied. "I charged at the northerners and I was lucky—they didn't shoot me. Then, when the lieutenant who commanded this company got shot at Ramblerton, they made our sergeant a lieutenant, and they made me a sergeant."

"A sergeant. A blond sergeant." The laborer who spoke might have been talking about a black unicorn or some other prodigy of nature.

The blond who'd called to Rollant in the language that wasn't Detinan asked, "And when you give an order, do the Detinans obey?"

All the blonds leaned forward, eagerly hanging on the answer. They all sighed ecstatically when he nodded. He couldn't blame them. What blond trapped in serfdom in the north didn't dream of turning the tables on his liege lord? Rollant knew he had, back when he was bound to Baron Ormerod's estate outside of Karlsburg.

"They do *now*," he told them.

"Now?" They all echoed that. A big, burly blond in rags asked, "Why didn't they before?"

Rollant wished the man hadn't asked that question. Reluctantly, he gave back the truth: "Because I had to beat up one of them to convince them I deserved to wear my stripes."

"Ahhh!" They all said that together, too.

"Wait!" Rollant held up a hand. With desperate urgency, he said, "Do you know what'll happen if *you* try to beat up Detinans?" The blond laborers shook their heads. "They'll give *you* stripes—stripes on your backs," he told them. "Or they may nail you to crosses. Don't try. You can't get away with it."

They frowned. The burly one asked, "Why could you, then? That's not right."

"Why could I?" Now Rollant was the one doing the echoing. "I'll tell you why. Because I've killed northerners. All the men in my company knew I could do that. They'd seen me do it. They'd seen I could fight and didn't run away. The only question left was whether I was tough enough to lick them, and I showed them I could do that, too, when one of our Detinans wouldn't obey me. If you haven't done all the other things, don't try this, or you'll be sorrier than you ever imagined you could be, and no one will help you."

He wondered if they were really listening, or if one of them would try to hit a Detinan overseer he didn't like right in the eye. He hoped they wouldn't be so stupid, but you never could tell.

Maybe they would just try to strip off their color-less clothes and get the Detinans to give them gray tunics and pantaloons instead. They might even succeed; King Avram's armies seemed permanently hungry for men. But if the blonds expected promotion to be easy or quick, they were doomed to disappointment. It was probably easier for them to end up dead than to end up as corporals, let alone sergeants. Rollant shrugged. Still, if they wanted to try, why shouldn't they?

He looked across the Franklin again. Ned's unicornriders kept right on patrolling the north bank. They probably kept right on being convinced that Geoffrey was the rightful King of Detina, too, and that blonds were serfs by nature. But, as far as the larger scheme of things went, what Ned of the Forest's troopers were convinced of mattered less and less with each passing day.

"Lollygagging around again, are you?" a deep voice rumbled behind Rollant.

He turned and saluted. "Oh, yes, sir, Lieutenant Joram," he replied. "You know all blonds are shiftless and lazy, same as you know all blonds are a pack of dirty, yellow cowards."

Joram opened his mouth to answer that, then closed it again. Before saying anything, the newly commissioned officer rumbled laughter. Only after he'd got it out of his system did he remark, "Gods damn it, Rollant, there are still plenty of Detinans who *do* know that, or think they do."

"Yes, sir." Rollant nodded. "But are you one of them?"

"Well, that depends," Joram said judiciously. "There's a difference, you know, between whether you were lollygagging around on account of you're a shiftless, cowardly blond and whether you were lollygagging around just in a general sort of way."

"Oh, yes, sir." Rollant nodded again. "That's the

truth. There is that difference. The Detinans you were talking about, though, *they* can't see it."

"Before you rubbed my nose in it, I would have had trouble seeing it myself," Joram said. "Some blonds *are* shiftless cowards."

"That's true, too, sir. So are some Detinans."

Joram grunted. Detinans prided themselves on being a warrior race. After a moment, Joram's big head bobbed up and down. "And *that's* the truth. So, Sergeant . . . in a general sort of way, *were* you lollygagging around?"

If Rollant had admitted it while still a common soldier, his reward would have been extra duty of some sort: chopping wood or digging a latrine trench or filling canteens. As a sergeant, he was supposed to be immune to such little oppressions. But he'd been a common soldier longer than he'd been an underofficer. "Sir, I don't know what you're talking about," he said blandly.

"I'll bet you don't!" Joram laughed again, a laugh so big and booming, Rollant wondered if the riders on the far side of the Franklin could hear it. But they just kept on riding. The company commander said, "Blond or not, you're sure as hells an old soldier, aren't you?"

Rollant shrugged. "I've been doing this a while now," he said, "but any serf would tell you how much of a fool you have to be before you admit anything that puts you in trouble."

"You don't need to be a serf to learn that—though I don't suppose it hurts," Joram said.

"Now that you're an officer, sir, have you heard anything about whether we'll cross the Franklin and finish the traitors once and for all?" Rollant asked.

That made Joram laugh yet again, but this time without much in the way of amusement in his voice. "Just because they gave me one epaulet doesn't mean they tell me anything," he answered. "If I had my way, we'd already be pushing those bastards out of Honey—

I hear that's where they finally went and ran to. But even though I'm a lieutenant, I don't have my way."

"For whatever it may be worth to you, I'd do the same," Rollant said. "Of course, I'm only a sergeant and I'm only a blond, so I *really* don't have my way."

"No, I don't suppose you do," Joram agreed. "But tell me this—when the war started, before you joined the army, did you ever think you'd say something like, 'I'm only a sergeant'?"

"No, sir, can't say that I did," Rollant admitted. "What I wonder now is how things will be for my children, and for *their* children. I don't want them to have to go through a lot of the things I've had to put up with because of the way I look."

Joram nodded his big, heavy-featured head once more. "Don't blame you a bit. If I were a blond, I'd say the same gods-damned thing. Since I'm not a blond, I'll say something else instead: don't expect miracles. The gods don't dole 'em out very often. If you figure everything's going to be perfect on account of we've gone and whipped false King Geoffrey, you'll wind up disappointed."

Now Rollant laughed. "Sir, I'm a blond. It's a miracle I believe in miracles, if you know what I mean."

"I think maybe I do." Lieutenant Joram smacked him on the back, hard enough to stagger him. "Never mind miracles, then. Believe that we've won this war whether we go over the Franklin or not, and that we'll go on from there."

Everyone kept saying the same thing. It wasn't so much that Rollant believed it was wrong, for he didn't. After the fight in front of Ramblerton, no northern army worthy of the name survived east of the Green Ridge Mountains. But he wanted to be in at the death, to *see* false King Geoffrey's realm fail. Hearing that it happened somewhere else later on didn't have the same feel, the same meaning. *Yes, I want victory in my own hands*, he thought, and then, *How very, very Detinan I'm getting*.

John the Lister had done a lot of hard and dangerous things during the War Between the Provinces. He'd got his detachment through the battle of Poor Richard, and wrecked the Army of Franklin in the process. His men had played a major role in the victory in front of Ramblerton, and in the pursuit that followed. And now here he was talking, negotiating terms of surrender for . . . a postmaster?

The postmaster in question, a wizened, bespectacled little man named Ithran, had taken care of letters and parcels going into and out of the town of Warsaw. He'd done that before the war, and he'd done it under the auspices of false King Geoffrey during the war, and he wanted to go on doing it now that King Avram's authority had come to northern Franklin. What he didn't want to do was swear an oath of allegiance to Avram.

"Well, that's simple enough," John told him. "If you don't, your town will have a new postmaster fast as we can find one."

Ithran writhed like a man who needed to run to the jakes. "It's not fair," he whined. "With the war just about over, who else would I be loyal to?"

"I don't know. I don't want to find out. Neither does his Majesty," John replied. "No penalty will fall on you if you don't swear the oath. King Avram is a merciful man—more merciful than he ought to be, I often think. But if you cannot swear loyalty to him by the Thunderer and the Lion God and the rest of the heavenly host on Mount Panamgam beyond the sky, you will not stay postmaster in Warsaw."

"But—" Ithran threw his hands in the air. He must have seen that John the Lister meant what he said. "All right. All *right*! I'll swear. Do I give you my oath?"

"No. You give it to the priests. They're the proper ones to hold it. Ask in our encampment," John said. "Someone will tell you where to find them."

"I'll do that. Thank you." Despite the polite words, Ithran sounded anything but grateful. Still fuming, he scuttled out of John's presence.

John reminded himself to check to make sure Ithran *had* sworn the oath before letting him open up the post office in Warsaw. Even if he did swear it, John judged he wouldn't do so with anything even approaching sincerity. He had, after all, already sworn allegiance first to King Buchan and then to false King Geoffrey. After that, how important would he reckon one more oath? But John was not charged with enforcing sincerity, only the law King Avram had ordained.

And, once the oath was sworn, the priests wouldn't be the only ones holding it. The gods would also keep it in their hands. While that might not matter in this world, it should in the next. Several of the seven hells had particularly . . . interesting sections reserved for oathbreakers.

That was one reason why John the Lister didn't fret much about Ithran's sincerity (though he did wish Major Alva had never told him about the Inward Hypothesis, which made the gods seem weaker than they should). The other was that, as the postmaster himself had said, the war was nearly over, false King Geoffrey nearly beaten. If no one could carry on the fight for Geoffrey, Ithran and all the people like him would have to stay loyal to Avram.

A runner came up to John and stood at attention, waiting—ostentatiously waiting—to be noticed. When John nodded, the young soldier in gray saluted and said, "Sir, you are ordered to report to Lieutenant General George's pavilion right away."

"Oh, I am, am I?" John said. "What's this all about?"

The runner shrugged. "I don't know, sir. I was just told to deliver the message, and now I've done it."

"I'm on my way, then." John wondered if the runner could have told him more than he had. Rumor and gossip always swirled through the camp. John shrugged broad shoulders. He'd find out soon enough.

Doubting George stood waiting for him outside the pavilion. The commanding general didn't look particularly happy, but then George never looked particularly happy. He returned John's salute in an absentminded way.

"Reporting as ordered, sir," John said. "What's going on? Will we cross the Franklin and chase the traitors after all?"

"No." Doubting George shook his head. "This army will do no such thing. The new orders I have from Georgetown make that perfectly clear."

"Oh, dear. Too bad," John said. "We really ought to finish smashing up the Army of Franklin and Lieutenant General Bell, or whoever's in charge of it if Bell really has resigned."

"The chowderhead *is* gone," George said. "No doubt about that at all. I don't know who the traitors will appoint in his place. I don't know how much it matters, either, not with these orders I've got."

John the Lister frowned. "What *are* your orders, sir?" Whatever they were, they seemed to have sucked all the vitality out of the commanding general. John couldn't remember ever having seen him so low, not even after the disaster by the River of Death. George had been a tower of strength then; without him, General Guildenstern's whole army, and the southron war effort east of the mountains, might well have gone to pieces in the aftermath of the defeat.

Now he said, "Your wing, Brigadier, is to be detached from my army and sent to General Hesmucet

in the west, to go to Croatoan and join him after he
moves south through Palmetto Province toward
Marshal Bart at Pierreville."

"My . . . entire wing? With me in charge of it?" John
the Lister had trouble believing his ears.

But Doubting George's heavy, pain-filled nod assured
him he'd heard correctly. "That is what the order says.
I suppose I should congratulate you." He held out his
hand. "You'll get to be in at the very end, to see everything false King Geoffrey has left fall to bits."

Automatically, John took the proffered hand. He
said, "But why are they leaving you behind, sir? If
anybody's earned the right to be there, you're the man."

"Not according to what the orders say. They're not
happy with me over in Georgetown. No, they're not
happy at all."

"Why the hells not?" John asked in honest amazement. He knew his own career was rising while George's
stumbled, and he rejoiced that he *was* moving up in the
world and in the army, but this left him baffled. "What
could they ask you to do that you haven't done?"

"Well, for one thing, they're still grumbling because
they think I took too long to hit the Army of Franklin
in front of Ramblerton. They don't seem to care that
I shattered it when I did hit it, and they're annoyed
with me for not pursuing harder and not destroying
it altogether."

That last touched John the Lister's honor, too. "By
the Thunderer's prick, sir, don't they know you're up
here on the Franklin?" he asked angrily. "Don't they
know how many traitors we've killed, how many we've
captured?"

"If they don't, it's not because I haven't told them,"
Doubting George replied. "But whether they want to
listen is another question, gods damn it. You know how
easy it is to be a genius when you're running a campaign

from a few hundred miles away from where the real fighting is, and how simple it is to blame the poor stupid sod who's actually there for not being perfect."

"Yes, sir." Like any officer in the field, John knew that all too well.

"All I can say is, it's a good thing Geoffrey has the same disease, or worse, or we'd be in a lot more trouble than we are." George spat in disgust. "But . . . so it goes. And so you go. And may good fortune go with you. Considering the dribs and drabs that are left of the traitors' armies, I expect it will."

John expected that, too, and for the same reason. "Thank you, sir," he said. "Thank you very much. And what will you be doing?"

"Well, I'm ordered to stay here with the rest of my army for now," the commanding general replied. "You notice I'm not *ordered* to pursue Bell, even though they say they're unhappy that I haven't. What I figure will happen is, they'll keep on detaching pieces from my army till I haven't got much left. Then, maybe they'll order me after what's left of the Army of Franklin. And if I have trouble, they'll blame me for it." He shrugged. "Like I say, so it goes."

"Army politics is a nasty business," John said sympathetically. Doubting George's glum prediction sounded all too likely to him.

With another shrug, George said, "It won't change who wins the war, not now it won't. I console myself with that. Of course, once we *have* won, they'll probably ship me out to the steppe to fight the blond savages instead of letting me help hold down the traitors."

"Urgh!" was all John the Lister said to that. Garrison duty at some dusty castle in the middle of nowhere? Command of a regiment at most, after leading an army tens of thousands strong? He looked down at his wrists. If he got orders like that with the rank among the regulars he now held, he'd think about slashing them. And George was a lieutenant general of regulars, not just a brigadier.

But the other officer surprised him, saying, "If that's where they send me, I'll go. Why the hells not? The blonds are honest enemies, not like some of the ones I've got in Georgetown."

"Er—yes." John thought George was being indiscreet. No, he didn't just think so. He *knew* George was being indiscreet. If he let word get back to Georgetown about what the general commanding had said . . . well, what difference would it make? If George didn't care whether they sent him to the trackless east, it would make no difference at all.

The power of indifference, John the Lister thought. Indifference was a power he'd never contemplated before, which made it no less real. *Trust Doubting George to come up with a weapon like that.*

"I have my orders," George said, "and now you have yours. Go get your wing ready to travel, Brigadier. I know you'll show Hesmucet he didn't take all the good soldiers with him when he set out to march across Peachtree."

"I'll do that, sir," John promised. "And I'm sorry things didn't turn out better for you."

"I doubt it," Doubting George said. "What you wish is that Marshal Bart would've named *you* commanding general here instead of trying to ship Baron Logan the Black here from the west. Then you would've smashed Bell in front of Ramblerton, and you would've been the hero. Eh? Am I right or am I wrong?"

"You're right," John mumbled, embarrassed he had to admit it. "Why didn't you do more to call me on it back then?" George *had* warned him, but hadn't made it so plain he *knew* what was going on in his mind.

With one more massive shrug, the general commanding said, "We had to beat Bell first. Now we've done that, so whether we squabble among ourselves doesn't matter so much." His smile was strangely wistful. "To the victors go the spoils—and the squabbles over them."

"Yes, sir." John the Lister gave Doubting George a salute that had a lot of hail-and-farewell in it. "Believe me, sir, I'll have the men in tiptop shape when we go west to join up with General Hesmucet."

Now Doubting George looked and sounded as sharp and cynical as he usually did: "Oh, I do believe you, Brigadier. After all, if the soldiers perform well, you look good because of it."

Nodding, John saluted again and beat a hasty retreat. He'd served alongside George before serving under him. He wouldn't be sorry to get away, to serve under General Hesmucet again. Yes, Hesmucet could be difficult. But, from everything John the Lister had seen, any general worth his pantaloons was difficult. Hesmucet, though, had a simple driving energy John liked. Doubting George brooded and fretted before he struck. When he finally hit, he hit hard. That his army stood by the southern bank of the Franklin proved as much. Still, his long wait till all the pieces he wanted were in place had driven everyone around him to distraction.

Hesmucet, now, Hesmucet had blithely set out across Peachtree Province toward Veldt without even worrying about his supply line, let alone anything else. He'd taken a chance—taken it and got away with taking it. John tried to imagine Doubting George doing the like.

And then, just when he was about to dismiss his present but not future general commanding as an old foof, he remembered George had had the idea for tramping across Peachtree weeks before Hesmucet latched on to it and made it real. John scratched his head. What did that say? "To the hells with me if I know," he muttered. The more you looked at people, the more complicated they got.

John had hardly returned to his own command before a major came running up to him and asked, "Sir, is it really true we're going to Croatoan?"

"How the hells did you know that?" John stared. "Lieutenant General George just this minute gave me my orders."

The major didn't look the least bit abashed. "Oh, it's all over camp by now, sir," he said airily. "So it is true, eh?"

"Yes, it's true." John's voice, by contrast, was heavy as granite. "Gods damn me if I know why we bother giving orders at all. Rumor could do the job twice as well in half the time."

"Wouldn't be surprised, sir." Trying to be agreeable, the major accidentally turned insulting instead. He didn't even notice. Saluting, he went on, "Well, the men will be ready. I promise you that." He hurried away, intent on turning his promise into reality.

John the Lister gaped, then started to laugh. "Gods help the traitors," he said to nobody in particular. Then, laughing still, he shook his head. "No, nothing can help them now."

Officers set above Doubting George had given him plenty of reason to be disgusted all through the War Between the Provinces. There were times, and more than a few of them, when he'd worried more about his own superiors than about the fierce blue-clad warriors who followed false King Geoffrey. But this . . . this was about the hardest thing George had ever had to deal with.

He'd done everything King Avram and Marshal Bart wanted him to do. He'd kept Bell and the Army of Franklin from reaching the Highlow River. He'd kept them from getting into Cloviston at all. They'd hardly even touched the Cumbersome River, and they'd never come close to breaking into Ramblerton.

Once he'd beaten them in front of the capital of Franklin, he'd chased them north all through the province. He'd *broken* the Army of Franklin, broken it to bits. Much the biggest part of the force Bell had brought into Franklin was either dead or taken captive. Bell had resigned his command in disgrace. What was left of that command wasn't even styled the Army of Franklin any more; it wasn't big enough to be reckoned an army.

And for a reward, Doubting George had got . . . "A good kick in the ballocks, and that's it," the commanding general muttered in disgust, staring across the Franklin at Ned of the Forest's unicorn-riders. *They* knew what he'd done to the Army of Franklin. Why the hells didn't the fancy-pantaloons idiots back in Georgetown?

Beside George, Colonel Andy stirred. "It isn't right, sir," he said, looking and sounding for all the world like an indignant chipmunk.

"Tell me about it," George said. "And while you're at it, tell me what I can do about it." Andy was silent. George had known his adjutant would be. He'd known why, too: "There's *nothing* I can do about it."

"Not fair. Not right." Andy looked and sounded more indignant than ever. "By the Lion God's mane, sir, if it weren't for you, King Avram wouldn't have been able to carry on the fight here in the east."

That did exaggerate things, as Doubting George knew. Voice dry, he answered, "Oh, Marshal Bart and General Hesmucet might've had a little something—

just a little something, mind you—to do with it, too.
And a good many thousand soldiers, too."

"I know what the trouble is," Andy said hotly. "It's
because you're from Parthenia, sir. That isn't right,
either, not when we're fighting to hold Detina together."

"Even if you're right, I can't do anything about it
now," George said. "Only thing I ever could have done
about it was fight for Grand Duke Geoffrey instead
of King Avram, and I do believe I'd've sooner coughed
up a lung."

He feared Andy had a point, though. A lot of southrons distrusted him because almost everyone in his
province (with the exception of the southeast, which was
now East Parthenia, a province of its own) *had* gone
over to Geoffrey. And the Parthenians who followed
Geoffrey called him a traitor to their cause. As far as
he was concerned, they were traitors to the Detinan
cause, but they cared not a fig for his opinion.

He tried not to care about theirs, either. It wasn't
easy; they'd been his neighbors, his friends—his relatives—before the war began. Now, even though some
of them still were his relatives, they despised him to
a man.

No, not quite. He shook his head. He knew that
wasn't quite true. Duke Edward of Arlington had
chosen to fight for his province rather than for a united
Detina, but he still respected those who'd gone the
other way. Duke Edward, of course, was no man of
the ordinary sort.

People said King Avram had offered command of
his armies to Duke Edward when the war began. Duke
Edward, though, had counted Parthenia above the
kingdom as a whole. Doubting George wondered how
things would have gone had Edward gone with Detina,
as he had himself. He suspected Geoffrey's forces
wouldn't have lasted long without their great general—

and with him leading the other side. But that was all moonshine. George had enough trouble dealing with what really was.

Across the river, the unicorn-riders went back and forth, back and forth, on their endless patrols. Bell hadn't had the faintest notion what he was doing, or so it often seemed to George. And yet Bell had gone to the military collegium at Annasville. Ned of the Forest, by contrast, had never been anywhere near the military collegium or any other place that had anything to do with soldiering. He'd first joined Geoffrey's side as a common soldier. Yet he was as dangerous a professional as anybody on either side. George doubted anyone could have run the rear-guard skirmishes during Bell's retreat any better than Ned had.

If Ned hadn't done quite so well, the Army of Franklin might have been completely destroyed. That might have sufficed to make Marshal Bart happy. Then again, it might not have. Bart seemed most determined not to be happy with Doubting George. George knew why, too. He'd committed the unforgivable sin for a subordinate: he'd bucked his superior's orders, and he'd proved himself right in doing it. No wonder Bart was breaking up his army and taking it away from him a piece at a time.

Doubting George was so intent on his gloomy reflections, he didn't notice someone had come up beside him till a polite cough forced him to. "Sorry to disturb you, sir," Major Alva said apologetically. "I know how important a reverie can be when you're trying to work things through."

"A reverie?" George snorted. "I don't believe I could come up with a good chain of thought right now. By the Thunderer's beard, I don't believe I could even come up with a good link. And you accuse me of reverie? Ha!"

The mage blinked. "Oh. Well, can you answer a question for me?"

"I can always answer questions, Major. Of course, whether the answers make any sense depends on what questions you ask."

"Uh, of course." Alva took half a step away from Doubting George, as if realizing he was dealing with a lunatic who might be dangerous. But he did ask his question: "Is it true that I'm ordered to Palmetto Province with John the Lister, the way I went to Summer Mountain and Poor Richard with him?"

Although the general commanding wished he could give an answer that made no sense, he had to nod. "Yes, Major, that is true. You're specifically mentioned in the orders sending John west. I wish I could tell you otherwise, because I'd like to keep you here. You've done splendid work for me. Don't think I haven't noticed."

"Thank you, sir," Alva said. "If you want to know what I think, I think it's a shame you don't get to do more here."

"So do I, now that you mention it," Doubting George said. "But that's not how things have worked out. All I can do about it is make sure the traitors don't get loose in spite of everything."

"I don't believe you have much to worry about there," Alva said.

"I don't believe I do, either, but that doesn't mean I won't be careful. It doesn't mean I won't be twice as careful, as a matter of fact," George replied. "The worst things happen when you're sure you've got nothing to worry about. And if you don't believe me, ask General Guildenstern." He waved, as if inviting the wizard to do just that. "Go ahead, Major. Ask him."

"Uh, I can't ask him, sir," Alva said nervously. "He isn't here." He might have feared the general commanding had forgotten Guildenstern was off in the east fighting blond savages on the steppe.

But Doubting George hadn't forgotten. He remembered all too well. "No, he isn't here," he agreed. "And the reason he isn't here is, he was sure he had Thraxton the Braggart whipped. He was sure the traitors were trundling up to Marthasville as fast as they could run. He was sure he didn't have a single, solitary thing to worry about. He was sure—and he was wrong. I don't intend to make that mistake. With the three men King Avram leaves me, I'll keep an eye on whatever the traitors still have up in Honey. They may lick me, but they won't catch me napping."

Alva pondered that. "You make good sense, sir. I wish they'd given lessons like that when I was studying sorcery. I'd be better off for them."

"But that isn't a lesson in sorcery," George said. "It's a lesson in life, a lesson in common sense. Are you telling me they don't teach mages common sense? That shocks me, that does."

"Well, that's not just what I meant. I—" Alva broke off and gave Doubting George a dirty look. "You're making fun again," he said accusingly.

With one of his broad-shouldered shrugs, George said, "I can either make fun or I can start yelling and cursing and pitching a fit. Which would you rather?"

"Me? I think it would be entertaining if you pitched a fit." Alva tried to project an air of childlike innocence. He didn't have too much luck.

"You would," Doubting George told him. "Now why don't you disappear, so I can go back into my—what did you call it?—my reverie, that was it."

"But you said it wasn't a reverie, sir," Alva said.

"It might be, if I give it a chance."

"But if it wasn't one in the first place, then you can't very well go *back* into it, can you?"

"Did you study wizardry, or at a collegium of law?" George rumbled.

To his surprise, Major Alva laughed out loud. "Can you imagine me a barrister, sir, or even a solicitor?" he asked, and Doubting George laughed, too, for he couldn't. With a half-mocking salute, Alva did leave.

And there stood Doubting George, looking at the rain-swollen waters of the Franklin, looking at Ned's unicorn-riders, looking at the ignominious conclusion to what should have been glorious instead. It *had* been glorious, in fact. The only trouble was, they couldn't see the glory back in Georgetown. Or maybe they could, but they didn't think it glittered brightly enough. *Is this a reverie?* George wondered. He doubted it. He just felt as chilly and gloomy as the winter's day all around him.

Hoofbeats brought him back to himself. He looked around, blinking a couple of times. Maybe it had been a reverie after all. Up came Hard-Riding Jimmy. The brash young commander of unicorn-riders swung down out of the saddle, tied his mount to a low-hanging branch, and came over to Doubting George. He saluted crisply.

Returning the salute, George said, "And what can I do for *you*?"

"Sir, I've just received orders from Georgetown," Jimmy said.

Excitement thrummed in his voice. George could see it in his stance. "What sort of orders?" the commanding general asked, though Jimmy's delight gave him a pretty good idea.

And, sure enough, Jimmy answered, "Detached duty, sir. My whole contingent of unicorn-riders. I'm ordered to go down into Dothan, smash up everything in my path, and hound Ned of the Forest to death." He sounded quiveringly eager to be about it, too.

Doubting George was also quivering—quivering with fury. "Congratulations, Brigadier. I hope you do it, and I think you can." He wasn't angry at Jimmy, or not directly. "These orders came straight to you?"

"Uh, yes, sir. They did." Now Jimmy knew what the trouble was. "Do you mean to say you didn't get them?"

"That is exactly what I mean to say," George growled. "By now, the butchers dismembering the carcass of my army must suppose I'm dead, for they don't even bother letting me know before they hack off another limb. At least they had the courtesy to tell me when they took John the Lister away from me."

Hard-Riding Jimmy turned red. He stroked one end of his long, drooping mustaches. "I'm sorry, sir. I assumed you would know before I did."

"Ha!" Doubting George said. "Marshal Bart doesn't think I deserve to know my own name, let alone anything else."

"Well . . ." The commander of unicorn-riders was too excited about what he was going to do to worry much about his superior's woes. "I can't wait to come to grips with Ned, not when I'm getting reinforced, all my men will have quick-shooting crossbows, and he can't afford to send his troopers scattering like quicksilver. He'll have to defend the towns in my path, because the manufactories in them make crossbows and catapults and such for the traitors. He'll have to defend them, and I aim to take them away from him and burn them to the ground."

Southron brigadiers had been talking like that when they went up against Ned of the Forest since the war was young. Most of the brigadiers who talked like that had come to grief in short order. Doubting George doubted whether Hard-Riding Jimmy would, though. He was a good officer, had a swarm of good men armed with fine weapons that had already proved their worth—and the north, now, was visibly coming to the end of its tether.

"May the gods go with you," George said. "I wish I were going with you, too, but I can't do a gods-damned thing about that."

"I wish this had been handled more smoothly," Jimmy said. "I feel real bad about it."

"Nothing you can do. Nothing I can do, either," Doubting George answered. "When you do go to Dothan with your detached command, though, you make sure you *do* whip those traitor sons of bitches, you hear me?"

"Yes, sir!" Hard-Riding Jimmy saluted once more. "I'll do it, sir." He got back onto his unicorn and rode away.

Doubting George stared after him. Then the commanding general turned and kicked a small stone into the Franklin. It splashed a couple of times before sinking without a trace. *Might as well be my career*, George thought gloomily. *Not all the sons of bitches are traitors. Too gods-damned many of 'em are on King Avram's side.*

These days, Ned of the Forest often felt he was the only officer in Honey—indeed, the only officer in Great River Province and Dothan put together—who was behaving as if he felt the north could still win the war. In a sour sort of way, that was funny, for Bell's disaster in front of Ramblerton had thrown the last log on the pyre of his hopes.

But, as far as he was concerned, the fight had to go on, hope or no hope. King Geoffrey hadn't surrendered. Geoffrey, in fact, kept loudly insisting that he wouldn't surrender, that he would sooner turn bush-whacker than surrender. Ned, a master bushwhacker if ever there was one, had his doubts about that, but he kept quiet about them.

His unicorn-riders kept patrolling north of the Franklin. A few of them sneaked across the river and raided southron outposts on the far bank. *They* behaved as if the war still were the close, hard-fought struggle it had always been.

Not so the footsoldiers who remained in Honey, the remnants of the once-proud Army of Franklin. Every day, a few—or, on a lot of days, more than a few—of them slipped out of their encampments, heading for home.

Lieutenant General Richard the Haberdasher, the general who'd taken over for Bell, summoned Ned to his headquarters in the best hostel in town. Richard, a belted earl, was King Geoffrey's brother-in-law and had a blood connection to King Zachary the Rough and Ready, now some years dead. Despite his blue blood, he'd proved a capable soldier, and had done some hard fighting in the northeast.

To do any more fighting with what had been the Army of Franklin, Ned was convinced, Earl Richard would have to be more than a capable soldier. He'd have to be able to raise the dead. But all Ned did on walking into Richard's suite was salute and say, "Reporting as ordered, your Grace."

Richard the Haberdasher was tall—though not quite so tall as Ned—and handsome. He was in his late thirties, four or five years younger than the commander of unicorn-riders. "I have a favor to ask of you, Lieutenant General," he said.

"What do you need?" Ned asked.

"I want you to put a cordon around Honey," Richard said. "These desertions have got to stop. Can you do that?"

"Yes, I can," Ned of the Forest answered. "And I will." He was glad to see Richard trying to take matters in hand. *About time*, he thought. Still, he couldn't help adding, "You could do it with footsoldiers, too, you know."

"I could, but I'd rather not," Earl Richard said. "I'm not sure I can rely on them. Your men, though—your men I can count on. And so, if it's all right with you, I'd sooner do that."

"All right. I'll take care of it." Ned wished he could disagree with Richard the Haberdasher. That would have meant the remaining fragments of the broken Army of Franklin were in better shape than they really were. The commander of unicorn-riders felt he had to add, "If I set some of my troopers to riding patrols around Honey, that means I can't use those fellows against the southrons."

"Yes, I know," Richard answered. "But it also means I'll have more pikemen and crossbowmen to send against them when I find the chance." He seemed to hear what he'd just said, to hear it and think he had to retreat from it. "If I find the chance, I should say."

Ned of the Forest nodded. Bell's successor was proving he had a better grasp on reality than the man he'd replaced. Had the one-legged officer kept his command here, he probably would have been planning yet another headlong assault on the southrons. He seemed to have wanted the Army of Franklin as thoroughly maimed as he was himself. But Richard the Haberdasher clearly realized the days of storming to the attack were gone forever for these soldiers.

"We have to do all we can to hold the manufactories in Dothan and the smaller ones here in Great River Province," Richard said. "With Marthasville and Veldt gone, they're the most important ones we've got left this side of Nonesuch."

"I understand," Ned said. "And with Marthasville and Veldt gone, gods only know how anything they make in Nonesuch'll get out here to the east. That means the ones hereabouts count for even more than they would otherwise."

"True. Every word of it true." Earl Richard hesitated, then said, "May I ask you something else? I swear by the Thunderer's strong right hand that whatever you answer won't go beyond the walls of this room."

The walls of that room were covered by a garishly flowered wallpaper that couldn't have been much uglier if it tried. Ned of the Forest didn't like to think of anything that hideous listening to him, but he nodded again. "Go right ahead."

"Thank you." After another long pause, Richard said, "What do you think of our chances of carrying on the war?"

"Well . . ." Ned puffed out his cheeks, then sighed loud and long and hard enough to make the flames of the candles on Richard's desk dance. "Well, I don't know how things are in the west. I've heard this and that and the other thing, but I don't *know*, so I shouldn't talk about that. Here in the east . . . hereabouts, would you be asking me to ride patrol against our own deserters if things were going the way they were supposed to?"

He waited. Richard the Haberdasher also waited, to see if he had anything else to say. When the nobleman decided no more was coming, he clicked his tongue between his teeth. "All right. That's a fair answer. Thank you."

"You're welcome. I wish I could've had something different to tell you." Ned sketched a salute and strode out of the room with the lurid wallpaper. He wondered if Richard would call him back. The other general didn't.

When Ned ordered patrols out against deserters, he rode out with them. He never sent his men to any duty he wouldn't take himself. And, before long, the squad with which he rode came across deserters: three men in the ragged ruins of blue uniforms sneaking away from Honey across the muddy fields around the town.

Ned spurred his unicorn toward them. The rest of the squad followed. The three footsoldiers froze in dismay. "What the hells do you think you're doing?" Ned roared, aiming a crossbow at the leading man's face.

The footsoldier looked at his pals. They looked back at him, as if to say, *He asked you, so you answer him.* The scruffy soldier gathered himself. "I reckon we're going home," he said, apparently deciding he might as well be hung for a sheep as for a lamb.

"I reckon you're gods-damned well *not*," Ned of the Forest thundered. "I reckon all three of you sorry sons of bitches are going to turn around and go back to Honey. I reckon I'll put a crossbow quarrel through your brisket if you don't, too."

"You might as well go ahead and shoot us," the soldier replied. "Won't make any difference to the war either way." Defiantly, he added, "Won't make any difference if we go home, neither."

He was right. Ned had known the war was lost for weeks. He felt a certain embarrassment at not being able to admit as much to the would-be deserter, and tried to cover that embarrassment with bluster: "By the Lion God's pointed toenails, where would we be if everybody in King Geoffrey's army acted the way you gutless bastards are doing?"

"Where?" the footsoldier answered. "About where we're at now, I reckon. Don't see how we could be much worse off, and that's the gods' truth."

One of the other unkempt soldiers plucked up enough courage to add, "That's right."

And so it was, but Ned didn't intend to admit it. "You don't get moving back to Honey right this minute,

I'll *show* you how you could be worse off. You want to try me? Get the hells out of here, before I decide to crucify you on the spot to give the other cowardly fools in this army a taste of what they can expect if they try running away."

They blanched and turned around and started back toward the sad, sorry encampment of what had been the Army of Franklin. A couple of years before, when the war still seemed an even affair, Ned really would have crucified deserters. He'd done it a couple of times. A couple of years before, though, soldiers like these would never have thought of abandoning their army. They'd been through everything flesh and blood could bear, they'd seen hope slaughtered on the battlefield, and they'd had enough.

Ned turned back to the other unicorn-riders. "Come on," he said. "Let's see how many others who want to run away we can catch."

"Yes, sir," said the sergeant commanding the squad. By the way he said it, his heart wasn't in what they were doing. He proved as much by adding, "When we run into poor miserable bastards like those fellows, though, can't we just look the other way?"

"That's not why we're out here riding around," Ned said. "We've got a job to do, and we're going to do it." Earl Richard the Haberdasher had thought his men were especially reliable. Ned had thought so himself. Now, suddenly, he wasn't so sure. Was their hope failing, too?

Maybe it was. The sergeant said, "Not a whole hells of a lot of point to getting killed now, is there?"

"If you worry about getting killed, maybe you shouldn't have turned soldier in the first place," Ned of the Forest said coldly.

The sergeant was a typical swarthy Detinan. Not only that, his thick black beard grew up to just below his eyes. Even so, Ned could see him flush. He said, "I've never run away from anything, Lord Ned, and I'm not about to start now. But I'm not a blind man, either. If we were whipping the gods-damned southrons, would we be up here in Great River Province riding circles around stinking Honey to keep our poor, miserable footsoldiers from running away?"

Only one answer to that was possible, and Ned gave it: "No." But he went on, "Irregardless of whether we're winning or losing, we've got to keep fighting hard. Otherwise, we're not just losing—we've lost."

That sergeant was also as stubborn as any other freeborn Detinan. He said, "Well, sir, I reckon we can lose even if we *do* keep fighting hard. We fought like hells in front of Ramblerton, and a whole fat lot of good it did us."

He wasn't wrong about that, either. Again, Ned said the only thing he could: "Lieutenant General Bell is gone. We won't make the mistakes we did on that campaign, not any more we won't."

"Of course we won't, gods damn it." The sergeant was as plain-spoken as any other freeborn Detinan, too. "We can't make those mistakes any more. We haven't got enough men left *to* make 'em."

One more painful truth. Ned of the Forest shrugged. "You can either do the best you can as long as you've got a unicorn under your butt, or else I'll muster you out and send you home right this minute. You won't be a deserter, on account of I'll give you a discharge."

He waited. If the sergeant really was fed up and called him on that, he would have to let him go. But the underofficer said, "Oh, I'll stick. You won't be rid of me that easy. But I'll be gods-damned if I like the way things are going."

"I don't reckon anybody does—except the southrons, I mean," Ned said. "But we're still here, and we've still got our crossbows. If we quit, King Avram wins. To hells with me if I want to make things that easy for him. Now come on."

This time, he didn't give the sergeant a chance to reply. He urged his own unicorn up to a trot. The squad—including the sergeant—followed him. Ned wasn't completely comfortable when he stayed in the saddle too long. Old wounds pained him. He didn't grumble about them. They didn't keep him from getting about, or from fighting. There, if nowhere else, he sympathized with Lieutenant General Bell. Poor Bell had been a fine officer leading a brigade when he was all in one piece. He'd been a disaster in the larger commands he'd got after he was wounded. How much did the endless swigs of laudanum and the inability to go forward and see for himself have to do with that? More than a little, Ned feared.

A fine mist began drifting down from a lead-gray sky. Even this far north, where winters were relatively mild, this time of year the land seemed dead. Trees and bushes stood bare-branched, skeletal. Grass was yellow and brown, dry stalks bent and broken. Somewhere off in the distance, a raven's croak sounded like the chuckle of a demon mocking the hopes of man.

Ned's troopers muttered among themselves. He knew what they were muttering about, too: they were wishing they hadn't heard the raven. The big black birds had an evil reputation, no doubt because they ate carrion. Ned felt a certain amount of superstitious dread, too, but he suppressed it. He had other things, things of the real world, to worry about, and for him things of the real world always counted for more than ghosts and spirits and haunts.

Would the desertions stop? How much difference would it make if they did? Would Doubting George or Hard-Riding Jimmy try to push past the Franklin

River and finish off the remnants of the Army of Franklin here in Honey? If they did, what could Ned's unicorn-riders do to stop them? Anything at all?

We've got to keep trying, Ned thought. *If we don't, then this war will end, and sooner, not later. The serfs'll be off the land forever, and the southrons'll go around telling 'em they're just as good as real Detinans.* Ned squared his broad shoulders and shook his fist toward the south in stubborn defiance. *Can't have that, gods damn it.*

Marthasville again. Rollant hadn't expected to see the biggest city in Peachtree Province again, not till John the Lister's men got the order to move west and rejoin General Hesmucet's army. Even after boarding the glideway carpet in northern Franklin, Rollant hadn't expected to stop in Marthasville for very long. But here he was, cooling his heels in the town for a second day now. Too many glideway carpets had come into the city all at once, from east and west and north and south, and the officers in charge of such things were still untangling the snarl.

Before the war—and even during it, as long as false King Geoffrey's men held the place—Marthasville had had pretensions of being a big city. Those pretensions made Rollant, who lived in New Eborac City, *the* metropolis of Detina, laugh. More than half the streets here were nothing but red dirt—red mud, at this season of the year. Cobblestones would have done wonders to improve them, but nobody'd bothered with—or been able to afford—cobblestones here. That by itself would have been plenty to take Marthasville out of the big-city class, as far as Rollant was concerned.

And Marthasville now wasn't what it had been before Hesmucet captured it from the traitors. Hesmucet had

burned it before setting out on his march across
Peachtree to Veldt, and his siege engines had had their
way with it even before it fell into his hands. Blackened ruins lined the muddy streets.

Here and there, people were already rebuilding.
Elegant homes and fancy shops might have perished
in the flames, but shacks built from salvaged lumber
and tents sprouted everywhere. A forest fire burned
oaks and maples, but toadstools and poison sumac
sprang up where they'd stood. The shabby new struc-
tures catered to soldiers: they were saloons and brothels
and gambling dens, all designed to separate southrons
from silver as swiftly as they could.

Provost marshals patrolled the streets, but they could
do only so much, especially now with the glideway
snarl. Men in gray tunics and pantaloons wanted what
the northerners were selling. If some of them ended
up poisoned by bad spirits, or poxed or rolled in the
brothels, or fleeced in the gambling dens, they didn't
seem to care. Every bit of it was part of having a good
time.

Nobody in Marthasville knew what to make of
Rollant. A blond with sergeant's stripes? Northerners
stared. Some of the Detinans from Marthasville glared.
Rollant smiled back. Why not? He had the power of
King Avram's army behind him, and King Avram's army
had proved itself mightier than anything in the north.

The blonds who lived and worked in Marthasville
stared at Rollant—and at the stripes on his sleeve—
too. But they didn't glare. He always collected a caravan
of little blond boys who followed him through the
streets. They did their best to imitate his marching
stride, a best that was usually pretty funny. Blond men
doffed their hats and bowed as if he were a marquis.
And the smiles some of the blond women sent his way
acutely reminded him of how long ago he'd left Norina.

Not for the first time, Smitty teased him about that: "If you don't want 'em, by the Sweet One's sweet place, steer some of 'em my way. That one little sweetie back there . . ." His hands shaped an hourglass in the air.

Rollant knew exactly which girl Smitty meant. He'd noticed her, too. He hadn't fooled around on his wife, but he wasn't blind. He said, "I'm not stopping you from chasing her." Even that took a certain effort. Detinans in the north had taken advantage of blond women too freely for too long to let him feel easy about encouraging any Detinan man to make advances to a woman of his people.

He knew more than a little relief when Smitty shook his head. "She didn't even see me," his comrade said mournfully. "But you . . . she looked like she wanted to have you for breakfast."

"Don't talk that way," Rollant said. When Smitty did, he felt the urges he was trying to ignore, and all the more acutely, too.

"How shall I talk? Like this?" Smitty put on what he imagined to be a northern accent. Still using it, he went into lascivious detail about what he would have liked to do with the pretty blond girl. Rollant wanted to clout him over the head with a rock. That seemed to be the only way to make him shut up.

"I never thought I'd be glad to get back on the glideway carpet and away from this place," Rollant said at last.

"It won't make any difference," Smitty said. "Wherever we go in the north, blonds look at you like you're the Thunderer come to earth." He held up a hand. "I take it back. I expect it'll make *some* difference, on account of gods only know when we'll see another girl that fine."

"If you need a woman so bad, wait your turn at a brothel," Rollant said.

Smitty shrugged. "I've done it now and again, but a willing girl's more fun than one you've got to pay. That way, she wants it, too. She's not just . . . just going through the motions, you might say."

"All right. I won't argue with you about that," Rollant said. "It's one of the reasons I steer clear of these women. They don't care much about *me*. If I weren't a sergeant, they wouldn't look twice. They care about the stripes."

"Well, so do you," Smitty said.

Rollant grunted. That crossbow quarrel had hit the target, sure enough. He was proud of the sergeant's stripes not least because they showed what he'd done in a Detinan-dominated world. How could he be surprised if other blonds saw them the same way?

"Yaaa! You stinking blond!" The shout came from an upstairs window. "You don't know who your father was!"

When Rollant looked up, he saw no one in the window. Whoever had yelled at him lacked the courage of his convictions. "Of course I do," Rollant shouted back. "He's the fellow who paid your mother three coppers. She'd remember—it's twice her going rate."

That set Smitty giggling. Rollant wondered if an enraged northerner would come boiling out of the false-fronted wooden building, ready to do or die for his mother's honor, if any. But everything stayed quiet after the initial jeer. Smitty said, "Well, I guess your old man got his money's worth."

"Right." Rollant's answering smile was tight. For centuries, Detinans had made free with blond women. But if a blond man presumed to look at a Detinan woman, let alone to touch her, dreadful things were liable—no, were sure—to happen to him. Back in Palmetto Province, Baron Ormerod's wife had been a famous beauty. Whenever Rollant was anywhere near her, he'd kept his eyes to the ground to make sure he didn't anger her or his liege lord. So had every other male serf with an ounce of brains in his head. Ormerod hadn't been a particularly nasty overlord. With some things, though, no one dared take chances.

Even in New Eborac City, Rollant treated Detinan women with exaggerated deference. He paid attention to them as customers, not as women. That wasn't just because he was a married man. He'd found some of them attractive. Some of them, by the looks and gestures they'd given him, found him attractive, too. But he'd never had the nerve to do anything about it, even if it would have helped pay back debts hundreds of years old. If it went wrong, if he guessed wrong, or if a woman just changed her mind or felt vindictive . . . He would have been lucky to last long enough to be crucified. A mob might have pulled him out of prison and taken care of matters on the spot.

"Let's go back," Smitty said suddenly. "I've seen more of this miserable place than I ever wanted to."

"Suits me fine," Rollant answered. "The traitors were so proud of Marthasville. They thought it was a big thing. Only goes to show they didn't really know what a big thing is."

When they got to the glideway depot, Lieutenant Joram collared both of them. "We're moving west again soon. Get the men out of the dives and onto the carpets, fast as you can."

In the end, they all went together. One man, or even two, was too likely to be ignored, maybe to get knocked over the head. Anybody who tried to take out Joram, Rollant, and Smitty at once would have a fight on his hands, though.

They hauled blind-drunk soldiers out of taverns and poured them onto the waiting carpets. They hauled soldiers out of brothels, too: some smug and sated, others frustrated because they were taken away before they could worship the Sweet One. One of those tried to slug Joram. Instead of ordering him held for court-martial, the company commander knocked him cold, slung him over his shoulder, and lugged him back to the depot.

Some of the women in the brothels were Detinans, not blonds. That surprised Rollant, who'd assumed every harlot in the north came from his own people. His being there in a uniform with three stripes on his sleeve surprised the whores, too. One of the Detinans, perhaps the best-looking woman in the waiting room in the place he and Smitty went to while Joram was dealing with the coldcocked soldier, called out to him: "You want to try something you never did before, Yellowhair?" She stood up and waggled her hips to show exactly what she meant. The silk shift she wore was so thin, so transparent, Rollant wondered why she'd bothered putting it on. On the other hand, she might have looked even more naked with it than she would have without it.

Staring at her, he almost forgot the question she'd asked. Only when the other women jeered at him did he remember and shake his head. "I'm here to get men from my company out, not to dally myself," he managed.

That brought more jeers and catcalls. "You've got a lot of gods-damned nerve, taking business away from us like that," a blond harlot said.

"By the Sweet One's . . . teeth, haven't you got enough?" Rollant asked.

"Come upstairs with me," urged the Detinan woman in the transparent shift. Rollant shook his head again, even if his eyes never left her. She saw that—she couldn't very well help seeing it. A slow smile spread across her face. Her lips were very red, very inviting.

She said, "On the house, Yellowhair. Come on. It'll be something different for both of us. Is it true what they say about blond men?" She was looking at him, too, but not at his face.

"On the house?" Three other women lounging on the couches in the waiting room said it at the same time, in identical tones of astonishment. By that astonishment, Rollant guessed how big a compliment he'd just got. In a brothel, what could be more perverse than lying with a man for nothing?

Somehow, Rollant shook his head once more. "I'm— I'm a married man," he said.

That might have been the funniest thing the whores ever heard. They clung to one another, howling with laughter. Smitty spoke up: "If he doesn't want you, sweetheart, I'll take you up on that."

"Corporal!" Rollant said. "We haven't got time."

"I won't take long," Smitty said blandly.

But the Detinan harlot shook her head. "Not unless you pay me the going rate, soldier. There's nothing special about *you*."

"Hells there's not," Smitty said, angry now. "Just let me—" He took a step forward. Rollant grabbed him as two very large, very muscular bouncers sprang into the waiting room.

"Get away!" Rollant told them. He had to wrestle with Smitty, who was furious and not making the slightest effort to hide it. "Calm down, gods damn it!" Rollant said. "We didn't come in for that anyway."

"All right. You're right." Smitty quit trying to break away from him. "Odds are I'd end up poxed anyway."

The harlots all screeched furiously. The bouncers advanced on Smitty. They both carried stout bludgeons. Rollant let go of his comrade. Smitty's shortsword hissed from the scabbard. So did Rollant's. The bouncers stopped. "Good thinking," Rollant told them. "We're all free Detinans here, right? We can all speak our minds, right?"

One of the bouncers jerked his thumb toward the door. "I'm speaking *my* mind: get the hells out of here."

"Have we got all our men out of the rooms here?" Rollant asked Smitty.

"Yes, Sergeant, we do. They're waiting for us in the hall." By the respect in Smitty's voice, Rollant might have been Marshal Bart. That must have irked the bouncers, who were doubtless men from Peachtree Province. It didn't irk them quite enough to make them do anything but glower, though, which was lucky—for them. After the worst false King Geoffrey's soldiers could do to him, Rollant didn't fear a couple of whorehouse toughs.

He and Smitty led the unsatisfied customers from the brothel back to the glideway terminal. The men in gray climbed up onto the carpets, some resigned to leaving, others glum. An hour passed, and nothing happened. "Gods damn it, Sergeant, we could've had our fun," one of the frustrated soldiers complained.

"I had my orders," Rollant said with a shrug. "You're not happy, take it up with Lieutenant Joram." The soldier stopped grumbling. Nobody wanted to complain to Joram. He'd been a sergeant too long; the men knew what sort of firepot would burst if they pushed him too far.

Sooner or later, they may start thinking that way about me. Rollant liked the idea. He didn't think it was all that likely to come true, though. Joram could roar like the Thunderer come down to earth. That had never been Rollant's way. In the north, blonds who roared at Detinans ended up gruesomely dead, and the lesson had stuck. He seemed to manage just the same.

The glideway carpet started west and south. Rollant settled himself against the motion. Palmetto Province ahead. He'd left a fugitive serf. He was coming back a conqueror. "And a sergeant," he said softly. Yes, he'd already won a lot of battles. The carpet picked up speed.

XII

"Tell it to me again," Ned of the Forest said. "I want to make sure I've got it straight."

"All right, Lord Ned." The man who'd come north from southern Dothan nodded. He looked weary. He had the right to look that way, too: he'd traveled hard, and dodged the southrons' patrols till he finally reached country King Geoffrey's men ruled. "I seen them southron sons of bitches ride out. They ain't that far in back of me, neither. If they wasn't looping around to hit you some funny way or other, reckon they would've got here ahead of me."

"Hard-Riding Jimmy's men, you're talking about," Ned said, to nail it down tight. "*All* of Hard-Riding Jimmy's men."

"That's about the size of it." The fellow who'd brought the news nodded again. "Hells of a lot of bastards in gray uniforms, every gods-damned one of 'em riding a white unicorn." He didn't even seem to notice his accidental near-rhyme.

Ned of the Forest wasn't inclined to play literary critic, either. "That's not good news," he said—an understatement if ever there was one. Hard-Riding Jimmy's force of unicorn-riders badly outnumbered his own. To make things worse, every southron carried one of those quick-shooting crossbows that made him much more deadly than anyone with an ordinary weapon. Ned plucked at his chin beard, then asked, "They have any footsoldiers with 'em?"

"I don't know for certain," the man from Dothan replied. "Only thing I can tell you is, I didn't see none. Just riders—lots and lots of riders."

"Lots and lots of riders," Ned echoed unhappily. "They were heading for the Franklin River? Aiming to cross it and get farther up into Dothan?"

"Can't tell you for certain," the other man said. "All I know for certain is, them buggers is on the move. If you don't stop 'em, Lord Ned, who the hells is going to?"

"Nobody," Ned answered with a mournful sigh. "Nobody at all." He nodded to the informant. "I do thank you for bringing me the news." He wished the news hadn't happened, so the other man wouldn't have needed to bring it. Such wishes, though, were written in water. Ned took a certain not quite modest pride in realizing as much. Hard-Riding Jimmy's move was real. Now Ned had to find some way to stop it.

He knew where Jimmy would be heading: toward the manufactories in Hayek and the other nearby towns. If the southrons could seize them or wreck them, where would King Geoffrey's men in this part of the realm get the crossbows and quarrels and engines and firepots they needed to carry on the fight against the southrons? *We won't get 'em anywhere, in that case*, Ned thought. *And if we don't, then it's really all over.*

By noon the next day, his own force of unicorn-riders was hurrying west out of Great River Province. Richard the Haberdasher had promised to send foot-soldiers after them. Ned had thanked him without believing a word of it. For one thing, Ned doubted the crossbowmen and pikemen who'd survived the advance to Ramblerton and the retreat from it were in any sort of fighting shape even now. For another, they were bound to get to Dothan too late to do much good.

Ned wondered if *he* would get to Dothan too late to do much good. In winter, roads turned into quag-mires. That worked a hardship on both sides, for it also slowed Hard-Riding Jimmy. But streaming away from Hayek and the other towns full of manufactories was a great flood of refugees who clogged the roads even worse than the mud did. The people of Dothan knew Jimmy was coming, and didn't want to get in his way.

"Bastard's burning everything in his path, same as that other bugger done did over in Peachtree," one man said. Others fleeing the southrons nodded, adding their own tales of horror.

Being who and what he was, Ned of the Forest needed longer than he might have to notice one thing about the flood of refugees: they were almost all Detinans, with hardly any blonds. This part of Dothan, though, held about as many blonds as it did ordinary Detinans. Ned wondered what that meant, but not for long. It meant the serfs were either staying put and waiting on the land for Jimmy to sever their ties to their liege lords, or else they were fleeing toward Jimmy and not toward Ned.

Attached to his command, he had a wagon train staffed by several dozen serfs. They'd been with him since the earliest days of the war. Some of the blonds were men Ned had caught, but who'd appealed to him because of the way they'd escaped or the way they handled themselves. Others had sought him out: men who wanted an overlord, perhaps, but not the one they'd got by custom.

They'd done a lot of things for Ned: carried supplies, doctored, foraged, and even occasionally picked up a crossbow and taken a few potshots at the southrons. He'd promised to cut their bonds to the land and to him when the war ended. "Well, boys," he said now, "we've been through a lot together these past four years, haven't we?"

"Sure have, Lord Ned," Darry rumbled. Ned of the Forest was a big man. Darry stood half a head taller, and was broader through the shoulders. The blond had not an ounce of fat on him anywhere; he was hard as a boulder. Several other men nodded.

"You know I promised you I'd set you up as yeoman farmers when the war was done if you stuck with me till then," Ned went on. Before the war, blond yeomen had been exceedingly rare in the north, but there had been a few.

His crew of blonds nodded again, this time more or less in unison. They weren't his serfs, not in any formal sense of the word. He had no noble blood; he owned no estates to which serfs were tied. But for all practical purposes, he was their liege lord, and they gave him more loyalty than most real nobles ever got. They could have fled or betrayed him to the southrons countless times. They could have, but they hadn't.

Clever Arris raised an eyebrow. Ned nodded for him to speak. Arris was only about half Darry's size, but had twice his brains. If he'd been born a Detinan, he might have made a general himself. Instead, he worried about unicorns and asses and scrounging—and about feathering his own nest, which he'd done quite nicely. Now he said, "If you grant us land, Lord Ned, will the grant be good?"

"What? You reckon Lord Ned'd cheat us?" Anger darkened Darry's face. He clenched a massive fist. "I ought to break your face for you."

Ned held up a hand. "It's all right, Darry. I'm not mad." Arris, he noted, hadn't flinched. That might have meant he'd figured Ned would protect him. Or it might have meant he'd stashed a knife in his boot. Ned wouldn't have been surprised either way. The commander of unicorn-riders continued, "He means, if I grant you land and the gods-damned southrons win, will they recognize what I've done?"

"If the gods-damned southrons win . . ." Even now, Darry's frown showed he had trouble imagining that. Being Ned's partisans, he and his comrades were stalwart partisans of the north, too.

"*Will* they win, Lord Ned? *Can* they?" a blond named Brank asked. He sounded as if he didn't want to believe it, either.

"They can. They probably will," Ned answered. "But I think the grants will be good anyhow. They're on lands up near Luxor that I owned before the fighting started. I didn't get 'em while Geoffrey was King." He feared nothing done while Geoffrey ruled in the north would stand now that Avram was returning to power here. Then he added, "And you boys are blonds. The southrons'll likely be happy with you on account of that. You may even have it easier than if you were ordinary Detinans, in fact."

Darry's rugged, blunt-featured face furrowed into another frown as he tried to imagine having it easier than a Detinan. Several of the other blonds laughed to show what they thought of the idea. Arris said, "Don't bet on it, Lord Ned."

Ned of the Forest shrugged. "Maybe you're right.

I don't know for sure. But the reason I'm telling you is, we're moving against Hard-Riding Jimmy now. He's liable to lick us. Hells, he's liable to smash us." He'd never said anything like that before; the words hurt. "If you want to take your grants now and head for Luxor, I'll give 'em to you. Nobody's ever going to say you boys didn't meet your end of the bargain."

Arris said, "I'll stick, Lord Ned. I reckon I've got a better chance of getting my land if you're there to say I deserve it." One by one, the rest of the blonds nodded. Arris had more brains than the others, and they had brains enough to know it.

But did the sly serf see everything that might happen? "They could put a bolt through my brisket tomorrow, you know. Or they could wait till the war's over, call me a real traitor, and nail me to a cross."

All the blonds shook their heads. "Oh, no, Lord Ned," Darry said. "Nothing like that'd ever happen to you." None of them seemed to think it was possible. Ned wished he didn't. To the blonds, he was something not far from a god, or perhaps from a demon: something more than an ordinary man, anyhow. The scars he bore proved crossbow quarrels thought differently, though. And King Avram's men wanted him dead; General Hesmucet had growled there could be no peace in eastern Franklin till he was. If they won the war—no, *when* they won the war—what would stop them from making their wishes come true? Nothing he could see.

He bowed to the blonds with as much courtesy as if they were King Geoffrey and his courtiers. There were times when he respected them much more than Geoffrey and that crowd of useless parasites in Nonesuch. "Thank you kindly, boys," he said. "We'll all do what we can to come out of this in one piece, that's all."

His riders met those of Hard-Riding Jimmy outside the town of Hayek. That was a town King Geoffrey had to hold. Both sides fought as dragoons, not as unicorn-riders in the strict sense of the term. They used their mounts to get where they were were going quickly, but they fought on foot. Scouts rode back to Ned, worried looks on their faces. "He's got a hells of a lot of troopers with him, Lord Ned," one of them said.

Ned of the Forest already knew that. He saw how long and thick a column of men Hard-Riding Jimmy led. "We've licked three times as many as we've got before," he said, which was true. "We can do it again."

He hoped he sounded as if he believed that. He wasn't so sure, though. Jimmy's riders had the bit between their teeth. They'd tasted victory, and they liked it. And they had those quick-shooting crossbows no northern artisan had been able to match. That made their effective numbers even greater than their actual ones.

At Ned's shouted commands, his soldiers took the best defensive position they could. He'd never been able to spend men with the lavish prodigality of a commander of footsoldiers. Now, especially, every man he lost was one he could never have back again. Jimmy, on the other hand, looked to have been substantially reinforced since the battle in front of Ramblerton.

The southrons stormed forward, plainly hoping to overwhelm Ned's men by weight of numbers and by the blizzard of bolts they put in the air. It didn't happen; Ned's veterans had been through too many fights to fail to take advantage of the ground. They gave back a murderous volley that knocked the southrons onto their heels.

"That's the way!" Ned shouted as his troopers frantically reloaded. He wondered whether the southrons would try to rush his position again. He hoped so. If they did, he could keep killing them by swarms.

But, having been repulsed once, they paused out of crossbow range. Ned could almost see their officers' surprise. *Oh*, they might have been saying as they pointed toward his line and talked among themselves. *These northerners still have some fight left in them. After everything we saw down in Franklin, who could have imagined that?*

Fighting flared again half an hour later. Ned would have liked to go forward himself and drive Hard-Riding Jimmy's men while they were still shaken by their reverse. He would have liked to, but he didn't dare. If his men left the safety of their shooting pits and trenches, the southrons' quick-shooting crossbows would pincushion them. He knew it, and hated the knowledge.

When the southrons tried his position again, they treated it with the respect of men who knew they would be in for a brawl. He could have done without the compliment. Hard-Riding Jimmy was as lavishly supplied with engines as he was with men and unicorns. Firepots flew through the air trailing smoke. They burst in and around Ned's lines. Men screamed when flames poured over them. Repeating crossbows sent endless streams of quarrels hissing through the air just at breastwork height. Any man who stuck his head up to shoot was asking to take a bolt in the face. Captain Watson answered back as best he could, but was able to do little to suppress the enemy's shooting.

Under cover of that bombardment, Jimmy's troopers advanced again. This time, they came in loose order, moving up in short rushes and then dropping to take advantage of whatever cover the ground offered. Watching them, Ned cursed. They knew what they were doing, all right. And they could do it, too.

And then, as the shooting heated up, a soldier from the left came dashing up to Ned. "They've got a column nipping around our flank, Lord Ned!" he cried. "They're mounted and riding like hells. If they hit us from the side or behind, it'll be the second day at Ramblerton all over again."

"Gods damn it!" Ned of the Forest shouted. But, however much he cursed, he could see the dust the enemy unicorn-riders were raising. The messenger was right. If they got where they wanted to go, they could wreck his army. He said what he had to say: "Fall back! Fall back, you bastards! We can't hold 'em here!"

If his men couldn't hold the southrons here, they couldn't hold Hayek, either. And if the north lost Hayek, another big log thudded onto the pyre of King Geoffrey's hopes. Ned swore again, in anger at least half aimed at himself. He'd had a good notion this would happen when he began the campaign. Now it was here, and the end of everything looked closer by the day.

The scryer who came up to Doubting George had the sense to wait to be noticed. George took his own sweet time, but finally nodded to the man in the gray robe. "Yes? And what exciting news have you got for me today?"

"Sir, I just got word from Hard-Riding Jimmy's scryer," the mage replied. "He's taken Hayek and burnt it to the ground."

"What? Hard-Riding Jimmy's scryer has done that? What a remarkable fellow he must be."

"No, no, no!" Doubting George's scryer started to explain, then sent the general commanding a reproachful look. "You're having me on, sir."

"Would I do such a thing?" George said. "Heaven forfend!"

"Er, yes, sir," the scryer said warily. "But isn't that good news? Hard-Riding Jimmy licked Ned of the Forest—licked him high, wide, and handsome—and he took Hayek, and now he's heading on up toward Clift. Isn't it grand?"

"Well, to the hells with me if I don't want to see Clift burnt to the ground," Doubting George said. Few men who backed King Avram would have said anything else. Clift was where Grand Duke Geoffrey put a crown on his head and started calling himself King Geoffrey. If that didn't make the capital of Dothan deserve whatever happened to it, George couldn't think of anything that would.

The scryer waited to see if George would have anything more to say. When the commanding general didn't, the young man in the gray robe shrugged and walked away. George said something then. He said several somethings, in fact, all of them pungent and all of them low-voiced so no one but him could hear them.

Indeed, Hard-Riding Jimmy was doing wonderful things—as an independent commander. John the Lister's wing was going to help throw logs on the pyre in the west—under Hesmucet's command. Another couple of brigades that had fought well in front of Ramblerton were now marching on Shell—under the command of Brigadier Marcus the Tall.

Doubting George did some more muttering. "No good deed goes unpunished," he said. He'd saved Avram's hopes in the east with his stand at the fight by the River of Death. He'd smashed Lieutenant General Bell in front of Ramblerton, wrecked the Army of Franklin beyond hope of rescue or repair, murdered false King Geoffrey's chances east of the mountains . . . and what had he got for it? His command pruned like a potted plant, and very little else.

Colonel Andy came up to him. George set his teeth. Andy was going to be sympathetic. George could tell, just by the way his adjutant carried himself; by the way he pursed his lips; even by the way he took a deep breath and then let it out, as if he stood by a sickbed and didn't want to talk too loud.

"You'll have heard, I suppose?" Andy said.

"Oh, yes." Doubting George nodded. "Hard-Riding Jimmy's scryer has gone and done great things."

Andy frowned. "His *scryer*, sir? I don't understand."

"Never mind," George said. "But isn't it remarkable how a man becomes a genius—a paladin—the instant he escapes my command?"

"What's remarkable," Andy said, swelling up in righteous wrath, "is how Marshal Bart keeps nibbling away at your command. Remarkable *and* disgusting, if anyone wants to know what *I* think."

No one did—no one who mattered, anyhow. Doubting George knew as much. Colonel Andy surely did, too. The only opinion that counted was Bart's, and Bart didn't want George in charge of anything much any more. King Avram could have overruled Bart, but Avram hadn't raised up a Marshal of Detina to go around overruling him afterwards.

"With me or without me, Colonel, we *are* going to whip the traitors," George said. "I console myself with that."

Colonel Andy nodded. "Yes, sir. We are. But you ought to play a bigger part. You've earned the right, by the Lion God's talons."

"I think I have, too." Doubting George sighed. "Marshal Bart doesn't, and he and King Avram are the only ones who matter. Bart thinks I'm slow because I waited for all my men before I hit Bell and the Army of Franklin. I think I was just doing what I had to do. And we won, gods damn it."

"That's right, sir. We sure did." Colonel Andy still had plenty of confidence in George. The only trouble was, Colonel Andy's confidence didn't matter. Bart's did. And Bart had decided other men could do a better job. He was the Marshal of Detina. He had the right to do that. And if George didn't care for it, what could he do? Nothing. Not a single, solitary thing.

"Baron Logan the Black," George muttered. At least he'd been spared that humiliation. To be ousted by a man who wasn't even a professional soldier . . . But it hadn't happened. He *had* gone forward. He *had* won. He *had* got no credit for it. Nor, by all appearances, would he ever.

He found out exactly how true that was at supper. He'd just sat down to a big plate of spare ribs (though he doubted the pig they'd come from had thought them spares) when a scryer came in and said, "Sir, Marshal Bart wants to speak to you right away."

"He would." Doubting George didn't want to speak to the Marshal of Detina. What a mere lieutenant general wanted in such circumstances mattered not at all. "Well, run along and tell him I'm coming." He cast a last longing glance at the spare ribs before heading off to the scryers' pavilion.

There was Bart's image, staring out of a crystal ball. Bart wasn't an impressive man to look at. In a crowd, he tended to disappear. But no one could deny he had a driving sense of purpose, a refusal to admit he *could* be defeated, that had served Detina well. "Good evening, Lieutenant General," he said now when he spotted George. "How are you?"

"Hungry, sir, if you want to know the truth," George answered. "What can I do for you at suppertime?"

If the barb bothered Bart—if Bart even noticed it *was* a barb—he gave no sign. He said, "I want you to move your force to Wesleyton in western Franklin as soon as is practicable. The less delay the better. You must be in place there in two weeks' time."

"Move the force I have left, you mean," Doubting George said.

"Yes, that's right," Bart agreed, again ignoring the sarcasm. "I have an important task for you there."

"Do you?" George said. "I thought my sole and entire function in this army was to stay where I am and grow moss. What else am I supposed to be doing?"

"Before too long, I aim to commence operations against Duke Edward of Arlington," Bart replied, still impassive. "If he is dislodged from the works covering Pierreville, he is likely to retreat eastward. Your men in Wesleyton will keep him from using western Franklin as a refuge, and you will be able to hold him until I can catch up with him with the bulk of my force and destroy the Army of Southern Parthenia."

He was as calm as if talking about the qualities of pine boards. But he meant every word of it. Of that Doubting George had no doubt at all. The idea left him slightly—no, more than slightly—stunned. Ever since the beginning of the War Between the Provinces, the Army of Southern Parthenia had been a fearful prodigy to all of King Avram's generals and armies that had to face it. It had been . . . but it was no more. Bart had its measure.

And for that, Doubting George admitted to himself, the nondescript little man who wouldn't believe false King Geoffrey's armies could beat him deserved to be Marshal of Detina.

Whether he deserved it or not, though, what he had in mind failed to delight George. "You want me to go to Wesleyton and sit there, just in case Duke Edward happens to come my way?"

"That's right." Bart nodded, pleased that he understood.

"Of course, since you will be there with your army, Edward's less likely to come that way. He's slippery as a barrister, Edward is, and so we've got to make sure he's shut up tight."

"I . . . see," George said slowly. "Isn't there anything more useful I could be doing than sitting around in Wesleyton impersonating a cork?"

"I don't believe so," Bart answered. "It's a useful thing to do, and the other pieces of your army are off doing different useful things in other places. This seems a good enough thing for the men you still have with you to do."

"A good enough thing," Doubting George echoed. "Gods damn it, Bart, we were more than 'good enough' not so long ago."

"Finally, yes. But you could have whipped Bell sooner. You should have whipped Bell sooner. Instead, you had King Avram and me half out of our minds with worry that the Army of Franklin would get around you and head for the Highlow River."

"Well, Marshal, if his Majesty thought that—and especially if *you* thought that, you *were* out of your minds, and not just halfway, either," George said. "Bell wasn't going anywhere, and neither was his army. He'd come as far as he could. If you'd had a look at his men, you could have seen that for yourself. I did. And I knew what I saw, too," George said.

Did something glint in Marshal Bart's eyes? George wasn't sure. The marshal had perhaps the deadest pan in Detina, too. Bart said, "You are entitled to your opinion, Lieutenant General. I am also entitled to mine. My opinion is that sending you to Wesleyton is the best thing I can do right now, given the way the war is going. Carry out your orders."

"Yes, sir," Doubting George said woodenly.

Bart turned to his scryer. His image vanished from

the crystal ball. George refrained from picking up the ball and chucking it into the Franklin River. He couldn't have said why he refrained from chucking it into the river, but refrain he did. Afterwards, he decided it had to prove he was a more tolerant man than even he would have imagined.

"Carry out your orders." In his mouth, the commonplace soldierly phrase somehow turned into a curse. Bart had the right to tell him to do it—had the right and used it. *And I reserve the right to reckon Bart is a first-class son of a bitch*, Doubting George thought.

That didn't eliminate the need to do as Bart said, worse luck. The general commanding—not that George had so very much left to command any more—turned and strode out of the scryers' tent. None of the mages in there said a word to him. In fact, they all seemed to be pretending they were somewhere else. Scryers, like other sorcerers, often missed emotions they should have seen. What Doubting George felt was too raw, too obvious, for even a scryer to miss.

Colonel Andy bustled up to George before he'd gone very far from the pavilion. Someone must have told the adjutant George had been summoned. "Well?" Andy asked expectantly. "What did he have to say for himself now?"

"Wesleyton is lovely this time of year, don't you think?" George answered.

"Wesleyton?" His adjutant gaped. "What the hells has Wesleyton got to do with anything? Who in his right mind would want to go to Wesleyton? It's not even a good place to die, let alone to live."

"No doubt you're right, Colonel." Doubting George couldn't help smiling, no matter how miserable he was. "Miserable or not, though, that's where we're going: you and I and as much of my army as Marshal Bart has graciously let me keep."

"Are we?" Colonel Andy said, and the commanding general nodded. Andy asked, "And *why*, pray tell, are we going to Wesleyton? I understand why Whiskery Ambrose went there last year: to take it away from the traitors. But we've held it ever since. What's the point of sending a whole lot more men there now?" Doubting George explained Marshal Bart's reasoning. His adjutant looked like a chipmunk who'd just bitten down on a cast-iron acorn. "That's one of the strangest things I've ever heard, sir. How likely is it that the Army of Southern Parthenia's going to come running in our direction?"

"Not very, not as far as I can see," George answered. "But Bart's right—it *could* happen. Now he'll have somebody in place to make sure Duke Edward doesn't get far if he tries it."

"Yes, sir. So he will." Andy didn't seem delighted at the prospect. "And isn't that a wonderful use for the army that broke the traitors' backs out here? Just a *wonderful* fornicating use."

"He *is* the Marshal of Detina. He *can* give the orders. He *has* given them, as a matter of fact. We need to obey them. You'll want to draw up plans to shift us to the western part of the province—glideway lines, supply dumps, and such."

"Oh, I have them," Andy said. "You don't need to worry about that."

Doubting George stared. "You . . . have them? Even to Wesleyton?"

"Yes, sir." Andy nodded. "That's what an adjutant is for: making plans, I mean. Most of them end up in the trash. That's how things work, too. But one will come in handy every now and again. Excuse me, please—I'll start things gliding." He saluted and hurried off.

Behind him, Doubting George started to laugh.

Now I know what an adjutant does, he thought. *And if only someone would tell me what a commanding general is for . . .*

Here in the west, the war looked and felt different. That was John the Lister's first thought when his wing moved through Georgetown on the way to the coast of Croatoan and a rendezvous with General Hesmucet's hard-driving army. Things seemed cramped here, without the room to maneuver that had marked the fighting in the east.

Georgetown itself appeared confident the war was won. Engineers had been fortifying the capital of Detina ever since the War Between the Provinces broke out. Castles and earthworks and trenches littered the landscape for miles around the heart of the city. If the Army of Southern Parthenia had ever come this far, it would have had to fight its way through all of them to get to the Black Palace.

When that thought crossed John's mind, he suddenly remembered that a detachment from the Army of Southern Parthenia *had* tapped at those fortifications only the summer before, till forces detached from Marshal Bart's army pushed them back. What a difference a bit more than half a year made! Now Jubal the Late's detachment was smashed, the valley he'd guarded so long a smoking ruin that could no longer feed Duke Edward's men, and the Army of Southern Parthenia penned up and hungry in Pierreville. That army would see southern Parthenia no more, nor Georgetown, either.

John the Lister's eye went to the Black Palace. The home of Detina's kings—of Detina's rightful kings, anyhow—towered over the city. Looking out from the battlements of the Black Palace, King Avram could see a long way. He could look on Parthenia to the north and on the loyal provinces to the south (even if crossbowmen and pikemen had been required at the start of the war to keep Peterpaulandia loyal).

Now everything looked likely to turn out for the best. A couple of years earlier, John wouldn't have bet on that. Twice Duke Edward of Arlington had invaded the south; once Count Thraxton the Braggart had pushed an army down into Cloviston, too. Even men of the stoutest loyalty to King Avram could hardly be blamed for fearing that Geoffrey might yet forge a kingdom of his own.

It hadn't happened, though. It hadn't, and now it wouldn't. The end was visibly at hand. Geoffrey, Duke Edward, and Count Joseph the Gamecock were all stubborn men. They hadn't given up yet. *That's why my wing's come west*, John thought: *to make them give up*.

He'd found his way back to his hostel while hardly even noticing in which direction his feet were going. Anyone who was anyone—anyone who had pretensions of being anyone—stayed at the House of the Rat when he came to Georgetown. For one thing, it had the softest beds and finest kitchen of any establishment in the city. For another, it lay right at the edge of the joyhouse quarter, with brothels to suit every purse and every taste within easy walking distance.

Fighting Joseph had stayed at the House of the Rat. Rumor said he'd enjoyed the nearby attractions, too. Knowing Fighting Joseph, John the Lister suspected rumor was true. And Marshal Bart had stayed at the House of the Rat. Rumor said he'd almost got a dreadful upstairs room because no one recognized him till he signed the guestbook. Knowing Bart, John suspected rumor there was also true.

Bart was supposed to be coming down from Pierre-ville to confer with him. The Marshal of Detina had already delayed the meeting once. John took the delay in stride. He was sleeping and eating in fancy style at King Avram's expense. He would have to spend his own money in the joyhouses, but every man had to sacrifice a little now and then. There was a war on, after all.

At the desk, John asked, "Any messages for me?"

"I'm sure *I* don't know," the clerk there replied, fixing John with a fishy stare. "Who *are* you, anyway?"

"John the Lister, brigadier of the regulars," John answered proudly.

He'd hoped that would impress the desk clerk. He rapidly discovered *nothing* impressed the clerk. With a yawn, the fellow said, "I've seen plenty of those before you. You can't expect me to recognize everybody." But he did condescend to look and see if John had any messages. With a grudging grunt, he passed the officer from the east a scrap of paper. "Here you are."

"Thank you so much," John said. The desk clerk proved immune to sarcasm, too. *I might have known*, John thought. When he unfolded the scrap of paper, he brightened. "Oh, good. It's from Marshal Bart."

That at least kept the scrawny little man behind the desk awake enough to ask,

"What has he got to say?"

"We're going to have supper here tonight," John answered before he realized he didn't have to tell this annoying creature anything. Gathering himself, he added, "You'd better inform the kitchens so they can fix up something extra fine for the Marshal of Detina."

But the desk clerk only sneered. "Shows how much *you* know. Whatever he orders, Marshal Bart'll want it with all the juices cooked out of it. He always does. Cooking fancy for him is just a waste of time."

Defeated, John the Lister went off to his room. He

emerged at sunset, to meet Bart in the lobby. If he hadn't worked with the Marshal of Detina in Rising Rock, he wouldn't have recognized him. As things were, he almost didn't. Bart wore a common soldier's plain gray tunic with epaulets fasted on very much as an afterthought: no fancy uniform for him. His boots were old and muddy. His face? He could have been a teamster as readily as the most eminent soldier Detina had produced in the past three generations.

"Good to see you, Brigadier," Bart said, an eastern twang in his voice. "Your men have done some fine work, and I know they'll do more once they get to Croatoan and link up with General Hesmucet."

"Thank you very much, sir," John replied. "Shall we go into the dining room?"

"I suppose so," Marshal Bart said. "Have to eat, I reckon." He sounded completely indifferent. That nasty, nosy little desk clerk, gods damn him, had had it right.

In the dining room, the blond waiter fawned on Bart—and, incidentally, on John the Lister as well. Basking in reflected glory, John chose a fancy seafood stew and a bottle of wine. Bart ordered a beefsteak.

"Don't you care for anything finer, sir?" John asked.

"Not me." Bart turned back to the waiter. "Make sure the cook does it up gray all the way through. No pink, or I'll send it back." The blond nodded, and hurried away. To John, Bart said, "I can't abide the sight of blood. I never have been able to."

"Uh, yes, sir," John said, reflecting that that was an odd quirk for a man who'd commanded most of the bloodiest fights in Detinan history.

As if thinking along with him, Bart remarked, "I've seen too much blood already. I don't need to look at more on my plate."

"Yes, sir," John said again. The waiter brought the wine and filled his goblet, then set the bottle on the table between the two officers. John reached for it. "Shall I pour you some?"

"No, thanks," Marshal Bart answered. "I will take a drink every now and again, but only every now and again. I used to like it too well—I daresay you'll have heard about that—so now I'm very careful about how much I pour down."

John felt self-conscious about drinking when the Marshal of Detina wouldn't, but Bart waved for him to go on. His first taste of the wine removed his lingering hesitation. The House of the Rat had an excellent cellar. The cooks worked fast, too. The waiter fetched John's stew and a beefsteak that looked as if it had just come from a long stay in the hottest of the seven hells.

Bart attacked the beefsteak with gusto, though it was so thoroughly cooked, he had to do some serious work with his knife to hack through it. He said, "You'll know Joseph the Gamecock is operating against General Hesmucet in Palmetto Province. Operating as best he can, I should say, because Hesmucet outnumbers him at least three to one. Your job will be to go up to Croatoan by sea, hit Joseph in the rear or in the flank as opportunity arises, and join forces with Hesmucet. Then, if the war has not ended before you get there, you will come up to Pierreville and help me finish off Duke Edward of Arlington."

That made John take another big sip of wine. "Finish off Duke Edward of Arlington," he echoed, awe in his voice. "That hardly seems real."

"Oh, it *is* real, all right," Bart said. "Real as horseradish. We are going to whip the traitors, and we are going to do it pretty quick. I have no doubts about that, none at all."

He'd never had any doubts about that, which made him unique among King Avram's officers. And he'd

been right. Time and time again, he'd been right. He
didn't look like much. He didn't sound like much. But
he won. That was why Avram had made him Marshal
of Detina. And he'd kept hammering till even Duke
Edward and the Army of Southern Parthenia were
visibly coming to the end of their tether.

Doubts, John thought. Then he heard himself saying,
"Doubting George isn't very happy with you, you know."

"Yes, I do know that." Bart paused to take another
bite of his leathery beefsteak. Once he'd choked it
down, he went on, "I am sorry about it, too. George
is a good man, a sound man. When it comes to holding off the foe, there is not a better man in all of
Detina. But when it comes to going after him . . . When
it comes to going after him, George is too gods-damned
slow. That is the truth. I am sad to say it, but it is the
truth. There at Ramblerton, he should have struck Bell
two weeks before he did. He would have won."

Since John the Lister thought the same, he could
only nod. That sufficed, anyhow. If he said unkind
things about Doubting George, Bart would see it as
backbiting. Instead, he spooned up a plump, juicy
oyster. *Better this than burnt meat*, he thought.

At a table not far away, a good-looking young man
began cursing King Avram, careless of the many gray-
clad soldiers in the dining room. John the Lister
scowled. "Who is that noisy fool?" he asked.

To his surprise, Bart seemed unconcerned. "That is
Barre the actor," he answered. "He is Handsome
Edwin's younger brother. He loves lost causes, so
naturally he adores false King Geoffrey."

"Does he?" John the Lister said in a voice as neu-
tral as he could make it. "How serious is he about
adoring Geoffrey? Should he be doing it inside a cell
somewhere instead of in the dining room of the House
of the Rat?"

"Folks who know him better than I do say he is nothing but wind and air, and that he would not harm a fly," Bart answered. "Putting him in prison would stir up more trouble than he is likely to cause, so he stays loose."

"I see," said John, who liked none of what he saw or heard.

Barre went on ranting. He didn't sound like an actor. He sounded like a crazy man. "Thus always to tyrants!" he shouted, and thumped his fist down on the table in front of him.

"Maybe they could lock him up for being a lunatic," John said hopefully.

Marshal Bart shook his head with just the hint of a smile. "You have been in the east a long time, John. Things are . . . different here in Georgetown. It took me a while to get used to it, too. A lot of men here favor Geoffrey. King Avram does not get upset about it as long as they keep it to talk, and they mostly do. There were serfs on the estates hereabouts till the war started, you know. In a lot of ways, this is more a northern town than one full of southrons."

John had heard that. He hadn't wanted to believe it. Evidently, it was true no matter what he wanted. He said, "They ought to clean out all those traitors, and crucify the worst of 'em."

Now Marshal Bart gave him an odd look. "I said something not much different from that when I first got here, too, Brigadier. But King Avram would not— will not—hear of it. He says victory will cure what ails them. After we whip false King Geoffrey, we will all be Detinans together again, and we will have to live with one another. When you look at it that way, it is hard to say he is wrong."

"Maybe." But John the Lister cocked his head to one side and listened to young Barre a little longer.

"To the hells with me, though, if I think that mouthy son of a bitch has any business running loose."

"Well, I would be harder than Avram is myself," Bart allowed. "But he *is* the King of Detina. We have fought this whole war to show the northerners that that is what he is. If he gives an order to let people like that alone, what can we do but leave them alone? Without turning into traitors ourselves, I mean?"

John thought that over. With a scowl, he said, "You know what, sir? I'm gods-damned glad I'm just a soldier. I don't have to worry about things like that."

"Some soldiers do," Bart said. "When Fighting Joseph was head general here, he talked about seizing the throne after he won some victories."

"It's a wonder Avram didn't take his head," John said.

"Avram heard about it, but he only laughed," Bart replied. "He said that if Fighting Joseph gave him the victories, he would take his chances with the usurpation. Then Duke Edward whipped the stuffing out of Joseph at Viziersville, and that was the end of *that* kind of talk. Our job is to make sure the traitors do not pull off any more little stunts like Viziersville, and we are strong enough to do it. That is why I brought your wing west. We will manage."

We will manage. It wasn't a flashy motto, nothing for soldiers to cry as they charged into battle. But it was a belief that Marshal Bart had turned into a truth, and a truth none of King Avram's other generals had ever been able to find. John the Lister nodded. "Yes, sir," he said.

However much Lieutenant General Bell didn't want to admit it even to himself—perhaps especially to himself—General Peegeetee had been right about how things were in Nonesuch. Like most Detinans (and all the more because he was a healer's son), Bell had spent time in sickrooms that held people who were going to die. Walk into such a room and you could see death brooding there, sometimes even before the bedridden patient knew the end drew near. Nonesuch was like that now.

King Geoffrey still made bold speeches. To listen to him, victory lay right around the corner. To look around in Nonesuch was to know Geoffrey was whistling in the dark. Everyone's eyes fearfully went to the north, where Duke Edward and the Army of Southern Parthenia had ever more trouble holding Marshal Bart and his men in gray away from the last couple of glideway lines that fed the city—and, not so incidentally, the army. If Bart seized those glideways, Nonesuch—and Duke Edward—would commence to starve.

And even if Bart didn't seize the glideways, how much would it matter in the end? Everything was scarce. Everything was expensive. Prices had been bad in Great River Province. They were worse here, much worse. Almost everything cost ten or twenty times what it had before the war began. Bell understood why, too, for the coins Geoffrey put out these days, though called silver, were copper thinly washed with the more precious metal. Bell didn't like using them, either.

If a man had King Avram's silver money, he could buy whatever he pleased, and at a civilized price. That also said too much about how the war was going.

For the time being, King Geoffrey was still feeding and housing Bell. Even if Bell had renounced command of the Army of Franklin, he remained a lieutenant general in his chosen sovereign's service. How much Geoffrey welcomed that service at the moment was an open question. He did not publicly renounce it, though.

Not publicly renouncing Bell's service and feeding

and housing him were as far as Geoffrey went. Time after time, Bell tried to secure an audience with the king. Time after time, he found himself rebuffed. At length, his temper fraying, he growled to a flunky, "I don't believe his Majesty wants to talk to me."

The flunky, who remained as toplofty as if Geoffrey's armies had overrun New Eborac City, looked at him from hooded eyes. "What ever could have given you that impression, Lieutenant General?"

Bell glowered back. "I'm having trouble believing the king has all this many meetings and such-like things."

"Are you? What a pity," the servitor murmured. "Some people will believe anything."

"What's that supposed to mean?" Bell asked.

"Why, what it said, of course," the other man replied.

He refused to be pushed. He was as agile with words as a dueling master with sabers. After a while, Bell gave up and went away. That that might have been what King Geoffrey's secretary had in mind never occurred to him.

But Bell, almost by accident, figured out a response to Geoffrey's evasions. Since the king would not see him, since the king would not hear him, he started telling his story to anyone else who might listen. That included his fellow officers in Geoffrey's capital, the nobles who thronged into Nonesuch to be near the king, and the merchants and gamblers who kept trying to get rich when everyone else got poorer and hungrier by the day. Bell talked—and talked, and talked.

After several days of this, everybody in Nonesuch was talking about what had happened in front of Ramblerton—and talking about Bell's version of what had happened there. That version, perhaps not surprisingly, gave Bell as much credit as could be salvaged from what had befallen the north.

The rumors Bell had started soon reached King Geoffrey's ears. And Geoffrey, who'd spent much of the war trying to strangle rumors, was naturally unenthusiastic about having more start. He didn't summon Bell to him to discuss the officer's reinstatement: he summoned him to try to get him to shut his mouth.

To Lieutenant General Bell, the difference in the two possible reasons for the summons was academic. That Geoffrey had summoned him to the citadel of Nonesuch was all that mattered. Bell was earnest, Bell was aggressive, but Bell had the political sense of a watermelon. Worse, he was completely unaware he had the political sense of a watermelon. As far as he was concerned, the summons represented a vindication of sorts.

Grim-faced guards in blue stood outside the citadel in Geoffrey's capital. For the life of him, Bell couldn't figure out why they looked so grim. They were here on ceremonial duty, weren't they? If they'd been in the trenches of Pierreville with the Army of Southern Parthenia facing Marshal Bart's army, they would have had some excuse for long faces. As things were? Not likely!

Well fortified with laudanum, Bell hitched along on crutches past the guards and into the citadel. King Geoffrey's throne resembled nothing so much as a gilded dining-room chair. *Well, how much does Geoffrey resemble a king?* Bell asked himself. But the answer to that formed in his mind at once: *more than Avram does, by the Lion God's fangs!*

Had Bell not been mutilated, he would have had to bow low before his sovereign. As things were, he contented himself with a nod and a murmured, "Your Majesty."

"Lieutenant General," Geoffrey replied, his voice colder than winter.

Bell waited for the king to order a blond servitor to bring him a chair. The king did no such thing. As Bell stood there, taking weight on his left leg and right crutch, Geoffrey glowered down at him from that cheap-looking throne. That was when the general began to suspect how angry at him the king really was. Bell should have been sure of that from the moment the second day's fighting in front of Ramblerton went wrong. He should have, but he hadn't, in spite of General Peegeetee's warning. After the wounds he'd taken, though, the prospect of facing down a king fazed him not in the least.

"Considering what you did to my kingdom, Lieutenant General, you have gall and to spare, complaining of your treatment at my hands," Geoffrey said at last.

"You named me commander of the Army of Franklin to fight," Bell said, "or so I inferred, at any rate. Since the moment I replaced Joseph the Gamecock, that is what I endeavored to do."

"I named you commander of the Army of Franklin to fight *and to win*," King Geoffrey said. "Instead, you threw your men away, so that the Army of Franklin exists no more. I do not thank you for that, or for misliking the fact that I accepted your resignation the instant you tendered it."

"I served the north proudly, and the best I knew how," Bell said. "I faced our foes, and fought them in my own person. The wounds I bear prove it . . . your Majesty."

"No one has ever questioned your courage, Lieutenant General," Geoffrey answered. "Your wisdom and your judgment, on the other hand . . ."

"You knew what sort of man I was when you placed me in command, or so I must believe," Bell said. "If you did not expect me to challenge the foe wherever I found him, you should have chosen another."

"I not only expected you to challenge the enemy, I expected you to destroy his armies," King Geoffrey said. "I did not expect you to destroy your own."

"No one can make war without suffering losses. Anyone who thinks he can is a fool," Bell said. "The enemy had more men, more siege engines, and, in the last fight, more quick-shooting crossbows than we did. He was better fed and better shod. We fought with the greatest of courage. We hurt him badly. In the end, we did not achieve quite the success I would have desired."

By then, Lieutenant General Bell had considerable practice in making disasters sound palatable. *Not quite the success I would have desired* seemed bloodless enough, especially if whoever was listening didn't know what had followed from that so-called incomplete success. King Geoffrey, unfortunately, knew in intimate detail. "Gods help us if you'd been defeated, then!" he exclaimed. "The eastern provinces probably would have fallen right off the map."

"Your Majesty, I resent the imputation," Bell said stiffly.

"Lieutenant General, I don't care," Geoffrey answered. "I have no army worth the name left between the Green Ridge Mountains and the Great River. Marthasville has fallen. Hesmucet has torn the living heart out of Peachtree Province, as if he were a blond priest sacrificing a bloody goat. Franklin and Cloviston will likely never see my soldiers again. And whom do I have to thank for these accomplishments, which must surely make King Avram grateful? You, Lieutenant General, you and no one else."

Had Bell won great victories, he would have wanted to share credit with no one else. He was more inclined to be generous about sharing blame. "No one else?" he rumbled. "What about the officers who could not get me grain or shoes or crossbow bolts? What about the officers who could not get me reinforcements when I needed them so desperately? What about the subordinate commanders who let me down again and again? I could not fight the southrons all by myself, though often it seemed I had to try."

"What good would reinforcements have done you?" King Geoffrey asked poisonously. "You would only have thrown them away along with the rest of your men."

"I am so very sorry, your Majesty," Bell said with just as much venom. "You have been such a perfect paragon of leadership, a paladin of proficiency, all through our struggle. If not for your blunders—"

"*You* were my worst blunder!" the King screamed. "Next to you, even Joseph the Gamecock looks like a soldier."

"Next to you, even Avram looks like a king," Bell retorted, a true measure of how disgusted he was.

They stared at each other in perfect mutual loathing. "You are dismissed," Geoffrey said in a voice clotted with fury. "Get out of my sight. If you ever come into my sight again, I shall not answer for the consequences."

"You already have plenty of consequences to answer for," Bell jeered. "And if you crucify me, how long will you last before Avram crucifies you?"

Geoffrey turned pale, not from fear but from fury. "I am going to win this war," he insisted. "I shall yet rule a great kingdom."

"Oh, yes. Indeed, your Majesty. And I am going to win the mile run at the Great Games next year." Bell cursed his mutilation not because he wouldn't win that race but because he couldn't turn and stomp out of King Geoffrey's throne room. The slow progress he made on crutches wasn't the same.

He wondered if he'd pushed Geoffrey too far. If the king decided to have him seized and crucified to encourage the others, what could he do about it? *Not much* was the obvious answer. A one-armed, one-legged swordsman was not an object to strike fear into the hearts of palace guards.

But for the click of Bell's crutch tips on the stone floor and the thump of his shoe, all was silence absolute. *Maybe Geoffrey's had an apoplexy and fallen over dead*, Bell thought hopefully. He didn't turn around to look. For one thing, turning around on crutches was commonly more trouble than it was worth. For another, he was all too liable to fall victim to disappointment if he did turn. And so he didn't.

He got out of the throne room. He got out of the citadel. He made his hitching way back to his hostel. Only when he'd sat down in his room did he remember he'd come to Nonesuch not to give Geoffrey a piece of his mind (he didn't have that many pieces to spare) but to seek reinstatement.

Reinstatement he would not get now. That was plain. He'd commanded his last army for King Geoffrey. "Well, it's Geoffrey's loss, gods damn him," Bell muttered. He remained convinced he'd done everything he could—he remained convinced he'd done everything anyone could—to serve the north well. If things hadn't always gone quite the way he would have wished . . . Well, if they hadn't, that couldn't possibly have been his fault. His subordinate commanders had botched too many fights the Army of Franklin should have, would have, won if only they'd followed his clear orders.

If they weren't a pack of blundering fools, he thought, *why did so many of them end up dead at Poor Richard? They got what they deserved, by the Thunderer's hairy fist!*

And one of these days—one of these days before too long, too—King Geoffrey would also get what he deserved. Bell could see that plainly now. Anyone coming into Nonesuch after long absence could see the kingdom was dying on its feet. Only someone who stayed here nearly all the time, like Geoffrey, could have any possible doubts on that score. *We'll all be stuck with Avram, and we'll all be stuck with blonds*.

Hating the idea but not knowing what he could do about it, Bell took his little bottle of laudanum off his belt. He yanked out the stopper and swigged. Healers sometimes gasped and turned pale when he told them how much laudanum he took every day. He didn't care. He needed the drug. It held physical torment at something close to arm's length. A good stiff dose also helped him avoid dwelling on any of the many things he didn't care to contemplate.

He caressed the smooth glass curve of the laudanum bottle as if it were the curve of a lover's breast. Till he was wounded, he'd never known how marvelous a drug could be. He tried to imagine his life these days without laudanum—tried and, shuddering, failed. Without laudanum, he wasn't truly alive.

"And I never would have known if I hadn't been wounded," he murmured. "I would have missed all—this." He caressed the bottle again. Laudanum made him real. Laudanum made him clever. As long as he had laudanum, everything that had happened to him, every single bit of it, was all worthwhile.

Captain Gremio had seen more in the way of warfare than he'd ever wanted. Now, in his own home province, he saw the final ruin to which the hopes of the north had come. Colonel Florizel's soldiers had joined with the forlorn handful of men Count Joseph the Gamecock was using to try to hold back the great

flood tide of General Hesmucet's advance. With the
addition of Florizel's veterans, Joseph the Gamecock
now had a forlorn double handful of men.

Handful or double handful, what Joseph didn't have
was enough men.

Hesmucet's soldiers ranged through Palmetto Province almost as they pleased. Joseph had hoped the
swamps and marshes in the north near Veldt would
slow the southrons down as they swarmed south
toward Parthenia. Building roads through the trackless wilderness, the southrons had broken through the
difficult country faster than Joseph or any other
northerner imagined possible.

Now Karlsburg, where the War Between the Provinces began and where Gremio lived, was lost. It wasn't
that Hesmucet's men had captured the place. They
hadn't. They'd simply passed it by, heading for Hail,
the provincial capital, and leaving a trail of devastation in their wake. Karlsburg would belong to Avram's
men as soon as they bothered to occupy it. At the
moment, they were showing it the ultimate contempt:
they weren't even wasting their time to conquer it.

As a regimental commander, Gremio could hope to
get answers to questions that would have kept his men
guessing. When Count Joseph's men camped outside
of Hail one chilly night that made the place seem to
live up to its name, he asked Colonel Florizel, "Sir, is
there any chance we can hold them out of this city?"

Florizel looked at him for a long time before shaking
his head. "No, Captain. We couldn't hold them out if
we had twice our men and they had half of theirs. We
are ruined. We are finished. We are through."

That would have hit Gremio harder if he hadn't
already expected it. "What *can* we do, sir?" he asked.

"Fall back through Hail. Destroy whatever's in there
that the gods-damned southrons might be able to use.

Stop on the south bank of the next river we come to. Pray to the gods that we can delay Hesmucet for a few hours. If we're very, very lucky, maybe we can even delay him for a whole day. Then we fall back to the river after that and pray to the gods again." Florizel, who'd carried so much on his broad, sturdy shoulders for so long, sounded like a man altogether bereft of hope.

Gremio had been without hope for a long time. He'd hoped to borrow a little from his strong-hearted superior. Finding none, he gave Florizel his best salute and went back to his regiment. "What's the news, sir?" Sergeant Thisbe asked, perhaps hoping to borrow some from him.

"The news is . . . bad, Sergeant," Gremio answered, and relayed what Colonel Florizel had said.

Thisbe frowned. "You're right, sir. That doesn't sound good. If we can't hang on to Hail, what's the point of going on with the war?"

"You would do better to ask that of King Geoffrey than of me," Gremio said. "His Majesty might be able to answer it. I, on the other hand, have no idea."

"All right, sir," the underofficer said. "I won't give you any more trouble about it, then. Seems to me we've got trouble enough."

"Seems to me you're right," Gremio said. "I wish you weren't, but you are."

If they had tried to fight in Hail, they would have been quickly surrounded and destroyed. That was obvious. Like Doubting George's army after the fight in front of Ramblerton, General Hesmucet's force kept extending tentacles of soldiers, hoping to trap its foes. As Joseph the Gamecock had in Peachtree Province, he traded space for time. The difference here was, he really couldn't afford to lose any more space at all, and he—along with the north—was fast running out of time.

Old men and boys and women cursed Joseph's soldiers as they marched south through Hail. A white-bearded fellow pointed to the governor's palace and shouted at Gremio, who stood out perhaps because of his epaulets: "That's where we started! That's where we said we wouldn't be part of Detina any more, not if gods-damned Avram was going to take our serfs off the land where they belong. Doesn't that mean anything to you?"

"It means a great deal to me, sir," Gremio answered stiffly.

"Then why the hells are you running away instead of fighting to save it?" the old man howled.

"Why? Because we *can't* save it," Gremio said. "If we try, we'll lose the palace and we'll lose this army, too. This way, the army lives to fight" —*or to run*, he thought— "another day."

He didn't convince the man with the white beard. He hadn't thought he would. The local kept right on yammering complaints and protests. That, of course, did him no good at all. Meanwhile, Joseph the Gamecock's army went about wrecking everything in Hail that might have been of some use to General Hesmucet. They set the arsenal ablaze: it had more sheaves of crossbow quarrels and more squat, deadly firepots than the soldiers could take with them. Up in flames they went, to keep the southrons from seizing them and flinging them at Joseph's men.

Bolt after bolt of indigo-dyed wool and cotton cloth burned, too. Hesmucet's men might dye it gray and turn it into their tunics and pantaloons. Better they didn't have the chance. So said Joseph, and no one disobeyed. More fires rose up to the heavens.

Joseph had almost waited too long. His little army was just pulling out of Hail at sunset as the vanguard of Hesmucet's much bigger army entered the provincial capital. Gremio's regiment stopped for the night a few miles south of town, when it got too dark to march any farther. Campfires flickered to life.

Sergeant Thisbe pointed back toward Hail. "Look!"

Fire made the northern horizon glow red and yellow and orange, though light had leaked out of the rest of the sky. "The town is burning," Gremio said dully, less sad and surprised than he'd ever dreamt he might be. "Maybe our fires got loose. Maybe the southrons are torching it. What difference does it make now? What difference does anything make now?"

"How can we go on?" Thisbe asked. "The place where everything started . . . in the southrons' hands and burning? How *can* we go on?"

Gremio looked north toward those flickering flames, which leaped higher every moment. Everything in Hail was going to burn; nothing could be plainer than that. And nothing could be plainer than the answer to Thisbe's question, either. Gremio looked around. No one but the underofficer was paying the least attention to what he said. "We can't go on any more," he replied. "What's the use? It's over. It's done. It's broken. We've lost. The sooner this cursed war ends, the better."

There. He'd said it. That he'd said it felt oddly liberating. He waited to hear what Sergeant Thisbe would say now that he'd said it. The underofficer looked at him for a long moment, then slowly nodded. "Yes, sir," Thisbe said after perhaps half a minute's silence, and then, "If that's how you feel, what do you aim to do now?"

"I'm going home," Gremio answered. "That's the best thing I can think of to do." Now he was the one who hesitated before asking, "Will you come with me?"

"Yes, sir," the sergeant said again, this time right away. "I'd be pleased to come along, if you're sure you want the company." Thisbe again waited a moment before asking, "Will you tell Colonel Florizel before you go?"

"No." Gremio shook his head. "That would only put the weight on him, not on me, where it belongs. This is *my* choice. Florizel's not a blind man, and not nearly so stupid as I thought when I first got to know him. If—no, when—we run into each other after the war, I'll explain myself then, but I won't need to do much explaining."

"Yes, sir," Thisbe said one more time.

They left Joseph the Gamecock's army in the gray half-light before dawn the next morning. Fires from the burning Hail still lit the sky. A sentry challenged them. Someone was still alert and doing his job the best way he knew how. Gremio didn't know whether to laugh or to cry. He gave his name and rank. The sentry said, "Advance and be recognized." As soon as the fellow saw his epaulets, he nodded and said, "Pass on, sir—and you, too, Sergeant."

"Thank you," Thisbe answered, with no trace of irony Gremio could hear.

Leaving the army was easy. Gremio wasn't sure how hard evading Hesmucet's men would prove. He hurried west, out of the southrons' line of march, reasoning they would be more interested in Joseph's army than in a couple of stragglers from it. His reasoning wasn't always what he wished it would be, but he turned out to be right about that. He saw men in gray in the distance three or four times. They probably saw him, too, but they kept on moving south. Two soldiers already out of the fight didn't matter to them.

And Gremio and Thisbe weren't the only stragglers on the road: nowhere near. Others were getting away from Joseph's army, too. Civilians were fleeing the wrath Hesmucet's men were showing against Palmetto

Province—and the greater wrath those civilians feared he would show. And blonds were on the road, straggling seemingly just for the joy of straggling. If they weren't bound to their liege lords' estates any more, they would go wherever they pleased. That was what their feet seemed to be saying, anyhow.

Both Gremio and Thisbe still carried crossbow and shortsword. That made the other wanderers through the ruins of King Geoffrey's hopes—and those of Palmetto Province—walk wide around them, which suited Gremio fine.

"What do you reckon Karlsburg'll be like?" Thisbe asked. "You think anything'll be left of it at all?"

"I don't know," was all Gremio could say. "We'll find out when we get there."

Thisbe nodded. "Makes sense."

Gremio wondered whether anything made sense. The estate he and Thisbe passed that afternoon made him doubt it. Serfs worked in the fields and garden plots there as if the War Between the Provinces had never started, let alone taken this disastrous turn for King Geoffrey's cause. He wondered what the liege lord had told his blonds. Whatever it was, they seemed to believe it. That would probably last till the first gray-uniformed southron found the place. It hadn't happened yet.

After tramping on till nightfall, Gremio and Thisbe camped by the side of the road. The sergeant made a little fire. They didn't have much to eat—only some bread Gremio had brought with him. He hadn't wanted to take much, for the men who stayed behind were every bit as needy as he was. Once they'd eaten, they rolled themselves in their blankets on opposite sides of the fire and fell asleep.

Two more days of marching (and a little judicious hen-stealing) brought them to the outskirts of Karlsburg.

A troop of gray-clad unicorn-riders trotted up the road toward them. Thisbe started to reach for a crossbow bolt, then hesitated. "We can't fight them all, sir," the underofficer said. "What now?"

"Let's see what they do," Gremio answered.

The southron unicorn-riders made no overtly hostile move. They reined in just in front of Gremio and Thisbe. Their captain looked the two northerners over, then asked, "You boys out of the war?"

Resignedly, Gremio nodded. "Yes, we're out of it."

"All right," the southron said. "Throw down your crossbows, then, and your quarrels. You can keep the shortswords. They don't matter. Go into town. Swear the oath of allegiance to King Avram. Take off the epaulets and the stripes. Go on about your business. No one will bother you if you don't bother anyone."

Thunk. Thunk. The crossbows, so long carried, so much used, went into the roadway. The sheaves of bolts followed. They rattled as they fell. Gremio strode on toward his home town without looking back. Thisbe followed. Nodding, the southron captain and his troopers resumed their patrol. To them, it was nothing but routine.

Coming into Karlsburg wasn't routine, not for Gremio. His home town hadn't burned. That was something, anyhow. But southron soldiers clogged the streets. And most of the soldiers in gray in Karlsburg were blonds. They grinned and swaggered as they marched. Ordinary Detinans stayed out of their way. How many old scores had the blonds already settled? Maybe better not to know.

A businesslike lieutenant—a Detinan, not a blond—accepted Gremio and Thisbe's oaths of allegiance to King Avram. The promises and the punishments in the oath were both milder than Gremio had expected. The lieutenant offered a scissors. "Cut off your emblems of rank," he said. "They don't matter any more. You're civilians again."

Once the job was done, Gremio returned the scissors to him. "Thank you," he managed.

"You're welcome," the brisk Detinan answered. "Good luck to you."

Out in the street, Gremio took Thisbe's hands. "This is the time," Gremio declared. "I've waited too . . . long already. I won't wait another minute, confound it. Will you marry me, Sergeant?"

Thisbe smiled. "I've waited a long time, too," she said, "but you can't ask me that."

"What?" Gremio didn't know whether he'd burst with fury or with mortification. "Why the hells not?"

"Because I'm not a sergeant any more, that's why." Thisbe touched the spot on her tunic sleeve where the stripes had stayed for so long. "The lieutenant said so, remember?"

"Oh." Gremio felt foolish. "You're right, of course. Well, in that case . . . Will you marry me—darling?"

"You bet I will," Thisbe said, and if anybody found anything odd about two soldiers kissing on the streets of Karlsburg, he kept quiet about it.

A LONG TIME AGO,
IN A REPUBLIC FAR,
FAR AWAY . . .

Advance and Retreat is a work of fiction. Not one of
the characters depicted herein bears any resemblance
to any real person, living or dead. A good thing, too,
says I; some of the characters depicted herein aren't the
sort you would want in your drawing room, even if you
weren't in there drawing at the time. Nonetheless, I
have been ~~browbeaten into~~ prevailed upon by my
editors to offer up a note of sorts for that handful of
stubborn skeptics who don't believe in disclaimers (and
to say shame on you, too).

After losing Atlanta—and, with it, most of the Civil
War that mattered—John Bell Hood skirmished with
Sherman's men throughout northern Georgia before
withdrawing into Alabama to refit what was left of the

Army of Tennessee. Sherman went east, toward Savannah and the Atlantic. Hood, in due course, went north, hoping to get up into Kentucky and, at the very least, create large amounts of chaos for the Union.

In Nashville, Tennessee, with what Sherman hadn't taken east on the march across Georgia, sat George Thomas. To oppose Hood, he needed to gather up garrisons in Tennessee, Kentucky, and Missouri, and to mold them into a cohesive force. To gain time to do this, he sent John Schofield south with a detachment from his army to delay Hood's northward progress.

Hood forced Schofield to withdraw from his position at Columbia, Tennessee, and got on his flank and in his rear as he retreated past Spring Hill. Something went wrong with the attack he planned, though. His subordinates said his orders weren't clear. He said they didn't obey properly. Schofield escaped and reached Franklin, on the south bank of the Harpeth River. (Yes, I know the geography in the American Civil War differs slightly from that of War Between the Provinces in the Kingdom of Detina. See, I told you you were reading fiction.) Hood, frustrated at the failure farther south, ordered an attack, at least as much from that frustration as for any real military reason, especially since Schofield intended to retreat anyhow.

Hood's generals wanted to show how brave they were, since his reaction to Spring Hill left them feeling insulted. They paid for their bravery with their lives; H.B. Granbury, O.F. Strahl, States Rights Gist, John Adams, and Patrick Cleburne died on the field, while John C. Carter was mortally wounded. Confederate soldiers got into Schofield's position, but could not break it. He did pull out that night, leaving his wounded in Hood's hands. It was, technically, a victory, but a victory that wrecked the Army of Tennessee. That army moved up to just in front of Nashville anyhow, and there could go no farther. Thomas had too many men for even Hood to try to outflank him and get up into Kentucky. Hood sat before the city, hoping to make Thomas attack him and to defeat him once he came out of his works, which were the most formidable west of the Appalachians.

Thomas, meanwhile, waited to get all his scattered command into place, and then had to wait further because of a nasty ice storm. The delay did not sit well with U.S. Grant. He kept ordering Thomas to attack at once, and Thomas kept saying he would as soon as he was ready. Grant, for once more jittery than imperturbable, finally sent John Logan to the west to take command if Thomas hadn't attacked by the time he got there, and then set out to follow Logan himself.

Logan had got to Louisville and Grant to Washington when Thomas did bestir himself. Hood got his wish, and doubtless then wished he hadn't. In the first day's fighting in front of Nashville, Thomas drove Hood's army back to the ridge line farther south. In the second day's fighting, Union cavalry general James Wilson's men got behind the Army of Tennessee and attacked it from the rear while Thomas' infantry hit it from the front. Hood's men broke and fled. Only a brilliant rearguard action commanded by Nathan Bedford Forrest kept Thomas from entirely destroying the Army of Tennessee; as things were, its fragments reassembled in Tupelo, Mississippi, for all practical purposes out of the war—not that there was much war left between the Appalachians and the Mississippi after that crushing defeat.

Hood tendered his resignation, which Jefferson Davis accepted. Richard Taylor, son of former President Zachary Taylor, took over what was left of the Confederate forces. Some men were sent east to help Joseph Johnston try to slow Sherman in his march through the Carolinas. He had little luck. Grant, still dissatisfied with Thomas, detached various elements of his commands and put them to other uses. Schofield was sent to North Carolina to join up with General Sherman, who was storming north to join the Army of the Potomac. Wilson, that spring, smashed Forrest's cavalry and destroyed Selma and other industrial towns in northern Alabama. The Civil War was all but over.

Some of you may note that John Bell Hood's memoirs are also entitled *Advance and Retreat*. Well, so what? That is, of course, just another coincidence.

TIME SCOUTS CAN DO

In the early part of the 21st century disaster struck—an experiment went wrong, bad wrong. The Accident almost destroyed the universe, and ripples in time washed over the Earth. Soon, the people of the depopulated post-disaster Earth learned that things were going to be a little different.... They'd be able to travel into the past, utilizing remnant time strings. It took brave pioneers to map the time gates: you can zap yourself out of existence with a careless jump, to say nothing of getting killed by some rowdy downtimer who doesn't like people who can't speak his language. So elaborate rules are evolved and Time Travel stations become big business.

But wild and wooly pioneers aren't the most likely people to follow rules... Which makes for great adventures as Time Scouts Kit Carson, Skeeter Jackson, and Margo Carson explore Jack the Ripper's London, the Wild West of the '49 Gold Rush, Edo Japan, the Roman Empire and more.

The Time Scout series
by Robert Asprin & Linda Evans

Time Scout	87698-8	$5.99	___
Wagers of Sin	87730-5	$5.99	___
Ripping Time	57867-7	$6.99	___
The House that Jack Built	31965-5	$6.99	___
For King & Country (HC)	7434-3539-7	$24.00	___